A PROMISE TO PROTECT

NEW YORK TIMES BESTSELLING AUTHOR

SUZANNE BROCKMANN

Previously published as *Taylor's Temptation*

HARLEQUIN® SELECTS™

Recycling programs
for this product may
not exist in your area.

ISBN-13: 978-1-335-40653-8

A Promise to Protect
First published in 2001 as Taylor's Temptation.
This edition published in 2021.
Copyright © 2001 by Suzanne Brockmann

Gut Instinct
First published in 2014. This edition published in 2021.
Copyright © 2014 by Barb Han

This edition published by arrangement with Harlequin Books S.A.

For questions and comments about the quality of this book,
please contact us at CustomerService@Harlequin.com.

Harlequin Enterprises ULC
22 Adelaide St. West, 41st Floor
Toronto, Ontario M5H 4E3, Canada
www.Harlequin.com

Printed in U.S.A.

CONTENTS

A PROMISE TO PROTECT   7
Suzanne Brockmann

GUT INSTINCT   275
Barb Han

Suzanne Brockmann is an award-winning author of more than fifty books and is widely recognized as one of the leading voices in romantic suspense. Her work has earned her repeated appearances on the *New York Times* bestseller list, as well as numerous awards, including Romance Writers of America's #1 Favorite Book of the Year and two RITA® Awards. Suzanne divides her time between Siesta Key and Boston. Visit her at suzannebrockmann.com.

Books by Suzanne Brockmann

Not Without Risk
Night Watch
Taylor's Temptation
Get Lucky
Identity: Unknown
The Admiral's Bride
Hawken's Heart
Harvard's Education

Visit the Author Profile page at
Harlequin.com for more titles.

A PROMISE
TO PROTECT

Suzanne Brockmann

In loving memory of Melinda Helfer,
RT Book Reviews reviewer—a friend of mine,
and a friend of all romance.

The first time I met Melinda was at an
RWA book signing years ago—right after
Prince Joe and *Forever Blue* had come out. She
rushed up to me, dropped to the floor in front of my
table and proceeded to kowtow! She told me she
loved those two books, and couldn't wait for the
next installment in the Tall, Dark & Dangerous series
to be released. She was funny, enthusiastic and
amazingly intelligent—a fierce and passionate
fan of all romance, and a good friend.

Melinda, this one's for you.
(But then again, I think you probably knew
that all my TDD books were written for you!)
You will be missed.

Acknowledgments

Special thanks to Mary Stella of the
New Jersey Romance Writers, friend and
fellow writer, for her help in creating a
suitable match for Bobby Taylor.

Prologue

"It was amazing." Rio Rosetti shook his head, still unable to wrap his mind around last night's explosive events. "It was absolutely amazing."

Mike and Thomas sat across from him at the mess hall, their ham and eggs forgotten as they waited for him to continue.

Although neither of them let it show, Rio knew they were both envious as hell that he'd been smack in the middle of all the action, pulling his weight alongside the two legendary chiefs of Alpha Squad, Bobby Taylor and Wes Skelly.

"Hey, Little E., get your gear and strap on your blue-suede swim fins," Chief Skelly had said to Rio just six hours ago. Had it really only been six hours? "Me and Uncle Bobby are gonna show you how it's done."

Twin sons of different mothers. That's what Bobby

and Wes were often called. Of *very* different mothers. The two men looked nothing alike. Chief Taylor was huge. In fact, the man was a total animal. Rio wasn't sure, because the air got kind of hazy way up by the top of Bobby Taylor's head, but he thought the chief stood at least six and a half feet tall, maybe even more. And he was nearly as wide. He had shoulders like a football player's protective padding, and, also like a football player, the man was remarkably fast. It was pretty freaky, actually, that a guy that big could achieve the kind of speed he did.

His size wasn't the only thing that set him apart from Wes Skelly, who was normal-size—about Rio's height at five-eleven with a similar wiry build.

Bobby was at least part Native American. His heritage showed in his handsome face and in the rich color of his skin. He tanned a real nice shade of brown when he was out in the sun—a far nicer shade than Rio's own slightly olive-tinged complexion. The chief also had long, black, straight hair that he wore pulled severely from his face in a single braid down his back, giving him a faintly mystical, mysterious air.

Wes, on the other hand, was of Irish-American descent, with a slightly reddish tint to his light brown hair and leprechaun-like mischief gleaming in his blue eyes.

No doubt about it, Wes Skelly came into a room and bounced off the walls. He was always moving—like a human pinball. And if he wasn't moving, he was talking. He was funny and rude and loud and not entirely tactful in his impatience.

Bobby, however, was the king of laid-back cool. He was the kind of guy who could sit perfectly still, without fidgeting, just watching and listening, sometimes for hours, before he gave voice to any opinions or comments.

But as different as they seemed in looks and demeanor, Bobby and Wes shared a single brain. They knew each other so well they were completely in tune with the other's thoughts.

Which was probably why Bobby didn't do too much talking. He didn't need to. Wes read his mind and spoke—incessantly—for him.

Although when the giant chief actually *did* speak, men listened. Even the officers listened.

Rio listened, too. He'd learned early on in SEAL training, long before he got tapped to join SEAL Team Ten's legendary Alpha Squad, to pay particular attention to Chief Bobby Taylor's opinions and comments.

Bobby had been doing a stint as a BUD/S instructor in Coronado, and he'd taken Rio, along with Mike Lee and Thomas King, under his extremely large wing. Which wasn't to say he coddled them. No way. In fact, by marking them as the head of a class filled with smart, confident, determined men, he'd demanded more from them. He'd driven them harder than the others, accepted no excuses, asked nothing less than their personal best— each and every time.

They'd done all they could to deliver, and—no doubt due to Bobby's quiet influence with Captain Joe Catalanotto—won themselves coveted spots in the best SEAL team in the Navy.

Rewind to six hours ago, to last night's operation. SEAL Team Ten's Alpha Squad had been called in to assist a FInCOM/DEA task force.

A particularly nasty South American drug lord had parked his luxury yacht a very short, very cocky distance outside of U.S. waters. The Finks and the DEA agents couldn't or maybe just didn't want to for some reason—Rio wasn't sure which and it didn't really matter to him—snatch the bad dude up until he crossed that invisible line into U.S. territory.

And that was where the SEALs were to come in.

Lieutenant Lucky O'Donlon was in charge of the op—mostly because he'd come up with a particularly devious plan that had tickled Captain Joe Cat's dark sense of humor. The lieutenant had decided that a small team of SEALs would swim out to the yacht—named *Swiss Chocolate*, a stupid-ass name for a boat—board it covertly, gain access to the bridge and do a little creative work on their computerized navigational system.

As in making the yacht's captain think they were heading south when they were really heading northwest.

Bad dude would give the order to head back toward South America, and instead they'd zoom toward Miami—into the open arms of the Federal task force.

It was just too good.

Bobby and Wes had been selected by Lieutenant O'Donlon to gain covert access to the bridge of the yacht. And Rio was going along for the ride.

"I knew damn well they didn't need me there," he told Thomas and Mike now. "In fact, I was aware I was slowing them down." Bobby and Wes didn't need to talk, didn't need to make hand signals. They barely even looked at each other—they just read each other's minds. It was so freaky. Rio had seen them do similar stuff on a training op, but somehow out in the real world it seemed even more weird.

"So what happened, Rosetti?" Thomas King asked. The tall African-American ensign was impatient—not that he'd ever let it show on his face. Thomas was an excellent poker player. Rio knew that firsthand, having left the table with empty pockets on more than one occasion.

Most of the time Thomas's face was unreadable, his expression completely neutral, eyelids half-closed. The combination of that almost-bland expression and his scars—one bisecting his eyebrow and the other branding one of his high cheekbones—gave him a dangerous edge that Rio wished his own far-too-average face had.

But it was Thomas's eyes that made most people cross the street when they saw him coming. So dark-brown as to seem black, his eyes glittered with a deep intelligence—the man was Phi Beta Kappa *and* a member of the Mensa club. His eyes also betrayed the fact that despite his slouched demeanor, Thomas King was permanently at Defcon Five—ready to launch a deadly attack without hesitation if the need arose.

He was Thomas. Not Tommy. Not even Tom. *Thomas.* Not one member of Team Ten ever called him anything else.

Thomas had won the team's respect. Unlike Rio, who somehow, despite his hope for a nickname like Panther or Hawk, had been given the handle Elvis. Or even worse, Little Elvis or Little E.

Holy Chrysler. As if Elvis wasn't embarrassing enough.

"We took a rubber duck out toward the *Swiss Chocolate*," Rio told Thomas and Mike. "Swam the rest of the way in." The swift ride in the little inflatable boat through the darkness of the ocean had made his heart pound. Knowing they were going to board a heavily guarded yacht and gain access to her bridge without anyone seeing them had a lot to do with it. But he was also worried.

What if he blew it?

Bobby apparently could read Rio's mind almost as easily as he read Wes Skelly's, because he'd touched Rio's shoulder—just a brief squeeze of reassurance—before they'd crept out of the water and onto the yacht.

"The damn thing was lit up like a Christmas tree and crawling with guards," Rio continued. "They all dressed alike and carried these cute little Uzi's. It was almost like their boss got off on pretending he had his own little army. But they weren't any kind of army. Not even close. They were really just street kids in expensive uniforms. They didn't know how to stand watch, didn't know what to look for. I swear to God, you guys, we moved right past them. They didn't have a clue we were there—not with all the noise they were making and the lights shining in their eyes. It was so easy it was a joke."

"If it were a joke," Mike Lee asked, "then what's Chief Taylor doing in the hospital?"

Rio shook his head. "No, that part wasn't a joke." Someone on board the yacht had decided to move the party up from down below and go for a midnight swim. Spotlights had switched on, shining down into the ocean, and all hell had broken loose. "But up until the time we were heading back into the water, it was a piece of cake. You know that thing Bobby and Wes can do? The telepathic communication thing?"

Thomas smiled. "Oh, yeah. I've seen them look at each other and—"

"This time they didn't," Rio interrupted his friend. "Look at each other, I mean. You guys, I'm telling you, this was beyond cool—watching them in action like this.

There was one guard on the bridge, okay? Other than that, it was deserted and pretty dark. The captain and crew are all below deck, right? Probably getting stoned with the party girls and the guests. So anyway, the chiefs see this guard and they don't break stride. They just take him temporarily out of the picture before he even sees us, before he can even make a sound. Both of them did it—together, like it's some kind of choreographed move they've been practicing for years. I'm telling you, it was a thing of beauty."

"They've been working with each other for a long time," Mike pointed out.

"They went through BUD/S together," Thomas reminded them. "They've been swim buddies from day one."

"It was perfection." Rio shook his head in admiration. "Sheer perfection. I stood in the guard's place, in case anyone looked up through the window, then there'd be someone standing there, you know? Meanwhile Skelly disabled the conventional compass. And Bobby broke into the navigational computers in about four seconds."

That was another freaky thing about Bobby Taylor. He had fingers the size of ballpark franks, but he could manipulate a computer keyboard faster than Rio would have thought humanly possible. He could scan the images that scrolled past on the screen at remarkable speeds, too.

"It took him less than three minutes to do whatever it was he had to do," he continued, "and then we were out of there—off the bridge. Lucky and Spaceman were in the water, giving us the all-clear." He shook his head, remembering how close they'd been to slipping silently away into the night. "And then all these babes in bikinis came running up on deck, heading straight for us. It was the absolute worst luck—if we'd been anywhere else on the vessel, the diversion would've been perfect. We would've been completely invisible. I mean, if you're an inexperienced guard are you going to be watching to see who's crawling around in the shadows or are you going to pay attention to the beach bunnies in the thong bikinis? But someone decided to go for a swim off the starboard side—right where we were hiding. These heavy-duty searchlights came on, probably just so the guys on board could watch the women in the water, but wham, there we were. Lit up. There was no place to hide—and nowhere to go but over the side."

"Bobby picked me up and threw me overboard," Rio admitted. He must not have been moving fast enough—he was still kicking himself for that. "I didn't see what happened next, but according to Wes, Bobby stepped in front of him and blocked him from the bullets that started flying while they both went into the water. That was when Bobby caught a few—one in his shoulder, another in the top of his thigh. He was the one who was hurt, but he pulled both me and Wes down, under the water—out of sight and out of range."

Sirens went on. Rio had been able to hear them along with the tearing sound of the guards' assault weapons and the screams from the women, even as he was pulled underwater.

"That was when the *Swiss Chocolate* took off," Rio said. He had to smile. "Right for Miami."

They'd surfaced to watch, and Bobby had laughed along with Wes Skelly. Rio and Wes hadn't even realized he'd been hit. Not until he spoke, in his normal, matter-of-fact manner.

"We better get moving, get back to the boat, ASAP," Bobby had said evenly. "I'm shark bait."

"The chief was bleeding badly," Rio told his friends. "He was hurt worse even than he realized." And the water hadn't been cold enough to staunch the flow of his blood. "We did the best we could to tie off his leg, right there in the water. Lucky and Spaceman went on ahead—as fast as they could—to connect with the rubber duck and bring it back toward us."

Bobby Taylor had been in serious pain, but he'd kept moving, slowly and steadily through the darkness. Apparently, he'd been afraid if he didn't keep moving, if he let Wes tow him back to the little rubber boat, he'd black out. And he didn't want to do that. The sharks in these waters *did* pose a serious threat, and if he were unconscious, that could have put Rio and Wes into even more significant danger.

"Wes and I swam alongside Bobby. Wes was talking the entire time—I don't know how he did it without swallowing a gallon of seawater—bitching at Bobby for playing the hero like that, making fun of him for getting shot in the ass—basically, just ragging on him to keep him alert.

"It wasn't until Bobby finally slowed to a crawl, until he told us he wasn't going to make it—that he needed help—that Wes stopped talking. He took Bobby in a lifeguard hold and hauled ass, focusing all his energy on getting back to the rubber duck in record time."

Rio sat back in his seat. "When we finally connected with the boat, Lucky had already radioed for help. It wasn't much longer before a helo came to evac Bobby to the hospital.

"He's going to be okay," he told both Thomas and

Mike again. That was the first thing he'd said about their beloved chief's injuries, before they'd even sat down to breakfast. "The leg wound wasn't all that bad, and the bullet that went into his shoulder somehow managed to miss the bone. He'll be off the active-duty list for a few weeks, maybe a month, but after that..." Rio grinned. "Chief Bobby Taylor will be back. You can count on that."

Chapter 1

Navy SEAL Chief Bobby Taylor was in trouble.

Big trouble.

"You gotta help me, man," Wes said. "She's determined to go, she flippin' hung up on me and wouldn't pick up the phone when I called back, and I'm going wheels-up in less than twenty minutes. All I could do was send her email—though fat lotta good that'll do."

"She" was Colleen Mary Skelly, his best friend's little sister. No, not *little* sister. *Younger* sister. Colleen wasn't little, not anymore. She hadn't been little for a long, long time.

A fact that Wes didn't seem quite able to grasp.

"If *I* call her," Bobby pointed out reasonably, "she'll just hang up on me, too."

"I don't want you to call her." Wes shouldered his seabag and dropped his bomb. "I want you to go there."

Bobby laughed. Not aloud. He would never laugh in his best friend's face when he went into overprotective brother mode. But inside of his own head, he was rolling on the floor in hysterics.

Outside of his head, he only lifted a quizzical eyebrow. "To Boston." It wasn't really a question.

Wesley Skelly knew that this time he was asking an awful lot, but he squared his shoulders and looked Bobby straight in the eyes. "Yes."

Problem was, Wes didn't know just how much he was asking.

"You want me to take leave and go to Boston," Bobby didn't really enjoy making Wes squirm, but he needed his best friend to see just how absurd this sounded, "because you and Colleen got into another argument." He still didn't turn it into a question. He just let it quietly hang there.

"No, Bobby," Wes said, the urgency in his voice turned up to high. "You don't get it. She's signed on with some kind of bleeding-heart, touchy-feely volunteer organization, and next she and her touchy-feely friends are flying out to flippin' Tulgeria." He said it again, louder, as if it were unprintable, then followed it up by a string of words that truly were.

Bobby could see that Wes was beyond upset. This wasn't just another ridiculous argument. This was serious.

"She's going to provide earthquake relief," Wes continued. "That's lovely. That's wonderful, I told her. Be Mother Teresa. Be Florence Nightingale. Have your goody two-shoes permanently glued to your feet. But stay *way* the hell away from Tulgeria! Tulgeria—the flippin' terrorist capital of the world!"

"Wes—"

"I tried to get leave," Wes told him. "I was just in the captain's office, but with you still down and H. out with food poisoning, I'm mission essential."

"I'm there," Bobby said. "I'm on the next flight to Boston."

Wes was willing to give up Alpha Squad's current assignment—something he was really looking forward to, something involving plenty of C-4 explosives—to go to Boston. That meant that Colleen wasn't just pushing her brother's buttons. That meant she was serious about this. That she really was planning to travel to a part of the world where Bobby himself didn't feel safe. And he wasn't a freshly pretty, generously endowed, long-legged—*very* long-legged—redheaded and extremely female second-year law student.

With a big mouth, a fiery temper and a stubborn streak. No, Colleen's last name wasn't Skelly for nothing.

Bobby swore softly. If she'd made up her mind to go, talking her out of it wasn't going to be easy.

"Thank you for doing this," Wes said, as if Bobby had already succeeded in keeping Colleen off that international flight. "Look, I gotta run. Literally."

Wes owed Bobby for this one. But he already knew it. Bobby didn't bother to say the words aloud.

Wes was almost out the door before he turned back. "Hey, as long as you're going to Boston…"

Ah. Here it came. Colleen was probably dating some new guy and… Bobby was already shaking his head.

"Check out this lawyer I think Colleen's dating, would you?" Wes asked.

"No," Bobby said.

But Wes was already gone.

* * *

Colleen Skelly was in trouble.

Big trouble.

It wasn't fair. The sky was far too blue today for this kind of trouble. The June air held a crisp sweetness that only a New England summer could provide.

But the men standing in front of her provided nothing sweet to the day. And nothing unique to New England, either.

Their kind of hatred, unfortunately, was universal.

She didn't smile at them. She'd tried smiling in the past, and it hadn't helped at all.

"Look," she said, trying to sound as reasonable and calm as she possibly could, given that she was facing down six very big men. Ten pairs of young eyes were watching her, so she kept her temper, kept it cool and clean. "I'm well aware that you don't like—"

"'Don't like' doesn't have anything to do with it," the man at the front of the gang—John Morrison—cut her off. "We don't want your center here, we don't want *you* here." He looked at the kids, who'd stopped washing Mrs. O'Brien's car and stood watching the exchange, wide-eyed and dripping with water and suds. "You, Sean Sullivan. Does your father know you're down here with *her*? With the hippie chick?"

"Keep going, guys," Colleen told the kids, giving them what she hoped was a reassuring smile. *Hippie chick.* Sheesh. "Mrs. O'Brien doesn't have all day. And there's a line, remember. This car wash team has a rep for doing a good job—swiftly and efficiently. Let's not lose any customers over a little distraction."

She turned back to John Morrison and his gang. And they *were* a gang, despite the fact that they were all in their late thirties and early forties and led by a respectable local businessman. Well, on second thought, calling Morrison *respectable* was probably a little too generous.

"Yes, Mr. Sullivan does know where his son is," she told them levelly. "The St. Margaret's Junior High Youth Group is helping raise money for the Tulgeria Earthquake Relief Fund. All of the money from this car wash is going to help people who've lost their homes and nearly all of their possessions. I don't see how even *you* could have a problem with that."

Morrison bristled.

And Colleen silently berated herself. Despite her efforts, her antagonism and anger toward these Neanderthals had leaked out.

"Why don't you go back to wherever it was you came from?" he told her harshly. "Get the hell out of our neighborhood and take your damn bleeding-heart liberal ideas and stick them up your—"

No one was going to use that language around her kids. Not while she was in charge. "Out," she said. "Get out. Shame on you! Get off this property before I wash your mouth out with soap. And charge you for it."

Oh, that was a big mistake. Her threat hinted at violence—something she had to be careful to avoid with this group.

Yes, she was nearly six feet tall and somewhat solidly built, but she wasn't a Navy SEAL like her brother and his best friend, Bobby Taylor. Unlike them, she couldn't take on all six of these guys at once, if it came down to that.

The scary thing was that this was a neighborhood in which some men didn't particularly have a problem with hitting a woman, no matter her size. And she suspected that John Morrison was one of those men.

She imagined she saw it in his eyes—a barely tempered urge to backhand her—hard—across the face.

Usually she resented her brother's interference. But right now she found herself wishing he and Bobby were standing right here, beside her.

God knows she'd been yelling for years about her independence, but this wasn't exactly an independent kind of situation.

She stood her ground all alone, wishing she was holding something more effective against attack than a giant-size sponge, and then glad that she wasn't. She was just mad enough to turn the hose on them like a pack of wild dogs, and that would only make this worse.

There were children here, and all she needed was Sean or Harry or Melissa to come leaping to her aid. And they would. These kids could be fierce.

But then again, so could she. And she would not let these children get hurt. She would do whatever she had to do, including trying again to make friends with these dirt wads.

"I apologize for losing my temper, Shantel," she called to one of the girls, her eyes still on Morrison and his goons. "Run inside and see if Father Timothy's coming out with more of that lemonade soon. Tell him to bring six extra paper cups for Mr. Morrison and his friends. I think we could probably all use some cooling off."

Maybe that would work. Kill them with kindness. Drown them with lemonade.

The twelve-year-old ran swiftly for the church door.

"How about it, guys?" Colleen forced herself to smile

at the men, praying that this time it would work. "Some lemonade?"

Morrison's expression didn't change, and she knew that this was where he was going to step forward, inform her he didn't want any of their lemonade—expletive deleted—and challenge her to just try washing out his mouth. He'd then imply—ridiculously, and solely because of her pro bono legal work for the HIV Testing and AIDS Education Center that was struggling to establish a foothold in this narrow-minded but desperately needy corner of the city—that she was a lesbian and offer to "cure her" in fifteen unforgettable minutes in the closest back alley.

It would almost be funny. Except for the fact that Morrison was dead serious. He'd made similar disgusting threats to her before.

But now, to her surprise, John Morrison didn't say another word. He just looked long and hard at the group of eleven-and twelve-year-olds standing behind her, then did an about face, muttering something unprintable.

It was amazing. Just like that, he and his boys were walking away.

Colleen stared after them, laughing—softly—in disbelief.

She'd done it. She'd stood her ground, and Morrison had backed down without any interference from the police or the parish priest. Although at 260 pounds, Father Timothy was a heart attack waiting to happen. His usefulness in a fist fight would be extremely limited.

Was it possible Morrison and his clowns were finally hearing what she was saying? Were they finally starting to believe that she wasn't going to let herself be intimidated by their bogus threats and ugly comments?

Behind her the hoses were still silent, and she turned around. "Okay, you guys, let's get back to—"

Colleen dropped her sponge.

Bobby Taylor. It was Bobby Taylor. Standing right there, behind her, in the St. Margaret's parking lot. Somehow, some way, her brother's best friend had materialized there, as if Colleen's most fervent wishes had been granted.

He stood in a Hawaiian shirt and cargo shorts, planted in a superhero pose—legs spread and massive arms crossed in front of his equally massive chest. His eyes were hard, and his face stony as he still glared in the direction John Morrison and his gang had departed. He was wearing a version of his "war face."

He and Wes had completely cracked Colleen up on more than one occasion by practicing their "war faces" in the bathroom mirror during their far-too-infrequent visits home. She'd always thought it was silly—what did the expression on their faces matter when they went into a fight?—until now. Now she saw that that grim look on Bobby's usually so-agreeably handsome face was startlingly effective. He looked hard and tough and even mean—as if he'd get quite a bit of enjoyment and satisfaction in tearing John Morrison and his friends limb from limb.

But then he looked at her and smiled, and warmth seeped back into his dark-brown eyes.

He had the world's most beautiful eyes.

"Hey, Colleen," he said in his matter-of-fact, no-worries, easygoing voice. "How's it going?"

He held out his arms to her, and in a flash she was running across the asphalt and hugging him. He smelled faintly of cigarette smoke—no doubt thanks to her brother, Mr. Just-One-More-Cigarette-Before-I-Quit—and coffee. He was warm and huge and solid and one of very few men in the world who could actually make her feel if not quite petite then pretty darn close.

As long as she'd wished him here, she should have wished for more. Like for him to have shown up with a million-dollar lottery win in his pocket. Or—better yet—a diamond ring and a promise of his undying love.

Yes, she'd had a wild crush on this man for close to ten years now. And just once she wanted him to take her into his arms like this and kiss her senseless, instead of giving her a brotherly noogie on the top of her head as he released her.

Over the past few years she'd imagined she'd seen appreciation in his eyes as he'd looked at her. And once or twice she could've sworn she'd actually seen heat—but only when he thought both she and Wes weren't looking. Bobby was attracted to her. Or at the very least she wished he were. But even if he were, there was no way in hell he'd ever act on that attraction—not with Wes watching his every move and breathing down his neck.

Colleen hugged him tightly. She had only two chances each visit to get this close to him—once during hello and once during goodbye—and she always made sure to take full advantage.

But this time he winced. "Easy."

Oh, God, he'd been hurt. She pulled back to look up at him, and she actually had to tilt her head. He was that tall.

"I'm a little sore," he told her, releasing her completely and stepping back, away from her. "Shoulder and leg. Nothing serious. You got me in the dead perfect spot, that's all."

"I'm sorry."

He shrugged. "It's no big deal. I'm taking some down time to get back to speed."

"What happened—or can you not tell me?"

He shook his head, smiling apologetically. He was such a good-looking man. And that little smile... What would he look like with his thick hair loose from the single braid he wore down his back? Although, she realized, he wasn't wearing a braid today. Instead, he wore his hair pulled back into a simple ponytail.

Every time she saw him, she expected him to have his hair cut short again. But each time it was even longer.

The first time they'd met, back when he and Wes were training to become SEALs, he'd had a crew cut.

Colleen gestured to the kids, aware they were all still watching. "Come on, gang, let's keep going here."

"Are you all right?" Bobby stepped closer to her, to avoid the spray from the hose. "What's the deal with those guys?"

"You're why they left," she realized suddenly. And even though mere minutes ago she'd wished desperately for Bobby's and her brother's presence, she felt a flare of anger and frustration. Darn it! She'd wanted Morrison's retreat to be because of her. As nice as it would be, she couldn't walk around with a Navy SEAL by her side every minute of every day.

"What was that about, Colleen?" Bobby pressed.

"Nothing," she said tersely.

He nodded, regarding her steadily. "It didn't feel like 'nothing.'"

"Nothing *you* have to worry about," she countered. "I'm doing some pro bono legal work for the AIDS Education Center, and not everyone is happy about it. That's what litigation's all about. Where's Wes? Parking the car?"

"Actually, he's—"

"I know why you're here. You came to try to talk me out of going to Tulgeria. Wes probably came to forbid me from going. Hah. As if he could." She picked up her sponge and rinsed it in a bucket. "I'm not going to listen to either of you, so you might as well just save your breath, turn around and go back to California. I'm not fifteen anymore, in case you haven't noticed."

"Hey, I've noticed," Bobby said. He smiled. "But Wes needs a little work in that area."

"You know, my living room is completely filled with boxes," Colleen told him. "Donations of supplies and clothing. I don't have any room for you guys. I mean, I guess you can throw sleeping bags on the floor of my bedroom, but I swear to God, if Wes snores, I'm kicking him out into the street."

"No," Bobby said. "That's okay. I made hotel reservations. This week is kind of my vacation, and—"

"Where *is* Wes?" Colleen asked, shading her eyes and looking down the busy city street. "Parking the car in Kuwait?"

"Actually." Bobby cleared his throat. "Yeah."

She looked at him.

"Wes is out on an op," he told her. "It's not quite Kuwait, but…"

"He asked *you* to come to Boston," Colleen realized. "For him. He asked you to play big brother and talk me out of going to Tulgeria, didn't he? I don't believe it. And you *agreed*? You jerk!"

"Colleen, come on. He's my best friend. He's worried about you."

"And you don't think I worry about him? Or you?" she countered hotly. "Do *I* come out to California to try to talk you out of risking *your* lives? Do *I* ever say, don't be a SEAL? No! Because I respect you. I respect the choices and decisions you make."

Father Timothy and Shantel emerged from the church kitchen with a huge thermos of lemonade and a stack of cups.

"Everything all right?" Father T. asked, eyeing Bobby apprehensively.

Bobby held out his hand. "I'm Bobby Taylor, a friend of Colleen's," he introduced himself.

"A friend of my brother, Wes's," she corrected him as the two men shook hands. "He's here as a surrogate brother. Father, plug your ears. I'm about to be extremely rude to him."

Timothy laughed. "I'll see if the other children want lemonade."

"Go away," Colleen told Bobby. "Go home. I don't want another big brother. I don't *need* one. I've got plenty already."

Bobby shook his head. "Wes asked me to—"

Damn Wes. "He probably also asked you to sift through my dresser drawers, too," she countered, lowering her voice. "Although I'm not sure what you're going to tell him when you find my collection of whips and chains, my black leather bustier and matching crotchless panties."

Bobby looked at her, something unrecognizable on his face.

And as Colleen looked back at him, for a moment she spun out, losing herself in the outer-space darkness of his eyes. She'd never imagined outer space could be so very *warm.*

He looked away, clearly embarrassed, and she realized suddenly that her brother wasn't here.

Wes wasn't here.

Bobby was in town *without Wes.* And without Wes, if she played it right, the rules of this game they'd been playing for the past decade could change.

Radically.

Oh, my goodness.

"Look." She cleared her throat. "You're here, so… let's make the best of this. When's your return flight?"

He smiled ruefully. "I figured I'd need the full week to talk you out of going."

He was here for a whole week. Thank you, Lord. "You're not going to talk me out of anything, but you cling to that thought if it helps you," she told him.

"I will." He laughed. "It's good to see you, Colleen."

"It's good to see you, too. Look, as long as there's only one of you, I can probably make room in my apartment—"

He laughed again. "Thanks, but I don't think that would be a very good idea."

"Why waste good money on a hotel room?" she asked. "After all, you're practically my brother."

"No," Bobby said emphatically. "I'm not."

There was something in his tone that made her bold. Colleen looked at him then in a way she'd never dared let herself look at him before. She let her gaze move down his broad chest, taking in the outline of his muscles, admiring the trim line of his waist and hips. She looked all the way down his long legs and then all the way back up again. She lingered a moment on his beautiful mouth, on his full, gracefully shaped lips, before gazing back into his eyes.

She'd shocked him with that obvious once-over. Well, good. It was the Skelly family motto: everyone needs a good shocking every now and then.

She gave him a decidedly nonsisterly smile. "Glad we got that established. About time, huh?"

He laughed, clearly nervous. "Um…"

"Grab a sponge," she told him. "We've got some cars to wash."

Chapter 2

Wes would kill him if he found out.

No doubt about it.

If Wes knew even *half* the thoughts that were steam-rolling through Bobby's head about his sister, Colleen, Bobby would be a dead man.

Lord have mercy on his soul, the woman was hot. She was also funny and smart. Smart enough to have figured out the ultimate way to get back at him for showing up here as her brother's mouthpiece.

If she were planning to go anywhere besides Tulgeria, Bobby would have turned around. He would have headed for the airport and caught the next flight out of Boston.

Because Colleen was right. He and Wes had absolutely no business telling her what she should and shouldn't do. She was twenty-three years old—old enough to make her own decisions.

Except both Bobby and Wes had been to Tulgeria, and Colleen hadn't. No doubt she'd heard stories about the warring factions of terrorists that roamed the dirt-poor countryside. But she hadn't heard Bobby and Wes's stories. She didn't know what they'd seen, with their own eyes.

At least not yet.

But she would before the week was out.

And he'd take the opportunity to find out what that run-in with the local chapter of the KKK had been about, too.

Apparently, like her brother, Wes, trouble followed Colleen Skelly around. And no doubt, also like Wes, when it didn't follow her, she went out and flagged it down.

But as for right now, Bobby desperately needed to regroup. He had to go to his hotel and take an icy-cold shower. He had to lock himself in his room and away— far away—from Colleen.

Lord save him, somehow he'd given himself away. Somehow she'd figured out that the last thing that came to mind when he looked at her was brotherly love.

He could hear her laughter, rich and thick, from the far end of the parking lot, where she stood talking to a woman in a beat-up station wagon, who'd come to pick up the last of the junior-size car washers.

The late-afternoon sunlight made Colleen's hair gleam. With the work done, she'd changed into a summer dress and taken down her ponytail, and her hair hung in shimmering red-gold waves around her face.

She was almost unbearably beautiful.

Some people might not agree. And taken individually, most of the features of her face were far from perfect.

Her mouth was too wide, her cheeks too full, her nose too small, her face too round, her skin too freckled and prone to sunburn.

Put it all together, though, and the effect was amazing.

And add those heartstoppingly gorgeous eyes...

Colleen's eyes were sometimes blue, sometimes green, and always dancing with light and life. When she smiled—which was most of the time—her eyes actually twinkled. It was corny but true. Being around Colleen Skelly was like being in the middle of a continuous, joyful, always-in-full-swing party.

And as for her body...

Ouch.

The woman was beyond hot. She wasn't one of those anemic little bony anorexic girls who were plastered all over TV and magazines, looking more like malnourished 12-year-old boys. No, Colleen Skelly was a woman—with a capital *W*. She was the kind of woman that a real man could wrap his arms around and really get a grip on. She actually had hips and breasts—and not only was that the understatement of the century, but it was the thought that would send him to hell, directly to hell. 'Do not pass Go, do not collect two hundred dollars,' do not live another minute longer.

If Wes ever found out that Bobby spent any amount of time at all thinking about Colleen's breasts, well, that would be it. The end. Game over.

But right now Wes—being more than three thousand miles away—wasn't Bobby's problem.

No, Bobby's problem was that somehow *Colleen* had realized that he was spending far too much time thinking about her breasts.

She'd figured out that he was completely and mind-lessly in lust with her.

And Wesley wasn't around to save him. Or beat him senseless.

Of course, it was possible that she was just toying with him, just messing with his mind. *Look at what you can't have, you big loser.*

After all, she was dating some lawyer. Wasn't that what Wes had said? And these days, wasn't *dating* just a euphemism for *in a relationship with?* And that was really just a polite way of saying that they were sleeping together, lucky son of a bitch.

Colleen glanced up from her conversation with the station-wagon mom and caught him looking at her butt.

Help.

He'd known that this was going to be a mistake back in California—the second the plea for help had left Wes's lips. Bobby should have admitted it, right there and then. *Don't send me to Boston, man. I've got a crippling jones for your sister. The temptation may be too much for me to handle, and then you'll kill me.*

"I've gotta go," Bobby heard Colleen say as she straightened up. "I've got a million things to do before I leave." She waved to the kids in the back. "Thanks again, guys. You did a terrific job today. I probably won't see you until I get back, so…"

There was an outcry from the back seat, something Bobby couldn't make out, but Colleen laughed.

"Absolutely," she said. "I'll deliver your letters to Analena and the other kids. And I'll bring my camera and take pictures. I promise."

She waved as the station wagon drove away, and then

she was walking toward him. As she approached, as she gazed at him, there was a funny little smile on her face.

Bobby was familiar with the full arsenal of devious Skelly smiles, and it was all he could do not to back away from this one.

"I have an errand to run, but after, we could get dinner. Are you hungry?" she asked.

No, he was terrified. He sidled back a bit, but she came right up to him, close enough for him to put his arms around. Close enough to pull her in for a kiss.

He couldn't kiss her. *Don't you dare*, he ordered himself.

He'd wanted to kiss her for years.

"I know this great Chinese place," she continued, twinkling her eyes at him. "Great food, great atmosphere, too. Very dark and cool and mysterious."

Oh, no. No, no. Atmosphere was the dead-last thing he wanted or needed. Standing here on the blazing-hot asphalt in broad daylight was bad enough. He had to clench his fists to keep from reaching for her. No way was he trusting himself around Colleen Skelly someplace dark and cool and mysterious.

She touched him, reaching up to brush something off his sleeve, and he jumped about a mile straight up.

Colleen laughed. "Whoa. What's with you?"

I want to sink back with you on your brightly colored bedspread, undress you with my teeth and lose myself in your laughter, your eyes and the sweet heat of your body.

Not necessarily in that order.

Bobby shrugged, forced a smile. "Sorry."

"So how 'bout it? You want to get Chinese?"

"Oh," he said, stepping back a bit and shifting around to pick up his seabag and swing it over his shoulder, glad he had something with which to occupy his hands. "I don't know. I should probably go try to find my hotel. It's the Sheraton, just outside of Harvard Square?"

"You're sure I can't talk you into spending the night with me?"

It was possible that she had no idea how suggestive it was when she asked a question like that, combined with a smile like that.

On the other hand, she probably knew damn well what she was doing to him. She was, after all, a Skelly.

He laughed. It was either that or cry. *Evasive maneuvers, Mr. Sulu.* "Why don't we just plan to have lunch tomorrow?"

Lunch was good. Lunch was safe. It was businesslike and well lit.

"Hmm. I'm working straight through lunch tomorrow," she told him. "I'm going to be driving the truck all day, picking up donations to take to Tulgeria. But I'd love to have breakfast with you."

This time it wasn't so much the words but the way she said it, lowering her voice and smiling slightly.

Bobby could picture her at breakfast—still in bed, her hair sexily mussed, her gorgeous eyes heavy-lidded. Her mouth curving up into a sleepy smile, her breasts soft and full against the almost-transparent cotton of that innocent little nightgown he'd once seen hanging in her bathroom...

Everything about her body language was screaming for him to kiss her. Unless he was seriously mistaken, everything she was saying and doing was one great big, giant green light.

God help him, why did she have to be Wes Skelly's little sister?

* * *

Traffic was heavy through the Back Bay and out toward Cambridge.

For once, Colleen didn't mind. This was probably the last time for a while that she'd make this drive up Comm. Ave. and over the BU bridge. It was certainly the last time she'd do it in this car.

She refused to feel remorse, refused even to acknowledge the twinge of regret that tightened her throat every time she thought about signing over the title. She'd done too much pro bono work this past year. It was her fault entirely, and the only way to make ends meet now was to sell her car. It was a shame, but she had to do it.

At least this final ride was a memorable one.

She glanced at Bobby Taylor, sitting there beside her, looking like the perfect accessory for a lipstick-red 1969 Ford Mustang, with his long hair and exotic cheekbones and those melted-chocolate eyes.

Yeah, he was another very solid reason why she didn't mind at all about the traffic.

For the first time she could remember, she had Bobby Taylor alone in her car, and the longer it took to reach Harvard Square, the better. She needed all the time she could to figure out a way to keep him from getting out when they arrived at his hotel.

She'd been pretty obvious so far, and she wondered just how blatant she was going to have to be. She laughed aloud as she imagined herself laying it all on the table, bringing it down to the barest bottom line, asking him if he wanted to get with her, using the rudest, least-elegant language she knew.

"So…what are you going to do tonight?" she asked him instead.

He glanced at her warily, as if he were somehow able to read her mind and knew what she really wanted to ask him.

"Your hair's getting really long," she interrupted him before he could even start to answer. "Do you ever wear it down?"

"Not too often," he told her.

Say it. Just say it. "Not even in bed?"

He hesitated only briefly. "No, I usually sleep with it braided or at least pulled back. Otherwise it takes forever to untangle in the morning."

She hadn't meant while he slept. She knew from the way he wasn't looking at her that he was well aware of what she had meant.

"I guess from your hair that you're still doing the covert stuff, huh?" she asked. "Oops, sorry. Don't answer that." She rolled her eyes. "Not that you would."

Bobby laughed. He had a great laugh, a low-pitched rumble that was always accompanied by the most gorgeous smile and extremely attractive laughter lines around his eyes. "I think it's fine if I say yes," he told her. "And you're right—the long hair makes it kind of obvious, anyway."

"So is Wes out on a training op or is it the real thing this time?" she asked.

"I don't know that myself," he admitted. "Really," he added as she shot him a skeptical glance.

The traffic light was red, and she chewed her lip as she braked to a stop and stared at the taillights of the cars in front of them. "It worries me that he's out there without you."

When she looked at him again, he was watching her. And he actually held her gaze for the first time since they'd gotten into her car. "He's good at what he does, Colleen," he told her gently. She loved the way he said her name.

"I know. It's just… Well, I don't worry so much when he's with you." She forced a smile. "And I don't worry so much about you when you're with him."

Bobby didn't smile. He didn't do much of anything but look into her eyes. No, when he looked at her like that, he wasn't just looking into her eyes. He was looking into her mind, into her soul. Colleen found herself holding her breath, hypnotized, praying that he would like what he saw. Wishing that he would kiss her.

How could he look at her like that—and the way he'd looked at her in the church parking lot, too—and then *not* kiss her?

The car behind her honked, and she realized that the light had changed. The line of traffic had already moved. She fumbled with the stick shift, suddenly afraid she was making a huge fool of herself.

One of Wes's recent emails had mentioned that Bobby had finally ended his on-again, off-again relationship with a woman he'd met in Arizona or New Mexico or someplace else equally unlikely, considering the man spent most of his waking hours in the ocean.

Of course, that so-called *recent* email from her brother had arrived nearly two months ago. A lot might've happened in the past two months. Bobby could well have hooked up with someone new. Or gotten back together with what's-her-name. Kyra Something.

"Wes told me you and Kyra called it quits." There was absolutely no point in sitting here wondering. So what if she came across as obvious? She was tired of guessing. Did she have a chance here, or didn't she? Inquiring minds wanted to know.

"Um," Bobby said. "Yeah, well… She, uh, found someone who wasn't gone all the time. She's actually getting married in October."

"Oh, yikes." Colleen made a face at him. "The *M* word." Wes always sounded as if he were on the verge of a panic attack when that word came up.

But Bobby just smiled. "Yeah, I think she called to tell me about it because she was looking for a counteroffer, but I just couldn't do it. We had a lot of fun, but…" He shook his head. "I wasn't about to leave the teams for her, you know, and that's what she wanted." He was quiet for a moment. "She deserved way more than I could give her, anyway."

"And you deserve more than someone who'll ask you to change your whole life for them," Colleen countered.

He looked startled at that, as if he'd never considered such a thing, as if he'd viewed himself as the bad guy in the relationship—the primary reason for its failure.

Kyra Whomever was an idiot.

"How about you?" he asked. "Wes said you were dating some lawyer."

Oh, my God. Was it possible that Bobby was doing a little fishing of his own?

"No," she said, trying to sound casual. "Nope. That's funny, but… Oh, I know what he was thinking. I told him I went to Connecticut with Charlie Johannsen. Wes must've thought…" She had to laugh. "Charlie's longtime companion is an actor. He just got cast in a new musical at Goodspeed-at-Chester."

"Ah," Bobby said. "Wes will be relieved."

"Wes never wants me to have any fun," she countered.

"How about you?" She used Bobby's own words. "Are you seeing someone new?"

"Nope. And Wes isn't, either."

Okay. She would talk about Wes. She'd gotten the info she'd wanted.

"Is he still carrying the torch for—" What was her name? "Laura?"

Bobby shook his head. "You'll have to ask him about that."

Yeah, like Wes would talk to her about this. "Lana," she remembered. "He once wrote me this really long email all about her. I think he was drunk when he wrote it."

"I'm sure he was." Bobby shook his head. "When you talk to him, Colleen, it's probably better not to mention her."

"Oh, my God, is she dead?"

"No. Do you mind if we talk about something else?"

He was the one who'd brought up Wes in the first place. "Not at all."

Silence.

Colleen waited for him to start a new topic of conversation—anything that wasn't about Wes—but he just sat there, distracted by the sight of the river out the window.

"Do you want to go see a movie later?" she finally asked. "Or we could rent a video. I've got an appointment at six-thirty with a guy who wants to buy my car. If everything goes right, I'll be done by seven-thirty, easy."

That got his attention, just the way she knew it would. "You're selling your car? *This* car?"

When she was fifteen, sixteen, seventeen, this Mustang was all she could talk about. But people's priorities changed. It wasn't going to be easy to sell it, but she refused to let it be the end of her world—a world that was so much wider now, extending all the way to Tulgeria and beyond.

She made herself smile at him. "I am. Law school's expensive."

"Colleen, if you need a loan—"

"I've got a loan. Believe me I've got *many* loans. I've got loans to pay off loans. I've got—"

"It took you five years to rebuild this car. To find authentic parts and—"

"And now someone's going to pay top dollar for a very shiny, very well-maintained vintage Mustang that handles remarkably badly in the snow. I live in Cambridge, Massachusetts. I don't need a car—especially not one that skids if you so much as whisper the word *ice*. My apartment's two minutes from the T, and frankly, I have better things to spend my money on than parking tickets and gasoline."

"Okay," he said. "Okay. I have an idea. I've got some money saved. I'll lend you what you need—interest free—and we can take the next week and drive this car back to your parents' house in Oklahoma, garage it there. Then in a few years when you graduate—"

"Nice try," Colleen told him. "But my travel itinerary has me going to Tulgeria next Thursday. Oklahoma's not exactly in the flight path."

"Think about it this way—if you don't go to Tulgeria, you get to keep your car and have an interest-free loan."

She took advantage of another red light to turn and look at him. "Are you attempting to bribe me?"

He didn't hesitate. "Absolutely."

She had to laugh. "You really want me to stay home?

It's gonna cost you. A million dollars, babe. I'll accept nothing less."

He rolled his eyes. "Colleen—"

"Put up or shut up."

"Seriously, Colleen, I've been to Tulgeria and—"

"I'm *dead* serious, Robert. *And* if you want to lecture me about the dangers of Tulgeria, you've got to buy me dinner. But first you've got to come with me while I sell my car—make sure the buyer's really a buyer and not some psycho killer who answers vintage car ads in the *Boston Globe*."

He didn't hesitate. "Of course I'll come with you."

Jackpot. "Great," Colleen said. "We'll go take care of business, then drop your stuff at your hotel before we grab some dinner. Is that a plan?"

He looked at her. "I never really stood a chance here, did I?"

She smiled at him happily. "Nope."

Bobby nodded, then turned to look out the window. He murmured something that Colleen wasn't quite sure she caught, but it sounded an awful lot like, "I'm a dead man."

Chapter 3

Dark, cool and mysterious.

Somehow, despite his best intentions, Bobby had ended up sitting across from Colleen in a restaurant that was decidedly dark, cool and mysterious.

The food *was* great. Colleen had been right about that, too.

Although she didn't seem to be eating too much.

The meeting with the buyer had gone well. The man had accepted her price for the car—no haggling.

It turned out that that meeting had been held in the well-lit office of a reputable escrow agent, complete with security guard. Colleen had known damn well there was absolutely no danger from psycho killers or anyone else.

Still, Bobby had been glad that he was there while the buyer handed over a certified check and she handed over the title and keys to the Mustang.

She'd smiled and even laughed, but it was brittle, and he'd wanted to touch her. But he hadn't. He knew that he couldn't. Even just a hand on her shoulder would have been too intimate. And if she'd leaned back into him, he would have put his arms around her. And if he'd done that there in the office, he would have done it again, later, when they were alone, and there was no telling where that might lead.

No, strike that. Bobby knew damn well it would lead to him kissing her. And that could and would lead to a full meltdown, a complete and utter dissolving of his defenses and resolve.

It made him feel like a total skeeve. What kind of friend could he be to Colleen if he couldn't even offer her the most basic form of comfort as a hand on her shoulder? Was he really so weak that he couldn't control himself around her?

Yes.

The answer was a resounding, unchallenged *yes*.

No doubt about it—he was scum.

After leaving the escrow office, they'd taken the T into Harvard Square. Colleen had kept up a fairly steady stream of conversation. About law school. About her roommate—a woman named Ashley who'd gone back to Scarsdale for the summer to work in her father's law office, but who still sent monthly checks for her share of the rent, who didn't have the nerve to tell her father that, like Colleen, she'd far rather be a public defender and a pro bono civil litigant than a highly paid corporate tax attorney.

Bobby had checked into his hotel and given his bag and a tip to the bellhop. He didn't dare take it up to his room himself—not with Colleen trailing behind, no way.

That transaction only took a few minutes, and then they were back out in the warm summer night.

The restaurant was only a short walk into Harvard Square. As he sat down across from Colleen, as he gazed at her pretty face in the dim candlelight, he'd ordered a cola. He was dying for a beer, but there was no way he'd trust himself to have even one. If he was going to survive this, he needed all of his wits about him.

They talked about the menu, about food—a nice safe topic—for a while. And then their order came, and Bobby ate while Colleen pushed the food around on her plate.

She was quiet by then, too. It was unusual to be around a Skelly who wasn't constantly talking.

"Are you okay?" he asked.

She looked up at him, and he realized that there were tears in her eyes. She shook her head. But then she forced a smile. "I'm just being stupid," she said before the smile wavered and disappeared. "I'm sorry."

She pushed herself out of the booth and would have rushed past him, toward the rest rooms at the back of the restaurant, if he hadn't reached out and grabbed her hand. He slid out of the bench seat, too, still holding on to her. It took him only a second to pull more than enough dollars to cover the bill out of his pocket and toss it onto the table.

This place had a rear exit. He'd automatically noted it when they'd first came in—years of practice in preparing an escape route—and he led her to it now, pushing open the door.

They had to go up a few steps, but then they were outside, on a side street. It was just a stone's throw to Brattle Street, but they were still far enough from the circus-like atmosphere of Harvard Square on a summer night to have a sense of distance and seclusion from the crowds.

"I'm sorry," Colleen said again, trying to wipe away her tears before they even fell. "I'm stupid—it's just a stupid car."

Bobby had something very close to an out-of-body experience. He saw himself standing there, in the shadows, next to her. Helplessly, with a sense of total doom, he watched himself reach for her, pull her close and enfold her in his arms.

Oh, dear Lord, she was so soft. And she held him tightly, her arms around his waist, her face buried in his shoulder as she quietly tried not to cry.

Don't do this. Get away from her. You're asking for trouble.

He must've made some kind of awful strangled sound because Colleen lifted her head and looked up at him. "Oh, no, am I hurting you?"

"No," he said. No, she was *killing* him. And count on Colleen to worry about someone else during a moment when most people wouldn't have been thinking of anyone but themselves.

Tears glistened on her cheeks and sparkled in her eyelashes, and the tip of her nose was red. Bozo the Clown, he and Wes had teased her whenever she'd cried back when she was thirteen.

She wasn't thirteen anymore.

Don't kiss her. Don't do it.

Bobby clenched his teeth and thought about Wes. He pictured the look on his best friend's face as he tried to explain. *See, she was right there, man, in my arms, and her mouth looked so soft and beautiful, and her body was so warm and lush and...*

She put her head back against his shoulder with a sigh, and Bobby realized he was running his fingers through the silk of her hair. She had hair like a baby's, soft and fine.

He knew he should make himself stop, but he couldn't. He'd wanted to touch her hair for more than four years now.

Besides, she really seemed to like it.

"You must think I'm a loser," she murmured.

"No."

She laughed softly. "Yeah, well, I am. Crying over a car. How dumb can I be?" She sighed. "It's just… When I was seventeen, I'd imagined I'd have that car forever—you know, hand it down to my grandchildren? I say it now, and it sounds stupid, but it didn't feel stupid back then."

The deal she'd just made gave her twenty-four hours to change her mind.

"It's not too late," he reminded her. He reminded himself, too. He could gently release her, take one step back, then two. He could—without touching her again—lead her back to the lights and crowd in Harvard Square. And then he'd never even have to mention anything to Wes. Because nothing would have happened.

But he didn't move. He told himself he would be okay, that he could handle this—as long as he didn't look into her eyes.

"No, I'm selling it," she told him, pulling back slightly to look up at him, wiping her nose on a tissue she'd taken from her shoulder pack. "I've made up my mind. I need this money. I loved that car, but I love going to law school, too. I love the work I do, I love being able to make a difference."

She was looking at him so earnestly he forgot about not looking into her eyes until it was too late. Until the earnest look morphed into something else, something loaded with longing and spiked with desire.

Her gaze dropped to his mouth, and her lips parted slightly, and when she looked once again into his eyes, he knew. She wanted to kiss him nearly as much as he wanted to kiss her.

Don't do this. Don't...

He could feel his heart pounding, hear the roar of his blood surging through his body, drowning out the sounds of the city night, blocking out all reason and harsh reality.

He couldn't not kiss her. How could he keep from kissing her when he needed to kiss her as much as he needed to fill his lungs with air?

But she didn't give him a chance to lean down toward her. She stood on her tiptoes and brushed her mouth across his in a kiss that was so achingly sweet that he thought for one paralyzingly weak-kneed moment he just might faint.

But she stepped back just a little to look at him again, to smile hesitantly into his eyes before reaching up, her hand cool against the too-hot back of his neck as she pulled his head down to kiss him again.

Her lips were so soft, so cool, so sweetly uncertain, such a contrast to the way his heart was hammering and to the tight, hot sensation in his rib cage—as if his entire chest were about to burst.

He was afraid to move. He was afraid to kiss her back, for fear he'd scare her to death with his hunger for her. He didn't even know how to kiss like this—with such delicate tenderness.

But he liked it. Lord, he liked it an awful lot. He'd had his share of women who'd given him deep, wet, soul kisses, sucking his tongue into their mouths in a decidedly unsubtle imitation of what they wanted to do with him later, in private.

But those kisses hadn't been even a fraction as sexy as what Colleen was doing to him right now.

She kissed his mouth, his chin and then his mouth again, her own lips slightly parted. She barely touched him. In fact, she touched him more with her breath— soft, unsteady puffs of air that caressed him enticingly.

He tried to kiss her the same way, tried to touch her without really touching her, skimming his hands down her back, his palms tingling from the almost-contact. It made him dizzy with anticipation.

Incredible anticipation.

She touched his lips with her tongue—just the very tiniest tip of her tongue—and pleasure crashed through him. It was so intense that for one blindingly unsteady moment he was afraid he might actually have embarrassed himself beyond recovery.

From just a kiss.

But he hadn't. Not yet, anyway. Still, he couldn't take it anymore, not another second longer, and he crushed her to him, filling his hands with the softness of her body, sweeping his tongue into her mouth.

She didn't seem to mind. In fact, her pack fell to the ground, and she kissed him back enthusiastically, welcoming the ferocity of his kisses, winding her arms around his neck, pressing herself even more tightly against him.

It was the heaven he'd dreamed of all these years.

Bobby kissed her, again and again—deep, explosively hungry kisses that she fired right back at him. She opened herself to him, wrapping one of her legs around his, moaning her pleasure as he filled his hand with her breast.

He caught himself glancing up, scanning a nearby narrow alleyway between two buildings, estimating whether it was dark enough for them to slip inside, dark enough for him to unzip his shorts and pull up her skirt, dark enough for him to take her, right there, beneath someone's kitchen window, with her legs around his waist and her back against the roughness of the brick wall.

He'd pulled her halfway into the alley before reality came screaming through.

Wes's sister. This was Wes's *sister*.

He had his tongue in Wes's sister's mouth. One hand was filled with the softness of Wes's sister's derriere as he pressed her hips hard against his arousal. His other hand was up Wes's sister's shirt.

Had he completely lost his mind?

Yes.

Bobby pulled back, breathing hard.

That was almost worse, because now he had to look at her. She was breathing hard, too, her breasts rising and falling rapidly, her nipples taut and clearly outlined beneath her shirt, her face flushed, her lips swollen and moist from his kisses.

But it was her eyes that almost killed him. They were smoky with desire, brimming with fire and unresolved passion.

"Let's go to my apartment," she whispered, her voice even huskier than usual.

Oh, God.

"I can't." His voice cracked, making him sound even more pathetic.

"Oh," she said. "Oh, I'm—" she shook her head "—I'm sorry, I thought... You said you weren't seeing anyone."

"No." He shook his head, tried to catch his breath. "It's not that."

"Then why stop?"

He couldn't respond. What could he possibly say? But shaking his head again wasn't a good enough response for Colleen.

"You really don't want to come back to my place and—"

"I can't. I just can't." He cut her off, unable to bear finding out just which words she would use to describe what they'd do if he did go home with her tonight. Whether she called it making love or something more crudely to the point, however she couched it, it would be a total turn-on.

And he was already *way* too turned on.

She took a step toward him, and he took a step back.

"You're serious," she said. "You really don't want to?"

He couldn't let her think that. "I want to," he told her. "God, I want to. More than you could possibly know. I just... I *can't*."

"What, have you taken some kind of vow of abstinence?"

Somehow he managed to smile at her. "Sort of."

Just like that she understood. He saw the realization dawn in her eyes and flare rapidly into anger. "Wesley," she said. "This is about my brother, isn't it?"

Bobby knew enough not to lie to her. "He's my best friend."

She was furious. "What did he do? Warn you to stay away from me? Did he tell you not to touch me? Did he tell you not to—"

"No. He warned me not even to *think* about it." Wes had said it jokingly, one night on liberty when they'd each had five or six too many beers. Wes hadn't really believed it was a warning he'd needed to give his best friend.

Colleen bristled. "Well, you know what? Wes can't tell *me* what to think, and *I've* been thinking about it. For a long time."

Bobby gazed at her. Suddenly it was hard to breathe again. A long time. "Really?"

She nodded, her anger subdued, as if she were suddenly shy. She looked everywhere but in his eyes. "Yeah. Wasn't that kind of obvious from the way I jumped you?"

"I thought I jumped you."

Colleen looked at him then, hope in her eyes. "Please come home with me. I really want you to—I want to make love to you, Bobby. You're only here for a week— let's not waste a minute."

Oh, God, she'd said it. Bobby couldn't bear to look at her, so he closed his eyes. "Colleen, I promised Wes I'd look out for you. That I'd take care of you."

"Perfect." She bent down to pick up her bag. "Take care of me. Please."

Oh, man. He laughed because, despite his agony, he found her funny as hell. "I'm positive he didn't mean it like that."

"You know, he doesn't need to find out."

Bobby braced himself and met her gaze. "I can't be that kind of friend to him."

She sighed. "Terrific. Now I feel like a total worm."

She started toward Brattle Street. "I think, considering all things, we should skip the movie. I'm going home. If you change your mind..."

"I won't."

"...you know where to find me." Bobby followed her about a dozen more steps, and she turned around. "Are you coming with me after all?"

"It's getting late. I'll see you home."

"No," Colleen said. "Thank you, but no."

Bobby knew not to press it. That look in her eyes was one he'd seen far too many times on a completely different Skelly.

"I'm sorry," he said again.

"Me, too," she told him before she walked away.

The sidewalk wasn't as crowded as it had been just a few hours ago, so Bobby let her get a good head start before he started after her.

He followed her all the way home, making certain she was safe without letting her see him again.

And then he stood there, outside her apartment building, watching the lights go on in her apartment, angry and frustrated and dying to be up there with her, and wondering what on earth he was going to do now.

Chapter 4

Colleen had printed out the email late last night, and she now held it tightly in her hand as she approached Bobby.

He was exactly where he'd said he would be when he'd called—sitting on the grassy slope along the Charles River, looking out at the water, sipping coffee through a hot cup with a plastic lid.

He saw her coming and got to his feet. "Thanks for meeting me," he called.

He was so serious—no easygoing smile on his face. Or maybe he was nervous. It was hard to be sure. Unlike Wes, who twitched and bounced off the walls at twice his normal frenetic speed when he was nervous, Bobby showed no outward sign.

He didn't fiddle with his coffee cup. He just held it serenely. He'd gotten them both large cups, but in his hand, large looked small.

Colleen was going to have to hold hers with both hands.

He didn't tap his foot. He didn't nervously clench his teeth. He didn't chew his lip.

He just stood there and breathed as he solemnly watched her approach.

He'd called at 6:30 this morning. She'd just barely fallen asleep after a night spent mostly tossing and turning—and analyzing everything she'd done and said last night, trying to figure out what she'd done wrong.

She'd come to the conclusion that she'd done *every-*thing wrong. Starting with crying over a motor vehicle and ending with darn near throwing herself at the man.

This morning Bobby had apologized for calling so early and had told her he hadn't been sure what time she was leaving for work today. He'd remembered that she was driving the truck, remembered their tentative plan to meet for breakfast.

Last night she'd wanted him to *stay* for breakfast.

But he hadn't—because of some stupid idea that by having a relationship with her, he'd be betraying Wes.

Wes, whose life he'd most likely saved, probably countless times. Including, so it seemed, one definite time just a few short weeks ago.

"I can't believe you didn't tell me you'd been *shot.*" Colleen didn't bother saying good morning. She just thrust the copy of Wes's email at him.

He took it and read it quickly. It wasn't very long. Just a short, fast, grammatically creative hello from Wes, who didn't report where he was, who really just wanted to make sure Bobby had arrived in Boston. He mentioned almost in passing that Bobby had recently been shot while out in the real world—the SEALs' nickname for a real mission or operation.

They had been somewhere they weren't supposed to be, Wes reported vaguely, and due to circumstances out of their control, they'd been discovered. Men with assault weapons started shooting, and Bobby had stepped in front of Wes, taking some bullets and saving his scrawny hide.

"Be nice to him," Wes had written to Colleen. "He nearly died. He almost got his butt shot off, and his shoulder's still giving him pain. Treat him kindly. I'll call as soon as I'm back in the States."

"If he can say all that in an email," Colleen told Bobby sternly, "you could have told me at least a *little* about what happened. You could have told me you were shot instead of letting me think you'd hurt yourself in some normal way—like pulling a muscle playing basketball."

He handed her the piece of paper. "I didn't think it was useful information," he admitted. "I mean, what good is telling you that a bunch of bad guys with guns tried to kill your brother a few weeks ago? Does knowing that really help you in any way?"

"Yes, because *not* knowing hurts. You don't need to protect me from the truth," Colleen told him fiercely. "I'm not a little girl anymore." She rolled her eyes. "I thought we cleared *that* up last night."

Last night. When some extremely passionate kisses had nearly led to getting it on right out in the open, in an alley not far from Harvard Square.

"I got coffee and muffins," Bobby said, deftly changing the subject. "Do you have time to sit and talk?"

Colleen watched as he lowered himself back onto the grass. Gingerly. Why hadn't she noticed that last night? She was *so* self-absorbed. "Yes. Great. Let's talk. You can start by telling me how many times you were shot and exactly where."

He glanced at her as she sat down beside him, amusement in his dark eyes. "Trust Wes to be melodramatic. I took a round in the upper leg that bled kind of heavily. It's fine now—no problem." He pulled up the baggy leg of his shorts to reveal a deeply tanned, enormously muscular thigh. There was a fresh pink scar up high on his leg. Where it would really hurt a whole lot to be shot. Where there were major veins—or were they arteries?—which, if opened, could easily cause a man to bleed to death very quickly.

Wes hadn't been melodramatic at all. Colleen couldn't breathe. She couldn't stop staring at that scar. Bobby could have died.

"It's my shoulder that's giving me the trouble," Bobby continued, pulling his shorts leg back down. "I was lucky I didn't break a bone, but it's still pretty sore. I've got limited mobility right now—which is frustrating. I can't lift my arm much higher than this."

He demonstrated, and Colleen realized that his ponytail wasn't a fashion statement after all. He was wearing his hair like that because he wasn't physically able to put it back in his usual neat braid.

"I'm supposed to take it easy," he told her. "You know, not push it for another week."

He handed her a cup of coffee and held open a bag that contained about a half a dozen enormous muffins. She shook her head. Her appetite was gone.

"Can you do me a favor?" she asked. "Next time you or Wes get hurt, even if it's just something really little, will you call me and let me know? Please? Otherwise I'm just going to worry about you all the time."

Bobby shook his head. "Colleen…"

"Don't *Colleen* me," she countered. "Just promise."

He looked at her. Sighed. "I promise. But—"

"No buts."

He started to say something, then stopped, shaking his head instead. No doubt he'd spent enough time around Skellys to know arguing was useless. Instead he took a sip of his coffee and gazed out at the river.

"How many times have you saved Wes's life?" she asked him, suddenly needing to know.

"I don't know. I think I lost count somewhere between two and three million." The laughter lines around his eyes crinkled as he smiled.

"Very funny."

"It's just not that big a deal," he said.

"It is to me," she returned. "And I'm betting it's a pretty big deal to my brother, too."

"It's really only a big deal to him because I'm winning," Bobby admitted.

At first his words didn't make sense. And then they made too much sense. "You guys keep score?" she asked in disbelief. "You have some kind of contest going…?"

Amusement danced in his eyes. "Twelve to five and a half. My favor."

"Five and a *half*?" she echoed.

"He got a half point for getting me back to the boat in one piece this last time," he explained. "He couldn't get a full point because it was partially his fault I needed his help in the first place."

He was laughing at her. Oh, he wasn't actually laughing aloud, but Colleen knew that, inside, he was silently chortling away.

"You know," she said with a completely straight face,

"it seems only fair that if you save someone's life that many times, you ought to be able to have wild sex with that person's sister, guilt free."

Bobby choked on his coffee. Served him right.

"So what are you doing tonight?" Colleen asked, still in that same innocent voice.

He coughed even harder, trying to get the liquid out of his lungs.

"'Be nice to him,'" she read aloud from Wes's email. She held it out for him to see. "See, it says it right there."

"That's *not* what Wes meant," Bobby managed to gasp.

"How do you know?"

"I *know*."

"Are you okay?" she asked.

His eyes were tearing, and he still seemed to have trouble breathing. "You're killing me."

"Good. I've got to go, so—" She started to stand up.

"Wait." He coughed again, tugging her back down beside him. "Please." He drew in a breath, and although he managed not to cough, he had to clear his throat several times. "I really need to talk to you about what happened last night."

"Don't you mean what *didn't* happen?" She pretended to be fascinated with her coffee cup, with folding up the little flap on the plastic lid so that she could take a sip without it bumping into her nose.

What had happened last night was that she had found out—the hard way—that Bobby Taylor didn't want her. At least not enough to take what she'd offered. At least not as much as she wanted him. It was possible he'd only used his fear of Wes's disapproval as an excuse to keep from going home with her. After all, it had worked, hadn't it? It had worked very well.

This morning she could only pretend not to care. She could be flip and say outrageous things, but the truth was, she was both embarrassed and afraid of what he might want to say to her.

Of course, if ever there were a perfect time for him to confess his undying love, it would be now. She supposed it *was* possible that he would haltingly tell her he'd fallen in love with her years ago, that he'd worshiped her from afar for all this time and now that they'd finally kissed, he couldn't bear to be apart from her any longer.

Bobby cleared his throat again. "Colleen, I, um… I don't want to lose you as a friend."

Or he could say that. He could give her the "let's stay friends" speech. She'd heard it before. It would contain the word *friend* at least seven more times. He would say *mistake* and *sorry* both at least twice and *honest* at least once. And he'd tell her that he hoped what happened last night wouldn't change things between them. Her friendship was very important to him.

"I really care about you," he told her. "But I have to be honest. What happened last night was, well, it was a mistake."

Yup. She'd definitely heard it before. She could have written it out for him on a three-by-five-card. Saved him some time.

"I know that I said last night that I couldn't…that we couldn't…because of *Wes* and, well, I need you to know that there's more to it than that."

Yeah, she'd suspected that.

"I can't possibly be what you really want," he said quietly.

Now *that* was different. She'd never heard that before.

"I'm not…" He started to continue, but then he shook his head and got back on track. "You mean too much to me. I can't take advantage of you, I *can't*. I'm ten years older than you, and—Colleen, I knew you when you were thirteen—that's just too weird. It would be crazy, it wouldn't go anywhere. It couldn't. *I* couldn't. We're too different and…" He swore softly, vehemently. "I really am sorry."

He looked about as miserable as she was feeling. Except he probably wasn't embarrassed to death. What had she been thinking, to throw herself at him like that last night?

She closed her eyes, feeling very young and very foolish—as well as ancient beyond her years. How could this be happening again? What was it about her that made men only want to be her friend?

She supposed she should be thankful. This time she got the "let's stay friends" speech *before* she'd gone to bed with the guy. That had been the lowest of a number of low-relationship moments. Or it should have been. Despite the fact that Bobby obviously cared enough not to let it get that far, he didn't care about her the way she wanted him to. And that hurt remarkably badly.

She stood up, brushing off the seat of her shorts. "I know you're probably not done. You still have one more *mistake* and another *sorry* to go, but I'll say 'em for you, okay? I'm sorry, too. The mistake was mine. Thanks for the coffee."

Colleen held her head up as she quickly walked away. And she didn't look back. She'd learned the hard way never to look back after the "let's stay friends" speech. And never to cry, either. After all, smart friends didn't cry when stupid, idiotic, completely clueless friends rejected them.

Tears welled in her eyes, but she forced them back. God, she was such a fool.

Bobby lay back on the grass and stared up at the sky.

In theory, telling Colleen that they should stay friends instead of rip each other's clothes off had seemed to be the least painful way of neatly dealing with something that was on the verge of turning into an emotional and physical bloodbath.

Physical—because if Wes found out that Bobby had messed with his little sister, he would have been mad enough to reach down Bobby's throat and rip his lungs out.

Bobby had been direct with Colleen. He'd been swift and, if not quite honest, he'd certainly been sincere.

Yet somehow he'd managed to hurt her. He'd seen it in her eyes as she'd turned and walked away.

Damn. Hurting her was the dead last thing he'd wanted to do.

That entire conversation had been impossibly difficult. He'd been on the verge of telling her the truth—that he hadn't slept at all last night, that he'd spent the night alternately congratulating himself for doing the right thing and cursing himself for being an idiot.

Last night she made it clear that she wanted him. And Lord knows that the last thing he honestly wanted was to stay mere friends with her. In truth, he wanted to get naked with her—and stay naked for the entire rest of this week.

But he knew he wasn't the kind of man Colleen Skelly needed. She needed someone who would be there for her. Someone who came home every night without fail. Someone who could take care of her the way she deserved to be taken care of.

Someone who wanted more than a week of hot sex.

He didn't want another long-distance relationship. He couldn't take it. He'd just gotten out of one of those, and it wasn't much fun.

And would be even less fun with Colleen Skelly—because after Wes found out that Bobby was playing around with his sister, Wes would come after him with his diving knife.

Well, maybe not, but certainly he and Wes would argue. And *Colleen* and Wes would argue. And that was an awful lot of pain, considering Bobby would spend most of his time three thousand miles away from her, him missing her with every breath he took, her missing him, too.

No, hurting Colleen was bad, but telling her the truth would hurt them both even more in the long run.

Chapter 5

Colleen had just finished picking up a load of blankets collected by a women's church group and was on her way to a half dozen senior centers to pick up their donations when a taxi pulled up. It stopped directly in front of her, blocking her exit from the parking lot with a TV-cop-drama squealing of brakes.

Her first thought was that someone was late to their own wedding. But other than the representative from the ladies' auxiliary who had handed over the bundles of blankets, the building had been silent and empty.

Her second thought was that someone was in a major hurry to repent their sins, probably before they sinned again. She had to laugh at that image, but her laughter faded as the absolute last person she'd expected to see here at the St. Augustus Church climbed out of the cab.

Bobby Taylor.

His hair had partially fallen out of his ponytail, and his face was covered with a sheen of perspiration, as if he'd been running. He ignored both his sweat and his hair as he came around to the passenger side of the truck's cab. She leaned across the bench seat, unlocked the door, and he opened it.

"Thank God," he said as if he really meant it. "I've been following you for an hour now."

More than just his face was sweaty. His shirt was as soaked as if he'd been running a marathon in this heat.

Wes. Her brother was the only reason she could come up with for Bobby to search her out so desperately. Wes had to have been injured. Or—please, God, no—dead.

Colleen flashed hot and then cold. "Oh, no," she said. "What happened? How bad is it?"

Bobby stared at her. "Then you haven't heard? I was ready to yell at you because I thought you knew. I thought you went out to make these pickups, anyway."

"Just tell me he's not dead," she begged him. She'd lived through one dead brother—it was an experience she never wanted to repeat. "I can take anything as long as he's not dead."

His expression became one of even more perplexity as he climbed into the air-conditioned cab and closed the door. "He?" he asked. "It was a woman who was attacked. She's in ICU, in a coma, at Mass General."

A woman? At Mass General Hospital…? Now it was Colleen's turn to stare at him stupidly. "You didn't track me down because Wes is hurt?"

"Wes?" Bobby shook his head as he leaned forward to turn the air conditioner fan to high. "No, I'm sure he's fine. The mission was probably only a training op.

He wouldn't have been able to send email if it were the real thing."

"Then what's going on?" Colleen's relief was mixed with irritation. He had a lot of nerve, coming after her like this and scaring her to death.

"Andrea Barker," he explained. "One of the chief administrators of the AIDS Education Center. She was found badly beaten—barely breathing—outside of her home in Newton. I saw it in the paper."

Colleen nodded. "Yeah," she said. "Yeah, I heard about that this morning. That's really awful. I don't know her that well—we talked on the phone only once. I've mostly met with her assistant when dealing with the center."

"So you *did* know she's in the hospital." Something very much like anger flashed in his eyes, and his usually pleasantly relaxed mouth was back to a hard, grim line.

Bobby Taylor was mad at her. It was something Colleen had never experienced before. She hadn't thought he was capable of getting mad—he was so laid-back. Even more mind-blowing was the fact that she truly had no clue what she'd done to get him so upset.

"The article went into some depth about the problem they've—*you've*— You're part of them, providing legal services at no cost, right? The problem *you've* been having establishing a center in this one particular neighborhood in Boston. The same neighborhood where you just happened to be threatened yesterday while having a car wash…?"

And Colleen understood. She laughed in disbelief. "You really think the attack on Andrea Barker had something to do with her work for the education center?"

Bobby didn't shout at her the way Wesley did when

he got mad. He spoke quietly, evenly, his voice danger-ously soft. Combined with the spark of anger in his eyes, it was far more effective than any temper tantrum Wes had ever thrown. "And you don't?"

"No. Come on, Bobby. Don't be so paranoid. Look, I heard that the police theory is she startled a burglar coming out of her house."

"I heard a partial list of her injuries," Bobby coun-tered, still in that same quietly intense voice. She had to wonder, what would ever set him off, make him raise his voice? What—if anything—would make this man lose his cool and detonate? If it ever happened, boy, look out. It would probably be quite an impressive show.

"They weren't the kind of injuries a woman would get from a burglar," he continued, "whose primary goal would have been to knock her down so he could run away as quickly as possible. No, I'm sorry, Colleen. I know you want to believe otherwise, but this woman was beaten deliberately, and if I know it, then the police know it, too. The burglar story is probably just some-thing they threw out to the press, to make the real per-petrator think he's home-free."

"You don't know that for sure."

"Yes," he said. "You're right. I don't know it abso-lutely. But I'm 99 percent sure. Sure enough to be afraid that, as the legal representative to the AIDS Education Center, you could be the next target. Sure enough to know that the last thing you should be doing today is driving a truck around all by yourself."

He clenched his teeth, the muscles jumping in his jaw as he glared at her. That spark of anger made his eyes cold, as if she were talking to a stranger.

Well, maybe she was.

"Oh. Right." Colleen let her voice get louder with her growing anger. What did he care what happened to her? She was just an idiot who'd embarrassed both of them last night. She was just his *friend*. No, not even. The real truth was that she was just some pain-in-the-butt sister of a friend. "I'm supposed to lock myself in my apartment because there *might* be people who don't like what I do? Sorry, that's not going to happen."

"I spoke to some people," Bobby told her. "They seem to think this John Morrison who threatened you yesterday could be a real danger."

"Some people?" she asked. "Which people? If you talked to Mindy in the center's main office—well, she's afraid of her own shadow. And Charlie Johannsen is no—"

"I dare you," Bobby said, "to look me in the eye and tell me that you're not just a little bit afraid of this man."

She looked at him. Looked away. "Okay. So maybe I am a *little*—"

"And yet you came out here, anyway. By yourself."

She laughed in his face. "Yeah, and like *you* never do anything that you're a little afraid of. Like jumping out of airplanes. Or swimming in shark-infested waters. That's a particularly tough one for you, isn't it, Bobby? Wes told me you have a thing about sharks. Yet you do it. You jump into the water without hesitation. You face down your fear and get on with your life. Don't be a hypocrite, Taylor, and expect me to do anything less."

He was trying hard to be patient. "I'm trained to do those things."

"Yeah, well, I'm a woman," she countered. "I've been trained, too. I've had more than ten years of experience dealing with everything from subtle, male innuendo to overt threats. By virtue of being female, I'm a little bit afraid almost every single time I walk down a city street—and I'm twice as afraid at night."

He shook his head. "There's a big difference between that and a specific threat from a man like John Morrison."

"Is there?" Colleen asked. "Is there really? Because I don't see it that way. You know, there have been times when I walk past a group of men sitting out on the front steps of their apartment building, and one of them says, 'Hey, baby. Want to…'" She said it. It was impossibly crude, and Bobby actually flinched. "'Get over here now,' they say. 'Don't make me chase you to get what I *know* you want to give me.'"

She paused for emphasis. Bobby looked appropriately subdued. "After someone," she said more quietly now, "some *stranger* says something like that to you—and if you want a real dare, then I dare you to find a woman my age who *hasn't* had a similar experience—you get a little—just a little—nervous just going out of your apartment. And when you approach a man heading toward you on the sidewalk, you feel a little flicker of apprehension or maybe even fear. Is he going to say something rude? Is he going take it a step further and follow you? Or is he just going to look at you and maybe whistle, and let you see from his eyes that he's thinking about you in ways that you don't want him to be thinking about you?

"And each time that happens," Colleen told him, "it's no less specific—or potentially unreal—than John Morrison's threats."

Bobby was silent, just sitting there, looking out the window.

"I'm so sorry," he finally said. "What kind of world

do we live in?" He laughed, but it wasn't laughter that had anything to do with humor. It was a burst of frustrated air. "The really embarrassing part is that I've been that guy. Not the one who actually says those things, I'd never do that. But I'm the one who looks and even whistles. I never really thought something like that might frighten a woman. I mean, that was *never* my intention."

"Think next time," she told him.

"Someone really said that to you?" He gave her a sidelong glance. "In those words?"

She nodded, meeting his gaze. "Pretty rude, huh?"

"I wish I'd been there," he told her. "I would've put him in the hospital."

He said it so matter-of-factly, but she knew it wasn't just an idle threat. "If you had been there," she pointed out, "he wouldn't have said it."

"Maybe Wes is right." Bobby smiled at her ruefully. "Maybe you *should* have a twenty-four-hour armed escort, watching your every move."

"Oh, no," Colleen groaned. "Don't *you* start with that, too. Look, I've got a can of pepper spray in my purse and a whistle on my key ring. I know you don't think so, but I'm about as safe as I can be. I've been keeping the truck doors locked, I've called ahead to set up appointment times, I've—"

"You forgot me," Bobby interrupted. "You should have called me, Colleen. I would have gladly come along with you right from the start."

Oh, perfect. She knew without even asking that he was not going to leave, that he was here in the cab of this truck until she made the last of her pickups, dropped off both the donations and the truck, and took the T back to Cambridge.

"Has it occurred to you that I might not be overly eager to spend the day with you?" she asked him.

She could see his surprise. He'd never dreamed she would be so blunt and to the point. Still, he recovered nicely. And he surprised her back by being equally straightforward.

"It's already too late for our friendship, isn't it?" he said. "I really blew it last night."

No way was she going to let him take the blame. "I was the one who kissed you first."

"Yeah, but I was the one who didn't stop you right then and there," Bobby countered.

She jammed the truck into gear, silently cursing herself for being stupid enough to have even just a little hope left to be crushed. Yet there it was, flapping about like a deflated balloon on the gritty floor of the truck, right next to her shredded pride and pulverized heart.

"I'm sorry," he said. "I should have been able to control myself, but I couldn't. I'm…"

Colleen looked at him. She didn't mean to. She didn't want to. God forbid he see the total misery that his words brought her reflected in her eyes. But there was something in his voice that made her unable to keep from turning her head.

He was looking at her. He was just sitting there, *looking* at her, and it was the exact same way he'd looked at her last night, right before he'd pulled her close and kissed the hell out of her. There was hunger in his eyes. Heat and need and *desire*.

He looked away quickly, as if he didn't want her to see those things. Colleen looked away, too, her mind and heart both racing.

He was lying. He'd lied this morning, too. He didn't want them to stay just friends any more than *she* did.

He hadn't given her the "let's stay friends" speech because he had an aversion to women like her, women who actually had hips and thighs and weighed more than ninety pounds, wet. He hadn't made that speech because he found her unattractive, because she didn't turn him on.

On the contrary...

With a sudden clarity that should have been accompanied by angelic voices and a brilliant light, Colleen knew.

She *knew.* Bobby had said there was more to it, but there wasn't. This was about Wes.

It was Wesley who had gotten in the way of her and Bobby Taylor, as surely as if he were sitting right there between them, stinking of stale cigarette smoke, in the cab of this truck.

But she wasn't going to call Bobby on that—no way. She was going to play—and win—this game, secure that she knew the cards he was holding in his hand.

Bobby wasn't going to know what hit him.

She glanced at him again as she pulled out of the parking lot. "So you really think Andrea's attack had something to do with her being an AIDS activist?" she asked.

He glanced at her, too, and this time he managed to keep his eyes mostly expressionless. But it was back there—a little flame of desire. Now that she knew what to look for, she couldn't help but see it. "I think until she comes out of that coma and tells the police what happened, we should err on the side of caution."

Colleen made herself shiver. "It's just so creepy—

the thought of her being attacked right outside of her own home."

"You don't have to worry about that. I'll go home with you after we're done here."

Jackpot. She had to bite the insides of her cheeks to keep from smiling. She somehow managed to twist her mouth around into a face of displeasure. "Oh," she said. "I don't know if that's necessary—"

"I'll check your place out, see what we can do to heighten the security," he told her. "Worst-case scenario, I'll camp out in the living room tonight. I know you probably don't want me to, but…"

No, indeed, she did *not* want him camped out in her living room tonight.

She wanted him in her bedroom.

"Wait," Colleen said, when Bobby would've opened the truck door and climbed down, after she parked outside the next senior center on her list. She was fishing around in her backpack, and she came up brandishing a hairbrush. "The wild hairstyle needs a little work."

He had to laugh. "That's so completely un-PC."

"What, telling you that your hair is a mess?"

"Very funny," he said.

"That's me," she said. "Six laughs a minute, guaranteed. Turn around, I'll braid it for you."

How had that happened? Ten minutes ago they'd been fighting. Bobby had been convinced that their friendship was badly strained if not completely over, yet now things were back to where they'd been when he'd first arrived yesterday.

Colleen was no longer completely tense, no longer

looking wounded. She was relaxed and cheerful. He would even dare to call her happy.

Bobby didn't know how that had happened, but he wasn't about to complain.

"You don't have to braid it," he said. "A ponytail's good enough. And all I really need help with is tying it back. I can brush it myself."

He reached for the brush, but she pulled it back, away from him.

"I'll braid it," she said.

"If you really want to." He let her win. What harm could it do? Ever since he'd gotten injured, he'd had to ask for help with his hair. This morning he'd gone into a beauty salon not far from his hotel, tempted to cut it all off.

Back in California, he'd gotten help with his hair each day. Wes stopped by and braided it for him. Or Mia Francisco—the lieutenant commander's wife. Even the captain—Joe Cat—had helped him out once or twice.

He shifted slightly in the seat so Colleen had access to the back of his head, reaching up with his good arm to take out the elastic.

She ran both the brush and her fingers gently through his hair. And Bobby knew immediately that there was a major difference between Colleen braiding his hair and Wes braiding his hair. They were both Skellys, sure, but that was where all similarities ended.

"You have such beautiful hair," Colleen murmured, and he felt himself start to sweat.

This was a bad idea. A very, very bad idea. What could he possibly have been thinking? He closed his eyes as she brushed his hair back, gathering it at his neck with her other hand. And then she was done brushing, and she just used her hands. Her fingers felt cool against his forehead as she made sure she got the last stray locks off his face.

She was going to braid his hair, and he was going to sit here, acutely aware of each little, last, barely-touching-him movement of her fingers. He was going to sit here, wanting her, thinking of how soft she'd felt in his arms just last night, how ready and willing and eager she'd been. She wouldn't have stopped him from pushing up her skirt and burying himself inside of her and—

Sweat trickled down his back.

What harm was there in letting her braid his hair?

None—provided no one at the Parkvale Senior Center had enough of their eyesight left to notice the uncomfortably tight fit of his pants.

Provided Colleen didn't notice it, either. If she did, she would realize that he'd lied to her. It wouldn't take her long to figure out the truth. And then he'd be a dead man.

Bobby tried thinking about death, about rats, about plague, about pestilence. He tried thinking about sharks—all those teeth, those mean little eyes coming right at him. He thought about the day—and that day *was* coming, since he was no longer in his twenties—when he'd have to leave the SEAL teams, when he'd be too old to keep up with the newer recruits.

None of it worked to distract him.

Colleen's gentle touch cut through it all. It was far more real than any of his worst-imagined nightmares.

Yet it was remarkably easy to picture her touching him like that all over—not just on his head and his hair and the back of his neck, but *all* over. Oh, man…

"If I were a guy," Colleen murmured, "and I had hair like this, I'd wear it down. All the time. And I would have women falling at my feet. Lining up outside my bedroom door. All the time."

Bobby choked. "What?"

"Most women can't keep their hands off guys with long hair," she explained. "Particularly good-looking guys like you who are completely ripped. Hey, did you pack your uniform?"

She thought he was good-looking and *ripped*. Bobby had to smile. He liked that she thought of him that way, even though he wasn't sure it was completely true. He was a little too big, too solid to get the kind of muscle definition that someone like Lucky O'Donlon had.

Now, there was a man who was truly ripped. Of course, Lucky wasn't here right now as a comparison, which was just as well. Even though he was married, women were still drawn to him like flies to honey.

"Hello," Colleen said. "Did you fall asleep?"

"No," Bobby said. "Sorry." She'd asked him something. "Um…"

"Your uniform?"

"Oh," he said. "No. No, I'm not supposed to wear a uniform while my hair's long—unless there's some kind of formal affair that I can't get out of attending."

"No this one's not formal," she told him. "It's casual— a bon voyage party at the local VFW the night before we leave. But there will be VIPs there—senators and the mayor and… I just thought it would be cool for them to meet a real Navy SEAL."

"Ah," he said. She was almost done braiding his hair, and he was simultaneously relieved and disappointed. "You want me to be a circus attraction."

She laughed. "Absolutely. I want you to stand around and look mysterious and dangerous. You'd be the hit of the party." She reached over his shoulder, her arm warm against his slightly damp, air-conditioner-chilled T-shirt. "I need the elastic."

He tried to hand it to her, and they both fumbled. It dropped into his lap. He grabbed it quickly—God forbid she reach for it there—and held it out on his open palm for her to take.

Somehow she managed to touch nearly every inch of his palm as she took the elastic.

"You know what you're asking, don't you?" he said. "I'll spend the evening fending off all kinds of personal questions. Is it true SEALs know how to rip out an opponent's throat with their bare hands? How many men have you killed? Have you ever killed anyone in hand-to-hand combat? Did you like it? Is it true SEALs are rough in bed?" He let out a burst of exasperated air. "As soon as people find out I'm a SEAL, they change, Colleen. They look at me differently. The men size me up, and the women…" He shook his head.

She laughed as she sat back, finally done. "Yeah, right, Taylor. You tell me that you and my brother haven't taken advantage of the way women react when they find out you're a SEAL."

"No," he said. "You're right. I *have* taken advantage—too many times. It's just…these days I don't get much enjoyment out of it. It's not real. You know, I didn't tell Kyra I was a SEAL until we were together for two months."

"Did she treat you differently when she found out?" Colleen asked. Her eyes were more green than blue today, so luminous and beautiful.

"Yeah, she did," he had to admit. "It was subtle, but it was there." And she'd slept with him that very same night. Coincidence? Maybe. But unlikely.

"I'm sorry," she said. "Forget I asked. You don't even have to come to this thing. It's just… I have to go, and since you're doing this twenty-four-hour bodyguard thing, I thought—"

"I'll call Harvard, have him send my uniform."

"No," she said. "You can go incognito. With your hair down. Wearing leather pants. I'll tell everyone you're a supermodel from Paris. See what kind of questions you get asked then."

Bobby laughed as Colleen climbed down from the cab of the truck. "Hey," he said, sliding across the seat and keeping her from closing the door by sticking out his foot. "I'm glad we're still friends."

"You know, I've been thinking about this friend thing," she said, standing there, hands on her hips, looking up at him. "I think we should be the kind of friends who have wild sex three or four times a day."

She shot him a smile and turned toward the seniors center.

Bobby sat there, staring after her, watching the sunlight on her hair and the gentle swaying of her hips as she walked away.

She was kidding.

Wasn't she?

God, maybe she wasn't.

"Help," he said to no one in particular as he followed her inside.

Chapter 6

Bobby caught Colleen by the arm and pulled her back, almost on top of him, almost down the stairs that led to her third-floor apartment.

At first she thought she'd won. At first she thought that all the little glances and smiles, and all the thinly veiled—and some not so thinly veiled at all—comments she'd made all afternoon were finally paying off, that she'd succeeded in driving him crazy. She thought he was pulling her toward him to kiss her, the way he'd kissed her in Harvard Square last night.

Yeah, right, Colleen. Dream on.

Kissing her was the last thing on his mind. "Stay behind me," he ordered, pushing her so that her nose was practically pressed into the broad expanse of his back.

She realized then that her apartment door was ajar.

Someone was in her apartment.

Andrea Barker had come home, too, to find someone breaking into her house.

And had been beaten so badly she was still in a coma.

Colleen grabbed Bobby—it was about as effective as grabbing an aircraft carrier. "Don't go in there!"

"I won't," he said. "At least not before I get you out of here." He was holding on to her then, too, turning toward her and practically lifting her up, about to carry her down the stairs.

For the first time in her life Colleen actually felt fragile and petite and in need of rescue.

She wasn't quite sure she liked it.

She was scared, yes. She didn't want Bobby charging in, a one-man assault team, to find John Morrison and his gang in her living room. At the same time, if John Morrison and his gang *were* in her apartment, she didn't want to run away and lose the opportunity to have them all arrested.

"Put me down," she ordered him. They could go downstairs, call the police from Mr. Gheary's apartment.

To her surprise he did put her down, none too gently pushing her away from him. As she struggled to regain her balance, she realized he was charging up the last few stairs toward her apartment door. Toward a man who was coming out.

Wearing an unbelievably loud plaid shirt.

"Bobby, don't!"

She wasn't the only one shouting.

The owner of that shirt was shouting, too, shrieking, really, in pure terror.

It was Kenneth. Bobby had him against the entryway wall, his face pressed against the faded wallpaper, his armed twisted up behind his back.

"Bobby, *stop*! He's a friend of mine," Colleen shouted, taking the stairs two at a time, just as the door to her apartment opened wide, revealing the equally wide eyes of Ashley and her brother, Clark. She did a double take. Ashley's blue-haired brother, Clark.

"What are you doing here?" she asked Ashley, who was supposed to be spending the entire summer working at her father's law firm in New York.

"I escaped from Scarsdale," Ashley said faintly, staring at Bobby, who still had Kenneth pinned, his feet completely off the ground. "Clark and Kenneth came and broke me out."

That explained the blue hair. Nineteen-year-old Clark knew he'd be seeing his extremely conservative father. Say no more.

"Bobby, meet my roommate, Ashley DeWitt," Colleen said. "Her brother, Clark, and his friend, Kenneth. Guys, this is my brother's friend, Chief Bobby Taylor."

"I'm your friend, too," Bobby reminded her as he gently lowered the kid back to the floor. "Sorry."

The kid was shaken, but he pulled himself together quickly. "That was...somewhat uncomfortable, but the adrenaline rush is quite nice, thanks."

"Kenneth's from England," Colleen told him.

"Yeah," Bobby said, following them all into her apartment. "I caught that from the accent."

Man, Colleen hadn't been kidding. It was worse in here than he'd imagined. The small living room was filled, in some cases from floor to ceiling, with boxes. Colleen was in the process of writing, in big, block letters, what seemed to be a Tulgerian address on each of them. As far as he could tell, she was only about a third of the way done.

"So you're a chief, huh?" Clark said as Bobby closed the door behind him. "What tribe?"

"Oh, God! Clark, he's not *that* kind of chief." Ashley gave Bobby an apologetic smile. She was what he thought of as a New York blonde. Average height and slender, with a figure that was just barely curvy enough to be considered feminine, but certainly not curvy enough to be lush. Everything about her was neat and perfectly in place, nothing too extreme. She was cool and beautiful—kind of the way a stone statue was cool and beautiful. You didn't mind looking, but you wouldn't want to touch.

Compared to Ashley, Colleen was a mess. Her hair was everywhere. Her smile was crooked. Her breasts looked as if they were about to explode out from under her T-shirt every time she moved. She was too much of everything—too tall, too stacked, too blunt, too funny, too into having a good time wherever she went. Laughter spilled out of her constantly. Her eyes were never the same color from one minute to the next, but they were always, *always* welcoming and warm.

Desire knifed through him so sharply he had to clench his fists.

"Forgive my brother," Ashley continued. "He's terminally stupid."

He yanked his gaze away from Colleen, aware he'd been staring at her with his tongue nearly hanging out. God, he couldn't let her catch him looking at her that way. If she knew the truth...

Who was he kidding? She'd probably already guessed the truth. And now she was trying to drive him slowly

insane with all those deep looks and the seemingly innocently casual way she touched him damn near constantly
in passing. A hand on his arm, on his knee. Fingers cool
against his face as she fixed a stray lock of his hair.
Brushing against him with her shoulder. Sitting so close
that their thighs touched.

And the things she said to him! She thought they
should be the kind of friends who had sex three or four
times a day. She'd only been teasing. She liked being
outrageous—saying things like that and trying to shake
him up.

That one had worked.

"I'm a chief petty officer," Bobby explained to the kid
with blue hair, working to keep up with the conversation.
That kid's name was Clark. He was Ashley's brother—
no doubt about that. He had the same perfectly sculpted
nose and chin, slightly differently shaped eyes that were
a warmer shade of gray. "I'm in the Navy."

"Whoa, dude," Clark said. "With long hair like that?"
He laughed. "Hey, maybe they'll take me, huh?"

"Bobby's a—" Colleen cut herself off, and Bobby
knew she was remembering all that he'd told her about
the way most people's attitudes changed when they
found out he was a SEAL. She looked at him and as
their eyes met he felt the small room shrink. It was as
if he'd been caught in the beam of a searchlight—he
and Colleen. Ashley, Clark and Kenneth vanished in the
darkness outside his peripheral vision. All he could see
was Colleen and her beautiful, laughing eyes.

They were very blue right now.

"Bobby's a very good friend of mine," she said softly,
instead of telling them he was a SEAL.

"I should join the Navy," Clark's voice cut through. "Wouldn't *that* tick the old man off?"

"I had big plans for tonight," Colleen said, still looking into Bobby's eyes. "I was going to cook dinner for Bobby and then seduce him by dancing naked in the kitchen."

There she went again. More teasing. She was laughing at him—probably at the look of shock on his face. But as she turned away, as the world opened up again to include the other three people in the room, Bobby got the feeling that she wasn't completely kidding. She'd had plans for tonight, and those plans *had* included him.

"I should go," he said, wanting to stay at least as much as he wanted to keep breathing. But he couldn't stay. No way.

"No," Ashley said swiftly. "We were just going out."

"No, we weren't," Clark said with disdain. "You are such a liar. You have a headache—so bad that Kenneth was going to the drugstore to get you some painkillers." He turned to Colleen. "Unless you've got some hidden here. Ash wouldn't let me search your bedroom."

"Gee, I don't know why," Colleen said. "Could it maybe have something to do with the fact that the last time you searched my room I got home and called the police because I thought I'd been vandalized? Besides, you wouldn't have found any. I don't get headaches. Did you look in the bathroom?"

"I'm feeling much better," Ashley interrupted. Bobby had just met her, but even he could tell that she was lying. "We're going out."

"But what about that letter you were going to write to Dad?"

"It can wait." Ashley motioned toward the door with

her head, making big eyes at her brother. "This is Bobby Taylor. Wes's friend?" Clark stared at her blankly, as only a younger brother can stare at an older sister. "The Navy SEAL…?"

"Oh," Clark said. "*Oh*. Right." He looked at Bobby. "You're a SEAL, huh? Cool."

Colleen's smile was rueful and apologetic. "Sorry," she told Bobby. "I tried."

Clark grinned at Kenneth. "Dude! You were almost killed by a Navy SEAL! You should definitely tell the girls at that party tonight. I bet one of 'em will go home with you."

"Ashley, you really don't have to go anywhere," Colleen said to her friend. "You look wiped. What happened? What'd your father do now?"

Ashley just shook her head.

"What's a Navy SEAL?" Kenneth asked. "And do you suppose if he actually *had* killed me then Jennifer Reilly might want to marry me? I mean, if you think she might go home with me if he *almost* killed me…"

"Oh, no way!" Clark countered. "I wasn't thinking Jenn Reilly, dude! Set your sights lower, man. Think B or C tier. Think Stacy Thurmond or Candy Fremont."

"You rank the women you know into *tiers*?" Colleen was outraged. "Get out of my house, scumball!"

"Whoa," Clark said, backing up and tripping over one of the boxes. "We don't *tell* 'em we rank 'em. We'd never say it to their faces. They don't know. Honest."

"Yes, they do," Colleen countered. "Believe me, they know."

"Who is this *we* to whom you keep referring, scumball?" Kenneth asked Clark.

"What tier am *I* in?" Colleen's voice was dangerously quiet.

"A," Clark told her quickly. "Absolutely. You are so completely, gorgeously, perfectly A."

Colleen cut him down with a single word—a pungent profanity that Bobby realized he'd never heard her use before. Unlike Wes, she didn't pepper her everyday speech with four-letter words. As a matter of fact, he couldn't remember the last time he'd heard her say damn or even hell. It was pretty remarkable actually, considering how prone she was to blurting out whatever was on her mind.

I think we should be the kind of friends who have wild sex three or four times a day. Help.

"Once when I was running down by the river," Colleen told Clark tightly, "I went past these two guys who were grading all the women who ran by. The wind carried their voices to me right at the exact moment they were checking me out. They gave me a C minus—probably about the equivalent of your lower C tier."

Bobby couldn't stay silent another second. "They were fools."

"They were…several words I will not lower myself to use," she said, chin held high, pretending that a C-minus ranking by a pair of strangers didn't bother her one bit. Pretending she was above that. Pretending that she hadn't been hurt.

"You're on my A list," Bobby said. The moment the words left his lips, he realized he'd just made a fatal mistake. Although he'd meant it as the highest compliment, he'd just admitted that he had an A list. And that would make him little better than…what had she called Clark? A scumball.

"That came out really wrong," he told her quickly as her eyes started to narrow.

Clark, the genius, stepped up to the plate. "See? All guys have lists. It's a guy thing," he protested, not old enough to know that all either of them could do now was grovel, apologize and pray for forgiveness. "It doesn't mean anything."

"Bobby, strangle him, strangle his strange, plaid-clothed little friend," Colleen ordered him, "and then strangle yourself."

"What I *meant* to say," Bobby told her, moving close enough to catch her chin with his hand, so she now had to look up into his eyes, "was that I find you as beautiful on the outside as you are on the inside."

The searchlight clicked back on, and the rest of the world faded. Colleen was looking at him, her eyes wide, her lips slightly parted. She was the only other person in the entire universe. No one and nothing else existed. He couldn't even seem to move his hand away from the soft smoothness of her face.

"Strangle me?" Bobby heard Kenneth protest, his voice faint, as if coming from a great distance. "Why strangle *me*? I don't put anyone into tiers, thank you very much."

"Yeah, because you can't see past Jenn Reilly," Clark countered, also from somewhere way back there, beyond Colleen's eyes and Colleen's lips. "For you, Jenn's got her own gigantic tier—and everyone else is invisible. You and Jenn are *so* not going to happen, man. Even if hell froze over, she would walk right past you and date Frosty the Snowman. And then she would call you later to tell you how it went because you guys are *friends.*

Sheesh. Don't you know friendship is the kiss of death between a man and a woman?"

"That was very sweet," Colleen told Bobby softly. "I forgive you."

She took his hand and kissed him, right on the palm, and Bobby felt something major snap in his chest.

Oh, God, he had to get out of here before it was too late. Before he reached for her and...

He turned away, forcing himself to focus on blue hair and a loud plaid. Anything but Colleen and her bone-melting smile.

"Yes, I'm thwarted by the curse of being the *friend.*" Kenneth sighed. "I'm double damned because Jennifer thinks I'm gay. I'm her *gay* friend. I've told her that I'm quite not, thanks, but..."

"*Every*one thinks you're gay," Clark countered. "Tell me honestly, bro," he asked Bobby. "When you first saw Kenneth—I mean, Kenneth, come on, man. Only a gay dude would call himself Kenneth instead of Ken or Kenny—when you first saw him, Bobby, didn't you think—" he held out his hands to frame Kenneth, like a movie director *"—gay?"*

Bobby didn't bother to answer. He'd spent far too much time around Wes, who was the same kind of hyped-up, whirlwind talker as this kid, to know that his answer wasn't really needed. Which was just as well, because he wasn't completely convinced that he'd be able to speak.

Every time he looked into Colleen's eyes, his hands started to sweat, his chest felt squeezed and his throat tightened up. He was in desperate trouble.

"You know, my father thinks you're gay, too," Clark

told Kenneth. "I enjoy that about you. You frighten him, dude."

"Well, I'm not gay," Kenneth said through clenched teeth.

Bobby cleared his throat experimentally. A few more times and he'd have his voice back. Provided he didn't look at Colleen again.

"Not that there's anything wrong with being gay," Kenneth added hastily, glancing at Bobby. "We should probably make sure we're not offending a gay Navy SEAL here—an extremely big, extremely tall gay Navy SEAL. Although I still am not quite certain as to exactly what a Navy SEAL might be."

Clark looked at Bobby with new interest. "Whoa. It never even occurred to me. *Are* you gay?"

For the first time in a good long number of minutes, there was complete and total silence. They were all looking at him. *Colleen* was looking at him, frowning slightly, speculation in her eyes.

Oh, great. Now she thought he'd told her he only wanted to be friends because he was—

He looked at her, wavering, unable to decide what to say. Should he just shut up and let her think whatever she thought, hoping that it would make her keep her distance?

Colleen found her voice. "Congratulations, Clark, you've managed to reach new heights of rudeness. Bobby, don't answer him—your sexual orientation is no one's business but your own."

"I'm straight," he admitted.

"I'm sure you are," Colleen said a little too heartily, implying that she suspected otherwise.

He laughed again. "Why would I lie?"

"I believe you," she said. "Absolutely." She winked at him. "Don't ask, don't tell. We'll just pretend Clark didn't ask."

Suddenly this wasn't funny anymore, and he laughed in disbelief. "What do you want me to do…?" Prove it? He stopped himself from saying those words. Oh, God.

She was giving him another of those killer smiles, complete with that two-thousand-degree incinerating heat in her eyes. Yes, she did want him to prove it. She didn't say it in words, but it was right there, written all over her face. She hadn't believed he was gay for one minute. She'd been baiting him. And he'd walked right into her trap. She waggled her eyebrows at him suggestively, implying that she was only teasing, but he knew better.

Help.

Please, God, let there be voice mail waiting for him, back in his hotel room. Please, God, let Wesley have called, announcing that he was back in the States and on his way to Boston. Please, God…

"Now that we've got *that* mystery solved, the two burning questions of the night that remain are why did you come back to Boston," Colleen said to her roommate, "and why blue?" She turned and looked at Clark's hair critically. "I'm not sure it's you…dude."

"What is a Navy SEAL?" Kenneth reminded her. "Burning question number three. I keep picturing beach balls and Seaworld, and I'm confident that's not quite right."

"SEALs are part of the U.S. military's special forces," Colleen said. "They're part of the Navy, so they spend a lot of time in and around the water—swimming, scuba diving, underwater demolition even. But SEAL stands for sea, air and land. They also jump out of airplanes and crawl across the desert and through the jungle, too. Most of the time no one knows that they're there. They carry great big guns—assault weapons, like commandos—but nearly all of their operations are covert." She looked at Clark. "Which means secret. Clandestine—99.9 percent of the time they insert and extract from their mission location without firing a single bullet."

She turned back to Bobby. "Did I miss anything vital? Besides the fact that you SEALs frequently kill people— usually with your bare hands—and that you're known for being exceedingly rough in bed?"

Bobby started to laugh. He couldn't help it. And then Colleen was laughing, too, with the others just staring at them as if they were crazy.

She was so alive, so full of light and joy. And in less than a week she was going to get on an airplane and fly to a dangerous place where she could well be killed. And, Lord, what a loss to the world that would be. The thought was sobering.

"Please don't go," he said to her.

Somehow she knew he was talking about the trip to Tulgeria. She stopped laughing, too. "I have to."

"No, you don't. Colleen, you have no idea what it's like there."

"Yes, I do."

Ashley pulled her brother and Kenneth toward the door. "Coll, we're going to go out for a—"

"No, you're not." Colleen didn't look away from Bobby. "Kick Thing A and Thing B out onto the street, but if you're getting one of your headaches, you're not going anywhere but to bed."

"Well then, I'll be in my room," Ashley said quietly. "Come on, children. Let's leave Aunt Colleen alone."

"*Hasta la vista*, baby." Clark nodded to Bobby. "Dude."

"Thanks again for not killing me," Kenneth said cheerfully.

They went out the door, and Ashley faded quietly down the hallway.

Leaving him alone in the living room with Colleen.

"I should go, too." That would definitely be the smart thing. As opposed to kissing her. Which would definitely be the opposite of the smart thing. But he couldn't seem to get his feet to move toward the door.

"You should come into the kitchen," she countered. "Where there are chairs that aren't covered with boxes. We can actually sit down."

She took his hand and tugged him into the kitchen. Somehow his feet had no problem moving in that direction.

"Okay," she said, sitting at the kitchen table. "Spill. What happened in Tulgeria?"

Bobby rubbed his forehead. "I wish it was that easy," he said. "I wish it was one thing. I wish I was wrong, but I've been there a half dozen times, at least, and each time was more awful than the last. It's bad and getting worse, Colleen. Parts of the country are a war zone. The government's lost control everywhere but in the major cities, and even there they're on shaky ground. Terrorist groups are everywhere. There are Christian groups, Muslim groups. They work hard to kill each other, and if that wasn't enough, there's in-fighting among each of the groups. Nobody's safe. I went into a village and—"

Lord, he couldn't tell her—not the details. He didn't

want to tell her *any* of it, but he made himself. He looked her straight in the eye and said it. "Everyone was dead. A rival group had come in and… Even the children, Colleen. They'd been methodically slaughtered."

She drew in a breath. "Oh, no!"

"We went in because there were rumors that one of the terrorist groups had gotten hold of some kind of chemical weapon. We were there to meet a team of Army Rangers, escort 'em out to a waiting submarine with samples of whatever they'd found. But they came up empty. These people had nothing. They had hardly any regular ammunition, let alone any kind of chemical threat. They killed each other with swords—these big machete-style things, with these curved, razor-sharp blades.

"No one is safe there." He said it again, hoping she was listening. "No one is safe."

She looked pale, but her gaze didn't waver. "I have to go. You tell me these things, and I have to go more than ever."

"More than half of these terrorists are zealots." He leaned across the table, willing her to hear him, to *really* hear him. "The other half are in it for the black market— for buying and selling anything. Including Americans. *Especially* Americans. Collecting ransom is probably the most lucrative business in Tulgeria today. How much would *your* parents pay to get you back?"

"Bobby, I know you think—"

He cut her off. "Our government has a rule—no negotiating with terrorists. But civilians in the private sector… Well, they can give it a go—pay the ransom and gamble that they'll actually get their loved one back.

Truth is, they usually don't. Colleen, please listen to me. *They usually don't get the hostages back.*"

Colleen gazed at him searchingly. "I've heard rumors of mass slaughters of Tulgerian civilians in retaliation by the local government."

Bobby hesitated, then told her the truth. "I've heard those rumors, too."

"Is it true?"

He sighed. "Look, I know you don't want to hear this, but if you go there you might die. *That's* what you should be worrying about right now. Not—"

"*Is* it true?"

God, she was magnificent. Leaning across the table toward him, palms down on the faded formica top, shoulders set for a fight, her eyes blazing, her hair on fire.

"I can guarantee you that the U.S. has special forces teams investigating that right this very moment," he told her. "NATO warned Tulgeria about such acts of genocide in the past. If they're up to their old tricks and if we find out about it—and if they are, we will, I guarantee it—then the U.S. ambassador and his staff will be pulled out of Tulibek immediately. The U.S. will cut all relations with the Tulgerian government. The embassy will be gone—potentially overnight. If that happens while you're there…"

Bobby took a steadying breath. "Colleen, if you go, you'll be in danger every minute of that entire week."

"I want to show you something," she said. "Don't go anywhere. I'll be right back."

Chapter 7

The photographs were in her bedroom. Colleen grabbed the envelope from her dresser, stopping to knock softly on Ashley's door on her way back to the kitchen.

"Come in."

The room was barely lit, with the shades all pulled down. Ash was at her computer, and despite the dim lighting, Colleen could see that her eyes were red and swollen. She'd been crying.

"How's the headache?" Colleen asked.

"Pretty bad."

"Try to sleep."

Ashley shook her head. "I can't. I have to write this."

"Write what?"

"A brief. To my father. That's the only way he'll ever pay attention to me—if I write him a legal brief. Isn't that pathetic?"

Colleen sighed. It *was* pathetic. Everything about Ashley's relationship with her father was pathetic. She'd actually gotten caller-ID boxes for all of their telephones, so they'd know not to answer when Mr. DeWitt called. Colleen loved it when her own father called.

"Why don't you do it later?" she said to her friend. "After the headache's gone."

Ashley's headaches were notoriously awful. She'd been to the doctor, and although they weren't migraines, they were similar in many ways. Brought on by tension and stress, the doctor had said.

Great ailment for a future lawyer to have.

"I'll help you with it," Colleen continued. "You need to tell me what happened—why you haven't called or emailed me since mid-May. I assume it's all connected?" It was. She could see that from the look on Ashley's face. "Just let me get rid of Bobby, okay?"

"Don't you dare!" Indignation gave Ashley a burst of energy. "Colleen, my God! You've had a thing for this guy for *years*! He's gorgeous, by the way. And huge. I mean, you told me he was big, but I had no idea. How tall is he?"

"I don't know exactly. Six-six? Maybe taller."

"His hands are like baseball mitts."

"Yeah," Colleen said. "And you know what they say about guys with big hands."

"They have big gloves," they said in unison. Colleen grinned, and Ashley even managed a weak smile. But it was fleeting.

"I can't believe my rotten timing. Of all the times to come running back to Cambridge and get in the way…" Ashley rested her forehead in her hands, elbows on her desk. "I saw him looking at you, Coll. All you have to do is say the word and he'll spend the night."

"He gave me the friends speech," Colleen told her.

"You're kidding!"

"Let's see—would that be something that I, designated best friend to the entire world's male population, would kid about? No, I don't think so."

"I'm sorry."

"Yeah, well..." Colleen forced a smile. "Personally I think he's lying—that he's got some kind of code-of-honor thing going, you know, because I'm his best friend's sister. I have to convince him that it's okay, that he doesn't have to fall in love and marry me—that I just want us to have some fun."

Although if he *did* happen to fall in love with her... No, she couldn't let herself think that way. That path was fraught with the perils of disappointment and frustration. All she wanted was to have fun, she reminded herself again, wishing the words hadn't sounded so hollow when she'd said them aloud.

"He's probably wondering what happened to you," Ashley pointed out.

Colleen went out the door, stopping to look at her friend, her hand on the knob. "I'll be back in about thirty minutes to get your full report on Scarsdale and your dear old dad."

"That's really not necessary—"

"I know you," Colleen said. "You're not going to sleep until we talk, so we're going to talk."

Bobby heard the door shut, heard Colleen coming back down the hall to the kitchen.

He'd heard the soft murmur of voices as she'd stopped to speak to her roommate.

The soundproofing in this old place was virtually nonexistent.

That meant that grabbing her when she came back into the room, and having hot, noisy sex right there, on top of the kitchen table was definitely not an option.

Oh, man, he had to get out of here.

He stood up, but Colleen came into the room, blocking his escape route.

"Sit," she ordered. "Just for a few more minutes. I want to show you something."

She took a photograph out of an envelope and slid it across the table toward him. It was a picture of a small girl, staring solemnly into the camera. She had enormous eyes—probably because she was so skinny. She was all narrow shoulders, with a pointy chin, dressed in ill-fitting clothes, with a ragged cap of dark-brown hair. She looked to be about six or seven years old, with the kind of desperate and almost feral air about her that would have made Bobby watch her from the corner of his eye had he happened upon her in the street. Yeah, he'd watch her, all right, *and* secure his wallet in an inside pocket.

"This was Analena," Colleen told him, "two years ago—before my student Children's Aid group adopted her."

She put another picture on the table. "This was taken just last month."

It was the same girl, only now her hair was longer—thick and glossy. She was smiling—laughing—as she ran across a field, kicking a soccer ball. Her cheeks were pink and healthy looking, and although she was still rail thin, it was because she was growing. She was gangly, gawky. She no longer looked as if she would snap in two. And the feral look was gone. She was a child again.

Colleen laid a letter in front of him—written in a large, loopy child's hand. "Dearest Colleen," he read silently:

> I dream last night that I visit you in U.S. of A. It such wonderful dream—I want to no wake up. I hope you okay that I gifted Ivan with futball you gifted me. He try to steal many times, I think, why not he keep?
>
> My English, she is getting better, no? It is gift from you—from America books and tape player and batteries you send. Blessed gift. More better than futball. Ivan make bad noise, don't think this. Still, I teach Ivan English words. Some day he thank me, thank you, also.
>
> Send more letter soon. Love, Analena.

Colleen pulled other photos from the envelope. They were pictures of other kids.

"Analena and about twenty-five other children live in an orphanage, St. Christof's, deep inside Tulgeria's so-called war zone," she told him, "which also happens to be the part of the country that sustained the most damage from the earthquake. My Children's Aid group has been corresponding—for over two years—with the nuns who run St. Christof's. We've been trying to find a legal loophole so we can get those children out of Tulgeria. These are unwanted children, Bobby. Most are of mixed heritage—and nobody wants them. The terrible irony is that we have lists of families here in the U.S. who want them desperately—who are dying to adopt.

But the government won't let them go. They won't pay to feed them, yet they won't give them up."

The pictures showed the bleakness of the orphanage. Boarded-up windows, peeling paint, bombed-out walls. These children were living in a shell of a former house. In all of the pictures, the nuns—some clad in old-fashioned habits, some dressed in American jeans and sneakers—were always smiling, but Bobby could see the lines of strain and pain around their eyes and mouths.

"When this earthquake happened," Colleen continued, still in that same soft, even voice, "we jumped at the chance to actually go in there." She looked Bobby squarely in the eyes. "Bringing relief aid and supplies to the quake victims is just our cover. We're really going in to try to get those children moved out of the war zone, to a safer location. Best-case scenario would be to bring them back to the States with us, but we know the chances of that happening are slim to none."

Bobby looked at her. "I can go," he said. "Colleen, I'll do this for you. I'll go instead of you."

Yes, that would work. He could get some of the other men in Alpha Squad to come along. Rio Rosetti, Thomas King and Mike Lee were all young and foolish. They'd jump at the chance to spend a week's vacation in the number-one most dangerous hot spot in the world. And Spaceman—Lieutenant Jim Slade. He was unmarried, too. He'd help if Bobby asked.

But no way would Bobby ask any of his married friends to spend any of their too-infrequent leave time away from their families, risking their lives.

"This could work," he told her, but she was already shaking her head.

"Bobby, I'm going." She said it firmly, absolutely,

calmly. As if this was a fact that wasn't going to change no matter what he said or did. "I'm the liaison with the Tulgerian minister of Public Health. I believe he's our one hope of getting those children moved out of immediate danger. He knows me, he trusts me—I'm going."

"If you're going, I'm going, too," he told her just as absolutely.

She shook her head. "No, you're not."

He sighed. "Look, I know you probably think I'm just interfering, but—"

Colleen smiled. "No, you don't understand. I'd love it if you could come along. Honest. It would be great. But be practical, Bobby. We're leaving in less than a week. It's taken us nearly three weeks to get permission to enter the country and bring aid—despite the fact that people there are wandering around hungry, their homes destroyed by this earthquake. You'll have to go through the same diplomatic channels and—"

"No, I won't."

She made a face at him. "Yeah, right. What, are you going to call some admiral and snap your fingers and…?"

"I won't snap my fingers at Admiral Robinson," Bobby told her. "That would be rude."

She stared at him. "You're serious. You're really going to call an *admiral*?"

He nodded as he glanced at his watch. It was a little too late to call tonight. The admiral and his wife, Zoe, had twins. Max and Sam.

The twins were pure energy in human form—as Bobby well knew. He baby-sat them once when the admiral and his wife were out in California, when their regular sitter had canceled at the last minute. Max and

Sam were miniature versions of their father. They both had his striking-blue eyes and world-famous smile.

Jake would've just finished reading them a story and putting them to bed. Bobby knew he would then go in search of his wife, maybe make them both a cup of herbal tea and rub her shoulders or feet…

"I'll call him tomorrow morning," Bobby said.

Colleen smiled. She didn't believe he was tight enough with an admiral to be able to give the man a call. "Well, it would be nice if you could go, but I'm not going to hold my breath." She gathered up the pictures and put them back in the envelope.

"How many people are going?" he asked. "You know, in your group?"

"About twelve."

Twelve unprepared, untrained civilians running around loose… Bobby didn't swear—at least not aloud.

"Most of them will actually be distributing supplies to the quake victims. They'll be hooking up with the Red Cross volunteers who are already in place in the country," she continued. "Of the twelve, there are five of us who'll be concentrating on getting those children moved."

Five was a much better, much more compact number. Five people could be whisked out of sight and removed from danger far more easily than twelve.

"Who's meeting you at the airport?" he asked.

"We've rented a bus and made arrangements to be picked up by the driver," she told him.

A bus. Oh, *man.* "How many guards?"

Colleen shook her head. "One. The driver insisted. We're still arguing over that. We don't want any guns. Our connection to the Red Cross—"

"Colleen, you'll need armed guards," he told her. "Way more than just one man hired by the driver. Three or four at the least. Even just for the short trip between the airport and your hotel. And you'll need twice as many if you're going up north."

"But—"

"The Red Cross means nothing in Tulgeria. In fact, it's often used as a bull's-eye for terrorists. Don't put the emblem on the bus, don't wear it on your clothes."

She was looking at him as if he were speaking Greek. "Are you serious?"

"Dead serious. And instead of a single bus, we should get you three or four Humvees. Something smaller and faster, that'll be less of a target."

"The bus is so that we can move the children if we get the opportunity," she told him.

Oh, damn. Yeah, they would definitely need a bus for that. "Okay," he said. "I'm going to do what I can to get Admiral Robinson involved—to make this an official operation for one of his Gray Group teams. But if it's official, there's a chance I won't be able to go. I'm still not 100 percent—"

"I'm not sure that's such a good idea," Colleen said. "If we go in there looking like some kind of commando team…"

"Whoever goes in with you, they'll be covert. There'll be three or four guys hanging around with assault weapons for show as if they were hired guards. But everyone else on the team will blend in with your group. I promise."

She looked at him. "You promise. Except you're not going to be there."

"I may not be there," he said. "But I'm sure as hell going to try."

Colleen smiled. "You know, every time someone says that they'll *try*, I think of that scene in *The Empire Strikes Back* with Luke Skywalker and Yoda. You know, the one where Yoda says, 'Try not. Do or do not.'"

"Yeah, I know that scene," Bobby told her. "And I'm sorry, but—"

She reached across the table and touched his hand. "No, don't apologize. I didn't mean to sound as if I were accusing you of anything. See, the truth is I've fought so many losing battles for so many years that I really appreciate someone who tries. In fact, a try is all I ever ask for anymore. It may not work out, but at least you know you gave it a shot, right?"

She wasn't talking about him coming to Tulgeria. She was talking about the way he'd kissed her. And the way he'd pushed her away, refusing to see where that kiss might lead. Refusing even to try.

Bobby wasn't sure what to say. He felt like the worst kind of coward. Too scared even to try.

Even when her hand was on top of his, her fingers so cool against the heat of his skin. Even when he wished with all of his heart that she would leave her hand right there for a decade or two.

But Colleen took her hand away as she stood. He watched as she placed the envelope with the pictures on the cluttered surface of a built-in desk in the corner of the room.

"You know, I've met most of the people who want to adopt these kids," she told him. "They're really wonderful. You look into their eyes, and you can see that they already love these children just from seeing their pictures, from reading their letters." Her voice wavered. "It just breaks my heart that those kids are in danger, that we can only *try* to help them. It kills me that there are no guarantees."

Bobby stood up. He didn't mean to. And as soon as he found himself on his feet, he forced himself to stop. To not move toward her, not take her into his arms. The last time he did that, he'd completely lost control.

But Colleen turned to face him. *She* came toward him. She reached for him, taking hold of both of his hands. "It's important to me that you know I'm not doing this purely to drive Wes crazy."

Her fingers were cool and strong and, again, he didn't want to let her go. *Help*. "I know."

But she didn't come any closer. She just smiled and squeezed his hands. "Good," she said as she released him. "So go. You're free. Escape. Lucky you—I need to hang with Ashley tonight. Guess I'll have to dance naked for you another night."

Her eyes sparkled as she laughed at him, at the pained look he couldn't keep off his face.

The door was right there. She'd given him permission to leave. He could have walked through it, walked out of her apartment, walked to a place where he—and she—were safe. Instead he didn't move. "Why do you keep doing that?"

She opted not to play dumb. She knew he was talking about her suggestive comments. "You're such an easy target and I want…"

"What?" He really wanted to know. Badly enough that he almost touched her again. Almost. "You want what, Colleen?"

"You."

He'd known she was gutsy. And when she teased,

she could be pretty outrageous. But he'd never expected her to say that.

She lowered her eyes as if she were suddenly shy. "I always have, you know."

She spoke barely loud enough for him to hear her, but he did. He heard. His ears were working perfectly. It was his lungs that were having trouble functioning.

"So now you know," she said quietly. When she looked up at him, her smile was rueful. "How's that for a powerful rebuttal to the 'I just want to be friends' speech?"

He couldn't respond. He didn't have any idea at all of what to say. She wanted him. She always had. He felt like laughing and crying. He felt like grabbing her, right there in the kitchen. He felt like running—as hard and as fast and as far as he possibly could.

"I figure either I'm right, and you didn't mean what you said this morning," she told him. "Or I'm wrong, and I'm a complete idiot who deserves humiliation and rejection twice in two days."

Bobby kept his mouth shut, wishing he *were* the kind of man who could just run for the door—and keep running when he hit the street. But he knew that he wasn't going to get out of there without saying *some*thing.

He just wasn't sure what that something should be. Tell the truth and admit he hadn't meant what he'd said? That was one hell of a bad idea. If he did that, she'd smile and move closer and closer and...

And he'd wake up in her bed.

And then Wes would kill him.

Bobby was starting to think he could maybe handle death. It would be worth it for a chance at a night with Colleen.

What he would never be able to live with was the look of betrayal in his best friend's eyes. He clamped his mouth shut.

"I know I act as if it's otherwise," Colleen continued, turning away from him and fiddling with half a dozen organic apples that were on the kitchen counter. As she spoke, she arranged them into a pattern. Big, then little, then big. "But I haven't had too much experience. You know. With men, I mean. In fact, all I've had are a couple of really crummy short-term relationships. I've never been with someone who really wants me—I mean other than for the fact that I'm female and convenient." With the apples neatly arranged in two perfect rows, she turned to face him, to look him in the eye. "I know you say you don't—want me, that is. But I see something really different when I look into your eyes. And… Bobby, I just want to know what that's like—to be made love to the way you kissed me last night. It felt so right and…"

She took a deep breath. Smiled shakily. "So. You've been warned. Now you know. You also know that I'm not going to be talked out of going to Tulgeria. So if your admiral guy doesn't come through for you, you can tell my brother you did everything you could to keep me off that plane. And you can go back to California with a clear conscience. And I think you probably should go— if you really did mean what you said about just wanting to be friends. If you stay, though, you better put on your fireproof suit. Because starting tomorrow I'm turning up the heat."

"You really said that?" Ashley laughed. "What did he do?"

After her little speech, Bobby hadn't grabbed her and

kissed her. But then again, Colleen hadn't really thought he would.

"What did he *say*?" Ash persisted.

"Nothing," Colleen told her friend. "He looked a little pale—kind of like he was going to faint. So I told him we'd talk more tomorrow and I pushed him out the door."

Truth was, she hadn't wanted to hear what he might have to say in response to her painfully honest confession.

She'd pretty much been flashing hot and cold by then herself—alternately clapping herself on the back for her bravery and deriding herself for pure stupidity.

What if she *were* completely wrong? What if she were completely misinterpreting everything she'd seen in his eyes? What if he hadn't really been looking at her with barely concealed longing and desire? What if it had just been a bad case of indigestion?

"I had to try," Colleen told Ashley—and herself as well.

Ash was sitting cross-legged on her bed, hugging her beat-up, raggedy stuffed bear—the one she'd been given when she was three and had chicken pox. The one she still slept with despite the fact that she'd just turned twenty-four.

It was ironic. Colleen's friend had everything. Money. A beautiful face. A slim, perfect body. Weight that didn't fluctuate wildly given her moods. A 4.0 grade point average. Impeccable taste.

Of course, Colleen had something Ashley didn't have. And Colleen wouldn't have traded that one thing for Ashley's looks and body, even if her friend had thrown in all the gold in Ft. Knox, too.

Not a chance.

Because Colleen had parents who supported her, 100 percent. She knew, without a doubt, that no matter what she did, her mom and dad were behind her.

Unlike Mr. DeWitt, who criticized Ashley nonstop.

Colleen couldn't imagine what it had been like growing up in that house. She could picture Ash as a little girl, desperately trying to please her father and never quite succeeding.

"Ashley, what's this? A Father's Day gift? A ceramic bowl? You made it yourself on the wheel in pottery class? Oh, well, next time you'll do much better, won't you?"

It was true, Colleen's own parents weren't perfect. No one's parents were. But hers loved her unconditionally. She'd never doubted that.

"You ready to talk about what happened?" she asked Ashley now.

Her friend sighed. "I'm so stupid."

Colleen just waited.

"There was a new associate in my father's firm," Ash finally said. "Brad Hennesey." Tears filled her eyes, and she tried to laugh. "God, I'm such an idiot. I can't even say his name without…" She gestured to her face.

Colleen handed her a box of tissues and waited while Ashley blew her nose.

"He was so nice," Ash told her. "I mean, I didn't expect him *not* to be nice to me, because I'm the boss's daughter, but he seemed so genuine, and…"

"Oh, no," Colleen said. She was pretty sure she knew where this was going, and she prayed she was wrong.

"I did something really dumb," Ash admitted. "We started dating, and he was so…" She laughed but it was loaded with pain. "Yeah, he was completely perfect—

smart and gorgeous with all those white teeth and that Land's End model body, and we loved the same books and movies, and… And I fell in love with him. God! How could I be so stupid?"

Colleen waited, praying that she was wrong.

"But then I found out that my father had hired him purposely. Brad was part of his plan to guarantee that I'd come home after law school and join the firm. He was going to be made partner instantly upon our engagement. I hear myself telling you this, and it sounds so ludicrous. Can you believe any of this?"

She could. She'd met Ashley's father. "Ah, Ash," Colleen said. "How did you find out?"

"Brad *told* me," Ashley said. "He confessed everything. He called me in the middle of the night and told me he had to see me. Right then. So he came over to the house and we went into the garden and… He was really upset and he told me he was in love with me. He said he'd fallen for me, and he told me that he had to come clean before it went any further, that he couldn't live with himself any longer."

"But that's good," Colleen countered. "Isn't it? He was honest when it mattered the most."

"Colleen, he accepted a position where the job description included tricking the boss's daughter into marrying him." Ashley was still aghast at the idea. "What kind of person would do that?"

"One who maybe saw your picture?" Colleen suggested.

Ashley stared at her as if she were in league with Satan.

"I'm not saying it's a good thing," she added quickly.

"But how bad could the guy be if he really did fall in love with you?"

"Did he?" Ashley asked darkly. "Or is he just saying that he did? Is this confession just another lie?"

Oh, ick. Colleen hadn't thought of it that way. But Ash was right. If *she* were trying to con someone into marrying her, she'd pretend to be in love with them, confess everything and beg for forgiveness. That would save her butt in the event that the truth ever did surface after the wedding.

"He slept with me, Colleen," Ashley said miserably. "And my father was *paying* him."

"Yeah," Colleen said, "I don't think your father was paying him to do that, though."

"It feels that way." Ashley was one of those women who still looked beautiful when she cried. "You know the really stupid thing?"

Colleen shook her head. "No."

"I didn't have the nerve to confront my father." Ashley's lip trembled. "I just ran away. I hid."

"But you're writing him a letter," Colleen pointed out. "That's a start."

"Clark keeps telling me I should take one of those assertiveness training courses. You know, the kind where you go out into the mountains with only a canteen of water and a hunting knife and come back after having killed a bear?"

Colleen laughed at the absurdity of that. "You'd take advice from a man with blue hair?"

Ash laughed, too. It was shaky, but it was laughter.

"You know what I think you should do?" Colleen said. "I think you should go back and have this raging, passionate affair with Brad. Flaunt it in your father's face.

Make it really public. And then, next May, when you graduate from law school, you dump the creep and flip your father the bird. You pass the California bar exam, and take a job as a public defender in East L.A. and you do pro bono work for the community on the side just to *really* tick him off. That's what *I* would do."

"You could do that?" Ashley asked. "Really? Have that kind of a relationship with a man without falling even further in love? Without getting in too deep?"

Colleen thought about Bobby Taylor, about what would happen if she did succeed in talking her way into his bed. She thought about waking up beside him, smiling into his beautiful eyes as he bent to kiss her. She thought about driving him to the airport and watching his broad back and his long, easygoing stride as he headed into the terminal, as he walked away. From her. Without looking back.

She thought about the way that would make her heart die inside of her. Just a little bit.

Just enough to change her forever.

"No," she said quietly. "I guess I couldn't, either."

Chapter 8

"Wait," Bobby said. "Zoe, no, if he's taking a day off, don't..." Bother him. But Zoe Robinson had already put him on hold.

"Hey, Chief!" Admiral Jake Robinson sounded cheerful and relaxed. "What's up? Zo tells me you're calling from Boston?"

"Uh, yes, sir," Bobby said. "But, sir, this can wait until tomorrow, because—"

"How's the shoulder?" the admiral interrupted. Admirals were allowed to interrupt whenever they wanted.

"Much better, sir," Bobby lied. It was exactly like Admiral Robinson to have made certain he'd be informed about the injuries of anyone on the SEAL teams—and to remember what he'd been told.

"These things take time." It was also like Robinson

to see through Bobby's lie. "Slow and steady, Taylor. Don't push it too hard."

"Aye, sir. Admiral, I had no idea that your secretary would patch me through here, to your home."

"Well, you called to talk to me, didn't you?"

"Yes, sir, but you're an *admiral*, sir, and—"

"Ah." Robinson laughed. "You wanted it to be harder to reach me, huh? Well, if you need me to, I'll call Dottie in my office and tell her to put you on hold for a half an hour."

Bobby had to laugh, too. "No, thank you. I'm just… surprised."

"I don't take everyone's call," Jake Robinson's voice was serious now. "In fact, Dottie's probably kissed off half a dozen captains, commanders and lieutenant commanders already this morning. But when I set up the Gray Group, Chief, I made a point to make myself available 24/7 to the men I call to go out on my missions. You work for me—you need me? You got me. You probably don't know it, but you were on a Gray Group mission when you were injured. That cycled your name to the top of the list."

"I wasn't told, but… I knew."

"So talk to me, Chief. What's going on?"

Bobby told him. "Sir, I've become aware of a situation in which a dozen U.S. citizens—mostly students from here in Boston—are about to walk into Tulgeria with a single, locally hired armed guard."

Robinson swore, loudly and pungently.

Bobby told the admiral about the earthquake relief organization. About the bus and the children in the orphanage. About the fact that these American Good Samaritans were not going to be talked out of making this trip.

"What's your connection to this group, Chief?" Robinson asked. "Girlfriend?"

"Negative, sir," Bobby said hastily. "No, it's Wes Skelly's sister. She's one of the volunteers who's going."

"What, did Skelly send you to Boston to talk her out of it?" Robinson laughed. "God, you're a good friend to him, Bobby."

"He's out of the country, Admiral, and I had the time. Besides, he'd do the same for me."

"Yeah, and I suspect *your* sister is a little easier to handle than this sister of Skelly's—what's her name?"

"Colleen, sir."

"Is Colleen Skelly as much like her brother as I'm imagining her to be, God help us all?"

Bobby laughed again. "Yes and no, sir. She's…" Wonderful. Beautiful. Amazingly sexy. Intelligent. *Perfect.* "She's special, sir. Actually, she reminds me of Zoe in a lot of ways. She's tough, but not really—it's just a screen she hides behind, if you know what I mean."

"Oh, yes. I do." The admiral laughed softly. "Oh, boy. So, I know it's none of my business, but does Wes know that you've got a thing for his sister?"

Bobby closed his eyes. Damn, he'd given himself away. There was no point in denying it. Not to Jake. The man may have been an admiral, but he was also Bobby's friend. "No, he doesn't."

"Hmm. Does *she* know?"

Good question. "Not really."

"Damn."

"I mean, she's incredible, Jake, and I think—no, I *know* she's looking for a fling. She's made that more than clear but I can't do it, and I'm…"

"Dying," Jake supplied the word. "Been there, done

that. If she really is anything like Zoe, you don't stand a chance." He laughed. "Colleen Skelly, huh? With a name like that, I'm picturing a tiny red head, kind of built like her brother—compact. Skinny. With a smart mouth and a temper."

"She's a redhead," Bobby said. "And you're right about the mouth and the temper, but she's tall. She might even be taller than Wes. And she's not skinny. She's…" Stacked. Built like a brick house. Lush. Voluptuous. All those descriptions felt either disrespectful or as if he were exchanging locker-room confidences. "Statuesque," he finally came up with.

"Taller than Wes, huh? That must tick him off."

"She takes after their father, and he's built more like their mother's side of the family. It ticks Colleen off, too. She's gorgeous, but she doesn't think so."

"Genetics. It's proof that Mother Nature exists," Jake said with a laugh. "She's got a strong sense of irony, doesn't she?"

"I need you to help me, sir." Bobby brought their conversation back to the point. "Colleen's determined to go to Tulgeria. This whole trip is an international incident waiting to happen. If this isn't something you want to get Alpha Squad or the Gray Group involved in, then I'm hoping you can give me—"

"It is," the admiral said. "Protection of U.S. citizens. In a case like this I like to think of it as preventative counterterrorism. The Tulgerian government will bitch and moan about it, but we'll get you in. We'll tell the local officials that we need two teams," he decided. "One'll accompany Colleen Skelly and her friends, the other'll go in covert. The timing is really good on this, Taylor. You're actually the one doing *me* the favor here."

Admiral Robinson didn't say it. He couldn't say it, but Bobby knew he was going to use this seemingly standard protection op as a chance to send in an additional highly covert and top-secret team on an entirely different mission. It was probably related to the ongoing investigation of those rumors that the Tulgerian government was mass slaughtering its own citizens.

God, what a world.

"Alpha Squad will be back from their current training op in three days, tops," Robinson continued. "I'll have them rerouted here to the East Coast—to Little Creek. We'll both meet them there, Chief, you'll fill them in and work out a plan, then bring them back up to Boston to hash out the details with Colleen Skelly and her idealistic friends."

The admiral wanted Bobby to be part of the op. "I'm sorry, sir," he said. "I may have misled you about the status of my shoulder. I still have limited movement and—"

"I'm thinking you're valuable because you've already established rapport with the civilians," Jake cut him off. "But I'll let it be your choice, Bobby. If you don't want to go—"

"Oh, no sir, I *want* to go." It was a no-brainer. He wanted to be there, himself, to make sure Colleen stayed safe.

Yes, it would have been easier to toss the entire problem into Admiral Robinson's capable hands and retreat, swiftly and immediately, to California. But Wes would be back in three days. Bobby could handle keeping his distance from Colleen for three days.

Couldn't he?

"Good," Jake said. "I'll get the ball rolling."

"Thank you, sir."

"Before you go, Chief, want some unsolicited advice?"

Bobby hesitated. "I'm not sure, sir."

The admiral laughed—a rich burst of genuine amusement. "Wrong answer, Taylor. This is one of those times that you're supposed to 'Aye, aye, sir' me, simply because I'm an admiral and you're not."

"Aye, aye, sir."

"Trust your heart, Chief. You've got a good one, and when the time comes, well, I'm confident you'll know what to do."

"Thank you, sir."

"See you in a few days. Thanks again for the call."

Bobby hung up the phone and lay back on his hotel room bed, staring up the ceiling.

When the time comes, you'll know what to do.

He already knew what he had to do.

He had to stay away from Colleen Skelly, who thought—God help them both—that she wanted him.

What did she know? She was ridiculously young. She had no clue how hard it was to sustain a relationship over long distances. She had no idea how difficult it was for *any*one to be involved with a SEAL, let alone someone ridiculously young. She was mistaking her desire for a physical relationship with a man she had a crush on, with her very real need for something more powerful and more permanent.

She said she wanted passion—well, he could give her that. He had no doubt. And maybe, if he were really lucky, she'd be so completely dazzled that she'd fall in love with him.

Yeah, right, *then* where would she be? In love with a man who spent most of his time out of the country with her brother—provided her brother would ever forgive him enough to speak to him again. But the key words there were *out of the country*. Colleen would get tired of *that* fast enough.

Eventually she'd be so tired of being second place in his life that she'd walk away.

And he wouldn't stop her.

But she'd want him to. And even though she was the one who left him, she'd end up hurt.

The last thing he wanted in the world was to leave her hurt.

Follow your heart. He would. Even though it meant killing this relationship before it even started. Even though it was the hardest thing he'd ever done.

Colleen slid the back door of the truck closed with a resounding bang.

"Okay," she said, as she attached a combination lock that was more to keep the door from bouncing open as they drove into Boston than to deter thieves. "Did someone lock my apartment?"

Kenneth looked blankly at Clark, and Clark looked blankly at Kenneth.

Colleen gave up on them and looked at Bobby, who nodded. "I took care of it," he said.

It was no surprise. He was dependable. Smart. Sexier than a man had the right to be at ten in the morning.

Their eyes met only briefly before he looked away—still it was enough to send a wave of heat through her. Shame. Embarrassment. Mortification. What exactly had she said to him last night? *I want you.* In broad daylight, she couldn't believe her audacity. What had she been thinking?

Still, he was here. He'd shown up bright and early this morning, hot cup of coffee in hand, to help lug all of the boxes of emergency supplies out of her living room and into the Relief Aid truck.

He'd said hardly anything to her. In fact, he'd only said, "Hi," and then got to work with Clark and Kenneth, hauling boxes down the entryway stairs and out to the truck. Bad shoulder or not, he could carry two at once without even breaking a sweat.

Colleen had spent the past ninety minutes analyzing that "Hi," as she'd built wall upon wall of boxes in the back of the truck. He'd sounded happy, hadn't he? Glad to see her? Well, if not glad to see her, he'd sounded neutral. Which was to say that at least he hadn't sounded *un*happy to see her. And that was a good thing.

Wasn't it?

Everything she'd said to him last night echoed in her head and made her stomach churn.

Any minute now they were going to be alone in the truck. Any minute now he was going to give her the friends speech, part two. Not that she'd ever been persistent and/or stupid enough before to have heard a part-two speech. But she had a good imagination. She knew what was coming. He would use the word *flattered* in reference to last night's no-holds-barred, bottom-line statement. He would focus on their differences in age, in background, in everything.

One major difference between them that she already knew was that she was an idiot.

Colleen climbed in behind the wheel and turned the key. Bobby got in beside her, picking her backpack up off the floor and placing it between them on the wide bench seat, like some kind of protective shield or definitive border.

She and her brother Ethan and her sister Peg, both who'd been closest to her in age among the seven Skelly children, had made similar boundaries in the far back seat of their father's Pontiac station wagon. Don't cross this line or else.

"Hey," Clark shouted over the roar of the diesel engine. "Can we bum a ride into Kenmore Square? You're going that way, right?"

"Sure," she said. "Squeeze in."

She felt Bobby tense. And then he moved. Quickly. He opened the passenger-side door, and would have leaped out to let the younger men sit in the middle—no doubt to keep from sitting pressed up against her—but Kenneth was already there, about to climb in.

As Colleen watched, Bobby braced himself and slid down the seat toward her.

She took her pack and set it on the floor, tucked between the seat and her door.

He moved as close as he possibly could without touching her. It was amazing, really, that he could be that close yet have absolutely no physical contact.

He smelled like baby shampoo and fresh laundry with a hint of the coffee that he seemed to drink each morning by the gallon. His hair was back in a ponytail again. She couldn't imagine him letting her braid it later today. She couldn't do it now, not the way they were sitting. And she knew that after Clark and Kenneth got out of the truck, Bobby wasn't going to let her get close enough to braid his hair ever again—not after what she'd said to him last night.

"Sorry," she said, her voice low. "I guess I must have embarrassed you to death last night."

"You scared me to death," he admitted, his voice pitched for her ears only. "Don't get me wrong, Colleen, I'm flattered. I really am. But this is one of those situations where what I want to do is completely different from what I should do. And should's got to win."

She looked up at him and found her face inches from his. A very small number of inches. Possibly two. Possibly fewer. The realization almost knocked what he'd just said out of her mind. Almost.

What he wanted *to do*, he'd said. True, he'd used the word *flattered* as she'd expected, but the rest of what he was saying was...

Colleen stared at that mouth, at those eyes, at the perfect chin and nose that were close enough for her to lean forward, if she wanted to, and kiss.

Oh, she wanted to.

And he'd just all but told her, beneath all those ridiculous *shoulds*, that he wanted her, too. She'd won. She'd *won*!

Look at me, she willed him, but he seemed intent upon reading the truck's odometer. *Kiss me.*

"I spoke to Admiral Robinson, who greenlighted U.S. military protection for your trip," he continued. "He wants me to remain in place as liaison with your group, and, well—" his gaze flicked in her direction "—I agreed. I'm here. I know what's going on. I have to stick around, even though I know you'd rather I go away."

"Whoa, Bobby." She put her hand on his knee. "I don't *want* you to go anywhere."

He glanced at her briefly again as he gently took her hand and deposited it back into her own lap. "The thing is…" He fixed his gaze on a point outside the truck. "I can't stay in the, uh—" he closed his eyes briefly "—the *capacity* in which you want me to stay."

She laughed in disbelief. "But that's crazy!"

He leaned forward to look out the passenger-side door, checking to see why Clark was taking so long to get in. Her roommate's brother was holding on to the door, blue head down, intent upon scraping something off the bottom of his shoe. "The admiral told me that Wes'll be back in about three days," Bobby told her.

Three days. That meant they didn't have a lot of time to—

"Once he's back, it'll be easier for me to, you know, do the right thing. Until then…"

"Do the right thing?" she repeated, loudly enough that Kenneth looked uncomfortable. "How could this," she gestured between them, "not be the *right thing* when everything about it feels so perfect?"

Bobby glanced back toward Kenneth and Clark before finally meeting and holding her gaze. "Please, Colleen, I'm begging you—don't make this more difficult for me than it has to be," he said, still softly, and she knew, just like that, that she hadn't won. She'd lost. He wanted her, too, but he was begging her—*begging* her—not to push this attraction that hung between them too far.

He wanted her, but he didn't want her. Not really. Not enough to let what he was feeling take priority over all their differences and all his asinine personal rules.

Colleen felt like crying. Instead she forced a smile. "Too bad, Taylor, it would have been amazingly great," she told him.

His smile was forced, too. He closed his eyes, as if he

couldn't bear looking at her, and shook his head slightly. "I know," he said. "Believe me, I know."

When he opened his eyes, he looked at her, briefly meeting her gaze again. He was sitting close—close enough for her to see that his eyes truly were completely, remarkably brown. There were no other flecks of color, no imperfections, no inconsistencies.

But far more hypnotizing than the pure, bottomless color was the brief glimpse of frustration and longing he let her see. Either on purpose or accidentally, it didn't matter which.

It took her breath away.

"I need about three more inches of seat before I can close this door," Clark announced. He shifted left in a move reminiscent of a football player's offensive drive, making Kenneth yelp and ramming Bobby tightly against Colleen.

Completely against Colleen. His muscular thigh was wedged against her softer one. He had nowhere to put his shoulder or his arm, and even though he tried to angle himself, that only made it worse. Suddenly she was practically sitting in the man's lap.

"There," Clark added with satisfaction as he closed the truck door. "I'm ready, dudes. Let's go."

Just drive. Colleen knew the smartest thing to do was to just drive. If traffic was light, it would take about fifteen minutes to reach Kenmore Square. Then Clark and Kenneth would get out, and she and Bobby wouldn't have to touch each other ever again.

She could feel him steaming, radiating heat from the summer day, from the work he'd just done, and he shifted, trying to move away, but he only succeeded in making her aware that they both wore shorts, and that his bare skin was pressed against hers.

She was okay, she told herself. She'd be okay as long as she kept breathing.

Colleen reached forward to put the truck into drive. Raising her arm to hold the steering wheel gave Bobby a little more space—except now his arm was pressed against the side of her breast.

He tried desperately to move away, but there was nowhere for him to go.

"I can't lift my arm enough to put it on the back of the seat," he said in a choked-sounding voice. "I'm sorry."

Colleen couldn't help it. She started to laugh.

And then she did the only thing she could do, given the situation. She threw the truck into Park and turned and kissed him.

It was obviously the last thing he'd expected. She could taste his disbelief. For the briefest moment he tried to pull away, but then she felt him surrender.

And then he kissed her back as desperately and as hungrily as she kissed him.

It was a kiss at least as potent as the one they'd shared in the alley. Did he always kiss like this, with his mouth a strange mix of hard and soft, with a voracious thirst and a feverish intensity, as if she were in danger of having her very life force sucked from her? His hands were in her hair, around her back, holding her in place so that he could claim her more completely. And claim her he did.

Colleen had never been kissed quite so possessively in all her life.

But, oh, she liked it. Very much.

Quiet, easygoing Bobby Taylor kissed with a delirious abandon that was on the verge of out of control.

He pulled her toward him, closer, tugging as if he wanted her on his lap, straddling him. As if he wanted...

"You know, on second thought, Kenneth, we might get to Kenmore faster on the T."

Oh, my *God*.

Colleen pulled back the same instant that Bobby released her.

He was breathing hard and staring at her, with a wild look in his eyes she'd never seen before. Not on him, anyway, the King of Cool.

"This is how you help?" he asked incredulously.

"Yes," she said. She couldn't breathe, either, and having him look at her that way wasn't helping. "I mean, no. I mean—"

"Gee, I'm sorry," Kenneth said brightly. "We've got to be going. Clark, *move* it."

"Clark, don't go anywhere," Colleen ordered, opening the door. "Bobby's going to drive. I'm coming around to sit on the other side."

She got out of the truck's cab, holding onto the door for a second while she waited for the jelly in her legs to turn back to bone.

She could feel Bobby watching her as she crossed around the front of the truck. She saw Clark lean forward, across Kenneth, and say something to him.

"Are you sure, man?" Clark was saying to Bobby as she opened the door.

"Yes," Bobby said with a definiteness that made her want to cry. Clark had no doubt asked if Bobby wanted the two of them to make themselves scarce. But Bobby didn't want them to leave. He didn't want to be alone with Colleen until he absolutely had to.

Well, she'd really messed *that* up.

As Bobby put the truck in gear, she leaned forward and said, across Clark and Kenneth, "I wasn't trying to make it worse for you. That was supposed to be like, I don't know, I guess a…a kind of a kiss goodbye."

He looked at her and it was a look of such total incomprehension, she tried to explain.

"It seemed to me as if we'd just decided that our relationship wasn't going to move beyond the…the, I don't know, platonic, I guess, and I just wanted—" She swore silently—words she'd never say aloud, words she usually didn't even *think*. This wasn't coming out right at all. *Just say it.* What was he going to do? Laugh at her for being so pathetic? "I just wanted to kiss you one last time. Is that so awful?"

"Excuse me," Clark said. "But that was a *platonic* kiss?"

Bobby's hair had come out of his ponytail. She must've done that when she'd wrapped her arms around his neck and kissed him as if there were no tomorrow. As she watched, he tried to gather it up with his right hand—his good arm. He settled for hooking it behind his ears.

"Dude. If *that* was a *platonic* kiss," Clark started, "then I want to see one that's—" Kenneth clapped his hand over his mouth, muffling the rest of his words.

"I'm sorry," Colleen said.

Bobby glanced up from the road and over at her. The mixture of remorse, anger, and whatever those other mysterious emotions were that seemed to glisten in his dark eyes, was going to haunt her dreams. Probably for the rest of her life. "I am, too."

Chapter 9

There were protestors. On the sidewalk. In front of the AIDS Education Center. With signs saying NIMBY. Not In My Back Yard.

Bobby, following Colleen's directions, had taken a detour after letting Clark and Kenneth out near Kenmore Square. Colleen had something to drop at the center—some papers or a file having to do with the ongoing court battle with the neighborhood zoning board.

She'd been filling up the silence in the truck in typical Skelly fashion, by telling Bobby about how she'd gotten involved doing legal work for the center, through a student program at her law school.

Although she'd yet to pass the bar exam, there was such a shortage of lawyers willing to do pro bono work like this—to virtually work for free for desperately cash-poor nonprofit organizations—student volunteers were allowed to do a great deal of the work.

And Colleen had always been ready to step forward and volunteer.

Bobby could remember when she was thirteen—the year he'd first met her. She was just a little kid. A tomboy—with skinned knees and ragged cutoff jeans and badly cut red hair. She was a volunteer even back then, a member of some kind of local environmental club, always going out on neighborhood improvement hikes, which was just a fancy name for cleaning up roadside trash.

Once, he and Wes had had to drive her to the hospital to get stitches and a tetanus shot. During one of her tromps through a particularly nasty area, a rusty nail went right through the cheap soles of her sneakers and into her foot.

It had hurt like hell, and she'd cried—a lot like the way she'd cried the other night. Wiping her tears away fast, so that, with luck, he and Wes wouldn't see.

It had been a bad year for her. And for Wes, too. Bobby had come home with Wes earlier that year—for a funeral. Wes and Colleen's brother, Ethan, had been killed in a head-on with a tree, in a car driven by a classmate with a blood-alcohol level high enough to poison him.

God, that had hurt. Wes had been numb for months after. Colleen had written to Bobby, telling him she'd joined a grief counseling group connected to Mothers Against Drunk Drivers. She'd written to ask Bobby to find a similar support group for Wes, who had loved Ethan best out of all his brothers and sisters, and was hurt the worst by the loss.

Bobby had tried, but Wes didn't want any of it. He ferociously threw himself into training and eventually learned how to laugh again.

"Pull over," Colleen said now.

"There's no place to stop."

"Double park," she ordered him. "I'll get out—you can stay with the truck."

"No way," he said, harshly throwing one of Wes's favorite—although unimaginative and fairly offensive—adjectives between the two words.

She looked at him in wide-eyed surprise. He'd never used that word in front of her before. Ever.

Her look wasn't reproachful, just startled. Still, he felt like a dirtball.

"I beg your pardon," he said stiffly, still angry at her for kissing him after he'd begged her—*begged* her—not to, angry at himself, as well, for kissing her back, "but if you think I'm going to sit here and watch while you face down an angry mob—"

"It's not an angry mob," she countered. "I don't see John Morrison, although you better believe he's behind this."

He had to stop for the light, and she opened the door and slipped down from the cab.

"Colleen!" Disbelief and something else, something darker that lurched in his stomach and spread fingers of ice through his blood, made his voice crack. Several of those signs were made with two-by-fours. Swung as a weapon, they could break a person's skull.

She heard his yelp, he knew she had, but she only waved at him as she moved gracefully across the street.

Fear. That cold dark feeling sliding through his veins was fear.

He'd learned to master his own personal fear. Sky diving, swimming in shark-infested waters, working with explosives that, with one stupid mistake, could tear a man into hamburger. He'd taken hold of that fear and controlled it with the knowledge that he was as highly skilled as a human being could be. He could deal with anything that came along—anything, that is, that was in his control. As for those things outside of his control, he'd developed a zen-like deal with the powers that be. He'd live life to its fullest, and when it was his turn to go, when he no longer had any other options, well then, he'd go—no regrets, no remorse, no panic.

He wasn't, however, without panic when it came to watching Colleen head into danger.

There was a lull in the traffic, so he ran the light, pulling as close to the line of parked cars in front of the building as possible. Putting on his flashers, he left the truck sitting in the street as he ran as fast as he could to intercept Colleen before she reached the protestors.

He stopped directly in front of her and made himself as big as possible—a wall that she couldn't get past.

"This," he said tightly, "is *the* last time you will *ever* disobey me."

"Excuse me," she said, her mouth open in outraged disbelief. "Did you just say...*disobey*?"

He'd pushed one of her buttons. He recognized that, but he was too angry, too upset to care. He was losing it, his voice getting louder. "In Tulgeria, you will not *move*, you will not lift a *finger* without my or Wes's permission. Do you understand?"

She laughed at him, right in his face. "Yeah, in your dreams."

"If you're going to act like a *child*—unable to control yourself—"

"What are you going to do?" she countered hotly. "Tie me up?"

"Yes, dammit, if I have to!" Bobby heard himself shouting. He was shouting at her. Bellowing. As loudly as he shouted in mock fury at the SEAL candidates going through BUD/S training back in Coronado. Except there was nothing mock about his fury now.

She wasn't in danger. Not now. He could see the protestors, and up close they were a far-less-dangerous-looking bunch than he'd imagined them to be. There were only eight of them, and six were women—two quite elderly.

But that was moot. She'd completely ignored his warning, and if she did that in Tulgeria, she could end up very dead very fast.

"Go on," she shouted back at him, standing like a boxer on the balls of her feet, as if she were ready to go a few rounds. "Tie me up. I dare you to try!" As if she honestly thought she could actually beat him in a physical fight.

As if she truly believed he would ever actually raise a hand against her or any other woman.

No, he'd never fight her. But there were other ways to win.

Bobby picked her up. He tossed her over his good shoulder, her stomach pressed against him, her head and arms dangling down his back. It was laughably easy to do, but once he got her there, she didn't stay still. She wriggled and kicked and howled and punched ineffectively at his butt and the backs of his legs. She was a big woman, and he wrenched his bad shoulder holding her in place, but it wasn't that that slowed him.

No, what made him falter was the fact that her T-shirt had gapped and he was holding her in place on his shoulder with his hand against the smooth bare skin of her back. He was holding her legs in place—keeping her from kicking him—with a hand against the silkiness of her upper thighs.

He was touching her in places he shouldn't be touching her. Places he'd been dying to touch her for years. But he didn't put her down. He just kept carrying her down the sidewalk, back toward the truck that was double parked in front of the center.

His hair was completely down, loose around his face, and she caught some of it with one of her flailing hands. Caught and yanked, hard enough to make his eyes tear.

"Ouch! God!" That was it. As soon as he got back to his room, he was shaving his head.

"Let! Me! Go!"

"You dared me," he reminded her, swearing again as she gave his hair another pull.

"I didn't think you were man enough to actually do it!"

Oh, ouch. That stung far worse than getting his hair pulled.

"Help!" she shrieked. "Someone *help!* Mrs. O'Hallaran!"

Mrs. who…?

"Excuse me, young man…"

Just like that, Bobby's path to the truck was blocked by the protestors.

One of the elderly women stood directly in front of him now, brandishing her sign as if it were a cross and he were a vampire. "What do you think you're doing?"

she asked, narrowing her eyes at him from behind her thick glasses.

Take Back the Night, the sign said. Neighborhood Safety Council.

"He's being a jerk, Mrs. O'Hallaran," Colleen answered for him. "A complete idiotic, stupid, male-chauvinist *jerk*. Put me down, *jerk*!"

"I know this young lady from church," the elderly woman—Mrs. O'Hallaran—told him, her lips pursed in disapproval, "and I'm certain she doesn't deserve the indignity of your roughhousing, sir."

Colleen punched him in the back as she kneed him as hard as she could. She caught him in the stomach, but he knew she'd been aiming much lower. She'd wanted to bring him to his knees. "Put me *down*!"

"Colleen, do you want us to call the police?" one of the two men asked.

She knew these people. And they knew her—by name. From church, the old lady had said. Colleen had never even remotely been in danger.

Somehow that only served to make him even more mad. She could have told him she knew them, instead of letting him think…

He put her down. She straightened her shirt, hastily pulling it back down over her exposed stomach, giving him a glimpse of her belly button, God help him.

She ran her fingers quickly through her hair, and as she did, she gave him a look and a smile that was just a little too smug, as if she'd won and he'd lost.

He forced himself to stop thinking about her belly button and glared at her. "This is just some kind of game to you, isn't it?"

"No," she said, glaring back, "this is my life. I'm a

woman, not a child, and I don't need to ask *any*one's permission before I 'so much as lift my finger,' thank you very much."

"So you just do whatever you want. You just walk around, doing whatever you want, *kissing* whoever you want, whenever you want—" Bobby shut himself up. What the hell did that have to do with this?

Everything.

She'd scared him, yes, by not telling him why she was so confident the protestors didn't pose a threat, and that fear had morphed into anger. And he'd also been angry, sure, that she'd completely ignored his warning.

But, really, most of his anger came from that kiss she'd given him, less than an hour ago, in front of her apartment building.

That incredible kiss that had completely turned him upside down and inside out and...

And made him want far more than he could take.

Worse and worse, now that he'd blurted it out, she knew where his anger had come from, too.

"I'm sorry," she said quietly, reaching up to push his hair back from his face.

He stepped away from her, unable to bear the softness of her touch, praying for a miracle, praying for Wes suddenly to appear. His personal guardian angel, walking down the sidewalk, toward them, with that unmistakable Skelly swagger.

Colleen had mercy on him, and didn't stand there, staring at him with chagrin and pity in her luminous blue-green eyes. God, she was beautiful.

And, God, he was so pathetic.

He'd actually shouted at her. When was the last time he'd raised his voice in genuine anger?

He couldn't remember.

She'd turned back to the protestors and was talking to them now. "Did John Morrison tell you to come down here with these signs?"

They looked at each other.

As Bobby watched, Colleen spoke to them, telling them about the center, reassuring them that it would be an improvement to the neighborhood. This wasn't an abortion clinic. They wouldn't be handing out copious handfuls of free needles or condoms. They would provide HIV testing and counseling. They would provide AIDS education classes and workshops.

She invited them inside, to introduce them to the staff and give them a tour of the facility, while Bobby stayed outside with the truck.

A parking spot opened up down the street, and as he was parallel parking the beast, the truck's phone rang. It was Rene, the coordinator from the Relief Aid office, wondering where they were. She had ten volunteers ready to unpack the truck. Should they wait or should she let them take an early lunch?

Bobby promised that Colleen would call her right back. He was a half a block away from the center when he saw the protestors take their signs and go home. Knowing Colleen, she'd talked half of them into volunteering at the center. The other half had probably donated money to the cause.

She came out and met him halfway. "I don't know why John Morrison is so determined to cause trouble. I guess I should be glad he only sent protestors this time, instead of throwing cinder blocks through the front windows again."

"Again?" Bobby walked her more swiftly toward the

truck, wanting her safely inside the cab and out of this wretched neighborhood. "He did that before?"

"Twice," she told him. "Of course, he got neighborhood kids to do the dirty work, so we can't prove he was behind it. You know, I find it a little ironic that the man owns a bar. And his place is not some upscale hangout... it's a dive. People go there to get seriously tanked or to connect with one of the girls from the local 'escort service,' which is really just a euphemism for Hookers R Us. I'm sure Morrison gets a cut of whatever money exchanges hands in his back room, the sleaze, and *we're* a threat to the neighborhood...? What's he afraid of?"

"Where's his bar?" Bobby asked.

She gave him an address that meant nothing to him. But with a map he'd find it easily enough.

He handed her the keys. "Call Rene on the cell phone and tell her you're on your way."

She tried to swallow her surprise. "You're not coming?"

He shook his head, unable to meet her eyes for more than the briefest fraction of a second.

"Oh," she said.

It was the way she said it, as if trying to hide her disappointment that made him try to explain. "I need to take some time to..." What? Hide from her? Yes. Run away? Absolutely. Pray that he'd last another two and a half days until Wes arrived?

"Look, it's all right," she said. "You don't need to—"

"You're driving me crazy," he told her. "Every time I turn around, I find myself kissing you. I can't seem to be able to stop."

"You're the only one of us who sees that as a bad thing."

"I'm scared to death to be alone with you," he admitted. "I don't trust myself to be able to keep the distance I need to keep."

She didn't step toward him. She didn't move. She didn't say anything. She just looked at him and let him see her wanting him. He had to take a step back to keep himself from taking a step forward, and then another step and another, and pulling her into his arms and…

"I've got to…" he said. "Go…"

He turned away. Turned back.

She still didn't say anything. She just waited. Standing there, wanting him.

It was the middle of the day, on the sidewalk of a busy city street. Did she really think he'd do something as crazy as kiss her?

Ah, God, he wanted to kiss her.

A goodbye kiss. Just one last time. He wanted to do it, to kiss her again, knowing this time that it would, indeed, be the last time.

He wanted—desperately—for her to kiss him the way she'd kissed him in the darkness of the backstreet off Harvard Square. So lightly. So sweetly. So perfectly.

Just one more time like that.

Yeah, like hell he could kiss her just one more time. If he so much as touched her again, they were both going to go up in flames.

"Get in the truck," he somehow managed to tell her. "Please."

For one awful moment he was certain she was going to reach for him. But then she turned and unlocked the door to the truck. "You know, we're going to have to talk about that 'obey' thing," she said. "Because if you don't lighten up, I'm going to recommend that we don't accept your admiral's protection. We don't have to, you know."

Oh, yes, they did. But Bobby kept his mouth shut. He didn't say another word as she climbed into the truck from the passenger's side, as she slid behind the wheel and started the big engine.

As he watched, she maneuvered the truck onto the street and, with a cloud of exhaust, drove away.

Two and a half more days.

How the hell was he going to survive?

Chapter 10

Colleen cleaned out her refrigerator.

She washed the bathroom floor and checked her email.

She called the center's main office to find out the status of Andrea Barker, who'd been attacked just outside her home. There was no change, she was told. The woman was still in a coma.

By 9:00, Bobby still hadn't called.

By 9:15, Colleen had picked up the phone once or twice, but each time talked herself out of calling his hotel.

Finally, at 9:45, the apartment building front door buzzer rang.

Colleen leaned on the intercom. "Bobby?"

"Uh, no." The male voice that came back was one she didn't know. "Actually, I'm looking for Ashley DeWitt?"

"I'm sorry," Colleen said. "She's not here."

"Look, I drove up from New York. I know she was coming here and… Hold on a sec," the voice said.

There was a long silence, and then a knock directly on her apartment door.

Colleen looked out through the peephole. Brad. Had to be. He was tall and slender, with dark-blond hair and a yacht-club face. She opened the door with the chain still on and gave him a very pointedly raised eyebrow.

"Hi," he said, trying to smile. He looked awful. Like he hadn't slept in about a week. "Sorry, someone was coming out, so I came in."

"You mean, you sneaked in."

He gave up on the smile. "You must be Colleen, Ash's roommate. I'm Brad—the idiot who should be taken out and shot."

Colleen looked into his Paul-Newman-blue eyes and saw his pain. This was a man who was used to getting everything he wanted through his good looks and charisma. He was used to being Mr. Special, to winning, to being envied by half of the world and wanted by the other half.

But he'd blown it, big-time, with Ashley, and right now he hated himself.

She shut the door to remove the chain. When she opened it again, she stepped back to let him inside. He was wearing a dark business suit that was rumpled to the point of ruin—as if he'd had it on during that entire week he hadn't been sleeping.

He needed a shave, too.

"She's really not here," Colleen told him as he followed her into the living room. "She went to visit her aunt on Martha's Vineyard. Don't bother asking, because I don't know the details. Her aunt rents a different house each summer. I think it's in Edgartown this year, but I'm not sure."

"But she *was* here. God, I can smell her perfume." He sat down, heavily, on the sofa, and for one awful moment Colleen was certain that he was going to start to cry.

Somehow he managed not to. If this was an act, he deserved an Oscar.

"Do you know when she'll be back?" he asked.

Colleen shook her head. "No."

"Is this your place or hers?" He was looking around the living room, taking in the watercolors on the walls, the art prints, the batik-patterned curtains, the comfortable, secondhand furniture.

"Most of this stuff is mine," Colleen told him. "Although the curtains are Ashley's. She's a secret flower child, you know. Beneath those designer suits is a woman who's longing to wear tie-dyed T-shirts."

"Did she, uh, tell you what I did?" Brad asked.

"Yup."

He cleared his throat. "Do you think…" He had to start again. "Do you think she'll ever forgive me?"

"No," Colleen said.

Brad nodded. "Yeah," he said. "I don't think she will, either." He stood up. "The ferry to the Vineyard is out of Woods Hole, right?"

"Brad, she went there because she doesn't want to see you. What you did was unconscionable."

"So what do *you* recommend I do?" he asked her. "Give up?" His hands were shaking as if he'd had too much coffee on the drive up from New York. Or as if he were going into withdrawal without Ashley around.

Colleen shook her head. "No," she said. "Don't give

up. Don't ever give up." She looked at the telephone—it still wasn't ringing. Bobby wasn't calling. That left only one alternative. She had to call him. Because *she* wasn't going to give up, either.

She followed Brad to the door.

"I quit my job," he told her. "You know, working for her father. If Ashley calls, will you tell her that?"

"If she calls," Colleen said, "I'll tell her you were here. And then, if she asks, I'll tell her what you said. But only if she asks."

"Fair enough."

"What should I tell her if she asks where you are?"

He started down the stairs. "Edgartown. Tell her I'm in Edgartown, too."

Bobby stared at the phone as it rang, knowing it was Colleen on the other end. Had to be. Who else would call him here? Maybe Wes, who had called earlier and left a message.

It rang again.

Bobby quickly did the math, figuring out the time difference.... No, it definitely wasn't Wes. Had to be Colleen.

A third time. Once more and the voice mail system would click on.

He reached for it as it began to ring that final time, silently cursing himself. "Taylor."

"Hi, it's me."

"Yeah," he said. "I figured."

"And yet you picked it up, anyway. How brave of you."

"What's happening?" he asked, trying to pretend that everything was fine, that he hadn't kissed her—again—

and then spent the entire afternoon and evening wishing he was kissing her again.

"Nothing," Colleen said. "I was just wondering what you were up to all day."

"This and that." Mostly things he didn't want to tell her. That when he wasn't busy lusting after her, he'd been checking out John Morrison, for one. From what Bobby could tell from the locals, Morrison was mostly pathetic. Although, in his experience, pathetic men could be dangerous, too. Mostly to people they perceived to be weaker than they were. Like women. "Is your door locked?"

Colleen lowered her voice seductively. "Is yours?"

Oh, God. "This isn't a joke, Colleen," he said, working hard to keep his voice even. Calm. It wasn't easy. Inside he was ready to fly off the handle, to shout at her again. "A woman you work with was attacked—"

"Yes, my door is locked," she said. "But if someone really wants in, they can get in, since my windows are all open wide. And don't ask me to close and lock them, because it's hot tonight."

It was. Very hot. Even here in his air-conditioned hotel room.

Funny, but it had seemed nice and cool right up until a few minutes ago. When the phone rang.

He'd showered earlier in an attempt to chill out, but his hair, still down around his shoulders, was starting to stick to his neck again. As soon as he got off the phone with Colleen, he'd put it into a ponytail.

Shoot, maybe he'd take another shower. A nice, freezing-cold one this time.

"Colleen," he said. Despite his attempts to sound

calm, there was a tightness to his voice. "Please don't tell me you sleep with your windows unlocked."

She laughed. "All right," she said. "I won't tell you."

Bobby heard himself make a strangled sound.

"You know, if you want me to be really, absolutely safe, you could come over," she told him. "Although, you've got air-conditioning over there, don't you? So you should really ask *me* to come to the hotel. I could take a cab and be there in five minutes."

He managed a word this time. "Colleen…"

"Okay," she said. "Right. Never mind. It's a terrible idea. Forget it. Just forget about the fact that I'm here, sitting on my bed, all alone, and that you're just a short mile away, sitting on yours, presumably also all alone. Forget about the fact that kissing you is on my list of the five most wonderful things I've ever done in my life and—"

Oh, man.

"I can't do it," he said, giving up on not trying to sound as desperate as he felt. "Dammit, even if you *weren't* Wes's sister, I'm only here for a few more days. That's all I could give you. I can't handle another long-distance relationship right now. I can't do that to myself."

"I'll take the days," she said. "Day. Make it singular if you want. Just once. Bobby—"

"I can't do that to you." But oh, sweet heaven, he wanted to. He *could* be at her place in five minutes. Less. One kiss, and he'd have her clothes off. Two, and… Oh, *man*.

"I want to know what it's like." Her voice was husky, intimate across the phone line, as if she were whispering in his ear, her breath hot against him. "Just once. No strings, Bobby. Come on…"

Yeah, no strings—except for the noose Wes would tie around his neck when he found out.

Wes, who'd left a message for Bobby on his hotel voice mail…

"Hey, Bobby! Word is Alpha Squad's heading back to Little Creek in a few days to assist Admiral Robinson's Gray Group in Tulgeria as part of some kind of civilian protection gig. Did you set that up, man? Let me guess. Leenie dug in her heels, so you called the Jakester. Brilliant move, my friend. It would be perfect—if Spaceman wasn't being such a total jerk out here on my end.

"He's making all this noise about finally getting to meet Colleen. Remember that picture you had of her? It was a few months ago. I don't know where you got it, but Spaceman saw it and wouldn't stop asking about her. Where does she go to school? How old is she? Yada-yada-yada, on and on about her hair, her eyes, her smile. Give me a break! As if I'd ever let a SEAL within twenty-five feet of her—not even an officer and alleged gentleman like Spaceman, no way. Look, I'll call you when we get into Little Creek. In the meantime, stick close to her, all right? Put the fear of God or the U.S. Navy into any of those college jerks sniffing around her, trying to get too close. Thanks again for everything, Bobby. I hope your week hasn't been too miserable."

Miserable wasn't even close. Bobby had left misery behind a long time ago.

"Maybe we should have phone sex," Colleen suggested.

"What?" Bobby dropped the receiver. He moved fast and caught it before it bounced twice. "No!"

She was laughing at him again. "Ah, come on.

Where's your sense of adventure, Taylor? What are you wearing? Isn't that the way you're supposed to start?"

"Colleen—"

She lowered her voice. "Don't you want to know what I've got on?"

"No. I have to go now." Bobby closed his eyes and didn't hang up the phone. *Yes.* Oh, man.

"My nightgown," she told him, her voice even softer. Slightly breathy now. Deep and husky, her voice was unbelievable even when she wasn't trying to give him a heart attack. Right now, she was trying, and it was pure sex. "It's white. Cotton." She left long pauses between her words, as if giving him plenty of time to picture her. "Sleeveless. It's got buttons down the front, and the top one fell off a long time ago, leaving it a little… daring, shall we say? It's old—nice and soft and a little worn-out."

He knew that nightgown. He'd seen it hanging on the back of her bathroom door the last time he and Wes had visited. He'd touched it by mistake when he'd come out of the shower, thinking it was his towel. It wasn't. It *was* very soft to the touch.

Her body, beneath it, would be even softer.

"Want me to guess what you're wearing?" she asked.

Bobby couldn't speak.

"A towel," she said. "Just a towel. Because I bet you just showered. You like to shower at night to cool down before you go to bed, right? If I touched you," her voice dropped another notch, "your skin would be clean and cool and smooth.

"And your hair's down—it's probably still a little damp, too. If I were there, I'd brush it out for you. I'd kneel behind you on the bed and—"

"If you were here," Bobby said, interrupting her, his voice rough to his own ears, "you wouldn't be brushing my hair."

"What would I be doing?" she shot back at him.

Images bombarded him. Colleen, flashing him her killer smile just before she lowered her head and took him into her mouth. Colleen, lying back on his bed, hair spread on his pillows, breasts peaked with desire, waiting for him, welcoming him as he came to her. Colleen, head back as she straddled him, as he filled her, hard and fast and deep and—

Reality intervened. Phone sex. Dear sweet heaven. What was she doing to him? Beneath the towel—yes, she was right about the towel he wore around his waist—he was completely aroused.

"What would you be doing? You'd be calling a cab to take you home," he told her.

"No, I wouldn't. I'd kiss you," she countered, "and you'd pick me up and carry me to your bed."

"No, I wouldn't," he lied. "Colleen, I have… I really have to go now. Really."

"Your towel would drop to the floor," she said, and he couldn't make himself hang up the phone, both dreading and dying to hear what she would say next. "And after you put me down, you'd let me look at you." She drew in a breath, and it caught—a soft little gasp that made him ache from wanting her. "I think you're the most beautiful man I've ever seen."

He wasn't sure if he wanted to laugh or cry. "I think you're crazy." His voice cracked.

"No. Oh, your shoulders are so wide, and your chest and arms…mmmmm." She made a sound deep in her throat that was so sexy he was sure he was going to die.

Stop this. Now. Somehow he couldn't make his lips form the words.

"And the muscles in your stomach, leading down to…" She made another sound, a sigh, this time. "Do you know how incredibly good you look naked? There's…so *much* of you. I'm a little nervous, but you smile at me, and your eyes are so soft and beautiful, I know you'd never hurt me."

Bobby stood up. His sudden, jerky movement was reflected in the mirror above the dresser, on the other side of the dimly lit room. He looked ridiculous standing there, his towel tenting out in front of him.

He must've made some anguished noise, because she quieted him. "Shhh. It's okay."

But it wasn't. Nothing about this was okay. Still, he couldn't hang up. He couldn't make her stop.

He couldn't stand the sight of himself like that, standing there like some absurd, pathetic clown, and he took the towel off, flinging it across the room. Only now he stood there naked. Naked and aching for someone he couldn't have. Not really.

"After I look at you for a long time…" Her voice was musical. Seductive. He could have listened to her read a phone book and gotten turned on. This was driving him mad. "I unbutton my nightgown. I've got nothing on underneath, nothing at all, and you know it. But you don't rush me. You just sit back and watch. One button at a time.

"Finally, I'm done, but… I'm shy." She was silent for a moment, and when she spoke again, her voice was very small. "I'm afraid you won't…like me." She was serious. She honestly thought—

"Are you kidding? I love your body," Bobby told her.

"I dream about you wearing that nightgown. I dream about—"

Oh, my God. What was he doing?

"Oh, tell me," she breathed. "Please, Bobby, tell me what you dream."

"What do you think I dream?" he asked harshly, angry at her, angry at himself, knowing he still wasn't man enough to hang up the phone and end this, even though he knew damn well that he should. "I dream exactly what you're describing right now. You in my bed." His voice caught on his words. "Ready for me."

"I am," she told him. "Ready for you. Completely. You're still watching, so I… I touch myself—where I'm dying for you to touch me."

She made a noise that outdid all of the other noises she'd been making, and Bobby nearly started to cry. Oh, man, he couldn't do this. This was Wes's sister on the other end of this phone. This was wrong.

He turned his back to the mirror, unable to look at his reflection.

"Please," she gasped, "oh, please, tell me what you dream when you dream about me."

Oh, *man.* "Where did you learn to do this?" He had to know.

"I didn't," she said breathlessly. "I'm making it up as I go along. You want to know what I dream about you?"

No. Yes. It didn't matter. She didn't wait for him to answer.

"My fantasy is that the doorbell rings, and you're there when I answer it. You don't say anything. You just come inside and lock the door behind you. You just look at me and I know. This is it. You want me.

"And then you kiss me, and it starts out so slowly, so

delicately, but it builds and it grows and it takes over everything—the whole world gets lost in the shadow of this one amazing kiss. You touch me and I touch you, and I love touching you, but I can't get close enough, and somehow you know that, and you make my clothes disappear. And you still kiss me and kiss me, and you don't stop kissing me until I'm on my back on my bed, and you're—" her voice dropped to a whisper "—inside of me."

"That's what I dream," Bobby whispered, too, struggling to breathe. "I dream about being inside you." Hell. He was going to burn in hell for saying that aloud.

Her breath was coming in gasps, too. "I love those dreams," she told him. "It feels *so* good..."

"Yes..."

"Oh, please," she begged. "Tell me more..."

Tell her... When he closed his eyes, he could see Colleen beneath him, beside him, her body straining to meet his, her breasts filling his hands and his mouth, her hair a fragrant curtain around his face, her skin smooth as silk, her mouth soft and wet and delicious, her hips moving in rhythm with his....

But he could tell her none of that. He couldn't even begin to put it into words.

"I dream of touching you," he admitted hoarsely. "Kissing you. Everywhere." It was woefully inadequate, compared to what she'd just described.

But she sighed as if he'd given her the verbal equivalent of the Hope Diamond.

So he tried again, even though he knew he shouldn't. He stood there, listening to himself open his mouth and say things he shouldn't say to his best friend's sister.

"I dream of you on top of me." His voice sounded distant and husky, thick with desire and need. Sexy.

Who would have thought he'd be any good at this? "So I can watch your face, Colleen." He dragged out her name, taking his time with it, loving the way it felt in his mouth, on his tongue. *Colleen.* "So I can look into your eyes, your beautiful eyes. Oh, I love looking into your eyes, Colleen, while you…"

"Oh, yes," she gasped. "Oh, Bobby, oh—"

Oh, *man.*

Chapter 11

Just after midnight the phone rang.

Colleen picked it up on the first ring, knowing it was Bobby, knowing that he wasn't calling for a replay of what they'd just done.

Pretended to do.

Sort of.

She didn't bother even to say hello. "Are you okay?"

He'd been so freaked out earlier that she'd made up an excuse to get off the phone, thinking he needed time alone to get his heart and lungs working again.

But now she was wondering if that hadn't been a mistake. Maybe what he'd really needed was to talk.

"I don't know," he answered her. "I'm trying to figure out which level of hell I'm going to be assigned to."

"He's able to make a joke," Colleen said. "Should I take that as a good sign?"

"I wasn't joking. Dammit, Colleen, I can't do that ever again. I can't. I shouldn't have even—"

"All right," she said. "Look, Guilt Man, let it go. I steamrolled over you. You didn't stand a chance. Besides, it's not as if it was real."

"No?" he said. "That's funny, because from this end, it sounded pretty authentic."

"Well, yeah," she said. "Sure. On a certain level it was. But the truth is, your participation was nice, but it wasn't necessary. All I ever really have to do is think about you. If you want to know the truth, this isn't the first time I've let my fantasies of you and me push me over the edge—"

"Oh, my God, don't tell me that!"

"Sorry." Colleen made herself stop talking. She was making this worse, telling him secrets that made her blush when she stopped to think about it. But his feelings of guilt were completely unwarranted.

"I've got to leave," he told her, his voice uncharacteristically unsteady. "I have to get out of here. I've decided—I'm going down to Little Creek early. I'll be back in a few days, with the rest of Alpha Squad."

With Wes.

One step forward, two steps back.

"I'd appreciate it if you didn't go into detail with my brother about—"

"I'm going to tell him that I didn't touch you. Much. But that I wanted to."

"Because it's not like I make a habit of doing that— phone sex, I mean. And since you obviously didn't like it, I'm not going to—"

"No," he interrupted her. "You know, if I'm Guilt Man, then you're Miss Low Self-Esteem. How could you even think I didn't like it? I loved it. Every excruciating minute. You are unbelievably hot, and you completely killed me. If you got one of those 900 numbers, you could make a fortune, but you damn well better not."

"You loved it, but you don't want to do it again?"

Bobby was silent on the other end of the line, and Colleen waited, heart in her throat.

"It's not enough," he finally said.

"Come over," she said, hearing her desire coat her voice. "Please. It's not too late to—"

"I can't."

"I don't understand why not. If you want me, and I want you, *why* can't we get together? Why does this have to be so hard?"

"If we were a pair of rabbits, sure," Bobby said. "It would be simple. But we're not, and it's not. This attraction between us…it's all mixed up with what I want, which is *not* to get involved with someone who lives three thousand miles away from me, and with what I want for you, which is for you to live happily ever after with a good man who loves you, and children if you want them, and a career that makes you jump out of bed with pleasure and excitement every single morning for the rest of your life. And if that's not complicated enough, there's also what I know *Wes* wants for you—which is more than just a man who loves you, but someone who will take care of you, too. Someone who's not in the Teams, someone who's not even in the Navy. Someone who can buy you presents and vacations and houses and cars without having to get a bank loan. Someone who'll *be* there, every morning, without fail."

"He also wants to make sure that I don't have any fun at all, the hypocrite. Making noise about how I have to wait until I'm married, when he's out there getting it on with any and every woman he can."

"He loves you," Bobby told her. "He's scared you'll end up pregnant and hating your life. Abandoned by some loser. Or worse—tied to some loser forever."

"As if I'd sleep with a loser."

Bobby laughed softly. "Yeah, well, I think I might fall into Wes's definition of a loser, so yes, you would."

"Ho," Colleen said. "Who's Mr. Low Self-Esteem now?"

"*Wes's* definition," he said again. "Not necessarily mine."

"Or mine," she countered. "It's definitely not mine."

"So, okay," he told her. "We toss the fact that I want to make love to you for about seventy-two hours straight into that mess of what you want and I want and Wes wants. Boom. What happens upon impact? You get lucky, I get lucky, which would probably be transcendental— no, not probably, *definitely.* So that's great…or is it? Because all I can see, besides the immediate gratification of us both getting off, is a boatload of pain.

"I risk getting too… I don't know, *attached* to someone who lives three thousand miles away from me.

"I risk my relationship with your brother…"

"You risk your relationship with your brother…

"You risk losing any opportunities that might be out there of actually meeting someone special, because you're messing around with me."

Maybe you're the special one. Colleen didn't dare say it aloud. He obviously didn't think so.

"I've got a flight into Norfolk that leaves Logan just after 1500 hours," he said quietly. "I'm going into the Relief Aid office in the morning. I've got a meeting set up at 1100 hours to talk about the security we're going to be providing in Tulgeria—and what we expect from your group in terms of following the rules we set up. I figured you'd want to sit in on that."

"Yeah," Colleen said. "I'll be there." And how weird was *that* going to be—meeting his eyes for the first time since they'd…since she'd… She took a deep breath. "I'll borrow a truck, after, and give you a lift to the airport."

"That's okay. I'll take the T." He spoke quickly.

"What, are you afraid I'm going to jump you, right there in the truck, in the airport's short-term parking lot?"

"No," he said. He laughed, but it was grim instead of amused. "I'm afraid I'm going to jump you. From here on in, Colleen, we don't go anywhere alone."

"But—"

"I'm sorry. I don't trust myself around you."

"Bobby—"

"Good night, Colleen."

"Wait," she said, but he'd already hung up.

One step forward, two steps back.

Okay. Okay. She just had to figure out a way to get him alone. Before 1500—3:00 p.m.—tomorrow.

How hard could *that* be?

The Relief Aid office was hushed and quiet when Bobby came in at 1055. The radio—which usually played classic rock at full volume—was off. No one was packing boxes of canned goods and other donations. People stood, talking quietly in small groups.

Rene pushed past him, making a beeline for the ladies' room, head down. She was crying.

What the…?

Bobby looked around, more carefully this time, but Colleen was nowhere in sight.

He saw Susan Fitzgerald, the group's leading volunteer, sitting at the row of desks on the other side of the room. She was on the phone, and as he watched, she hung up. She just sat there, then, rubbing her forehead and her eyes behind her glasses.

"What's going on?" he asked.

"Another quake hit Tulgeria this morning," she told him. "About 2 a.m., our time. I'm not sure how it happened, whether it was from a fire caused by downed power lines or from the actual shock waves, but one of the local terrorist cells had an ammunitions stockpile, and it went up in a big way. The Tulgerian government thought they were under attack and launched a counteroffensive."

Oh, God. Bobby could tell from the look on Susan's face that the worst news was coming. He braced himself.

"St. Christof's—our orphanage—sustained a direct hit from some sort of missile," Susan told him. "We lost at least half of the kids."

Oh, Christ. "Does Colleen know?"

Susan nodded. "She was here when the news came in. But she went home. Her little girl—the one she'd been writing to—was on the list of children who were killed."

Analena. Oh, God. Bobby closed his eyes.

"She was very upset," Susan told him. "Understandably."

He straightened up and started for the door. He knew damn well that Colleen's apartment was the last place he should go, but it was the one place in the world where he absolutely needed to be right now. To hell with his rules.

To hell with everything.

"Bobby," Susan called after him. "She told me you're leaving for Virginia in a few hours. Try to talk her into coming back here when you go. She really shouldn't be alone."

Colleen let the doorbell ring the same way she'd let the phone ring.

She didn't want to talk to anyone, didn't want to see anyone, didn't want to have to try to explain how a little girl she'd never met could have owned such an enormous piece of her heart.

She didn't want to do anything but lie here, on her bed, in her room, with the shades pulled down, and cry over the injustice of a world in which orphanages were bombed during a war that really didn't exist.

Yet, at the same time, the last thing she wanted was to be alone. Back when she was a kid, when her world fell apart and she needed a shoulder to cry on, she'd gone to her brother Ethan. He was closest in age to her—the one Skelly kid who didn't have that infamous knee-jerk temper and that smart-mouthed impatience.

She'd loved him, and he'd died, too. What was it with her…that made the people she loved disappear? She stared up at her ceiling, at the cracks and chips that she'd memorized through too many sleepless nights. She should have learned by now just to stop loving, to stop taking chances. Yeah, like that would ever happen. Maybe she was stupid, but that was one lesson she refused to learn.

Every single day, she fell in love over and over. When she walked past a little girl with a new puppy. When a baby stared at her unblinkingly on the trolley and then smiled, a big, drooly, gummy grin. When she saw an elderly couple out for a stroll, still holding hands. She lost her heart to them all.

Still, just once, she wanted more than to be a witness to other people's happy endings. She wanted to be part of one.

She wanted Bobby.

She didn't care when the doorbell stopped ringing and the phone started up again, knowing it was probably Bobby, and crying even harder because she'd pushed too hard and now he was leaving, too.

Because he didn't want her love, not in any format. Not even quick and easy and free—the way she'd offered it.

She just lay on her bed, head aching and face numb from the hours she'd already cried, but unable to stop.

But then she wasn't alone anymore. She didn't know how he got in. Her door was locked. She hadn't even heard his footsteps on the floor.

It was as if Bobby had just suddenly materialized, next to her bed.

He didn't hesitate, he just lay down right next to her and drew her into his arms. He didn't say a word, he just held her close, cradling her with his entire body.

His shirt was soft against her cheek. He smelled like clean clothes and coffee. The trace of cigarette smoke that usually lingered on his shirt and even in his hair had finally been washed away.

But it was late. If he was going to get to Logan in time to catch his flight to Norfolk… "You have to leave soon," she told him, trying to be strong, wiping her face and lifting her head to look into his eyes.

For a man who could make one mean war face when

he wanted to, he had the softest, most gentle eyes. "No." He shook his head slightly. "I don't."

Colleen couldn't help it. Fresh tears welled, and she shook from trying so hard not to cry.

"It's okay," he told her. "Go on and cry. I've got you, sweet. I'm here. I'll be here for as long as you need me."

She clung to him.

And he just held her and held her and held her.

As she fell asleep, still held tightly in his arms, his fingers running gently through her hair, her last thought was to wonder hazily what he was going to say when he found out that she could well need him forever.

Bobby woke up slowly. He knew even before he opened his eyes that, like Dorothy, he wasn't in Kansas anymore. Wherever he was, it wasn't his apartment on the base, and he most certainly wasn't alone.

It came to him in a flash. Massachusetts. Colleen Skelly.

She was lying against him, on top of him, beneath him, her leg thrown across his, his thigh pressed tight between her legs. Her head was on his shoulder, his arms beneath her and around her, the softness of her breasts against his chest, her hand tucked up alongside his neck.

They were both still fully dressed, but Bobby knew with an acceptance of his fate—it was actually quite calming and peaceful, all things considered—that after she awoke, they wouldn't keep their clothes on for long.

He'd had his chance for a clean escape, and he'd blown it. He was here, and there was no way in hell he was going to walk away now.

Wes was just going to have to kill him.

But, damn, it was going to be worth it. Bobby was going to die with a smile on his face.

His hand had slipped up underneath the edge of Colleen's T-shirt, and he took advantage of that, gliding his fingers across the smooth skin of her back, up all the way to the back strap of her bra, down to the waistband of her shorts. Up and back in an unending circle.

Man, he could lie here, just touching her lightly like this, for the rest of his life.

But Colleen stirred, and he waited, still caressing the softness of her skin, feeling her wake up and become as aware of him as he was of her.

She didn't move, didn't pull away from him.

And he didn't stop touching her.

"How long did I sleep?" she finally asked, her voice even huskier than usual.

"I don't know," he admitted. "I fell asleep, too." He glanced at the windows. The light was starting to weaken. "It's probably around 1900—seven o'clock."

"Thank you," she said. "For coming here."

"You want to talk about it?" Bobby asked. "About Analena?"

"No," she said. "Because when I say it out loud, it all sounds so stupid. I mean, what was I thinking? That I was going to bring her here, to live with me? I mean, come on—who was I kidding? I don't have room—look at this place. And I don't have money—I can barely pay my own bills. I couldn't live here without Ashley paying for half of everything. I had to sell my car to stay in law school. And that's *with* the school loans. And how am I supposed to take care of a kid while I'm going to school? I don't have time for an instant family—not now while I'm in law school. I don't have time for a husband, let alone a child. And yet…"

She shook her head. "When I saw her pictures and read her letters… Oh, Bobby, she was so alive. I didn't even get a chance to know her, but I wanted to—God, I wanted to!"

"If you had met her, you would have fallen completely in love with her." He smiled. "I know you pretty well. And she would've loved you, too. And you would have somehow made it work," he told her. "It wouldn't have been easy, but there are some things you just have to do, you know? So you do it, and it all works out. I'm sorry you won't get that chance with Analena."

She lifted her head to look at him. "You don't think I'm being ridiculous?"

"I would never think of you as ridiculous," he told her quietly. "Generous, yes. Warm. Giving. Loving, caring…"

Something shifted. There was a sudden something in her eyes that clued him in to the fact that, like him, she was suddenly acutely, intensely aware of every inch of him that was in contact with every inch of her.

"Sexy as hell," he whispered. "But never ridiculous."

Her gaze dropped to his mouth. He saw it coming. She was going to kiss him, and his fate would be sealed.

He met her halfway, wanting to take a proactive part in this, wanting to do more than simply be unable to resist the temptation.

Her lips were soft, her mouth almost unbearably sweet. It was a slow, languorous kiss—as if they both knew that from here on in, there was no turning back, no need to rush.

He kissed her again, longer this time, deeper—just in

case she had any last, lingering doubts about what was going to happen next.

But before he could kiss her again, she pulled away. There were tears in her eyes.

"I didn't want it to happen this way," she said.

He tried to understand what she was telling him, tried to rein himself in. "Colleen, if you don't want me to stay—"

"No," she said. "I do want you to stay. I want you. Too much. See, I lay awake last night, figuring out ways to get you back here. I was going to make something up, try to trick you into coming here after the meeting and then…"

Comprehension dawned. She'd gotten what she'd wanted. He was here. But at what price? An earthquake and a war. A body count that included people she'd loved.

"No," he told her, not wanting her to believe that. "I would've shown up here sooner or later. Even if I'd gotten on that plane—and I'm not sure I would have been able to—I would've called you from Little Creek tonight. I wouldn't have been able to resist."

She wiped her eyes with the heel of her hands. "Really?"

"The things you do to me with just a telephone… Man, oh, man."

Tears still clung to her eyelashes, and her nose was slightly pink. But she was laughing.

As he held her gaze, he remembered the things she said to him last night and let her see that memory reflected in his eyes. She blushed slightly.

"I've really never done that before," she told him. "I

mean, the phone part." She blushed again as she looked away, embarrassed by what she'd just again admitted.

He needed her to know what merely thinking about her—about that—did to him. He pulled her chin back so that she had to look into his eyes, as he answered her with just as much soul-baring honesty. "Maybe someday you'll let me watch."

Someday. The word hung between them. It implied that there was going to be more than just tonight.

"You don't do long-distance relationships," she reminded him.

"No," he corrected her. "I don't *want* to do it that way. I have in the past, and I've hated it. It's so hard to—"

"I don't want to be something that's hard," she told him. "I don't want to be an obligation that turns into something you dread dealing with."

He steeled himself, preparing to pull away from her, out of her arms. "Then maybe I should go, before—"

"Maybe we should just make love and not worry about tomorrow," she countered.

She kissed him, and it was dizzying. He kissed her back hungrily, possessively—all sense of laziness gone. He wanted her, now. He needed her.

Now.

Her hands were in his hair, freeing it completely from the ponytail that had already halfway fallen out. She kissed him even harder, angling her head to give him better access to her mouth—or maybe to give herself better access to *his* mouth.

Could she really do this?

Make love to him tonight and only tonight?

Her legs tightened around his thigh, and he stopped thinking. He kissed her again and again, loving the taste of her, the feel of her in his arms. He reached between them, sliding his hand up under her shirt to fill his hand with her breast.

She pulled back from him to tug at his T-shirt. She wanted it off, and it was easier simply to give up—temporarily—trying to kiss and touch as much of her as he possibly could, and take his shirt off himself. His shoulder was still stiff, and the only way he could get a T-shirt on or off was awkwardly. Painfully. One arm at a time.

Before he even got it off, she'd started on his shorts, her fingers cool against his stomach as she unfastened the button and then the zipper.

She had his shorts halfway down his legs by the time he tossed his shirt onto the floor.

He helped her, kicking his legs free, and then there he was. On her bed in only his briefs, while she was still fully clothed.

He reached for her, intending to rid her of her T-shirt and shorts as efficiently as she'd taken care of his, but she distracted him by kissing him. And then he distracted himself by touching her breasts beneath her shirt, by unfastening her bra and kissing her right through the cotton, by burying his face in the softness of her body.

It wasn't until he tried to push her shirt up over her breasts so that he could see her as well as touch and kiss, that he felt her tense.

And he remembered.

She was self-conscious about her body.

Probably because she wasn't stick thin like the alleged Hollywood ideal.

The hell with that—she was *his* ideal. She was curvaceous. Stacked. Voluptuous. She was perfection.

Man, if he were her, he would walk around in one of those little nonexistent tank tops that were so popular. She should wear one without a bra, and just watch all the men faint as she passed by.

Someday he'd get her one of those. She could wear it here, in the privacy of her room, if she didn't want to wear it in public. Man, he hadn't thought he could get any harder, any hotter, but just the thought of her wearing something like that, just because he liked it—just for him—heated him up another notch.

She would do it, too. After he made her realize that he truly worshiped her body, that he found her unbelievably beautiful and sexy, she would be just as adventurous about that as she was with everything else.

Phone sex. Sweet heaven.

Phone sex was all about words. About saying what he wanted, about saying how he felt.

He hadn't been very good at it—not like Colleen. Unlike her, words weren't his strong suit. But he had to do it again now. He had to use words to reassure her, to let her know just how beautiful he thought she was.

He could do it with body language, with his eyes, with his mouth and his hands. He could show her, by the way he made love to her, but even then, he knew she wouldn't completely believe him.

No, if he wanted to dissolve that edge of tension that tightened her shoulders, he had to do it with words.

Or did he? Maybe he could do a combination of both show *and* tell.

"I think you're spectacular," he told her. "You're incredible and gorgeous and…"

And he was doing this wrong. She wasn't buying any of it.

He touched her, reaching up beneath her shirt to caress her. He had the show part down. He wanted to taste her, and he realized with a flash that instead of trying to make up compliments filled with meaningless adjectives, he should just say what he wanted, say how he felt. He should just open his mouth and speak his very thoughts.

"I want to taste you right here," he told her as he touched her. "I want to feel you in my mouth."

He tugged her shirt up just a little, watching her face, ready to take it even more slowly if she wanted him to. But she didn't tense up, so he drew it up a little more, exposing the underside of her breast, so pale and soft and perfect. And then he forgot to watch her eyes because there was her nipple, peeking out. He'd been holding his breath, he realized, and he let it out in a rush. "Oh, yeah."

She was already taut with desire, and he lowered his head to do just what he'd described. She made a sound that he liked, a sound that had nothing to do with being self-conscious and everything to do with pleasure.

He drew her shirt up then, up and over her head, and she sat up to help him.

And there she was.

As he pulled back to look at her, he opened his mouth and let his thoughts escape.

Unfortunately, his expression of sincere admiration was one of Wes's favorite, more colorful turns of phrase.

Fortunately, Colleen laughed. She looked at him, looked at the expression he knew was on his face, the pure pleasure he let shine from his eyes.

"You're so beautiful," he breathed. "I've died and gone to heaven."

"Gee," she said, "and I don't even have my pants off."

He grabbed her by the waist of her shorts, flipping her back onto the bed and, as she whooped in surprised laughter, he corrected that.

In five seconds flat she was naked and he was kissing her, touching, loving the feel of all that smooth, perfect skin against him. And when he pulled back to really look at her, there wasn't a bit of tension in the air.

But this talking thing was working so well, why stop?

"Do you know what you do to me?" he asked her as he touched, kissed, explored. He didn't give her time to answer. He just took one of her own exploring hands, and pressed it against him.

"You are *so* sexy, that happens to me every time I see you," he whispered, looking into her eyes to let her see the intense pleasure that shot through him at her touch. "Every time I *think* of you."

She was breathing hard, and he pulled her to him and kissed her again, reaching between them to help her rid him of his briefs.

Her fingers closed around him, and he would have told her how much he liked that, but words failed him, and all he could do was groan.

She seemed to understand and answered him in kind as he slipped his hand between her legs. She was so slick and soft and hot, he could feel himself teetering on the edge of his self-control. He needed a condom. *Now.*

But when he spoke, all he could manage to say was her name.

Again she understood. "Top drawer. Bedside table."

He lunged for it, found it. An unopened, cellophane-wrapped box. He both loved and hated the fact that the box was unopened. Growling with frustration, he tried to rip the damned thing in half.

Colleen took it from his hands and opened it quickly, laughing at the way he fumbled the little wrapped package, getting in the way, touching and kissing him as he tried to cover himself.

Slow down. She'd told him herself that she hadn't had much experience. He didn't want to be too rough, didn't want to hurt her or scare her or…

She pulled him back with her onto the bed in a move that Xena the Warrior Princess would have been in awe of. And she told him, in extremely precise language, exactly what she wanted.

How could he refuse?

Especially when she kissed him, when she lifted her hips and reached between them to find him and guide him and…

He entered her far less gently than he'd intended, but her moan was one of pure pleasure.

"Yes," she told him as he pushed himself even more deeply inside her. "Oh, Bobby, yes…"

He kissed her, touched her, stroked her, murmuring things that he couldn't believe were coming out of his mouth, things that he loved about her body, things he wanted to do to her, things she made him feel—things that made her laugh and gasp and murmur equally sexy things back to him, until he was damn near blind with passion and desire.

Gentle had long-gone right out the window. He was filling her, hard and fast, and she was right there with him, urging him on.

She told him when she began to climax—as if he wouldn't know from the sound of her voice. As if he couldn't feel her shatter around him. Still, he loved that she told him, and her breathless words helped push him over the edge.

And just like that he was flying, his release rocketing through him with so much power and force he had to shout her name, and even that wasn't enough.

He wanted to tell her how she made him feel, about the sheer, crystal perfection of the moment that seemed to surround him, shimmering and wonderful, filling his chest until it was hard to breathe, until he wanted to cry from its pure beauty.

But there were no words that could describe how he felt. To do it justice, he would have to invent a completely new vocabulary.

Bobby realized then that he was lying on top of her, crushing her, completely spent. His shoulder felt as if he'd just been shot all over again—funny, he hadn't felt even a twinge until now and—

Colleen was crying.

"Oh, my God," he said, shifting off her, pulling her so that she was in his arms. "Did I hurt you? Did I…?"

"No!" she said, kissing him. "No, it's just…that was so perfect, it doesn't seem fair. Why should I be so lucky to be able to share something so special with you?"

"I'm sorry," he said, kissing her hair, holding her close. He knew she was thinking about Analena.

"Will you stay with me?" she asked. "All night?"

"I'm right here," he said. "I'm not going anywhere."

"Thank you." Colleen closed her eyes, her head against his chest, her skin still damp from their lovemaking.

Bobby lay naked in Colleen's bed, holding her close, breathing in her sweet scent, desperately trying to fend off the harsh reality that was crashing down around him.

He'd just made love with Colleen Skelly.

No, he'd just had *sex* with Colleen Skelly. He'd just got it on with Wes's little sister. He'd put it to her. Nailed her. Scored. That was the way Wes was going to see it—not sweetly disguised with pretty words like *making love.*

Last night he'd had phone sex with Colleen. Tonight he'd done the real deal.

Just one night, she wanted. Just one time. Just to find out what it would be like.

Would she stick to that? Give him breakfast in the morning, shake his hand and thank him for the fun experience and send him on his way?

Bobby wasn't sure whether to hope so or hope not. He already wanted too much. He wanted— No, he couldn't even think it.

Maybe, if they only made love this once, Wes would understand that it was an attraction so powerful—more powerful than both of them—that couldn't be denied. Bobby tried that on for size, tried to picture Wes's calm acceptance and rational understanding and—

Nah.

Wes was going to kill him. No doubt about that.

Bobby smiled, though, as he ran his hand down Colleen's incredible body. She snuggled against him, turning so that they were spooned together, her back to his front. He tucked his good arm around her, filling his hand with the weight of her breasts.

Oh, man.

Yeah, Wes was going to kill him.

But before he did, Bobby would ask them to put four words on his tombstone: It Was Worth It.

Chapter 12

Colleen woke up alone in her bed.

It was barely even dawn, and her first thought was that she'd dreamed it. All of it. Everything that had happened yesterday and last night—it was all one giant combination nightmare and raging hot fantasy.

But Bobby's T-shirt and briefs were still on her floor. Unless he'd left her apartment wearing only his shorts, he hadn't gone far.

She could smell coffee brewing, and she climbed out of bed.

Muscles she didn't even know existed protested—further proof that last night hadn't been a dream. It was a good ache, combined with a warmth that seemed to spread through her as she remembered Bobby's whispered words as he'd... As they'd...

Who knew that such a taciturn man would be able to express himself so eloquently?

But even more eloquent than his words was the expressiveness of his face, the depth of emotion and expressions of sheer pleasure he didn't try to hide from her as they made love.

They'd made love.

The thought didn't fill her with laughter and song as she'd imagined it would.

Yes, it had been great. Making love to Bobby had been more wonderful than she'd ever dared to dream. More special and soul shattering than she'd imagined. But it didn't begin to make up for the deaths of all those children. Nothing could do that.

She found her robe and pulled it on, sitting back on the edge of the bed, gathering her strength.

She didn't want to leave her room. She wanted to hide here for the rest of the week.

But life went on, and there were things that needed to be done for the children who'd survived. And in order to get them done, there were truths that had to be faced.

There were going to be tears shed when she went into the Relief Aid office. She was also going to have to break the news to the church youth group that had helped raise money for the trip. Those kids had exchanged letters and pictures with the children in Tulgeria. Telling them of the tragedy wasn't going to be easy.

And then there was Bobby.

He had to be faced, too. She'd lied to him. Telling him that she'd be content with only one night. Well, maybe it hadn't been a lie. At the time, she'd talked herself into believing it was possible.

But right now all she felt was foolish. Deceitful. Pathetic.

Desperate.

She wanted to make love to him again. And again. And again, and again.

Maybe he wanted her again, too. She'd read—extensively—that men liked sex. Morning, noon and night, according to some sources.

Well, it was morning, and she would never discover whether he was inclined to run away or to stay a little longer unless she stood up and walked out of this room.

She squared her shoulders and did just that. And after a quick pit stop in the bathroom—where she also made sure her hair wasn't making her look too much like the bride of Frankenstein—she went into the kitchen.

Bobby greeted her with a smile and an already-poured cup of coffee. "I hope I didn't wake you," he said, turning back to the stove where both oatmeal and eggs were cooking, "but I didn't have dinner last night, and I woke up pretty hungry."

As if on cue, her stomach growled.

He shot her another smile. "You, too, I guess."

God, he was gorgeous. He'd showered, and he was wearing only his cargo shorts, low on his hips. With his chest bare and his hair down loose around his shoulders, he looked as if he should be adorning the front of one of those romance novels where the kidnapped girl finds powerful and lasting love with the handsome warrior.

The timer buzzed, and as Colleen watched, the warrior look-alike in her kitchen used her pink-flowered oven mitts to pull something that looked remarkably like a coffee cake out of her oven.

It was. He'd baked a *coffee cake*. From scratch. He smiled at her again as he put it carefully on a cooling rack.

He'd set her kitchen table, too, poured her a glass of cranberry juice. She sat down as he served them both a generous helping of eggs and bowls of oatmeal.

It was delicious. All of it. She wasn't normally a fan of oatmeal, but somehow he'd made it light and flavorful instead of thick and gluey.

"What's on your schedule for today?" he asked, as if he normally sat across from her at breakfast and inquired about her day after a night of hot sex.

She had to think about it. "I have to drop a tuition check at the law school before noon. There's probably going to be some kind of memorial service for—"

She broke off abruptly.

"You okay?" he asked softly, concern in his eyes.

Colleen forced a smile. "Yeah," she told him. "Mostly. It's just…it'll take time." She took a deep breath. They'd been discussing her day. "I'll need to spend some time this afternoon spreading the word about the memorial service. And I should probably go into the Relief Aid office later, too. There's still a lot to do before we leave."

He stopped eating, his fork halfway to his mouth. "You're still planning on going…?" He didn't let her speak. He laughed and answered for her. "Of course you're still planning on going. What was I thinking?" He put down his fork. "Colleen, what do you want me to do? Do you want me to get down on my knees and beg you not to go?"

Before she could answer, he rubbed his forehead and swore. "I take that back," he continued. "I'm sorry. I shouldn't have said that. I'm a little…off balance today."

"Because…we made love last night?" she asked softly.

He looked at her, taking in her makeup-free face, her hair, the thin cotton of her robe that met with a deep vee between her breasts. "Yes," he admitted. "I'm a little nervous about what happens next."

She chose her words carefully. "What do you want to have happen next?"

Bobby shook his head. "I don't think what I want should particularly factor in. I don't even know what I want." He picked up his fork again. "So I'm just going to save my guilt for later and enjoy having breakfast with you—enjoy how beautiful you look in the morning."

He did just that, eating his eggs and oatmeal as he gazed at her. What he really liked was looking at her breasts—she knew that after last night. But he never just ogled her. Somehow, he managed to look at her in-offensively, respectfully, looking into her eyes as well, looking at her as a whole person, instead of just a female body.

She looked back at him, trying to see him the same way. He was darkly handsome, with bold features that told of his Native American heritage. He was handsome and smart and reliable. He was honest and sincere and funny and kind. And impossibly buff with a body that was at least a two thousand on a scale from one to ten.

"Why aren't you married?" she asked him. He was also ten years older than she was. It seemed impossible that some smart woman hadn't grabbed him up. Yet, here he was. Eating breakfast in her kitchen after spending the night in her bed. "Both you and Wes," she added, to make the question seem a little less as if she were wondering how to sign up for the role of *wife*.

He paused only slightly as he ate his oatmeal. "Marriage has never been part of my short-term plan. Wes's either. The responsibility of a wife and a family... It's pretty intense. We've both seen some of the guys really struggle with it." He smiled. "It's also hard to get married when the women you fall in love with don't fall in love with you." He laughed softly. "Harder still when they're married to someone else."

Colleen's heart was in her throat. "You're in love with someone who's married...?"

He glanced up at her, a flash of dark eyes. "No, I was thinking of...a friend." He made his voice lighter, teasing. "Hey, what kind of man do you think I am, anyway? If I could be in love with someone else while I messed around with you...?"

Relief made her giddy. "Well, I'm in love with Mel Gibson and *I* messed around with you last night."

He laughed, pushing his plate away from the edge of the table. He'd eaten both the pile of eggs and the mound of oatmeal and now he glanced over at the coffee cake, taking a sip of his cooling coffee.

"Is that really what we did last night?" Colleen asked him. "Messed around?" She leaned forward and felt her robe gap farther open. Bobby's gaze flickered down, and the sudden heat in his eyes made her breathless. *He* may claim not to know what was going to happen next, but *she* did. And it didn't have anything to do with the coffee cake.

"Yeah," he said. "I guess so. Isn't it?"

"I don't know," she said honestly. "I don't have a lot of experience to compare it to. Can I ask you something?"

Bobby laughed again. "Why do I get the feeling I should brace myself?"

"Maybe you better," she said. "It's kind of a weird question, but it's something I need to know."

"Oh, man. Okay." He put down his mug, held on to the table with both hands.

"Okay." Colleen cleared her throat. "What I want to know is, are you really good in bed?"

Bobby laughed in genuine surprise. "Wow, I guess not," he said. "I mean, if you have to ask…"

"No," she said. "Don't be dumb. Last night was incredible. We both know that. But what I want to know is if you're some kind of amazing superlover, capable of heating up even the most frigid of women—"

"Whoa," he said. "Colleen, you are so completely the *farthest* thing from frigid that—"

"Yes," she said, "that's what I thought, too, but…"

"But someone told you that you were," he guessed correctly. "Damn!"

"My college boyfriend," she admitted. "Dan. The jerk."

"I feel this overpowering urge to kill him. What did he tell you?"

"It wasn't so much what he said, but more what he implied. He was my first lover," she admitted. "I was crazy about him, but when we—I never managed to— You know. And he quit after the third try. He told me he thought we should just be friends."

"Oh, God." Bobby winced.

"I thought it had to be my fault—that there was something wrong with me." Colleen had never told all of this to anyone. Not even Ashley, who had heard a decidedly watered-down version of the story. "I spent a few years doing the nun thing. And then, about a year and a half ago…" She couldn't believe she was actually telling him this, her very deepest secrets. But she wanted to. She needed him to understand. "I bought this book, a kind of a self-help guide for sexually challenged women—I guess that's a PC term for frigid these days. And I discovered fairly early on that the problem probably wasn't entirely mine."

"So, you haven't—" Bobby was looking at her as if he were trying to see inside her head. "I mean, between last night and the jerk, you haven't…?"

"There's been no one else. Just me and the book," she told him, wishing she could read his mind, too. Was this freaking him out, or did he like the fact that he'd essentially been her first real lover? "Trying desperately to learn how to be normal."

"Yeah, I don't know," Bobby shook his head. "It's probably hopeless. Because I *am* somewhat legendary. And it's a real shame, but if you want to have any kind of satisfying sex life, you're just going to have to spend the rest of your life making love to me."

Colleen stared at him.

"That was a joke," he said quickly. "I'm kidding. Colleen, last night I didn't do anything special. I mean, it was *all* special, but you were right there with me, the entire time. Except…"

"What?" She searched his face.

"Well, without having been there, it's hard to know for sure, but…my guess is that you were—I don't know—*tense* at the thought of getting naked, and the jerk was a little quick on the trigger. He probably didn't give you time to relax before it was all over. And in my book, that's more his fault than yours."

"He was always telling me he thought I should lose weight," Colleen remembered. "Not in so many words. More like, 'Gee, if you lost ten pounds you'd look great in that shirt.' And, 'Why don't you find out what kind of diet Cindy Crawford is on and try that? Maybe that'll work.' That kind of thing. And you're right, I hated taking off my clothes in front of him."

Bobby just shook his head as he looked at her. God, when he looked at her like that, he made her feel like the most beautiful, most desirable woman in the world.

"I liked taking off my clothes for you," she told him softly, and the heat in his eyes got even more intense.

"I'm glad," he whispered. "Because I liked it, too."

Time hung as she gazed into his eyes, as she lost herself in the warmth of his soul. He still wanted her. He wanted more, too.

But then he looked away, as if he were afraid of where that look was taking them.

Guilt, he'd said before, and she knew if she didn't act quickly, he was going to walk out of her apartment and never come back. At least not without a chaperone.

"Don't move," she told him. She pushed her chair back from the table and stood up. "Stay right there."

She was down the hall and in the bedroom in a flash, grabbing what she needed.

Bobby turned to look at her as she came back into the kitchen, still sitting where she'd commanded him to stay. He quickly looked away from her, and she realized that her robe had slipped open even farther—the deep vee now extending all the way down to her waist.

She didn't adjust it, didn't pull it closed. She just moved closer, so that she was standing beside him. Close enough that she was invading his personal space.

But she didn't touch him. Didn't even speak. She just waited for him to turn his head and look up at her.

He did just that. Looked at her. Looked away again. Swallowed hard. "Colleen, I think—"

Now was definitely not the time for thinking. She sat on his lap, straddling him, forcing him to look at her. Her robe was completely open now, the belt having slipped its loose knot.

He was breathing hard—and trying not to. "I thought we decided this was going to be a one-night thing. Just to get it out of our systems."

"Am I out of your system?" she asked, knowing full well that she wasn't.

"No, and if I'm not careful, you're going to get under my skin," he admitted. "Colleen, please don't do this to me. I spent the night convincing myself that as long as we didn't make love again, I'd be okay. And I know it's a long shot, but even your brother might understand that something like this could happen between us—once."

His words would have swayed her—if he hadn't touched her, his hands on her thighs, just lightly, as if he couldn't stop himself, couldn't resist.

She shrugged her robe off her shoulders, and it fell to the floor behind her, and then there she was. Naked, in the middle of her kitchen, with daylight streaming in the windows, warming her skin, bathing her in golden sunshine.

Bobby's breath caught in his throat, and as he looked at her, she felt beautiful. She saw herself as if through his eyes, and she *was* beautiful.

It felt unbelievably good.

She shifted forward, pressing herself against him, feeling him, large and hard beneath his shorts. No doubt about it. He still desired her. He made a sound, low in his throat. And then he kissed her.

His passion took her breath away. It was as if he'd suddenly exploded, as if he needed to kiss her to stay alive, to touch as much of her as he possibly could or else he'd die. His hands were everywhere, his mouth everywhere else.

It was intoxicating, addicting—to be wanted so desperately. It was almost as good as being loved.

She reached between them and unfastened his shorts as she kissed him, taking him into her hand, pressing him against her, letting him know that she wanted him desperately, too.

She still held the condom she'd taken from her bedroom, although the little paper wrapper was tightly scrunched in her hand. She tore it open, and Bobby took it from her, covering himself and then—oh, yes!—he was inside of her.

He tried, but he couldn't keep from groaning aloud, from holding her close and burying his face in her breasts. She moved slowly, stroking him with her body, filling herself completely with him.

Making love to Bobby Taylor was just as amazing in the daylight as it had been last night.

She pulled back slightly to watch him as she moved on top of him, and he held her gaze, his eyes sparking with heat beneath heavy eyelids.

She couldn't get enough of him. She pressed against him, wanting more, wanting forever, wanting him never to leave, wanting this moment never to end.

Wanting him to fall in love with her as completely as she'd fallen in love with him.

Oh, no, what had she done? She didn't love him. She couldn't love him.

She must've made some kind of noise of frustration and despair, because he stood up. He just lifted himself from the chair, with her in his arms, with his body still buried deeply inside her. Even deeper now that he was standing.

Colleen gasped, and then had to laugh as he carried her—effortlessly, as if she weighed nothing—across the room, her arms around his neck, her legs now locked around his waist. He didn't stop until he'd pressed her up against the wall by the refrigerator. The muscles in his chest and arms stood out, making him seem twice as big. Making her seem almost small.

Still... "Don't hurt your shoulder," she told him.

"What shoulder?" he asked hoarsely, and kissed her.

It was so impossibly macho, the way he held her, her back against the wall, the way he possessed her so completely with his mouth. His kiss was far from gentle, and that was so exciting, it was almost ridiculous. Still, there was no denying that she found it sexy beyond belief, to be pinned here, like this, as he kissed her so proprietarily.

She was expecting more roughness, expecting sex that was hard and fast and wild, but instead he began a long, lingering withdrawal, then an equally deliberate penetration that filled her maddeningly slowly.

It was sexier than she could have dreamed possible—this man holding her like this, taking his time to take her completely. On his terms.

He kissed her face, her throat, her neck as if he owned her.

And he did.

She felt her release begin before she was ready for it, before he'd even begun that slow, sensuous slide inside of her for the third heart-stopping time. She didn't want this to end, and she tried to stop herself, to hold him still for a moment, but she was powerless.

And she didn't mind.

Because she loved what he was doing. She loved his strength and his power, loved the fact that he was watching her with such intense desire in his eyes.

Loved that even though he was pretending to be in control, she knew that he wasn't. She owned him as absolutely as he owned her. More.

She held his gaze while she melted around him, while she flew apart from wave upon endless wave of pleasure.

He smiled, a fierce, proud, fairly obnoxious male grin. It would have made her roll her eyes a day or so ago, but today she found she loved it. She loved being pure female to his pure male. It didn't mean she was weaker. On the contrary. She was his perfect match, his opposite, his equal.

"I loved watching you do that last night," he murmured as he kissed her again. "And I love it even more this morning."

He was her first real lover in the physical sense of the word. And he was also the first man she'd ever known who liked who she was—not merely the promise of the person he could mold her into becoming.

"I want to do that to you again," he said. "Right now. Is that okay with you?"

Colleen just laughed.

He lifted her away from the wall and carried her down the hall to her bedroom, kicking the door shut behind them.

Chapter 13

Bobby was floating.

He was in that place halfway between sleep and consciousness, his face buried in Colleen's sweet-smelling hair, his body still cradled between the softness of her legs.

So much for willpower. So much for resolving not to make love to her again. So much for hoping that Wes would forgive him for one little, single transgression.

Ah, but how he'd loved making love to her again. And no red-blooded, heterosexual man could've resisted the temptation of Colleen Skelly, naked, on his lap.

And really, deep in his heart, he knew it didn't matter. Wes was going to go ape over the fact that Bobby had slept with Colleen. Realistically, how much worse could it be to have slept with her twice? What difference could it possibly make?

To Wes? None. Probably. Hopefully.

But the difference it made to Bobby was enormous.

As enormous as the difference between heaven and hell.

Speaking of heaven, he was still inside of her, he realized, forcing himself to return to earth. Falling asleep immediately after sex was not a smart move when using condoms as the sole method of birth control. Because condoms could leak.

He should have pulled out of her twenty minutes ago. And for that matter, he should also have been aware that he was still on top of her, crushing her.

But she hadn't protested. In fact, she still had her arms tightly wrapped around him.

He shifted his weight, pulling away from her and reaching between them to...

Uh-oh. "Uh, Colleen...?" Bobby sat up, suddenly fully, painfully, completely alert.

She stirred, stretched, sexy as hell, a distraction even now, when he should have been completely nondistractible.

"Don't leave yet, Bobby," she murmured, still half asleep. "Stay for a while, please?"

"Colleen, I think you better get up and take a shower." Condoms sometimes did something far worse than leak. "The condom broke."

She laughed as she opened her eyes. "Yeah, right." Her smile faded as she looked into his eyes. "Oh, no, you're not kidding are you?" She sat up.

Silently he shook his head.

Twenty minutes. She'd been lying on her back for at least twenty minutes after he'd unknowingly sent his sperm deep inside of her.

Was it possible she already was pregnant? How quickly could that happen?

Quickly. Instantly—if the timing was right. In a flash, a heartbeat.

In a burst of latex.

"Well," Colleen said, her eyes wide. "These past few days have certainly been full of first-time experiences for me, and this one's no exception. What do we do about this? Is a shower really going to help at this point?"

Count on Colleen not to have hysterics. Count on her to be upbeat and positive and proactive in trying to correct what could well be the biggest, most life-changing mistake either one of them had ever made.

"Probably not," he admitted. "Although…"

"I'll take one right now, if you want me to. I'm not sure where I am in my cycle. I've never really been regular." She was sitting there, unconcerned about her nakedness, looking to him for suggestions and options and his opinion, with complete and total trust.

That kind of trust was an incredible turn-on, and he felt his body respond. How could that be? The disbelief and cold fear that had surged through his veins at his discovery should have brought about an opposite physical response—more similar to the response one had from swimming in an icy lake.

And his mental reaction to a broken condom should have included not even *thinking* about having sex for the next three weeks without shaking with fear.

But there was Colleen, sitting next to him on her bed, all bare breasts and blue-green eyes and quiet, steadfast trust.

Right now she needed him to be honest about this.

There was no quick fix. No miraculous solutions. "I think it's probably too late to do anything but pray."

She nodded. "That's what I figured."

"I'm sorry."

"It's not your fault," she said.

He shook his head. "It's not about fault—it's about responsibility, and I *am* responsible."

"Well, I am, too. You were coerced."

Bobby smiled, thinking of the way she'd sat on his lap, intending to seduce him, wondering if she had even the slightest clue that his last hope of resisting her had vanished the moment she'd appeared in the kitchen wearing only that robe.

"Yeah," he said, "as if that was really hard for you to do."

She smiled back at him, and his world shrank to a few square feet of her bed—to her eyes, her smile, her face and body.

"It was another one of those first-time endeavors for me," she told him. "I was proud of myself for not chickening out."

"You're a natural." His voice was husky. "But that's not what I meant. I meant it wasn't hard because when it comes to you, I'm a total pushover."

Just looking into her eyes like this made him want her again—badly enough that he wasn't able to keep it any kind of secret.

Colleen noticed and laughed softly. "Well now, *there's* an interesting, hedonistic approach to this problem." She crawled toward him, across the bed, her eyes gleaming and her smile filled with the very devil. "You know that old saying, when a door closes, somewhere a window opens? Well, how about, when a condom breaks, a window of opportunity opens?"

Bobby knew that wasn't necessarily true. He knew he should stop her, back away, stand up, do *any*thing but just sit there and wait for her to...

Too late.

Colleen sat up. "Oh, my God."

"Mmph," Bobby said, facedown on her bed.

It was 11:05. Fifty-five minutes to make it to her law school in the Fenway from Cambridge. Without a car, on the T. "Oh, my *God*!"

Bobby lifted his head. "What's the—"

She was already scrambling for the bathroom, climbing directly over him, inadvertently pushing his face back into the pillow.

"Mmmrph!"

"Sorry!"

Thanking the Lord—not for the first time today—that Ashley was still on the Vineyard, Colleen flew down the hallway stark naked and slapped on the bathroom light. One glance in the mirror and she knew she had to take a shower. Her hair was wild. And her face still held the satisfied look of a woman who'd kept her lover very busy all morning long.

She couldn't do anything about the face, but the hair she could fix with a fast shower.

She turned on the shower and climbed in before the water had a chance to heat up, singing a few operatic high notes in an attempt to counteract the cold.

"You all right?" Bobby had followed her in. Of course, she'd left the bathroom door wide open.

She peeked out from behind the shower curtain. He

was as naked as she was, standing in front of the commode with that utterly masculine, wide-spread stance.

"I have to take a tuition check to my law school," she told him, quickly rinsing her hair, loving the fact that he was comfortable enough to be in the bathroom with her, feeling as if they'd crossed some kind of invisible, unspoken line. They were lovers now—not just two people who had given in to temptation and made love once. "The deadline's noon today, and like a total idiot, I pushed it off until the last minute." Literally.

"I'll come with you."

She turned off the water and pulled back the curtain, grabbing her towel and drying herself as she rushed back to her bedroom. "I can't wait for you," she called to him. "I'm literally forty-five seconds from walking out the door."

She stepped into clean underwear and pulled her blue dress—easy and loose fitting, perfect for days she was running dangerously late—over her head, even though she was still damp. Feet into sandals.

"What do you know," Bobby said. "A woman who can go wheels-up in less than three minutes." He laughed. "I feel as if I should drop to my knees right now and propose."

Colleen was reaching for the tuition check, which she'd hidden for safety in her complete collection of Shakespeare, and she didn't freeze, didn't faint, didn't gasp and spin to face him, didn't let herself react at all. He was teasing. He didn't have a clue that his lightly spoken words had sent a rush of excitement and longing through her that was so powerful she'd nearly fallen over.

Oh, she was so stupid. She actually wanted…the impossible. As if he really would marry her. He'd told her just hours ago that staying single was part of his career plan.

She made herself smile as she turned around, as she stuffed the check and a book to read into her knapsack, as she checked to make sure she had money for the T, then zipped her bag closed.

"It's going to take me at least a few hours," she said, brushing out her wet hair as she headed back into the kitchen to grab an apple from the fridge. He followed her, followed her to the door, still naked and completely comfortable about that.

Colleen could picture him trailing her all the way out to the street. Wouldn't *that* give little old Mrs. Gibaldi who lived downstairs an eyeful?

She turned to face him. "I'd love it if you were still here when I got back. Wearing just that." She kissed him, lowered her voice, gave him a smile designed to let him read her very thoughts. "And if you think getting dressed in three minutes is fast, just wait and see how long it takes me to get *un*dressed."

He kissed her, pulling her into his arms, his hand coming up to cup her breast as if he couldn't not touch her.

Colleen felt herself start to dissolve into a puddle of heat. What would happen if she didn't get that check to the office on time?

She might have to pay a penalty. Or she'd get bumped from the admissions list. There were so many students wait-listed, the admissions office could afford to play hardball. Reluctantly, she pulled back from Bobby.

"I'll hurry," she told him.

"Good," he said, still touching her, looking at her as if she were the one standing naked in front of him, lowering his head to kiss her breast before he let her go. "I'll be here."

He wasn't in love with her. He was in lust.

And that was exactly what she'd wanted, she reminded herself as she ran down the stairs.

Except, now that she had it, it wasn't enough.

The phone was ringing as Bobby stepped out of Colleen's shower.

He grabbed a towel and wrapped it around himself as he went dripping into the kitchen. "'Lo?"

He heard the sound of an open phone line, as if someone were there but silent. Then, "Bobby?"

It was Wes. No, not just "It was Wes," but "Oh, God, it was Wes."

"Hey!" Bobby said, trying desperately to sound normal—as opposed to sounding like a man who was standing nearly naked not two feet from the spot where mere hours earlier he'd pinned Wes's sister to the wall as they'd... As he'd...

"What are you doing at Colleen's place?" Wes sounded funny. Or maybe Bobby just imagined it. Guilt had a way of doing that—making everyone sound suspicious.

"Um..." Bobby said. He was going to have to tell Wes about what was going on between him and Colleen, but the last thing he wanted was to break the news over the telephone. Still, he wasn't going to lie. Not to Wes. Never to Wes.

Fortunately—as usual—Wes didn't particularly want his question answered. "You are one hard man to get hold of," he continued. "I called your hotel room last night—late—and you were either AWOL or otherwise occupied, you lucky son of a bitch."

"Well," Bobby said, "yeah." He wasn't sure if Wes particularly cared what he was agreeing to, but the truth was he'd been AWOL, otherwise occupied *and* a lucky son of a bitch. "Where are you?"

"Little Creek. You need to get your butt down here, bro, pronto. We've got a meeting with Admiral Robinson at 1900 hours. There's a flight out of Logan that leaves in just under two hours. If you scramble, you can make it, easy. There'll be a ticket there, waiting for you."

Scrambling meant leaving before Colleen got back. Bobby looked at the kitchen clock and swore. Best-case scenario didn't get her back here for another ninety minutes. That's if she had no holdups—if the T ran like a dream.

"I'm not sure I can make it," he told Wes.

"Sure you can. Tell Colleen to drive you to the airport."

"Oh," Bobby said. Now, here was a secret he could divulge with no pain. "No. She can't—she sold her car."

"What?"

"She's been doing all this charity work—pro bono legal stuff, you know? Along with her usual volunteer work," Bobby told Wes. "She sold the Mustang because she was having trouble making ends meet."

Wes swore loudly. "I can't believe she sold that car. I would've lent her money. Why didn't she ask me for money?"

"I offered to do the same. She didn't want it from either one of us."

"That's stupid. Let me talk to the stupid girl, will you?"

"Actually," Bobby told Wes, "it's not stupid at all." And she wasn't a girl. She was a woman. A gorgeous, vibrant, independent, sexy woman. "She wants to do this her way. By herself. And then when she graduates, and passes the bar exam, she'll know—*she* did this. Herself. I don't blame her, man."

"Yeah, yeah, right, just put her on the phone."

Bobby took a deep breath, praying that Wes wouldn't think it was weird—him being in Colleen's apartment when she wasn't home. "She's not here. She had to go over to the law school for something and—"

"Leave her a message then. Tell her to call me." Wes rattled off a phone number that Bobby dutifully wrote on a scrap of paper. But he then folded it up, intending to put it into his pocket as soon as he was wearing something that had a pocket. No way was he going to risk Colleen calling Wes back before he himself had a chance to speak to him.

"Put it in gear," Wes ordered. "You're needed for this meeting. If Colleen's going to be stupid and insist on going to Tulgeria, we need to do this right. If you get down here tonight, we'll get started planning this op a full twelve hours earlier than if we wait to have this meeting in the morning. I want those extra twelve hours. This is Colleen's safety—her *life*—we're talking about here."

"I'm there," Bobby said. "I'll be on that flight."

"Thank you. Hey, I missed you, man. How's the shoulder? You been taking it easy?"

Not exactly, considering that for the past twenty-four hours he'd been engaged in almost nonstop, highly gymnastic sex. With Wes's precious little sister. Oh, God.

"I'm feeling much better," Bobby told the man who

was the best friend he'd ever had in his life. Not a lie—
it was true. The shoulder was still stiff and sore, and he
still couldn't reach over his head without pain, but he
was, without a doubt, feeling exceptionally good this
morning.

Physically.

Emotionally was an entirely different story. Guilt.
Doubt. Anxiety.

"Hey," Bobby said. "Will you do me a favor and pick
me up in Norfolk alone? There's something we need to
talk about."

"Uh-oh," Wes said. "Sounds heavy. You all right?
God—you didn't get some girl pregnant did you? I didn't
even know you were seeing anyone since you and Kyra
split."

"I didn't get anyone..." Bobby started to deny, but
then cut himself off. Oh, Lord, it was possible that he
had indeed gotten Colleen pregnant just this morning.
The thought still made him weak in the knees. "Just
meet my flight, okay?"

"Ho," Wes said. "No way can you make hints that
something dire is going down and then not tell me what
the—"

"I'll tell you later," Bobby said, and hung up the
phone.

Chapter 14

When Colleen got home, Clark and Kenneth were sitting in her living room, playing cards.

"Hey," Clark said. "Where's your TV?"

"I don't have a TV," she told him. "What are you doing here? Is Ashley back?"

"Nah. Mr. Platonic called us," Clark answered. "He didn't want you coming home to an empty apartment."

"He had to go someplace called Little Creek," Kenneth volunteered. "He left a note on your bed. I didn't let Clark read it."

Bobby had gone to Little Creek. He'd finally run away, leaving the two stooges behind as baby-sitters.

"Thanks," she said. "I'm home now. You don't have to hang here."

"We don't mind," Clark said. "You actually have food in your kitchen and—"

"Please, I need you to go," Colleen told them. "I'm sorry." She had no idea what Bobby had written in that note that was in her bedroom. She couldn't deal with reading it while they were in her living room.

And she couldn't deal with not reading it another second longer.

"It's cool," Clark said. "I was betting we wouldn't get the warmest welcome, since you're one of those liberated, I-can-take-care-of-myself babes and—"

She heard the door close as Kenneth dragged Clark out.

Colleen took her backpack into her bedroom. Bobby had cleaned up the room. And made the bed, too. And left a note, right on her pillow.

"I got a call and had to run," it said in bold block letters—an attempt by someone with messy penmanship to write clearly. "Heading to Little Creek—to a meeting I can't miss. I'm sorry (more than I can say!) that I couldn't stick around to kiss you goodbye properly, but this is what it's like—being part of Alpha Squad. When I have to go, I go, whether I want to or not."

He'd then written something that he'd crossed out. Try as she might, Colleen couldn't see beneath the scribbled pen to the letters below. The first word looked as if it might be *maybe*. But she couldn't read the rest.

"Stay safe!" he wrote, both words underlined twice. "I'll call you from Little Creek." He'd signed it "Bobby." Not "Love, Bobby." Not "Passionately yours, Bobby." Just "Bobby."

Colleen lay back on her bed, trying not to overanalyze his note, wishing he hadn't had to go, trying not to wonder if he were ever coming back.

He'd come back if she were pregnant. Maybe she

should wish she actually was. He'd insist that she marry him and…

The thought made her sit up, shocked at herself. What a terrible thing to wish for. She didn't want to be an obligation. A lifelong responsibility. A permanent mistake.

She wanted him to come back here because he liked being with her. And yes, okay—because he liked making love to her. She wasn't going to pretend their relationship wasn't based mostly on sex. Great sex. Incredible sex.

She knew that he liked making love to her. And so she would see him again, Colleen told herself. And when he called from Little Creek—if he called—she'd make herself sound relaxed. As if she wasn't a bundle of anxiety. As if she had no doubt that he would be back in her bed in a matter of a day or two. And as if her world wouldn't end if he didn't come back.

The phone rang, and she rolled to the edge of her bed, lying on her stomach to look at the caller ID box, hoping… *Yes.* It was Bobby. Had to be. The area code and exchange was from Little Creek. She knew those numbers well—Wes had been stationed there when he'd first joined the Navy. Back before he'd even met Bobby Taylor.

Bobby must've just arrived, and he was calling her first thing. Maybe this wasn't just about sex for him…

Colleen picked up the phone, keeping her voice light, even though her heart was in her throat. "Too bad you had to leave. I spent the entire T ride imagining all the different ways we were going to make love again this afternoon."

The words that came out of the phone were deafening and colorful. The voice wasn't Bobby's. It was her brother's. "I don't know who you think I am, Colleen, but you better tell me who you thought you were talk-ing to so that I can kill him."

"Wes," she said weakly. Oh, no!

"This is great. This is just great. Just what I want to hear coming out of the mouth of my little sister."

Her temper sparked. "Excuse me, I'm *not* little. I haven't been little for a long time. I'm twenty-three years old, thank you very much, and yes, you want to know the truth? I'm in a relationship that's intensely physical and *enormously* satisfying. I spent last night and most of the morning having wild sex."

Wes shouted. "Oh, my *God*! Don't tell me that! I don't want to hear that!"

"If I were Sean or...or..." She didn't want to say Ethan. Mentioning their dead brother was like stomp-ing with both feet on one of Wes's more sensitive but-tons. "Or *Frank*, you'd be *happy* for me!"

"Frank's a *priest*!"

"You know what I mean," Colleen countered. "If I were one of the guys in Alpha Squad, and I told you I just got lucky, you'd be slapping me on the back and con-gratulating me. I don't see the difference—"

"The difference is you're a girl!"

"No," she said, tightly. "I'm a *woman*. Maybe that's the basis of your relationship problems, Wes. Maybe until you stop seeing women as *girls*, until you treat them as *equals*—"

"Yeah, thanks a million, Dr. Freud. Like you even have a half a clue about my *problems*." He swore.

"I know you're unhappy," she said softly. "And angry almost all the time. I think you've got some unresolved issues that you've really got to deal with before—"

He refused to follow her out of this argument and into

a more personal, private discussion. "Damn straight I've got unresolved issues—and they're all about this jackass you've been letting take advantage of you. You probably think he loves you, right? Is that what he told you?"

"No," Colleen said, stung by his implications. "As a matter of fact he hasn't. He likes me, though. And he respects me—which is more than I can say about *you*."

"What, is he some geeky lawyer?"

"That's not your business." Colleen closed her eyes. She couldn't let herself get mad and tell him it was Bobby. If Bobby wanted to tell him, fine. But her brother wasn't going to hear it first from her. No way. "Look, I have to go. You know, paint myself with body oil," she lied just to annoy him. "Get ready for tonight."

It got the response she'd expected, through gritted teeth. "Col*leen*!"

"I'm glad you're back safely."

"Wait," he said. "I'm calling for a reason."

"No kidding? A reason besides sibling harassment?"

"Yeah. I have to go pick up Bobby at the airport, but before I leave, I need info on your contacts in the Tulgerian government. Admiral Robinson is going to run a quick check on everyone involved." Wes paused. "Didn't you get my message to call me?" he asked. "When I spoke to Bobby just before noon, I told him to leave a message for you and—"

Silence.

Big, long silence.

Colleen could almost hear the wheels in Wes's head turning as he put two and two together.

Colleen had spent—in her own words—"most of the morning having wild sex" with her mysterious lover.

Her brother had spoken to Bobby earlier. In Colleen's

apartment. Just before noon. As in the "just before noon" that occurred at the very end of a morning filled with wild sex.

"Tell me I'm wrong," Wes said very, very quietly— never a good sign. "Tell me it's not Bobby Taylor. Tell me my best friend didn't betray me."

Colleen couldn't keep quiet at that. "*Betray* you? Oh, my God, Wesley, that's absurd. What's between me and Bobby has nothing to do with you at all!"

"I'm right?" Wes lost it. "I *am* right! How could he *do* that, that son of a—I'm gonna kill him!"

Oh, *damn!* "Wes! Listen to me! It was *my* fault. I—"

But her brother had already hung up.

Oh, dear Lord, this was going to be bad. Wes was going to pick up Bobby from the airport and…

Colleen checked her caller-ID box and tried to call Wes back.

The flight to Norfolk was just long enough to set Bobby completely on edge. He'd had enough time to buy a book at the airport store, but he stared at the words on the page, unable to concentrate on the bestselling story.

What was he going to say to Wes?

"So, hey, nice to see you. Yeah, Cambridge was great. I liked it a lot—especially when I was having sex with your sister."

Oh, man.

Thinking about his impending conversation with Wes was making him feel edgy and unsettled.

Thinking about Colleen was making him crazy.

A glance at his watch told him that she had surely come back to her apartment by now.

If he hadn't left, she'd be naked, just as she'd promised, and he'd be buried deep inside of her and—

He shifted in his seat. Coach wasn't built for someone his size, and his knees were already pressed against the back of the seat in front of him. He was already uncomfortable as hell—thinking of Colleen wasn't going to help.

But as Bobby closed his eyes, he couldn't help but think of her.

It was probably good that he'd had to leave. If it had been left up to him, he never would have left. He would have just stayed there forever, in Colleen's bedroom, waiting for her to come and make love to him.

She had cast a spell over him, and he couldn't resist her. All she had to do was smile, and he was putty in her hands.

This way the spell was broken. Wasn't it? God, he hoped so. It would be just his luck to fall for another woman who didn't love him. Even better luck to fall for a woman who clearly only saw him as a sexual plaything. If he wasn't careful, his heart was going to get trashed.

Bobby tried to focus again on his book, tried to banish the image of Colleen, her eyes filled with laughter as she leaned forward to kiss him, as she pressed her body against him, as their legs tangled and…

Help.

He wanted her with every breath.

God, why couldn't he have felt this way about Kyra?

Because even back then, he was in love with Colleen.

Man, where had *that* thought come from? Love. God. This was already way too complicated without screwing it up by putting love into the picture.

In a matter of minutes Bobby was going to be hip

deep in a conversation with Wes that he was dreading with every ounce of his being. And Wes was going to warn him away from Colleen. *Don't go near her any more.* He could hear the words already.

If he were smart, he'd heed his friend.

If he weren't smart, if he kept thinking with his body instead of his brain, he was going to get in too deep. Before he even blinked, he would find himself in a long-distance relationship, God help him. And then it would be a year from now, and he'd be on the phone with Colleen again, having to tell her—again—that he wasn't going to make it out for the weekend, and she would tell him that was okay—again—but in truth, he'd know that she was trying not to cry.

He didn't want to make her cry—but that didn't mean he was in love with her.

And the fact that he wanted to be with her constantly, the fact that he missed her desperately even now, mere hours after having been in bed with her, well, that was just his body's healthy response to great sex. It was natural, having had some, to want more.

Bobby squeezed his eyes shut. Oh, God, he wanted more.

It wouldn't be too hard to talk Colleen into giving a bicoastal relationship a try. She was adventurous and she liked him. And, of course, he'd never had a long-distance relationship with someone who liked phone sex...

Bobby felt himself start to smile. Yeah, who was he kidding? Pretending he had any choice at all? Pretending that he wasn't going to spend every waking hour working on ways to get back to Cambridge to see Colleen. The truth was, unless she flat-out refused to see him again, he was going to be raking up the frequent flyer miles, big-time.

He was already in too deep.

And, jeez, if Colleen were pregnant…

Oh, hell. As the plane approached the runway for a landing, Bobby tried to imagine Wes's reaction to *that* news.

"Hey, man! Not only did I do the nasty with your sister more times than I can remember, but the condom broke and I probably knocked her up, ruining her dreams of finishing law school, condemning her to a life with a husband she doesn't particularly love, who isn't even around all that often, anyway. And how was *your* week?"

Bobby came off the plane the way he'd gotten on. With no luggage, wearing the same cargo shorts and shirt he'd worn over to Colleen's nearly a full twenty-four hours ago.

Not that he'd been wearing them for that entire time. On the contrary.

As he came out of the walkway that connected the plane to the terminal, he scanned the crowd, searching for Wes's familiar face.

And then, there he was. Wes Skelly. He was leaning against the wall, arms crossed in front of his chest, looking more like a biker than a chief in the elite U.S. Navy SEALs. He was wearing baggy green cargo pants with lots of pockets and a white tank top that showed off his tan and revealed the barbwire tattoo on his upper arm. His hair was long and messy. The longer it got, the lighter it looked as it was bleached by the sun, as the reddish highlights were brought out.

Bobby and Wes had been virtually inseparable for

nearly eleven years—even though they'd hated each other's guts at the outset of BUD/S training, when they'd been assigned together as swim buddies. That was something not many people knew. But Wes had earned Bobby's respect through the grueling training sessions—the same way Bobby earned Wes's. It took them a while, but once they recognized that they were made from the same unbreakable fabric, they'd started working together.

It was a case of one plus one equaling three. As a team, they were unstoppable. And so they became allies.

And when Wes's little brother Ethan had died, they'd taken their partnership a step forward and become friends. Real friends. Over the past decade that bond had strengthened to the point where it seemed indestructible.

But years of working with explosives had taught Bobby that indestructibility was a myth. There was no such thing.

And there was a very good chance that over the next few minutes, he was going to destroy ten years of friendship with just a few small words.

I slept with your sister.

"Hey," Wes said in greeting. "You look tired."

Bobby shrugged. "I'm okay. You?"

Wes pushed himself off the wall. "Please tell me you didn't check your luggage."

They started walking, following the stream of humanity away from the gate. "I didn't. I didn't bring it. There was no time to go back to the hotel. I just left it there."

"Bummer," Wes said. "Paying for a room when you don't even sleep there. That's pretty stupid."

"Yeah," Bobby agreed. *I slept with your sister.* How the hell was he supposed to say something like that? Just blurting it out seemed wrong, and yet there was no real graceful way to lead into a topic like that.

"How's Colleen?" Wes asked.

"She's—" Bobby hesitated. Beautiful. Heart-stoppingly sexy. Great in bed. Maybe carrying his baby. "Doing okay. Selling the car wasn't easy for her."

"Jeez, I can't believe she did that. Her Mustang… That's like selling a child."

"She got a good price. The buyer was a collector, and she was sure he'd take good care of it."

Wes pushed open a door that led toward the parking area. "Still…"

"Did Jake fill you in on the situation with this Tulgerian orphanage Colleen and her friends have been trying to move out of the war zone?" Bobby asked.

"Yeah, apparently the building was hit in some kind of skirmish a day or so ago. The place was pretty much destroyed, and the survivors were brought to a local hospital—but the place doesn't even have electricity or running water. We'll be going out there pretty much upon insertion in Tulgeria to move the kids back into the city."

"Good," Bobby said. "I'm glad the admiral's made that a priority. Wes, there's something you need to know…" The easy stuff first. "The little girl that Colleen was hoping to adopt was killed in that air strike."

Wes stared at him in the shadowy dimness of the parking garage. "Adopt?" he said, loud enough that his voice echoed. "She was going to *adopt* a kid? What, was she nuts? She's just a kid herself."

"No, she's not," Bobby said quietly. "She's a grown woman. And—" okay, here's where he had to say it

"—I should know. I've…uh, been with her, Wes. Colleen. And me."

Wes stopped walking. "Aw, come on, Bobby, you can do better than that. You've *been* with her? You could say *slept with*, but of course you didn't sleep much, did you, dirt wad? How about…" He used the crudest possible expression. "Yeah, that works. *That's* what you did, huh? You *son* of a…" He was shouting now.

Bobby stood there. Stunned. Wes had known. Somehow he'd already known. And Bobby had been too self-absorbed to realize it.

"I sent you there to take *care* of her," Wes continued. "And *this* is what you do? How could you do this to me?"

"It wasn't about you," Bobby tried to explain. "It was about me and— Wes, I've been crazy about her for years."

"Oh, this is fine," Wes had gone beyond full volume and into overload. "For *years*, and this is the first I hear of it? What, were you just waiting for a chance to get her alone, scumbag?" He shoved Bobby, both hands against his chest.

Bobby let himself get shoved. He could have planted himself and absorbed it, but he didn't. "No. Believe me I tried to stay away from her, but… I couldn't do it. As weird as it sounds, she got it into her head that she wanted me, and hell, you know how she gets. I didn't stand a chance."

Wes was in his face. "You're ten years older than she is, and you're trying to tell me that *she* seduced *you*?"

"It's not that simple. You've got to believe—" Bobby cut himself off. "Look, you're right. It *is* my fault. I'm more experienced. She offered, and God, I wanted her, and I didn't do the right thing. For *you*."

"Ho, *that's* great!" Wes was pacing now, a tightly wound bundle of energy, ready to blow. "Meaning you did the right thing for Colleen, is that what you're saying? How right is it, Bobby, that she sits around and waits for you, that she'll have half a life, pretending to be okay, but really terrified, just waiting to get word that something's happened to you? And say you *don't* get your head blown off on some op. Say you do make it home. Retire from the teams in a few years. Then what? How right is it that she's the one who makes more money working as a lawyer? How's she supposed to have kids? Put 'em in day care? That's just great."

Kids...day care... Bobby was shocked. "Wes, whoa, I'm not going to marry her."

Wes stopped short, turning to stare with his mouth open, as if Bobby'd just announced his plan to detonate a nuclear warhead over New York City. "Then what the hell were you doing with her, dirt wad?"

Bobby shook his head, laughing slightly in disbelief. "Come on. She's twenty-three. She's just experimenting. She doesn't want to *marry* me."

In hindsight, it was probably the laughter that did it.

Wes exploded. "You *son* of a bitch. You went into this with completely dishonorable intentions!" He put his shoulder into a solid right jab, right in Bobby's face.

Bobby saw it coming. He didn't dodge it or block it. He just stood there, turning his head only slightly to deflect the force of the blow. It rocked him back on his heels, but he quickly regained his balance.

"Wes, don't do this." There were people around. Getting into and out of cars. It wouldn't be long until someone called a security team, who would call the police, who would haul their butts to jail.

Wes hit him again, harder this time, an ear-ringing blow, and again Bobby didn't defend himself.

"Fight back, you bastard," Wes snarled.

"No."

"*Damn* it!" Wes launched himself at Bobby, hitting him in the exact place that would knock him over, take him down onto his back on the concrete. After years of training together, Wes knew his weak spots well.

"Hey!" The shout echoed against the concrete ceilings and walls as Wes hit him with a flurry of punches. "Hey, Skelly, back off!"

The voice belonged to Lucky O'Donlon. An SUV pulled up with a screech of tires, and O'Donlon and Crash Hawken were suddenly there, in the airport parking garage, pulling Wes off him.

And the three newest members of Alpha Squad, Rio Rosetti, Mike Lee and Thomas King climbed out of the back, helping Bobby to his feet.

"You okay, Chief?" Rio asked, his Italian street-punk attitude completely overridden by wide-eyed concern. The kid had some kind of hero worship thing going for both Bobby and Wes. If this little altercation didn't cure him of it forever, Bobby didn't know what would.

He nodded at Rio. "Yeah." His nose was bleeding. By some miracle it wasn't broken. It should have been. Wes had hit him hard enough.

"Here, Chief." Mike handed him a handkerchief.

"Thanks."

Crash and Lucky were both holding on tightly to Wes, who was sputtering—and ready to go another round if they released him.

"You want to explain what this is all about?" Crash was the senior officer present. He rarely used his officer voice—he rarely spoke at all—but when he did, he was obeyed instantly. To put it mildly.

But Wes wouldn't have listened to the president of the United States at this moment, and Bobby didn't want to explain any of this to anyone. "No, sir," he said stiffly, politely. "With all due respect, sir…"

"We got a call from your sister, Skelly," Lucky O'Donlon said. "She was adamant we follow you down here to the airport. She said she had good reason to believe you were going to try to kick the hell out of Taylor, here, and she didn't want either of you guys to get arrested."

"Did she say *why* I was going to kick the hell out of Taylor?" Wes asked. "Did she tell you what that *good reason* was?"

It was obvious she hadn't.

Bobby took a step toward Wes. "What we were discussing is not public information. Show some respect to your sister."

Wes laughed in his face, looked up at Crash and Lucky. "You guys know what this *friend* of mine did?"

Bobby got large. "This is between you and me, Skelly. So help me God, if you breathe a single word of—"

Wes breathed four words. He told them all, quite loudly, in the foulest possible language what Bobby had done with his sister. "Apparently, she's doing some *experimenting* these days. All you have to do is go to Cambridge, Massachusetts, and look her up. Colleen Skelly. She's probably in the phone book. Anyone else want to give her a go?"

Wes Skelly was a dead man.

Bobby jumped on top of him with a roar. The hell with the fact that Wes was being held in place by Lucky and Crash. The hell with everything. No one had the right to talk about Colleen that way. *No* one.

He hit Wes in the face, harder than he'd ever hit him before, then he tackled him. It was enough to take them down to the concrete—Lucky and Crash with them.

He hit Wes again, wanting to make him bleed.

The other SEALs were on top of him then, grabbing his back and his arms, trying to pull him away, but they couldn't stop him. No one could stop him. Bobby yanked Wes up by the front of his shirt as he got to his feet, hauling him away from Lucky and Crash, with Rio, Mike and Thomas clinging to him like monkeys.

He pulled back his arm, ready to throw another brain-shaking punch when another voice, a new voice, rang out.

"Stop this. *Right. Now.*"

It was the senior chief.

Another truck had pulled up.

Bobby froze, and that was all the other SEALs needed. Lucky and Crash pulled Wes out of his grip and safely out of range, and then, God, Senior Chief Harvard Becker was there, standing in between him and Wes.

"Thank you for coming, Senior," Crash said quietly. He looked at Bobby. "I answered the phone when Colleen called. She didn't say as much, but I correctly guessed the cause of the, uh, tension between you and Skelly. I anticipated that the senior's presence would be helpful."

Wes's nose was broken, and as Bobby watched—not without some grim satisfaction—he leaned forward slightly, his face averted as he bled onto the concrete floor.

Lucky stepped closer to Harvard. He was speaking

to him quietly, no doubt filling him in. Telling him that Bobby slept with Wes's sister.

God, this was so unfair to Colleen. She was going to Tulgeria with this very group of men. Who would all look at her differently, knowing that she and Bobby had…

Damn it, why couldn't Wes have agreed to talk this problem out…privately? Why had he turned this into a fist fight and, as a result, made Bobby's intimate relationship with Colleen public knowledge?

"So what do you want to do?" Harvard asked, hands on his hips as he looked from Bobby to Wes, his shaved head gleaming in the dim garage light. "You children want to move this somewhere so you can continue to beat the hell out of each other? Or you want to pretend to be grown-ups for a change and try working this out with a conversation?"

"Colleen doesn't sleep around," Bobby said, looking at Wes, willing him to meet his gaze. But Wes didn't look up, so he turned back to Harvard. "If he implies that again, Senior—or anything else even remotely disrespectful— I'll rip his head off." He used Wes's favorite adjective for emphasis.

Harvard nodded, his dark eyes narrowing slightly as he looked at Bobby. "Okay." He turned to Wes. "You hear that, Chief Skelly? Do you understand what this man is saying to you?"

"Yeah," Wes answered sullenly. "He'll rip my head off." He added his favorite adjective, too. "Let him try."

"No," Harvard said. "Those are the *words* he used, but the actual semantics—what he really means by saying those words—is that he cares a great deal for your sister. You fools are on the same side here. So what's it going to be? Talk or fight?"

"Talk," Bobby said.

"There's nothing to say," Wes countered. "Except from now on he better stay the hell away from her. If he so much as *talks* to her again, I'll rip *his* head off."

"Even if I wanted to do that," Bobby said quietly, "which I don't, I couldn't. I've got to talk to her again. There's more that you need to know, Skelly, but I'm not going to talk about it here in front of everyone."

Wes looked up, finally meeting Bobby's gaze, horror in his eyes. "Oh, my God," he said. "You got her pregnant."

"All right," Harvard commanded. "Let's take this someplace private. Taylor, in my truck. Rosetti, take Chief Skelly's keys, drive him to the base and escort him to my office. On the double."

"You're going to have to marry her."

Bobby sat back in his chair, his breath all but knocked out of him. "What? Wes, that's insane."

Wes Skelly sat across the table from him in the conference room on base that Harvard had appropriated and made into a temporary office. He was still furious. Bobby had never seen him stay so angry for such a long time.

It was possible Wes was going to be angry at Bobby forever.

He leaned forward now, glaring. "What's *insane* is for you to go all the way to Cambridge to *help* me and end up messing around with my sister. What's *insane* is that we're even having this conversation in the first place—that you couldn't keep your pants zipped. You got yourself into this situation. You play the game—you pay when you lose. And you lost big-time, buddy, when that condom broke."

"And I'm willing to take responsibility if necessary—"

"If necessary?" Wes laughed. "*Now* who's insane? You really think Colleen's going to marry you if she *has* to? No way. Not Colleen. She's too stubborn, too much of an idealist. No, you have to go back to Boston tomorrow morning. First thing. And make her think you *want* to marry her. Get her to say yes *now*—before she does one of those home tests. Otherwise, she's going to be knocked up and refusing to take your phone calls. And boy, won't *that* be fun."

Bobby shook his head. It was aching, and his face was throbbing where Wes's fists had connected with it—which was just about everywhere. He suspected Wes's nose hurt far worse; yet, both of their physical pain combined was nothing compared to the apprehension that was starting to churn in his stomach. Ask Colleen to marry him. God.

"She's not going to agree to marry me. She wanted a fling, not a lifetime commitment."

"Well, too bad for her," Wes countered.

"Wes, she deserves—" Bobby rubbed his forehead and just said it "—she deserves better than me."

"Damn straight she does," Wes agreed. "I wanted her to marry a lawyer or a doctor. I didn't want this for her—to be a Navy wife, like my mother." He swore. "I wanted her to hook up with someone rich, not some poor, dumb Navy chief who'll have to work double shifts to buy her a washer and dryer. Damn, if she's going to marry Navy, she should at least have been smart enough to pick an officer."

This wasn't a surprise. Wes had voiced his wishes for Colleen often enough in the past. The surprise came from how bad Bobby felt hearing this. "I wanted that for her, too," he told Wes quietly.

"Here's what you do," Wes told him. "You go to Colleen's and you tell her we had a fight. You tell her that I wanted you to stay the hell away from her. You tell her that you told me that you wouldn't—that you want to marry her. And you tell her that I flat-out forbid it." He laughed, but there wasn't any humor in it. "She'll agree to marry you then."

"She's not going to ruin her life just to tick you off," Bobby argued.

"Wanna bet?" Wes stood up. "After the meeting I'll get you a seat on the next flight back to Boston."

"Are you ever going to forgive me?" Bobby asked.

"No." Wes didn't turn around as he went out the door.

Chapter 15

Colleen came home from the Tulgerian children's memorial service at St. Margaret's to find Ashley home and no new messages on the answering machine. Bobby had called last night, while she was at a Relief Aid meeting, so at least she knew he'd survived his altercation with her brother. Still, she was dying to speak to him.

Dying to be with him again.

"Any calls?" she called to Ashley, who was in her room.

"No."

"When did you get back?" Colleen asked, going to her roommate's bedroom door and finding her...*packing*?

"I'm not back," Ashley said, wiping her eyes and her nose with her sleeve. She had been crying but she forced an overly bright smile. "I'm only here temporarily and I'm not telling you where I'm going because you might tell someone."

Colleen sighed. "I guess Brad found you."

"I guess you would be the person who told him where I was…?"

"I'm sorry, but he seemed sincerely broken up over your disappearing act."

"You mean broken up over losing his chances to inherit my share of DeWitt and Klein," Ashley countered, savagely throwing clothes into the open suitcase on her bed. "How could you even *think* I'd consider getting back together with him? My father hired him to be my husband, and he went along with it! Some things are unforgivable."

"People change when they fall in love."

"Not *that* much." She emptied her entire drawer of underwear into the suitcase. "I figured out how to get my father off my back. I'm dropping out of law school."

What? Colleen took another step into the room. "Ashley—"

"I'm going to go to bartending school and get a job dancing in some exotic bar like the women in that video we rented before I left for New York."

Colleen laughed in surprise. She quickly stopped when Ashley shot her a dark look.

"You don't think I'd be any good at it?"

"No," Colleen protested. "No, I think you'd be great. It's just… Isn't it a little late in your childhood to start sporting the career equivalent of—" she thought of Clark "—of blue hair?"

"It's never too late," Ashley said. "And my father deserves all the blue hair—symbolic or other—that he gets." She closed her suitcase, locked it. "Look, I'm going to send for the rest of my things. And I'll pay my share of the rent until you find a new roommate."

"I don't want a new roommate!" Colleen followed her into the living room. "You're my best friend. I can't believe you're so mad at me that you're leaving!"

Ashley set her suitcase down. "I'm not leaving because I'm mad at you," she said. "I'm not really mad at you at all. I just... I did a lot of thinking, and... Colleen, I have to get out of here. Boston's too close to my father in New York. And you know, maybe Clark's right. Maybe I should go to one of those survival training schools. Learn to swim with sharks. See if I can grow a backbone—although I suspect it's a little late for that."

"You have a *great* backbone."

"No, *you* have a great backbone. I'm really good at borrowing yours when I need it," Ashley countered. She pushed her hair back from her face, attempting to put several escaped tendrils neatly back into place. "I have to do this, Colleen. I've got a cab waiting..."

Colleen hugged her friend. "Call me," she said, pulling back to look into Ashley's face. Her friend's normally perfect complexion was sallow, and she had dark circles beneath her eyes. This Brad thing had truly damaged her. "Whenever you get where you're going, when you've had a little more time to think about this—call me, Ash. You can always change your mind and come back. But if you don't—well, I'll come out to visit and cheer while you dance on the bar."

Ashley smiled even though her eyes filled with tears. "See, everything's okay with you. Why couldn't *you* be my father?"

Colleen had teared up, too, but she still had to laugh. "Aside from the obvious biological problems, I'm not ready to be anyone's parent. I'm having a tough enough time right now keeping my own life straightened out."

And yet, she could well be pregnant. Right now. Right this moment, a baby could be sparking to life inside her. In nine months she could be someone's mother. Someone very small who looked an awful lot like Bobby Taylor.

And somehow that thought wasn't quite so terrifying as she'd expected it to be.

She heard an echo of Bobby's deep voice, soft and rumbly, close to her ear. *There are some things you just have to do, you know? So you do it, and it all works out.*

If she were pregnant, despite what she'd just told Ashley, she would make it work out. Somehow.

She gave her friend one more hug. "You liked law school," she told Ashley. "Don't cut off your nose to spite your face."

"Maybe I'll go back some day—anonymously."

"That'll look good on your diploma—Anonymous DeWitt."

"The lawyer with blue hair." Ashley smiled back at Colleen, wiping her eyes again before dragging her suitcase to the door.

The door buzzer rang.

"That's probably the cab driver," Ashley said, "wondering if I sneaked out the back door."

Colleen pushed the button for the intercom. "She'll be right down."

"Actually, I was hoping to come up." The voice over the ancient speaker was crackly but unmistakable, and Colleen's heart leaped.

Bobby.

"I thought you were the cab driver," she told him, leaning close to the microphone.

"You're not going anywhere, are you?" Did he sound worried? She hoped so.

"No," she said. "The cab's Ashley's."

She buzzed him into the lobby as Ashley opened the apartment door. From the sound of his footsteps, he took the stairs two at a time, and then there he was. Carrying *flowers*?

He was. He had what looked like a garden in his arms—an outrageous mix of lilies and daisies and big, bold, crazy-looking flowers for which she didn't know the names. He thrust them toward her as he quickly took the suitcase from Ashley's hands. "Let me get that for you."

"No, you don't need to—" But he was already down the stairs. Ashley looked helplessly at Colleen. "See? No backbone."

"Call me," Colleen said, and then Ashley was gone.

Leaving Colleen face-to-face with the flowers that Bobby had brought. For *her*.

She had to smile. It was silly and sweet and a complete surprise. She left the door ajar and went into the kitchen to find a vase. She was filling it with water when Bobby returned.

He looked nice, as if he'd taken special care with his appearance. He was wearing Dockers instead of his usual jeans, a polo shirt with a collar in a muted shade of green. His hair was neatly braided. Someone had helped him with that.

"Sorry I didn't call you last night. The meeting didn't end until well after midnight. And then I was up early, catching a flight back here."

He was nervous. She could see it in his eyes, in the tension in his shoulders—but only because she knew him so very well. Anyone else would see a completely relaxed, easygoing man, standing in her kitchen, dwarfing the refrigerator.

"Thanks for the flowers," she said. "I love them."

He smiled. "Good. I didn't think you were the roses type, and they, well, they reminded me of you."

"What?" she said. "Big and flashy?"

His smile widened. "Yeah."

Colleen laughed as she turned to give him a disbelieving look. Their eyes met and held, and just like that the heat was back, full force.

"I missed you," she whispered.

"I missed you, too."

"Kinda hard for you to take off my clothes when you're way over there."

He yanked his gaze away, cleared his throat. "Yeah, well. Hmmm. I think we need to talk before…" He cleared his throat. "You want to go out, take a walk? Get some coffee?"

She put the flowers into the water. "You're afraid if we stay here, we won't be able to keep from getting naked."

"Yes," he said. "Yes, I am."

Colleen laughed, opening the refrigerator. "How about we take a glass of iced tea to the roof?"

"Am I going to get the urge to jump you there?"

"Absolutely," she said as she poured the tea. "But unless you're an exhibitionist, you won't. There's a taller building right behind this one. There are about three floors of apartments that have a bird's-eye view of this roof."

She gave him one of the glasses and a kiss.

His mouth was soft and warm and wonderful, his

body so solid and strong, and she felt herself melt against him.

She looked up at him. "You sure you don't want to…?"

"Roof," he said. "Please?"

Colleen led the way, up the main staircase, through the exit door and out into the bright sunshine. A long-departed former tenant had built a sundeck, complete with large pots of dirt in which she and Ashley had planted flowers last May. It wasn't luxurious, but it was a far cry from the peeling tar paper on the neighboring buildings' roofs.

There was even a bench, placed strategically in the shade provided by the larger building next door.

Colleen sat down. Bobby sat, too—about as far away from her as he could manage.

"So I guess I should ask about my brother," she said. "Is he in intensive care?"

"No." Bobby looked down into his iced tea. "We *did* fight, though."

She knew. She could see the shadows of bruises on his face. "It must've been awful," she said quietly.

He turned to gaze at her, and her heart moved up into her throat. He had such a way of looking at her, as if he could see inside her head, inside her very heart and soul, as if he saw her completely, as a whole, unique, special person.

"Marry me."

Colleen nearly dropped her glass. *What?*

But she'd heard him correctly. He reached into his pocket and took out a jeweler's box. A *ring* box. He opened it and handed it to her—it was a diamond in a gorgeously simple setting, perfect for accenting the size of the stone. Which was enormous. It had to have cost him three months' pay.

She couldn't breathe. She couldn't speak. She couldn't move. Bobby Taylor wanted to marry her.

"Please," he said quietly. "I should have said, *please* marry me."

The sky was remarkably blue, and the air was fresh and sweet. On the street below, a woman shouted for someone named Lenny. A car horn honked. A bus roared past.

Bobby Taylor wanted to *marry* her.

And yes, *yes*, she wanted to marry him, too. *Marry* him! The thought was dizzying, terrifying, but it came with a burst of happiness that was so strong, she laughed aloud.

Colleen looked up at him then, into the almost palpable warmth of his eyes. He was waiting for her answer.

But she was waiting, too, she realized. This was where he would tell her that he loved her.

Except he didn't. He didn't say anything. He just sat there, watching her, slightly nervous, slightly…detached? As if he were waiting for her to say no.

Colleen looked hard into his eyes. He was sitting there, waiting, as if he expected her to turn him down.

As if he didn't really want her to marry him.

As if…

Her happiness fizzled, and she handed him the ring box. "Wes put you up to this, didn't he?" She saw the truth in his eyes. Oh, no, she was right. "Oh, Bobby."

"I'm not going to lie to you," he said quietly. "It *was* Wes's idea. But I wouldn't have asked if I didn't want to do it."

"Yeah," Colleen said, standing up and walking away

so that her back was to him. She couldn't bear to let him see her disappointment. "Right. You look really enthusiastic. Grim is more like it. 'I'm here to be sentenced to life in prison, your honor.'"

"I'm scared. Can you blame me for that?" he countered. She heard the ice tinkling in his glass as he set it down, as he stood up and moved directly behind her. But he didn't touch her. He just stood there, impossible to ignore.

"This is a big step," he said quietly. "A major life decision for both of us. And I'm not sure marrying me is the right thing for *you* to do. I don't make a lot of money, Colleen, and my job takes me all over the world. Being a Navy wife sucks—I'm not sure I want to do that to you. I don't know if I could make you happy enough to ignore all the negatives of being married to me. And, yes, that scares me."

He took a deep breath. "But the fact is, you could be pregnant. With my child. That's not something I can ignore."

"I know," she whispered.

"If you *are* pregnant, you *will* marry me," he told her, his quiet voice leaving no room for argument. "Even if it's only just for a year or two, if that's how you want to play it."

Colleen nodded. "If I'm pregnant. But I'm probably not, so I'm not going to marry you." She shook her head. "I can't believe you would *marry* me, just because Wes told you to." She laughed, but her throat ached, and she knew she was dangerously close to crying. "I can't decide if that makes you a really good friend or a total chump."

She headed for the door to the stairs, praying she

would make it into her apartment before her tears escaped. "I should get back to work."

God, she was a fool. If he'd been just a little more disingenuous, if he'd lied and told her he loved her, she would have given herself away. She would have thrown her arms around his neck and told him yes. Yes, she'd marry him, yes, she loved him, too.

She loved him so much…but there was no *too*.

"Colleen, wait."

Oh, damn, he was chasing her down the stairs. He caught her at her apartment door as she fumbled her key in the lock, as her vision blurred from her tears.

She pushed open the door, and he followed. She tried to turn away, but it was too late.

"I'm so sorry," he said hoarsely, engulfing her in his arms. "Please believe me—the last thing I wanted to do was upset you like this."

He was so solid, so huge, and his arms gave her the illusion of safety. Of being home.

He swore softly. "I didn't mean to make you cry, Colleen."

She just held him tightly, wanting them both just to pretend this hadn't happened. He hadn't asked her to marry him, she hadn't discovered just how much she truly loved him. Yeah, that would be easy to forget. He could return the ring to the jeweler's, but she didn't have a clue what she was going to do with her heart.

She did, however, know exactly what to do with her body. Yes, she was going to take advantage of every second she had with this man.

She pushed the door closed behind them and, wrapping her arms around his neck, pulled his head down for a kiss.

He hesitated—for about one-tenth of a second. Then, with a groan, he kissed her, too.

And Colleen stopped crying.

How the hell had *this* happened?

As Bobby awoke, he knew exactly where he was before he even opened his eyes.

He could smell the sweet scent of Colleen, feel her softness nestled against him.

Her windows were open, and a soft breeze from this perfect summer day caressed his naked behind. Colleen caressed him, too. She was running her fingers lightly up and down the arm he'd draped around her after she'd succeeded in completely wearing him out. Had they made love twice or three times?

How *had* that happened—even once? It didn't quite line up with him asking to marry her, and her getting angry because she saw clear through him, saw it had been Wesley's idea in the first place.

Except she hadn't been so much angry as *hurt*, and...

He lifted his face from her pillow to find her watching him. She smiled. "Hi."

He wanted her again. Just from one smile. Except it wasn't so much his body that reacted this time. It was his *heart* that expanded. He wanted to wake up to her smile every day. He wanted...

"You need to go," she said to him. "I have to pack for Tulgeria, and you're distracting me."

"I'll help you."

"Yeah, right." She laughed and leaned forward to kiss him. "Ten minutes of your *help*, you'll have me back in bed."

"Seriously, Colleen, I know exactly what you need to

take. No bright colors, no white, either, otherwise you're setting yourself up as a potential sniper target. Think drabs—browns, greens, beiges. I also don't want you to bring anything clingy—wear loose overshirts, okay? Long sleeves, long skirts—and you know this already. Right." Bobby laughed, disgusted with himself. "Sorry."

She kissed him again. "I love that you care."

"I do," he said, holding her gaze, wishing there was some way to convey just how much.

But the door buzzer rang, and Colleen gently extracted herself from his arms. She slipped on her robe. Man, he loved that robe. He sat up. "Maybe you should let me get the door."

But she was already out of the room. "I've got it."

Whoever had buzzed had gotten past the building's security entrance and was now knocking directly on the door to Colleen's apartment.

Where *were* his shorts?

"Oh, my God," he heard Colleen say. "What are *you* doing here?"

"What, I can't visit my own sister?" Oh, damn! It was Wes. "Sleeping in today, huh? Late night last night?"

"No," she said flatly. "What do you want, Wes? I'm mad at you."

"I'm looking for Taylor. But he better not be here, with you dressed like that."

The hell with his shorts. Bobby grabbed his pants, pulling them on, tripping over his own feet in his haste and just barely keeping himself from doing a nosedive onto the floor. His recovery made an incriminating *thump.*

Wes swore—a steady stream of epithets that grew

louder as he moved down the hall toward Colleen's bedroom.

Bobby was searching for his shirt among the sheets and blankets that spilled from the bed and onto the floor as Wes pushed the door open. He slowly straightened up, his hair wild around his shoulder, his feet bare and his shirt nowhere to be found.

Damn, there it was—over near Colleen's closet, near where he'd tossed his socks and shoes.

"Well, this is just beautiful," Wes said. His eyes were cold and hard—they were someone else's eyes. The Wes Skelly who'd been closer to him than a brother for years was gone. As Bobby watched, Wes turned to Colleen. "You're marrying this son of a bitch over my dead body."

Bobby knew Wes honestly thought that would make Colleen determined to marry him. "Wes—"

"You don't want me to marry him?" she asked innocently.

Wes crossed his arms. "Absolutely not."

"Okay," Colleen said blithely. "Sorry, Bobby, I can't marry you. Wes won't let me." She turned and went into the kitchen.

"What?" Wes followed, sputtering. "But you *have* to marry him. Especially now."

Bobby pulled on his shirt and grabbed his socks and shoes.

"I'm not marrying Bobby," Colleen repeated. "I don't *have* to marry Bobby. And there's nothing you can do to *make* me, thank you very much. I'm a grown woman, Wesley, who happens to be in a completely mutual, intimate relationship with a very attractive man. You either need to deal with that or get your negative opinions out of my apartment."

Wes was still sputtering. "But—"

She moved grandly from the kitchen to the door, opening it wide for him. "Leave."

Wes looked at Bobby. "No way am I leaving with him still here!"

"Then take him with you," Colleen said. "I have work to do." She pointed the way. "Go. Both of you."

Bobby moved, and Wes followed. But at the door Colleen stopped Bobby, kissed him. "Sorry about my brother the grouch. I had a lovely afternoon, thank you. I'll see you tonight."

If her intention was to infuriate her brother, she'd succeeded.

She closed the door behind them, with Bobby still holding his socks and shoes.

Wes gave him a scathing look. "What is *wrong* with you?"

How could he explain? He wasn't sure himself how it happened. Every time he turned around, he found himself in bed with Colleen. When it came to her, he—a man who'd set time-and-distance records for swimming underwater, a man who'd outlasted more physically fit SEAL candidates during BUD/S through sheer determination, a man who'd turned himself around from a huge man carrying quite a bit of extra weight into a solid, muscular monster—had no willpower.

Because being with her felt so right. It was *right.*

That thought came out of nowhere, blindsiding him, and he stood there for a moment just blinking at Wes.

"You were supposed to get her to marry you," Wes continued. "Instead you—"

"I tried. I was trying to—"

"That was *trying*?"

"If she's pregnant, she'll marry me. She agreed to that."

"Perfect," Wes said, "so naturally you feel inclined to keep trying to get her pregnant."

"Of course not. Wes, when I'm with her—"

"I don't want to hear it." Wes glared at him. "Just stay the hell away from her," he said, and clattered down the stairs. "And stay away from me, too."

Chapter 16

The early-afternoon meeting between Alpha Squad and the members of Relief Aid who were going to Tulgeria tomorrow had gone well.

Colleen had been afraid that some of the more left-wing group members would be opposed to protection from the U.S. military, but with the recent outbreak of violence in the dangerous country, there wasn't a single protest.

She'd sat quietly, listening to the information presented by the SEALs. Bobby and the squad's commander, Captain Joe Catalanotto, sat up on a desk in the front of the room, feet swinging, extremely casual, dressed down in shorts and T-shirts—just a coupla guys. Who also happened to be members of *the* most elite military force in the world.

Bobby did most of the talking—a smart move, since

he'd been working alongside most of the Relief Aid volunteers for the past few days. They knew and trusted him.

He warned them of the dangers they'd be encountering and the precautions and methods the SEALs would be taking to protect them, in his usual straightforward, quiet manner. And everything he said was taken very seriously.

The SEALs would maintain a low profile, blending in with the volunteers. Only a few would be obvious guards and carry obvious weapons.

After the meeting they'd mingled over iced tea and lemonade. She'd met many of the SEALs her brother had mentioned in his letters and emails down through the years. Joe Cat, Blue, Lucky, Cowboy, Crash. Some of the nicknames were pretty funny.

Spaceman. His real name was Jim Slade, and he was tall and good-looking in an earthy way, with craggy features and the kind of blue eyes that were perpetually amused. He'd followed her around for a while and had even invited her back to the hotel, to have dinner with him later.

Bobby had overheard that, and Colleen had expected him to step forward, to make some kind of proprietary move. But he hadn't. He'd just met Colleen's eyes briefly, then gone back to the conversation he'd been having with Relief Aid leader, Susan Fitzgerald.

And Colleen was bemused—more with her own reaction. It was stupid really. If Bobby had gotten all macho and possessive on her, she would have been annoyed. But since he hadn't, she found herself wondering why not. Didn't he *feel* possessive toward her? And wasn't *that* a stupid thing to wonder? She didn't want to be any man's possession.

She'd spoken to Bobby only briefly before he'd left for another meeting with his team, held back at the hotel. She'd stayed behind and helped discuss plans for TV news coverage of tonight's bon voyage party.

That meeting was brief, and Colleen was on the T, heading toward Cambridge before four o'clock. She was inside the lobby of Bobby's hotel by 4:15.

She used the lobby phone to dial his room.

Bobby answered on the first ring, and she knew right away that she'd woken him up.

"Sorry," she said.

"No, I was just catching a nap. Are you, um… Where are you?"

"Downstairs. Can I come up?"

Silence. She heard the rustle of sheets as he sat up. "How about you give me a few minutes to get dressed? I'll meet you in the bar."

"How about I come up?"

"Colleen—"

"Room 712, right? I'll be there in a sec."

"Colleen…" She'd hung up.

Bobby dumped the phone's handset into the cradle and lay back in his bed.

What was the point in getting dressed? She was coming up here. In five minutes—ten tops—she'd have him out of his clothes.

He threw back the covers, anyway, got up and pulled on his pants and a T-shirt. If he was quick enough, he'd meet her in the hall, outside the elevators. He pulled on his sneakers, checked himself in the mirror to make sure his hair hadn't completely fallen out of its braid.

He opened the door, and Colleen was standing there, ready to knock.

"Hi," she said. "Good timing."

She swept past him, into the room.

No, it was bad timing. The last place they should be right now was here, alone in his hotel room. If Wes found out, he'd be furious.

Bobby had been shaken by what had happened this morning. He truly had not intended to take advantage of Colleen, but he honest-to-God could not stop himself from climbing into her bed and making love to her.

Even though she didn't want to marry him.

Was he turning into some kind of prude in his old age? So what if she didn't want to marry him. She wanted to do him, and that was what mattered.

Wasn't it?

"I have a favor to ask," she told him now.

God, she looked beautiful, in a blue-flowered sleeveless dress that flowed almost all the way to the floor. He'd been hyperaware of her all throughout the afternoon's meeting—aware of how easy it would be to get her out of that dress, with its single zipper down the back.

Bobby crossed the room and opened the curtains, letting in the bright late-afternoon sunshine. "Name it," he said.

"I know we don't officially need your protection until we enter Tulgeria," she told him, "but remember I told you about that bon voyage party? It's tonight at the VFW right down the street from St. Margaret's—the church where I had that car wash?"

Bobby nodded. "I know St. Margaret's." It was in that same crummy 'hood where the AIDS Center was creating a controversy among the locals.

Colleen put her backpack down and came to help as he attempted to make the bed. "We just found out that the local Fox affiliate is sending TV cameras tonight. That's great news—we could use all the public support we can get." Together they pulled up the bedspread. "But…"

"But the cameras are going to attract attention in the neighborhood." Bobby knew just where she was heading. "You're afraid John Morrison's going to show up. Crash your party."

She nodded. "It wouldn't surprise me one bit if he caused trouble, just to get the news camera pointed in his direction."

He took a deep breath. "There's something I should probably tell you. Don't be angry with me, but I checked up on John Morrison. I was worried about you, and I wanted to know how much of a wild card he was."

"There's not much to find out," Colleen countered. "I did the same thing right after he and I…met. He served in the army, did a tour in Vietnam. There's an ex-wife and a kid somewhere in New York. He inherited his bar from his father, who got it from *his* father. He's dating one of his waitresses—she shows up in the ER every now and then for some stitches. After I found *that* out, I started carrying one of those little spray cans of mace."

"Good plan. He's got the potential to be violent," Bobby told her. "Oh, I meant to tell you—I got a call right before I left the hotel. The woman who was attacked—Andrea Barker—she came out of her coma. Turns out it was her ex-husband who beat her up. He ignored a restraining order and…"

Colleen touched his arm. "Andrea's out of her coma—that's great news."

He stepped back slightly. "So is the fact that it wasn't Morrison who put her into the hospital. That fits with what I found out about him—that he never leaves his neighborhood. He rarely leaves his bar. In fact, his drinking pals are all still talking about the trips he made to New York—one about a year ago, the other just a few months back. I also found out he used to be a member of St. Margaret's but he stopped going to church about a year ago. I played out a hunch and called his ex in New York, and sure enough, a year ago was when he found out his son was dying of AIDS."

Colleen closed her eyes. "Oh, no."

"Yeah. John, Jr., died two months ago. He was living with Morrison's ex-wife in the Bronx. She's worried about John. According to her, he's angry and ashamed that even when his son was dying, he couldn't acknowledge the kid, couldn't bring himself to visit. God forbid anyone find out his son was gay, you know? And that's the thing, Colleen. No one up here knows anything. They don't even know that his kid is dead. He hasn't spoken to anyone about this. They still come into the bar and ask how Johnny's doing—if he's gotten that big break as an actor, if he's on Broadway yet."

Oh, God. "The poor man."

"Regardless of that, this *poor man* is responsible for putting cinder blocks through the center's windows. If he gets near you tonight, his health will be at risk."

"You'll be there?" she asked.

"Absolutely. I'll bring some of the guys, too. Rio, Thomas and Mike. And Jim Slade. He'll definitely come. What time does it start?"

"Eight. The camera crew's due to arrive at 7:30."

"We'll be there at seven."

"Thank you." Colleen sat down on his bed. "I liked meeting Rio, Thomas and Mike... Lee, right?" She smiled. "They really think the world of you. Make sure you tell them what you told me about John Morrison. If he shows up, let's try to treat him with compassion."

"We'll get him out of there as quickly—and compassionately—as possible," he promised. "I'm glad you had a chance to meet them—they're good men. All the guys in the squad are. Although some are definitely special. The senior chief—Harvard Becker. Did you meet him? I'd follow him into hell if he asked."

"Big black man, shaved head, great smile?" she asked.

"That's Harvard. Hey, whatdya think of Slade? Spaceman?" Bobby tried to ask the question casually, as if he was just talking, as if her answer didn't matter to him. The stupid thing was, he wasn't sure if he wanted her to tell him that she liked the man or hated him.

Colleen was gazing at him. "I thought he was nice. Why?"

"He's a lieutenant," Bobby told her. "An officer who's probably going to get out of the Teams pretty soon. He's having a tough time with his knees and... He's not sure what he's going to do. For a while he was thinking JAG—you know, going to law school, getting a degree, doing a stint in the regular Navy as a lawyer. I just thought you'd, um, probably have a lot in common. You know, with you going to law school, too?"

Colleen shrugged. "Lawyers are boring."

"You're not. Slade's not, either."

She laughed. "Is there a reason you sound like you're trying to sell this guy to me?"

It was Bobby's turn to shrug. "He's a good man."

"You're a good man, too. A *very* good man."

She was gazing at him with that look in her eyes that made him crazy. And she smiled that smile that made his knees weak as she leaned back on her elbows. "So why are we talking about your friend? Why are we talking at all? Wouldn't you rather help me make Wes really mad—and spend the next half hour or so naked?"

Bobby was proud of himself. He didn't move toward her, didn't instantly strip off both his clothes and hers. "Colleen, I love being with you, you know that, but I don't want to be a pawn in this war you've got going with your brother."

She sat up, her smile instantly gone, wide-eyed. "Whoa—wait! Bobby, I was making a joke. I wasn't serious."

She wasn't serious. "That's part of the problem here," he told her quietly. "You and me, we're not serious, but Wes is. He doesn't want you messing around, not with a man that you don't have a serious shot at having a future with, you know? He thinks that's wrong and…" And Bobby was starting to think it was wrong, too.

It was one thing to have a casual sexual relationship with a woman who was older, someone his age, who lived near the Navy base, who'd maybe been through a nasty divorce and had no intention of repeating that mistake in the near future.

But with Colleen there were expectations.

Although, God help him, it sure seemed as if all the expectations were *his*.

"Wes thinks what we've got going is wrong? Well, what's *wrong*," Colleen countered hotly as she got to her feet, "is strong-arming your best friend into proposing marriage to your sister. What if I'd said yes? Would you have married me just because Wes told you to?"

"No," he said. He would have married her because he wanted to. Because unlike Colleen, this relationship was more to him than great sex. He turned away from her. "Look, maybe you should go."

She moved in front of him, forced him to look at her. "And do what?" she said sharply. "Have an early dinner with Jim Slade?"

He didn't nod, didn't say yes, but somehow the answer was written on his face. Slade was the kind of man she should be with. How could she meet men like him if she was wasting her time with Bobby?

"Oh, my God," she said. "You were, weren't you? You were trying to set me up with your friend." Her voice caught as she struggled not to cry, and as she gazed at him, she suddenly looked and sounded impossibly young and so very uncertain. "Bobby, what's going on? Don't you want me anymore?"

Oh, damn, he was going to cry, too. He wanted her more than he could ever say. He wanted her with every breath, with every beat of his heart. "I want to do what's right for you, Colleen. I need to—"

She kissed him.

God help him, she kissed him, and he was lost.

Again.

In truth, it was no ordinary kiss. It was fire and hunger and need. It was passion and fury, with a whole lot of anger and hurt thrown in. It consumed him completely, until doing the right thing was no longer an option but an impossibility. Sure, he'd do the right thing—if the right thing meant sweeping her into his arms and carrying her to his bed. If the right thing meant nearly ripping her dress in his haste to get it off her, of pushing down his pants and covering himself and thrusting, hard, inside of her as she clung to him, as she begged him for more.

More.

He was ready to give her all he had to give—body, heart and soul, and he did, disguising it as near-mindless sex, hard and rough and fast.

She called out his name as she climaxed, shaking around him, and he joined her in a hot rush of pleasure so intense it was almost pain.

And then there he was again. Back from that place of insanity and passion, back to this extremely familiar real world that was filled with rumpled bedclothes and mind-numbing guilt.

He swore. "I'm sorry," he whispered as he rolled off her.

She sat up on the edge of the bed instead of snuggling against him, and he realized she was getting dressed. Bra, dress, sandals. Her panties had been torn—damn, he'd done that—and she threw them in the garbage.

She ran her fingers through her hair, picked up her pack. "I'm sorry that you're sorry," she said quietly, "but… I'm a fool—I still want to see you later tonight. Will you come to my place after the thing at the VFW?"

Bobby didn't answer right away, and she looked at him. "Please?"

"Yes," he whispered, and she let herself out the door.

The elevator door opened, and Colleen found herself face-to-face with Wes.

He was getting off on this floor, Bobby's floor, followed by the trio of young SEALs she was starting to think of as The Mod Squad. Pete, Link and Mike Lee.

Wes's expression was grim, and Colleen knew that

she looked like a woman who'd just been with a man. She should have taken more time, should have gone into the bathroom and splashed water on her still-flushed face.

Except then she would have been in Bobby's room when Wes knocked on the door.

She went into the elevator, her head held high as her brother glared at her. "Don't worry," she told him. "You win. I'm not going to see him again after tonight."

They were leaving for Tulgeria in the morning. While they were there, she would be sharing a room with Susan and Rene, and Bobby would be in with one or two of the SEALs for the week. There would be no place to be alone, no time, either. Bobby would have no trouble avoiding her.

And after they got back to the States, he'd head for California with the rest of Alpha Squad.

He wasn't interested in a long-distance relationship.

She wasn't interested in one that created limitless amounts of anguish and guilt.

There was no way their relationship could work out. This was what he'd tried to tell her in his room. That was why he'd tried to spark her interest in his stupid friend.

What they'd shared—a few days of truly great sex— was almost over. It *was* over, and they both knew it in their hearts. It was just taking their bodies a little bit longer to catch up.

The elevator door closed, and Colleen put on her sunglasses, afraid of who else she'd run into on the way to the lobby, and unwilling to let them see her cry.

Bobby didn't answer the door.

He knew from the weight of the knock that it was Wes—the last person in the world he wanted to see.

No, Wes was the *second* to last person Bobby wanted to see right now. The first was Colleen. God forbid she see him and know that he'd been crying.

Man, he'd screwed this up, big-time. He should have stayed away from her. He should have taken the T to Logan and hopped the next flight to Australia. He should have hung up the phone that first night she'd called him. He should have—

"Open the damn door, Taylor. I know you're in there!"

Wes was the one person he should have been able to run to, the one person who could have helped him sort this out, to figure out what to do now that he'd completely messed it up by falling in love.

"I love her." Bobby said it aloud, to the door, knowing Wes couldn't hear him over the sound of his own knocking. "I'm in love with Colleen."

Still, it was a shock to speak the words, to admit these powerful feelings that he'd worked overtime to deny right from the very start.

Right from her nineteenth birthday, when he and Wes had taken Colleen and a group of her girlfriends from college to Busch Gardens. Bobby hadn't seen her in a few years, and suddenly there she was. All grown up. He'd gotten into an argument with her about some political issue, and she was so well-informed and so well-spoken, she'd convinced him that he was backing the wrong party. He'd fallen for her then—a girl-woman who wasn't afraid to tell a man that he was wrong.

Yeah, he'd loved her for years, but it wasn't until this past week, until they became lovers, that his love for her had deepened and grown into this complete, everlasting force. It was bigger than he was. It was all-consuming and powerful. He'd never felt anything like it in his entire life, and it scared the hell out of him.

"I can't say no to her," Bobby said to Wes, through the door. "She wants me to meet her tonight, and I'm going to be there, because, damn it, I can't stay away from her. It's tearing me up, because I know this isn't what you want for her. I know you wanted better. But if she came to me and told me she loved me, too, and that she wanted to marry me, I'd do it. Tonight. I'd take her to Vegas before she changed her mind. Yeah, I'd do it, even though I know what a mistake it would be for her.

"But she doesn't want to marry me." Bobby wiped his face, his eyes. "She only wants to sleep with me. I don't have to worry about her waking up seven years from now and hating her life. I only have to worry about spending the rest of *my* life wanting someone I can't have."

Bobby sat on the edge of the hotel room bed, right where Colleen had sat just a short time ago.

"God, I want her in my life," he said aloud. "What am I going to do, Wes?"

No one answered.

Wes had stopped knocking on the door. He was gone.

And Bobby was alone.

As the TV news cameras arrived, Colleen glanced at her watch. It was about 7:20.

Bobby and his friends were already there, already in place—Thomas and Jim Slade seemingly casually hanging out on the sidewalk in front of the church parking lot, Rio and Mike up near the truck that held the camera.

Bobby was sticking close to her in the crowd.

"There's a good chance if Morrison's going to try anything, he's going to target you," he explained. He was dressed in jeans and a white button-down shirt with a jacket over it, despite the heat.

"Are you wearing a jacket because you've got on a gun under there?" She had to ask.

He laughed. "I'm wearing a jacket because I'm here posing as a member of Relief Aid, and I wanted to look nice."

Oh. "You do," she said. "You look very nice."

"So do you." His gaze skimmed appreciatively down her denim skirt, taking in the yellow daisies that adorned her blouse. "You always do."

Time hung for a moment, as she fell into the bottomless depths of his eyes. But then he looked away.

"I'm sorry," Colleen said. "About this afternoon."

"No." He glanced at her. "I was the one who was—"

"No," she said. "You weren't."

His eyes were apologetic. "I can't come over tonight. I'm sorry, but…"

She nodded. Had to ask. "Are you sure?"

"No." He met her gaze again, smiled ruefully. "I mean, five minutes ago, yeah, I was sure. But here you are and…" He shook his head.

"Well, if you change your mind, I'll be home." Colleen tried to sound casual, tried to sound as if sharing this one last night with him didn't mean so much to her. She cleared her throat. "I should probably go inside pretty soon. If John Morrison were coming, he'd probably be here by now."

Famous last words.

"Hey! Hey, hippie chick! Nice party you're throwing here. What are we celebrating? The fact that you're going away and won't be around to annoy us for a whole week?"

It was John Morrison, and he was drunk, holding a bottle wrapped in a paper bag.

As Bobby stepped in front of her, he seemed to expand, and Colleen realized that a baseball bat was dangling from Morrison's other hand.

"How about we let those cameras cover some real news?" Morrison asked loudly—loudly enough for heads to turn in his direction.

Loudly enough for the other SEALs to move toward them. But the crowd was thick, and they were having trouble getting through the crush. As were the police officers who'd been assigned to keep traffic moving.

"I'm going down the street," Morrison continued, "just a block or so over, to that AIDS Center they're building down there. I'm going to break the windows in protest. We don't want it in our neighborhood. We don't want *you* in our neighborhood."

He pointed at Colleen with the baseball bat, swinging it up toward her, and just like that, it was over.

She barely saw Bobby move. Yet somehow he'd taken the bat away from Morrison and had the man down on the ground before she even blinked.

The other SEALs made the scene a few seconds before the police.

Bobby lifted Morrison to his feet, handed the man to Spaceman. "Take him inside. There are some empty rooms upstairs." He turned to Rio. "Find Father Timothy. Tell him it has to do with that matter I discussed with him earlier this week." He looked at Colleen. "You okay?"

She watched as Spaceman hustled Morrison inside. "Yeah. I don't think he was going to hurt me."

"What's going on here?" the police officer—a big,

ruddy-cheeked beat cop named Danny O'Sullivan—planted himself in front of them.

Bobby touched her arm and lowered his voice. "You want to press charges? Lifting the bat like that could be considered assault. At the least, we could get him for drunk and disorderly."

She met his gaze. "No." Not if Father Timothy was getting involved. Bobby had talked to Timothy earlier in the week, he'd said.

Be compassionate, she'd told him, just that afternoon. Obviously, he hadn't needed the reminder.

"Just a little outburst from a friend who had too much to drink," Bobby told O'Sullivan. He squeezed Colleen's arm. "You want to take it from here? I want to go inside to talk to Morrison."

She nodded, and he pulled Thomas King over. "Don't let Colleen out of your sight."

"Aye, aye, Chief."

The crowd parted for Bobby as Colleen turned back to the cop. "Really, Dan," she said. "Everything's fine. We'll see John gets home safely."

O'Sullivan looked at the bat that Mike Lee had picked up through narrowed eyes. "What, did Johnny want to get a game going or something?"

"Or something," Colleen agreed.

"Sometimes it does a body more harm than good to be protected by friends," O'Sullivan said.

"He's had a recent tragedy in his family," she told him. "He doesn't need a night in jail, Dan. He needs to talk to his parish priest."

O'Sullivan smiled as he shook his head. "I wish I were twenty-something and still believed I could save the world, one poor loser at a time. Good luck on your trip to Tulgeria." He nodded to Thomas, who was still standing beside her.

She glanced at Thomas, too. "Let's go inside."

Bobby was in an upstairs storage room, talking to John Morrison about Vietnam. He was much too young to have been there, but he must've been something of a historian, because he knew the names of the rivers and the towns and the battles in which Morrison had fought.

John Morrison was drunk, but not as drunk as Colleen had first thought. His speech was slightly slurred, but he was following the conversation easily.

As she listened, lingering with Thomas King just outside the door, the two men talked about Admiral Jake Robinson, who'd also served in 'Nam. Morrison knew of the man and was impressed that Bobby thought of him as a friend. They talked about Bobby's career in the SEAL units. They talked about Morrison's bar, and his father who'd served in a tank division in World War II—who had died just two years ago after a long struggle with cancer. They talked about elderly parents, about loss, about death.

And suddenly they were talking about Wes.

"My best friend is still jammed up from his little brother's death," Bobby told Morrison. "It happened ten years ago, and he still won't talk about it. It's like he pretends the kid never existed." He paused. "Kind of like what you're doing with John Jr."

Silence.

"I'm sorry for your loss," she heard Bobby say quietly. "But you've got to find a way to vent your anger besides taking out the windows at the AIDS Center. Someone's going to end up hurt, and that will make my friend Colleen Skelly—and you know who she is—unhappy. And if you make Colleen unhappy, if you hurt someone, if you hurt *her*, then I'm going to have to come back here and hurt *you*. This is not a threat, John, it's a promise."

His friend. She was his *friend* Colleen—not his lover, not his girlfriend.

And Colleen knew the truth. He'd told her right from the start—he wanted to be friends. And that's all they were, all they ever would be. Friends who had hot sex.

Despite his promise to hurt John Morrison, Bobby was, without a doubt, the kindest, most sensitive man she'd ever met. He was too kind to tell her again that he didn't love her, that he would never love her.

The sex they had was great, but he was the kind of man who would want more in a relationship than great sex.

She could hear Father Timothy coming, puffing his way up the stairs to talk to John Morrison, to try to set him on a path that would lead him out of the darkness into which he'd fallen.

The cynic in her knew that a talk with his priest probably wouldn't change anything. Morrison needed serious help. Chances were when he sobered up he'd be embarrassed and angry that the secret about his son's death had slipped out. Maybe he'd be angry enough to burn down the center.

Or maybe he'd go to grief counseling. She could almost hear Bobby's gentle voice telling her that maybe John Morrison would find peace and stop hating the world—and hating himself.

Father Timothy had almost reached the landing.

Colleen stepped closer to Thomas King, lowered her voice. "I need you to do me a favor and give Bobby a message for me."

Thomas nodded, his face serious to the point of grimness. That was his default expression. He was very black, very serious, very intense. He now turned that intensity directly upon her.

"Please tell him that I thought he probably shouldn't come to my place tonight." Good Lord, could she sound any more equivocal? "Tell him I'm sorry, but I don't want him to come over."

An expression outside of his serious and grim repertoire—one of disbelief—flashed across Thomas King's face and he suddenly looked his actual, rather tender age. "Maybe that's something you should tell Chief Taylor yourself."

"Please," she said. "Just give him the message."

Father Timothy had cleared the top of the stairs, and she went down, as swiftly as she could, before she changed her mind.

Chapter 17

They'd won.

Well, they weren't going to be able to bring the orphans back to the United States at the end of the week, but no one had really expected that. The Tulgerian government *had* given the Relief Aid volunteers permission to move the children to a location near the American Embassy. Paid for, of course, with American dollars.

The other good news was that the government was making it possible for American citizens to travel to the capital city, Tulibek, to petition to adopt. The older children in particular would be allowed to leave, for exorbitant adoption fees.

It *was* a victory—although it was a bittersweet one for Colleen. She was sitting, looking out the window, her forehead against the glass, as the bus moved steadily north, into the even more dangerous war zone.

Bobby watched her, well aware of what she was thinking. In a matter of minutes they would arrive at the hospital where the children had been taken after the orphanage had been destroyed. As they went inside, Analena wouldn't be among the children who rushed to greet her.

Yes, it was a bittersweet victory for Colleen.

It was a city bus—this vehicle they were in. Some of the hard plastic seats faced forward, some faced the center of the bus. There was space for people to stand, bars and straps to hold on to.

Colleen was facing forward, and the seat next to her was empty. He sat down beside her, wishing for the privacy that came with seats that had high backs. He lowered his voice instead. "You okay?"

She wiped her eyes, forced a smile. "I'm great."

Yeah, sure she was. He wanted to hold her hand, but he didn't dare touch her. "The past few days have been crazy, huh?"

She gave him another smile. "Yeah, I've been glad many times over that you and Alpha Squad are here."

God, he'd missed her. When Thomas King had given him her message—don't come over—he'd known that it was over between them. Right up until then he'd harbored hope. Maybe if he went to her and told her that he loved her... Maybe if he begged, she'd agree to keep seeing him. And maybe someday she'd fall in love with him, too.

"You and Wes are on friendlier terms again," she noted. "I mean, at least you seem to be talking."

Bobby nodded, even though that was far from the truth. The final insult in this whole messed-up situation was the damage he'd done to his decade of friendship with Wes. It seemed irreparable.

Wes was talking to him, sure—but it was only an exchange of information. They weren't sharing their thoughts, not the way they used to. When he looked at Wes, he could no longer read the man's mind.

How much of that was his own fault, his own sense of guilt? He didn't know.

"Life goes on, huh?" Colleen said. "Despite all the disappointments and tragedies. There's always good news happening somewhere." She gestured to the bus, to the four other Relief Aid volunteers who sat quietly talking in the back of the bus. "This is good news— the fact that we're going to bring those children back to a safer location. And, oh, here's some good news for you—I'm not pregnant. I got my period this morning. So you can stop worrying about Wes coming after you with a shotgun, huh?"

She wasn't pregnant.

Colleen tried to smile, but just managed to look… almost wistful? "You know, it's stupid, but I imagined if I was, you know, pregnant, the baby would be a boy who would look just like you."

She was kidding, wasn't she? Bobby tried to make a joke. "Poor kid."

"Lucky kid." She *wasn't* kidding. The look she was giving him was fierce. "You're the most beautiful man I've ever known, Bobby. Both inside and out."

He didn't know what to say. He didn't know what to think.

And Colleen went back to looking out the window. "Funny, isn't it, how one person's good news can be someone else's disappointment?"

"You're disappointed? About..." He had to search for the words. "You wanted to have a baby? But, Colleen, you said—"

"Not just any baby." When she looked at him, the tears were back in her eyes. "I wanted Analena. And I wanted *your* baby. I'd make a terrible mother, wouldn't I? I'm already playing favorites."

"Colleen. I'm..." Speechless.

"I had this stupid fantasy going," she said in a very small voice, almost as if she were talking to herself, not to him, "that I'd be pregnant, and you'd have to marry me. And then, after we were married, I'd somehow make you love me, too. But real life doesn't work that way. People who have to get married usually end up resenting each other, and I'd hate it if you ever resented me."

Make you. Love me. Too. Bobby wasn't sure, but he thought it was possible he was having a heart attack. His chest was tight and his brain felt numb. "Colleen, are you telling me—"

"Heads up, Taylor. We're getting close," Senior Chief Harvard Becker's voice cut through. "I need your eyes and ears with me right now."

Damn.

Colleen had turned her attention back to the drab scenery flashing past, outside the window.

Bobby stood up, shouldering his weapon, using every ounce of training he'd ever had to get his head back in place, to focus on the mission.

Rio Rosetti was nearby, and he caught Bobby's eye. "You okay, Chief? Your shoulder all right?"

His shoulder? "I'm fine," he said shortly. Dammit, he needed to talk to Wes. Just because Colleen loved him—and she only *maybe* loved him, he didn't know it for sure—didn't mean that gave him the right to go and ruin her life by marrying her. Did it?

"Okay, listen up," Captain Joe Catalanotto said for the benefit of the Relief Aid volunteers, the bus driver and the Tulgerian guard who was leading them down the unmarked roads to the hospital.

All of the SEALs knew precisely how this was going to go down. Swiftly and efficiently.

"We sent a small team in early, to do surveillance," Joe Cat continued. "One of those men will meet us on the road about a mile from the hospital, tell us if there's anything unusual to watch out for. If it's all clear, we'll pull up right outside the hospital doors, but everyone will stay in their seats. Another team will go in to check the place out, join forces with the rest of the surveillance team. Only when they secure entrances and give the all-clear do any of you get off this bus. Is that understood?"

A murmur of voices. "Yes, sir."

"At that point," Joe Cat said even though they'd already gone over it dozens of times, "you'll move from the bus to the building as quickly as possible. Once inside, you will stay close. You do not wander off under any circumstances."

"You all right?"

Bobby turned to see Wes right behind him.

"The bus driver will stay in the vehicle," Joe Cat continued. "The plan is to return to the bus with the children and nuns as quickly—"

"Your head's not here," Wes said quietly. "Come on, Bobby. Now's not the time to screw around."

"I'm in love with your sister."

"Ah, jeez, perfect timing," Wes muttered.

"I think she loves me, too."

"No kidding, genius. You're just figuring that out now?"

"If she'll have me, I'm going to marry her." Damn it, he was as good as any doctor or lawyer out there. He'd figure out a way to make money, to buy her the things she deserved. When she was with him, he could do *any-*thing. "I'm sorry, Wes."

"What are you crazy? You're *sorry*?" Wes stared at him. "You're apologizing for something I'd sell my left nut to have. If it were me in love with your sister, Bobby, you better believe I would have told you to flip off days ago." He shook his head in disgust.

"But you said…"

"Marry her," Wes said. "All right? Just don't do it right this second if you don't flipping mind. We're all a little busy, making sure these tourists stay alive—in case you haven't noticed?"

These tourists—including Colleen.

"I'll forgive you for damn near anything," Wes continued, "but if you get Colleen killed, I swear to God, you're a dead man."

Colleen. Killed.

Wham.

Just like that, Bobby's head was together. He was back and ready—200 percent ready—for this op, for keeping Colleen and the others safe.

"Yeah, that's more like it," Wes said, glancing up at him as he checked his weapon. "You're all here now."

Bobby leaned over to look out the windows, to scan the desolate countryside. "I love you, man. Do you really forgive me?"

"If you hug me," Wes said, "I'll kill you."

There was nothing out the window. Just rocks and dust. "I missed you, Wesley."

"Yeah," Wes said, heading toward the front of the bus. "I'm going to miss you, too."

Something was wrong.

Colleen shifted in her seat, trying to see the men having a discussion at the front of the bus.

They'd stopped, supposedly to pick up one of the SEALs who'd been sent ahead on surveillance.

But instead of picking him up and driving the last mile to the hospital at the outskirts of the small town, they'd all but parked here at the side of the road.

The SEAL had come onto the bus—it looked like the man who was nicknamed Lucky, allegedly from his past exploits with women. Yeah, that perfect nose was unmistakable despite the layers of dust and camouflage greasepaint. He was talking to the captain and the SEAL who, according to Wes, had actually gone to Harvard University—the senior chief who was almost as tall as Bobby. The other men were listening intently.

Susan came forward a few seats to sit behind Colleen. "Do you know what's going on?" she whispered.

Colleen shook her head. Whatever they were saying, their voices were too low. Please, God, don't let there be trouble.

"All right," the captain finally said. "We have a situation at the hospital. For a place that's supposedly staffed by a single doctor and four nuns, we've got twelve men inside, wearing surgical scrubs and long white coats—the better to hide their Uzis.

"We've ID'd them as members of two particularly nasty local terrorist cells. We're actually surprised they haven't blown each other to pieces by now—but apparently their goal of taking out a bus-load of hated Americans is more than enough to overcome their natural distaste for each other."

Colleen flashed hot and then cold. Terrorists. In the hospital with the nuns and the children. "Oh, my God," she breathed.

Behind her, she heard Rene start to cry. Susan moved back to sit with her.

Captain Catalanotto held up his hand. "We're going in there," he told them. "Covertly—that means secretly, without them knowing we're there. Lieutenant O'Donlon's report indicates these are amateur soldiers we're up against. We can take them out quickly. And we will.

"We're leaving Lieutenant Slade and Chiefs Taylor and Skelly here with you on the bus. They are in command, if there's an emergency, you will do as they say. I considered sending the bus back into Tulibek…"

He held up his hand again as there was a murmur of voices. It was amazing, really, how effective that was.

"But I made a command decision. I think you'll be safer right here until we secure the hospital. Once we have possession of that building, the bus will approach, but you will *not* leave the vehicle. We'll be going over the hospital inch by inch, making sure the terrorists didn't leave any booby traps or other nasty surprises. Our priority will be to check the children and get them out of there and onto the bus.

"Are there any questions?"

Susan Fitzgerald, head of Relief Aid, stood up. "Yes, sir. You've just basically told us that you and your men are going to sneak into a building where there are twelve terrorists with twelve machine guns waiting for you. I'm just curious, sir. Does your wife know about the danger you're going to be in this afternoon?"

For a moment there was complete silence on the bus. No one moved, no one breathed.

But then Captain Catalanotto exchanged a look with his executive officer, Lieutenant Commander McCoy. They both wore wedding rings. In fact, many of the men in Alpha Squad were married.

Colleen looked up and found Bobby watching her. As she met his eyes, he smiled very slightly. Ruefully. His mouth moved as he spoke to her silently from across the bus. "This is what we do. This is what it's like."

"Yeah, Dr. Fitzgerald," Captain Catalanotto finally said. "My wife knows. And God bless her for staying with me, anyway."

"I don't care," Colleen mouthed back, but Bobby had already looked away.

Colleen sat on the bus in silence.

Wes and Jim Slade both paced. Bobby stood, across the aisle from her. He was still, but he was on the balls of his feet—as if he were ready to leap into action at the slightest provocation.

Colleen tried not to look at him. God forbid she distract him. Still, he was standing close, as if he wanted to be near her, too.

"How much longer?" Susan Fitzgerald finally asked.

"We don't know, ma'am," Wes answered from the back of the bus. He touched his radio headset. "They'll open a channel we can receive at this distance only after they've got the place secure. Not until then."

"Will we hear gunshots?" one of the men, Kurt Freid-richson, asked.

"No, sir," Wes told him. "Because there'll be no weapons discharged. Alpha Squad will take them down without a struggle. I can guarantee that as much as I can guarantee anything in this world."

"This isn't the time for conversation," Bobby said quietly.

And once again there was silence.

"Jackpot," Wes said, into his radio headset. "Affirmative, sir. We copy that." He made an adjustment to his lip microphone. "We've been given the order to move toward the hospital. The building has been secured with no casualties."

"Oh, thank God," Colleen breathed. It was over. They were all safe—children, nuns, SEALs.

"Let's move it out," Spaceman—Jim Slade—said to the bus driver.

"No!" Wes shouted from the back of the bus. "Bobby!"

Colleen barely looked up, she barely had time to think, let alone react.

But the Tulgerian guard, the man who'd been hired by the bus driver to guide them to the hospital, had pulled a gun out of nowhere. He was sitting three rows up and across the aisle. She was the closest to him.

The closest target.

But Colleen got only a glimpse of the bottomless dark hole of the gun's barrel before Bobby was on top of her, covering her, pushing her down.

The noise was tremendous. A gunshot. Was that really what it sounded like? It was deafening. Terrifying.

A second one, and then a third. But Colleen couldn't see. She could only hear. Screaming. Was that her voice?

Wes, cursing a blue storm. Spaceman. Shouting. For a helo. Man down.

Man down? Oh, God.

"Bobby?"

"Are we clear?" That was Bobby's voice. Colleen could feel it rumbling in his chest.

But then she felt something else. Something wet and warm and...

"We're clear." Wes. "Jeezus!"

"Are you all right?" Bobby pulled back, off her and, thank God, she *was*. But she was covered with blood.

His blood.

"Oh, my God," Colleen said, starting to shake. "Don't die. Don't you dare die on me!"

Bobby had been shot. Right now, right this minute, he was bleeding his life away onto the floor of the bus.

"Of all the *stupid* things you've done," she said, "stepping in front of a loaded gun again—again—has to take the cake."

"I'm okay," he said. He touched her face, forced her to look into his eyes. They were still brown, still calm, still Bobby's eyes. "Breathe," he ordered her. "Stay with me, Colleen. Because I'm okay."

She breathed because he wanted her to breathe, but she couldn't keep her tears from spilling over. "You're bleeding." Maybe he didn't know.

He didn't. He looked down, looked amazed. "Oh, man."

Wes was there, helping him into the seat next to Colleen, already working to try to stop the flow. "God *damn*, you've got a lot of blood. Bobby, I can't get this to stop."

Bobby squeezed Colleen's hand. "You should get out of here." His voice was tight. "Because you know, it didn't hurt at first—probably from adrenaline, but God, oh my God, now it does, and you don't need to be here to see this. I don't want you here, Colleen. Please."

"I love you," she said, "and if you think I'm going anywhere right now—besides with you to a hospital—then you don't know me very well."

"He wants to marry you," Wes told her.

"Oh, wonderful timing," Bobby said, gritting his teeth. "Like this is the most romantic moment of my life."

"Yeah?" Colleen said, trying to help Wes by keeping Bobby still, by holding him tightly. "Well, too bad, because I'm marrying you whether you ask me or not."

"She said that she loved you," Wes countered.

"Don't die," Colleen begged him. She looked at her brother. "Don't you dare let him die!"

"How could I die?" Bobby asked. "I'm surrounded by Skellys. Death couldn't get a word in edgewise."

Wes shouted toward the driver. "Can we move this bus a little faster? I need a hospital corpsman and I need him *now*!"

Chapter 18

Bobby woke up in a U.S. Military hospital.

Someone was sitting beside his bed, holding his hand, and it took him a few fuzzy seconds to focus on...

Wes.

He squeezed his best friend's fingers because his throat was too dry to speak.

"Hey." Wes was on his feet almost immediately. "Welcome back."

He grabbed a cup, aimed the straw for Bobby's mouth. Hadn't they just done this a few months ago?

"The news is good," Wes told him. "You're going to be okay. No permanent damage."

"Colleen?" Bobby managed to say.

"She's here." Wes gave him another sip of water. "She went to get some coffee. Do you remember getting moved out of ICU?"

Bobby shook his head. He remembered…

Colleen. Tears in her beautiful eyes. *I love you…*

Had she really said that? Please, God, let it be true.

"You had us scared for a while there, but when they moved you into this room, you surfaced for a while. I was pretty sure you were zoned out on painkillers, but Colleen got a lot of mileage out of hearing your voice. She slept after that—first time in more than seventy-two hours. She really loves you, man."

Bobby looked into his best friend's eyes. He didn't say anything. He didn't have to. Wes always did enough talking for both of them.

"And you know, I love you, too," Wes told him. "And you know how I mean that, so no making any stupid jokes. I'm glad Colleen's not here right now, because I need to tell you that I know I was wrong. She doesn't need a doctor or a lawyer. That's garbage. She doesn't need an officer. She doesn't need money. Of all the women in the world, Colleen doesn't give a damn about money.

"What she needs, bro, is a man who loves her more than life itself. She needs you."

I love her. Bobby didn't have to say the words aloud. He knew Wes knew.

"The really stupid thing is," Wes continued, "that I probably knew that right from the start. You and Colleen. I mean, she was made for you, man. And you're going to make her really happy. She's been crazy about you forever.

"See, my big problem is that I'm scared," Wes admitted. "When I found out that you and she had——" He shook his head. "I knew right at that moment that you were going to marry her, and that things would never be the same. Because you'd be one of the guys who'd found what they were looking for, and I'd still be here, on the outside. Searching.

"You know, on that training op that you missed because of your shoulder, because you were in Cambridge—it was just me and a bunch of mostly married men. After the op, we had a night to kill before our flight back, and everyone went to bed early. Even Spaceman—he had to ice his knees, he's really hurting these days. Thomas King—he's worse than some of the married guys. He just goes and locks himself in his room. And Mike Lee's got a girl somewhere. So that leaves Rio Rosetti. Can you picture me and Rosetti, out on the town?"

Actually, Bobby could.

"Yeah, well, believe me, it sucked. He went home with some sweet young tourist that he should've stayed far away from, and I'm thinking about how that's me ten years ago, and how I'm looking for something different now. Something *you* managed to find.

"Scared and jealous—it's not a good combination. I hope someday you'll forgive me for the things I said."

"You know I already do," Bobby whispered.

"So marry her," Wes said. "If you don't, I'll beat you senseless."

"Oh, this is just perfect." Colleen. "Threatening to beat up the man who just saved your sister's life." She swept into the room, and everything was heightened. It was suddenly brighter, suddenly sharper, clearer. She smelled great. She looked gorgeous.

"I'm just telling him to marry you," Wes said.

Bobby used every ounce of available energy to lift his hand and point to Wes and then to the door. "Privacy," he whispered.

"Attaboy," Wes said, as he went out the door.

Colleen sat beside him. Took his hand. Her fingers were cool and strong.

"Colleen—"

"Shhh. We have plenty of time. You don't need to—"

It was such an effort to speak. "I want...now..."

"Bobby Taylor, will you marry me?" she asked. "Will you help me find a law school near San Diego, so I can transfer and be with you for the rest of my life?"

Bobby smiled. It was much easier to let a Skelly do the talking. "Yes."

"I love you," she said. "And I know you love me."

"Yes."

She kissed him, her mouth so sweet and cool against his.

"When you're feeling better, do you want to..." She leaned forward and whispered into his ear.

Absolutely. Every day, for the rest of their lives. "Yes," Bobby whispered, knowing from her beautiful smile that she knew damn well what he was thinking, glad that Wes wasn't the only Skelly who could read his mind.

Epilogue

"What time does the movie start?" Bobby asked as he cleared the Chinese food containers off the kitchen table.

"Seven thirty-five. We have to leave in ten minutes." Colleen was going through the mail, opening today's responses to the wedding invitations. She looked tired—she'd been getting up early to meet with the administrators of a local San Diego women's shelter who were in the process of buying a big old house. She was handling tomorrow morning's closing—pro bono, of course.

"Are you sure you want to go?" he asked.

She looked up. Smiled. "Yes. Absolutely. You've wanted to see this movie for weeks. If we don't go tonight…"

"We'll go another night," he told her. They were getting married. They had a lifetime to see movies together. The thought still made him a little dizzy. She loved him...

"No," she said. "I definitely want to go tonight."

Aside from her legal work, there were a million things to do, what with finding a new apartment big enough for the two of them and all the wedding plans.

They were getting married in four weeks, in Colleen's mother's hometown in Oklahoma. It was where the Skellys had settled after her dad had retired from the Navy. Colleen had only lived there her last few years of high school, but her grandparents and a whole pack of cousins were there. Besides, softhearted Colleen knew how important it was to her mother to see her daughter married in the same church in which she'd taken her own wedding vows.

But it made planning this wedding a real juggling act.

And no way was Bobby willingly going to let Colleen head back to Oklahoma for the next four weeks. No, he'd gotten real used to having her around, real fast. They were just going to have to get good at juggling.

She frowned down at the reply card she'd just opened. "Spaceman's not coming to the wedding?"

"No, he told me he's going in for surgery on his knees."

"Oh, rats!"

Bobby tried to sound casual. "Is it really that big a deal?"

Colleen looked up at him. "Are you jealous?"

"No."

"You are." She laughed as she stood up and came toward him. "What, do you think I want him there so I can change my mind at the last minute and marry him instead of you?" She wrapped her arms around his neck as she twinkled her eyes at him.

Something tightened in his chest and he pulled her more tightly to him. "Just try it."

"I was going to try to set him up with Ashley."

Ashley? And Jim Slade? Bobby didn't laugh. At least not aloud.

"Ashley DeWitt," Colleen said. "My roommate from Boston?"

"I know who she is. And… I don't think so, Colleen." He tried to be tactful. "She's not exactly his type. You know, icy blonde?"

"Ash is very warm."

"Yeah, well…"

She narrowed her eyes at him. "Her warmth has nothing to do with it. What you really mean is that she's too skinny. She's not stacked enough for Spaceman, is that what you're trying to say?"

"Yes. Don't you hate him now? Thank God he's not coming to the wedding."

She laughed and his chest got even tighter. He wanted to kiss her, but that would mean that he'd have to stop looking at her, and he loved looking at her.

"Didn't he have that friend who started that camp— you know, mock SEAL training for corporate executives?" she asked. "Kind of an Outward Bound program for business geeks? Someone—Rio, I think—was telling me about it."

"Yeah," Bobby said, settling on sliding his hand up beneath the edge of her T-shirt and running his fingers across the smooth skin of her back. "Randy Something—former SEAL from Team Two. Down in

Florida. He's doing really well—he's constantly understaffed."

"Ashley wants to do something like that," Colleen told him. "Can you find out Randy's phone number so I can give it to her?"

Ashley DeWitt, in her designer suits, would last about ten minutes in the kind of program Randy ran. But Bobby kept his mouth shut because, who knows? Maybe he was wrong. Maybe she'd kick butt.

"Sure," he said. "I'll call Spaceman first thing tomorrow."

Colleen touched his face. "Thank you," she said. And he knew she wasn't talking about his promise to call Spaceman. She'd read his mind, and was thanking him for not discounting Ashley. "I love you so much."

And that feeling in his chest got tighter than ever.

"I love you, too," he told her. He'd started telling her that whenever he got this feeling. Not that it necessarily made his chest any less tight, but it made her eyes soften, made her smile, made her kiss him.

She kissed him now, and he closed his eyes as he kissed her back, losing himself in her sweetness, pulling her closer, igniting the fire he knew he'd feel for her until the end of time.

"We'll be late for the movie," she whispered, but then whooped as he swung her up into his arms and carried her down the hall to the bedroom.

"What movie?" Bobby asked, and kicked the bedroom door closed.

* * * * *

USA TODAY bestselling author **Barb Han** lives in north Texas with her very own hero-worthy husband, three beautiful children, a spunky golden retriever/standard poodle mix and too many books in her to-read pile. In her downtime, she plays video games and spends much of her time on or around a basketball court. She loves interacting with readers and is grateful for their support. You can reach her at barbhan.com.

Books by Barb Han

Harlequin Intrigue

An O'Connor Family Mystery

Texas Kidnapping
Texas Target

Rushing Creek Crime Spree

What She Did
What She Knew
What She Saw

Crisis: Cattle Barge

Kidnapped at Christmas
Murder and Mistletoe
Bulletproof Christmas

Cattlemen Crime Club

One Tough Texan
Texas-Sized Trouble
Texas Witness
Texas Showdown

Visit the Author Profile page at Harlequin.com for more titles.

GUT INSTINCT

Barb Han

My deepest thanks to my editor, Allison Lyons, for challenging me and making me a better writer. To my agent, Jill Marsal, for her brilliant guidance and unfailing support. To Brandon, Jacob and Tori, for encouraging me to work hard and inspiring me to dream. To my husband, John, for walking this journey side by side with me—I love you. And a special thank-you to readers, and especially my girlfriend's mom, Linda Tumino, for being so very passionate about books.

Chapter 1

Luke Campbell bit back a groan. Why did Julie Campbell—correction, Julie *Davis*—have to interrupt a killer in the middle of one of his "projects"?

His ex-wife's landscaping business had brought her to the doorstep of one of the most devious serial murderers in Luke's career. A knot tightened in his gut as he pulled in front of her small redbrick town house in a North Dallas suburb, the one they'd shared, and parked his truck.

An emotion he refused to acknowledge kept him from opening the door and stepping into the frigid night. How many times had he wished he still lived in that house after he'd come home from active duty a wreck? How many times had he prayed he could go back and change the past since then? How many times had he missed the feel of her long silky legs wrapped around him, welcoming him home? *Too many.*

Hell, he wasn't there for a reunion. She was in jeopardy, and his job was to protect society from national-security threats and major criminals. Keeping her safe was the least he could do after the way he'd hurt her.

He stepped into the crisp evening air.

A young detective with a thick build and sun-worn face approached. "Evening, Special Agent Campbell. Not sure if you remember me, but I worked the Martin crime scene earlier."

"Detective Wells. Thank you. I appreciate the call." Luke shook the outstretched hand in front of him.

"I wouldn't normally bother you with something like this. My boss thought you'd be interested."

The young guy reported to Detective Garcia. Garcia's judgment was dead-on. "What do you have?"

He waved another detective over. "This is Detective Reyes."

Luke shook hands with the detective.

"Show him what was taped to Ms. Davis's window earlier," Detective Wells said.

The officer used tongs to hold out a standard-size piece of white paper. The words *I hope you enjoy your dance with the Devil. Be in touch soon, Rob* were handwritten.

"Whoever wrote this has good penmanship." Luke noticed. He took note of the capitalization of the word *Devil*. The tension between his shoulder blades balled and tightened as he reread the name. His killer, Ravishing Rob, never left a clue as to whom he would target next. If this was him, why would he change his M.O.?

One reason came to mind. Anger. Rob was meticulous. Julie had interrupted his ritual killing, which he'd described as more of a turn-on than sex. That might be enough to trigger a variation.

Luke couldn't ignore another possibility. This could be a copycat. Julie's picture had been splashed all over the news and internet.

Then again, Julie had black hair just like all Rob's targets.

He examined the neat print. Cursive would give more clues to Rob's personality. With his high IQ he was smart enough to know that, too, which made the capitalization of *Devil* even more poignant. "Whoever wrote this took his time."

Luke pulled an evidence bag from his glove box and pointed at the note. "I'll send this up for analysis."

The detectives nodded.

"Can you spare one of your uniformed men for the night? I'd like someone to keep watch on the alley behind her house."

"Sure thing," Detective Wells said. "I made some notes after interviewing Ms. Davis. Do you want to take a look?"

"Absolutely." Luke studied the page. He focused on the word *boyfriend*. The knot tightened in his gut. The thought of another man's arms wrapped around Julie ignited his possessive instincts. He still wanted her, needed her. Those selfish emotions had caused him to stay at the town house to be near her when he'd returned from Iraq a broken man. The front-row seat he'd had to her pain—the hell he'd caused—when he pushed her away day after day had forced him to man up and leave before he permanently damaged her. Intelligent and beautiful, she deserved so much more than him. He glanced up at the detectives who were waiting for his response to the report. Not wanting to give away his bone-deep reaction to her, he skimmed the rest and handed it back. "Good information. Send my office a copy of the report when it's filed."

Detective Wells gave a satisfied smile. "I'll keep a man outside tonight. Let me know if you need anything else."

"Will do." Luke turned and walked toward the house. A thought stopped him at the base of the stairs. What if she wasn't alone?

The detective's notes said she'd been dating a dentist on and off. Was he here?

Davis had been her maiden name, which meant she was still single. Even so, she might be *on* with the dentist again. After the day she'd had, he might be there with her in Luke's house. *Old house,* he corrected, ignoring the all-too-real tug of emotion at seeing the place again.

Taking the couple of steps to her porch in quick strides, he clenched his fists.

The thought of Ravishing Rob targeting Julie didn't do good things to Luke's head. He knocked on the door and his chest squeezed as he thought about seeing her again.

The solid hunk of wood swung open, and suddenly, there she was, his ideal combination of beauty and grace, staring at him with a shocked look on her face. He could see those long legs where her bathrobe split, her taut hips where the robe cinched. A hunger roared from deep within him. The reality of why he was there chased it away.

Her amber eyes stood out against pale skin. Even red-rimmed and puffy, their russet-coppery tint was every bit as beautiful as it had been the last time he'd seen her. Her shoulder-length hair was still inky black. His fingers itched to get lost in that curly abyss again. Muscle memory, he decided. Besides, the frown on her face and stress in her eyes said he was the last person she wanted to see.

Under the circumstances, he was her best bet.

She opened her mouth to speak, but her ringtone sounded. "Dammit. Hang on."

Bad sign. She only cursed when she was hanging on by a thread.

"May I?" He motioned for permission to enter.

Her gaze narrowed, but then she nodded and turned her back to him. She spoke directly into the phone. "I'm okay. No. I promise. You don't need to come over right now. I'll see you when you get off work."

Was she talking to her boyfriend? The last word stuck. Tasted bitter as hell, too.

One step inside and he almost lost his footing. A wave of nostalgia slammed into him. The furniture was in exactly the same spot as when he'd left. The coffee-colored leather sofa against the wall to his right. The flat-screen directly across from it mounted on the wall to his left. He could see all the way to the back door from where he stood. Same black pedestal dining table with avocado-green chairs tucked around it. The place looked completely untouched, except all the pictures of the two of them had been removed. She'd probably enjoyed stomping on the frames.

The town house might've looked the same, but it had a different air. Funny how out of place he felt in what used to be his own home.

He folded his arms, parted his feet in an athletic stance and stood next to the door. He wasn't there for a reunion. This was business. And no matter how much Julie looked as if she'd rather crawl out of her skin than be in the same room with him, he had a job to do.

She closed the call and whirled around on him, still wearing her angry expression. There was something else in her eyes there, too. Hurt? "Why did they send *you?*"

"I've been tracking this guy for the past two years. He's my case." He intentionally withheld the part about Ravishing Rob being the most ruthless killer Luke had come across so far in his FBI career.

Her eyes narrowed to such slits he couldn't figure out if she could see him anymore. Then again, she probably wanted to block him out altogether, and he couldn't blame her. She'd pleaded with him to stay, but he couldn't stand watching her pain when he had no way to heal either one of them.

With all the daggers shooting from her eyes, he couldn't tell if she was using anger to mask other emotions. Hurt? Fear? Regret?

"There's no one else they could've sent?" The hollow sound in her voice practically echoed.

"I'm afraid not."

"So the note's from him? You're sure?"

"I need to get a little more information from you to help me decide." Even though she'd already given her account to police and he'd read the jacket, he needed to hear her words. He needed to know what she thought she saw. Maybe she'd remember something that could help put this monster away or help Luke figure out if it was a copycat. "Tell me what happened when you arrived at the scene of the murder this morning."

She shivered, looked lost and alone. "My client Annie Martin wanted to meet with me to discuss landscaping after her new pool was installed. I brought a rendering with me and planned to give my presentation. It was a big project that would start in the spring, so I broke all the planting down into zones." She glanced up at him curiously as if she realized he didn't know the first thing about plants or landscaping, or care. "Sorry, I'm babbling. I'm sure you didn't come here to talk about the details of my business."

"I did," he said quickly. He covered a crime scene the same way, broke it down on a grid. "I want to hear everything even if you don't think it's important. You never know what might spark a memory. Something you didn't think of before when you talked to the police." His hopes she'd be more comfortable talking to him had diminished the second he saw her. He wanted to ask her how she was doing, but decided not to, even though he found he still really wanted to know, needed to know. He'd left things broken between them, and thoughts of the sadness in her eyes every time she'd looked at him still haunted him. Outside of this case, he had no right to know anything about her. Why was he already reminding himself of the fact?

"As soon as I pulled up to her house, I heard a noise. Like a muffled cry or something. I couldn't make it out for sure. She'd asked me to come around back in case she was with contractors for the pool, so I ran to make sure she was okay. I thought maybe she tripped or was hurt. But there was no one out there. She screamed again and I ran to the front door. Someone bolted from around the side of the house about the same time. He killed her, didn't he?"

He locked gazes with her and wished like anything he could protect her from the truth. He felt pained that she'd had to witness this and his heart went out to her. "Yes. You get a good look at him?"

"No." She hugged her arms to her body. "I didn't see anything. By then I heard an awful sound coming from inside. Sounded like an animal dying." She shivered.

He pulled out a pad and scribbled notes. Not that he needed a piece of paper to remember the details of their conversation. His memory was sharper than a switchblade. He needed something to look at besides her fearful eyes. Old instinct kicked in and he wanted to maim the person who'd made her feel that way, offer comfort she would certainly reject. "What happened next?"

"You want to sit down?" She moved to the couch and sat on the edge. She clasped her hands together and rocked back and forth. "It was bad, Luke."

The sound of his name rolling off her tongue was a bitter reminder of the comfort and connection he hadn't felt in a long time. He took a seat next to her but not too close.

Tears spilled down her cheeks. "I don't want to think about it again, let alone say the words out loud."

"I know how hard this is." Every muscle in his body tightened from wanting to reach out and comfort her. He didn't want to press further, but the information he gained could mean saving her life. "It's important you tell me everything. Do you want a cup of tea or something?" He made a move to stand.

"No. I'm fine." The uncertainty in her words made him freeze.

"Anything else you can give me might save another woman from going through this."

"We both know he's going to come after me next." Her voice shook with terror.

"I'm not certain it's him yet. Besides, I'll catch him first."

The suggestion of depending on him for anything after the way he'd hurt her set her eyes to infernos. "I didn't ask you to come."

"This is my territory. My guy. I know him better than anyone else."

"I didn't even know you were FBI." The exasperation in her voice made him clench his fists involuntarily.

"I didn't think it was appropriate to send you Christmas cards after your lawyer sent me papers." It was a low blow and he regretted saying the words as soon as they passed his lips. After all, he'd been the one to leave and force the divorce issue.

She looked straight through him. "I lost track of you after..."

This wasn't the time to talk about their past. It complicated the situation. He was professional enough to look beyond shared history and concentrate on doing his job. He focused his gaze on the opened laptop on the coffee table. There was a picture of Julie at the crime scene beneath the banner Breaking News. Damn. Another reminder that she'd been placed right there for the killer or any other lunatic to see.

The last time the local newspaper printed a story with the headline The Metroplex Murderer Strikes Again, Rob went off. He'd left a message on Luke's cell complaining about how common that made him seem. Luke still hadn't figured out how the man got his number. The man calling himself Ravishing Rob—someone who captivated and then decapitated—had done his research. Efforts to trace the call were futile. He'd used a burn phone. Rob was thorough. He also knew how to play the media.

Reporters had their uses. In this case, they might've issued Julie a death warrant. "You said earlier you didn't get a good look at him. Any idea as to general information like height? Build? Race?"

She shook her head. "I was so horrified. The whole thing shocked me. One minute I was planning to meet a client, like usual, and then I thought the worst-case scenario was that I'd walked into a robbery in progress. The next thing I know, I'm staring at a person whose throat had been slit. I'll never forget her eyes, pleading." She shivered again and tears streamed down her cheeks.

Luke had to grip the pencil tighter to stop himself from wiping them away. He didn't like seeing her cry. He'd seen those tears enough for a lifetime. If it didn't mean saving her life, he'd stop questioning. "When did you find the note?"

"This evening. I'd just gotten home from spending the day at the police station answering questions."

"What time?" he pressed. She might not have gotten a good look at Rob. Rob didn't know that. The reason he'd given himself the nickname Ravishing Rob churned in Luke's thoughts as he sat next to her. Rob had said he charmed his way into his victims' homes or cars before taking them hostage, torturing them and then beheading them with surgical precision. The bastard would never get the chance with Julie, no matter how much swagger he thought he had.

"I'm not sure. All I wanted to do when I first got home was take a shower and get out of those clothes I'd been wearing. I ate dinner alone, a bowl of soup. I decided to slip out and check the mail…and that's when I saw it."

He already knew she'd showered. The smell of her pineapple-and-coconut shampoo filled his senses when he breathed. That she'd eaten alone soothed a part of him it shouldn't. He scooted back and scribbled approximate times on his notepad. "Did you see any cars?"

She shrugged noncommittally, leaning into him for support. The vulnerability in her amber eyes ripped right through him. Damned if the past didn't come flooding back all at once, reminding him of old times they'd shared and the feelings he missed.

He had to remind himself their history wasn't the reason she was leaning on him now. She was scared.

"I'm not sure. You know how this street is. There's always someone parked out there. I didn't pay attention." She tapped her hand on her knee.

"I need you to think."

"I said I didn't know," she barked in the way she did when her nerves got the best of her.

Everything about her body language said she'd just frozen up on him. Fear could paralyze victims. Once the shock wore off, she'd forget. As it was, he had very little to go on. Anything she could give him might paint a more detailed picture, save her life. The profiler had said Rob probably kept something from each of his victims and liked to hunt. A saw was his favorite weapon, but he used guns when necessary to kill them before cutting their throats. He was also a perfectionist. Rob was most likely educated, a collector, and he had weapons. "Dammit, Julie. This is important."

"Don't you have anything from the scene you can use to figure out who it is? Hair sample? DNA?"

"Doubt it. The house is being combed, but I'm not expecting the crew to find anything. This guy's careful, meticulous. Even though you interrupted him, he had the presence of mind to ensure he didn't leave a witness." He didn't tell her the guy normally cut off the heads of his "projects," as he called them. Or about the half-open carton of orange juice they'd found sitting on the counter. Since Rob wasn't able to bleach his victim this time, maybe he'd left behind a print. Doubtful, but Luke hadn't given up hope completely. "A rookie was first on the scene. That doesn't help. I just came from there. If there was evidence, which I doubt, it's most likely gone." He stabbed his fingers through his hair. "Can you think of anything else? Anything different. Doesn't have to be about what you saw. Could be anything about the visit."

Julie's gaze widened. "I was supposed to meet with her on Thursday. She changed our appointment last minute."

"Did you mention that to the police?"

"No. I didn't think about it until just now."

Bingo. New information. "Did she say why she moved the appointment?"

"No. She sent me a text asking if I could come a day early. Said something came up last minute and she needed to leave town right away."

"How long did you have the original appointment on your calendar?" This guy watched his "projects" carefully. Hacked into their computers. Studied their movements. He knew them as intimately as he could without ever having met them face-to-face. At least in this case, he wasn't monitoring her phone.

"Weeks."

Must've been the change in schedule. Damn, if Julie had just kept the original appointment she'd be in the clear. This guy didn't like an audience. He was most likely planning a way to finish his interrupted work…on

Julie. Then again, any crazy with internet access could be targeting her right now. Luke glanced around. "How safe's the neighborhood?"

"I had an alarm installed after you left…"

He'd noticed the keypad earlier. "I think it's best if you stay with a friend for a while."

"I've already thought about that. I have someone coming over later to stay the night."

"Who?" He told himself the only reason he'd asked was to make sure it was someone who would have her back if the killer decided to strike. Not that Luke planned on being far away.

"A friend."

He said a quick prayer it was a female. The thought of another man sleeping in his bed shot a lightning bolt of anger down his spine. "Does this *friend* have a name?"

"Alice."

Relief he had no right to own washed over him. Alice hated him. But she was a helluva lot better than Herb, the dentist. "What time is she coming over?"

"She works until…" Julie checked her watch. Her hand shook. "Actually, she should be getting off soon. I'll give her a call."

Before he could debate his actions, he covered her hand with his. A current he refused to acknowledge pulsed up his arm. He didn't want to offer to stay in a place that brought back so many painful memories. He couldn't count how many times they'd made love on this very couch before he shipped off. Or how cold the leather was against his skin when he slept there every night after his return. "I doubt anything will happen tonight. He'll want time to regroup. I'll be right out front as precaution."

"All night?"

"Yes. I have an officer stationed out back, too." Luke was almost certain she wanted to poke his eyes out for ever having to look at him again. She still looked damn sexy. Her robe opened just enough for him to see she wore his old AC/DC T-shirt to bed. And since every muscle in his body screamed to reach out and touch her, he figured he'd better put a brick wall between them for safety's sake.

"With this cold front it'll be twenty degrees after the sun goes down. I can't let you do that. You'll freeze to death."

"I'll keep the heat on in my truck."

"It just seems silly for you to be out there when you could set up right here."

She must be awfully scared to make that offer. "I'm pretty certain I'm the last person you want to see. Let alone have sleeping under the same roof."

She folded her arms. He could've sworn he saw a flash of regret or sadness darken her features. "True."

He made a move to stand. Her hand on his arm stopped him. An electric volt shot through him, warming places it shouldn't.

"I thought if I ever saw you again, it would be for different reasons." Her lip quivered, but she compressed her mouth. Damn, it was still sexy when she was being stubborn.

"Yeah. Me, too. For the record, I don't like this any more than you do." Scratch that. He liked this situation boatloads less than anyone possibly could, even her. He'd be lying if he didn't admit to fantasizing about meeting up with her again once he got his head screwed on straight. This scenario had never once entered his imagination.

"Luke."

"Yeah."

"You look…better. I hope you don't mind me saying so."

He smiled and meant it. For some reason those words mattered to him.

"And you seem different now," she said. A melancholy note laced her tone.

The anger was gone from her voice completely now, but the sadness was far worse. Anger he could handle, fight head-to-head. He understood anger. Her sounding broken was a sucker punch to his solar plexus.

Her world had been turned upside down. She was reaching for comfort. He was still the same man she'd wanted to gut a few minutes ago. "Everyone changes a little, right?"

"Nope. Not everyone."

Was she referring to herself or Herb?

Reminders that he had no right to care didn't hold weight. He stood and walked to the door. "I'll check in with the officer stationed out back before I take my post."

Chapter 2

The last person Julie wanted to see after the hell she'd been through today was her ex-husband. How long had it been? Three years? Four?

Worse yet, the deep timbre in his voice still caused her nerves to fizz and her body to hum. The effect he'd had—correction, *still* had—on her was infuriating and not to mention completely out of place under the circumstances.

His expertly defined muscles on a six-foot-one-inch frame made for an imposing presence. Those golden eyes, light brown curly hair, dimpled chin and cheeks brought back memories of lying in bed long after she woke just so she could watch him sleep. Her body reacted to that.

Besides, *that* was a lifetime ago.

Her cell vibrated. She read the incoming text. Alice was on her way. *Good.*

Julie heated water in the microwave and made a cup of chamomile tea to calm herself and give her something to do besides think about her ex. Hadn't she spent enough time trying to get over him? And she was almost certain she had.

Almost.

She threw on a pair of yoga pants and curled up on the couch with the steaming brew. She was less than thrilled her ex had shown up. Even so, she wasn't stupid. He was FBI. She'd do whatever he said to stay alive.

There was some relief that he looked better than when he'd come back from Iraq. Then he'd been a shell of the once-charismatic, -vibrant and -sexy-as-hell man he'd been.

She still remembered the day she'd learned his tour was finished and he'd be coming home. She'd sat on this very couch, where they'd made love more times than she could count, and cried tears of joy.

Nothing had prepared her for the day Luke walked through that door.

She hugged the pillow into her stomach and took a sip of her hot tea.

The cool, courageous and fearless man she'd once stayed up all night talking to was gone. He looked as if he hadn't eaten or shaved or slept in weeks. His eyes were deep set. He'd been dehydrated, starved or both. He barely spoke when he walked through the door and then folded onto the couch.

His vacant expression had startled her the most.

He'd refused to talk. The only thing she knew for sure was something very bad had happened overseas. Her determination to be there for him solidified even though he gave her zero reasons to hang on. Julie Campbell didn't quit. Her father had sown those seeds years before and the crop was fully grown.

Even though Luke had shut her out completely, she was convinced she'd break through and find the real him again. The days had been long and fruitless. Then there were the nightmares. He'd wake drenched with sweat but refusing to talk about it. The slightest noise sent him to a bad place mentally—a prison, one he wouldn't allow her access to.

She held on to their relationship, to the past, as long as she could before there was nothing left between them but sadness and distance. Then he left.

Seeing him now, he looked different but stronger.

She sank deeper into the couch.

Living on his own must agree with him.

She heard a noise from out back and fear skittered across her nerves. She told herself to calm down. There was a police officer stationed out there and Luke covered the front. No one could hurt her. She was safe. Luke wouldn't allow anything to happen to her.

Even so, a warning bell sounded inside her. She turned out the light in the living room, slipped next to the curtain and peeked out the window. Luke's truck sat out front. Empty. He should be at his post by now. Where was he?

A knock at the back door caused her to jump.

Adrenaline had her running toward the kitchen, needing to know if Luke was there.

The tapping on the door increased and intensified, causing her heart to lurch into her throat.

She forced her rubbery legs to carry her the rest of the way into the kitchen.

"Julie" broke through the pounding noise. Luke's voice gave her strength to power forward.

She cracked the door.

He forced it all the way open and pushed his way inside. His weapon was drawn as he leaned his shoulder against the door for support. His dark eyes touched hers. "Thank God you're safe."

"What happened, Luke? What's wrong?"

"He's here." He tucked her behind him.

A scuffle sounded from the alley. Luke opened the door and bolted toward it.

Julie fought to keep pace, pushing her legs until her lungs burned.

They stopped at the sight of an officer's body lying twisted on the concrete, his radio the only noise breaking through the chilly air.

"Stay right behind me," Luke instructed as he scanned the alley for a threat, his weapon leading the way. "And watch for any movement around us."

She looked everywhere but at the officer, who she feared was too quiet to still be alive. She said a silent prayer for him.

When Luke had checked behind garbage cans and gaps in fences, he moved to the injured man. He dropped to the ground, bent over the officer and administered CPR as Julie kept a vigilant watch.

Luke leaned back on his heels after several intervals of compressions. He looked at her again and his horrified expression almost took her breath away.

"What else can we do? We can't leave him."

"There's nothing we can do now. I tried to revive him. He's gone." The sadness in his voice was palpable as he called it in. He glanced at the officer's empty holster and looked around. "His gun is missing."

A sob broke through before Julie could suppress it.

"We have to go," he said, then twined their fingers.

She noticed blood on his shirt and arms. She stuck close behind him as they bolted back through her house and toward the front door, his gun drawn.

"Alice is on her way," she said.

"We'll call her from my truck and tell her to turn around. I already notified local police. We can't stay here."

By the time they got to the front door, the silhouette of a man appeared against the front window.

Luke's grip tightened on her fingers, and he leveled his weapon at the man's chest.

Julie didn't realize she was holding her breath until the squawk of a police radio on the other side of the door broke the silence.

Luke tucked her behind him, placing his body between her and the officer, and opened the door. He pointed to the badge clipped on his belt. "I'm Special Agent Campbell, and I called for backup. Where'd you come from? I didn't hear your sirens."

"I received a call of an officer down and was told to proceed with caution until others arrived at the scene. I was nearby."

"He's in the alley," Luke said.

The officer thanked Luke, hopped off the porch and disappeared.

Several squad cars roared up the narrow street, descending on the once-quiet neighborhood in a swarm.

Relief washed over Julie. She glanced up in time to see Alice running toward them, looking panicked.

Julie let go of Luke's hand and embraced her friend on the stairs.

"What in hell is going on?" Alice demanded.

"He was here." Another sob broke through.

Alice's expression dropped in terror. "You don't mean...? How does he know where you live?"

"I don't know. He left a note on my window earlier and now a police officer is dead."

"What note?"

"I was planning to tell you about it when you got here. We weren't sure it was him before." Julie caught her friend giving Luke the once-over.

"That who I think he is?" Disdain parted her lips as her gaze stayed trained on Luke.

Julie nodded.

"What's he doing here?"

"This is his case. He's been tracking this guy for the past two years. He's the expert, so he's in charge." Julie hoped her friend didn't pick up on the change in her voice every time she spoke about her ex.

"Well, he isn't doing a very good job." Alice spoke loud enough for him to hear.

Julie took her friend arm in arm and turned to face the street, walking down the couple of steps to the sidewalk. "You can't know how much I appreciate you for coming. I didn't realize how dangerous this was when I called you earlier. I wasn't thinking straight. You have to go."

"Wait a minute. Are you worried about that killer coming after me, too?"

"I don't know what could happen next. This whole experience is surreal and I don't want to take any chances." Julie wished she could wake up from this nightmare. Except a little piece of her felt a sense of peace at seeing Luke again. She told herself it was only because she had to know he was all right. After the way they'd left things, she couldn't let him go completely.

"I'd feel better if you stayed with me for a few days," Alice said.

"It's safer for both of us if I stay with Luke. I'm sure he'll find this guy, and when he does, I can have my life back."

"How can you stand to be around him after what he put you through?" Alice asked, incredulous.

"It's different. This is work and our past is behind us," Julie lied. One glance in his direction released a thousand butterflies in her stomach. She rationalized the only reason that still happened was because her body remembered the passion between them. Their sex had surpassed earth-shattering, world-exploding-into-a-thousand-flecks-of-light hotness. The physical had never been an issue. She'd even lured him into bed one more time before he left, hoping they could build from there. The sex blazed, but after was all wrong.

They never got closure on their emotional connection, she reasoned. At least she hadn't. He, on the other hand, looked to be doing just fine.

Maybe a part of him regretted the quick marriage?

Whatever had happened overseas could've expedited his realization they were two strangers who had jumped too quickly into a lifetime commitment. Young people were known to be impetuous with their decisions, hearts.

Alice stared intently at Julie for a few seconds that seemed to drag into minutes. Then came "Well, if you're sure."

"I am."

"Don't worry about me. I'm a big girl," Alice reassured her.

"Yeah? Well, this guy won't care what you are," Julie said. The truth cut like a serrated knife. She looked to Luke for comfort, reassurance. For now, she wouldn't stress about the fact that one glance at him stopped the invisible band from tightening around her chest. Or that his touch warmed her in places it shouldn't.

"Tell me you're not staying here tonight," Alice said.

"I'm not."

Luke motioned for her to come back toward him. He hadn't stopped watching her since she'd stepped away, looking uncomfortable the second she left.

"Promise to stay safe," she said to Alice.

The short blonde nodded and gave Julie another hug.

"This will all be over soon and we'll have lunch at Mi Cocina again. Like normal people," she said. She pulled back and saw big tears filling her friend's eyes.

"Are you kidding?" Alice asked. "After this ordeal, we're going out for margaritas. Or maybe I'll skip the mixer and go straight to tequila shots."

Julie glanced up at Luke. He'd finished his conversation with the officers but kept his distance. He looked impatient for her to wrap things up.

"Take care of yourself. I'll be in touch," she said to Alice.

Her friend started down the sidewalk.

Luke was by Julie's side in a heartbeat. He must've noticed her shivering, not from cold but from the shock wearing off, because he put his arm around her shoulders. She fit perfectly, just exactly as she remembered. Body to body, the air thinned and then thrummed. Julie ignored the familiar rush of warmth traveling over her skin and making her legs rubbery.

"Where's your friend parked?" he asked.

Julie scanned the vehicles lining the street. "I don't see her car."

"Call her back."

Last thing Julie wanted was to witness a confrontation. "Why?"

"He's around here somewhere." He skimmed the street.

"Alice!"

Her friend stopped and turned.

Luke had already flagged an officer. "Do me a favor?"

"Sure thing," the cop said.

"See to it the blonde gets into her car, locks the doors, and then wait until she pulls away." He motioned toward Alice.

The officer nodded. "Sure thing."

Luke turned to Julie and said, "You okay with staying over at my place tonight until we find a suitable safe house?"

The thought of being alone with Luke at his place for an entire night sent a very different kind of shiver down her body. She downplayed it as her being cold. Looking him straight in the eyes, she asked, "Do you really think that's best?"

He didn't answer her. He had already started walking her toward the house. "Want to grab an overnight bag?"

She nodded. He escorted her inside, washed the blood off his hands and waited while she threw together a few items to get her through the next couple of days.

"Rob's one step ahead of me, if it's him. I don't want

to let you out of my sight until I'm certain you're protected," he said low, in practically a whisper, as he
walked her toward his truck.

His reasoning made sense. After the way he'd been
looking at her all night, she suspected he also probably
felt some sense of guilt about how he'd left things before.
Maybe he could catch a killer and ease his conscience
at the same time.

Maybe she'd get the closure she so desperately
needed.

Too many nights Luke Campbell had shown up in
her dreams, charming her. If she spent the night with
him, fixed the past, then maybe she'd be able to walk
away clean, too. And possibly be ready to start a life
with Herb. Or someone new. She doubted Herb would
want to see her again after she'd told him she needed
time to think.

Luke helped her into the truck and scanned the street
again before he climbed into the driver's seat.

She glanced back at her once-quiet neighborhood.

People were on their porches or standing at their front
windows watching the circus of lights. Police were urging them to go back inside and lock their doors. Knowing a cold-blooded killer stalked her, and seemed intent
on never letting up, made blood run cold in her veins.

"Wanna scoot a little closer? You're shivering again."

"I'm fine. It's just been a long day."

He turned the heater up. "Shock's wearing off. I'm
sorry this happened. If we saw each other again, I'd
hoped it would be under different circumstances."

If. He'd clearly had no plans to seek her out. Why did
that make her heart sink?

Because Luke was her only failure in life.

"Breathe in and out slowly," Luke said.

She did a few times. It helped calm her fried nerves. "Where'd you learn to do that?"

He shrugged, kept his gaze focused out the front window. "I took the military up on its offer to see a shrink. She was big on breathing."

Luke Campbell went to counseling? If he hadn't told her himself, she never would've believed it. "I'm shocked. You seemed so adamant about not involving doctors or having someone poke around in your head."

"I made a lot of mistakes when I came home from duty." A beat passed. "Some I could fix."

The power of that last sentence hit her like a tsunami. Perhaps he'd worked on the things he thought worth saving. Their marriage clearly didn't fall into that category. Anger burned through her. "When did you start therapy?"

"Not long before you… Doesn't matter. Point being, it helped." His tone was sharp, his words cutting.

"Before I what?" She couldn't let it go.

"Never mind." He flipped on the turn signal and then turned on the radio.

It was just like Luke to get all quiet as soon as they started talking about something personal. Hadn't that been the true failure in their marriage? He didn't trust her enough to open up.

Julie glanced in the side mirror. A white sedan turned a little too quickly at the same time they did. "Has that car been following us?"

Luke's gaze narrowed as he checked the rearview mirror. "I've been keeping an eye on him."

"Good. I thought my paranoia was in high gear after the day I've had."

"Most people wouldn't be able to hold it together as well as you have today. I'm really proud of you." His voice was low and masculine, and it sent unwelcome sensual shivers racing through her.

She rubbed her arms to stave off the goose bumps.

"Hold on tight." He cut a hard right without signaling. The white sedan didn't follow.

"Looks like I was imagining things. Sorry," Julie said, ignoring the electric current pulsing through her at being this near Luke again. Damn body.

"No need to apologize. He landed on my radar, too. Besides, I want you to suspect everyone and everything around you from here on out. I want you to take every precaution until I can put this whole ordeal behind you and restore your previous life."

What life? She almost said it out loud. She hadn't had much of an existence since he'd walked away.

Luke glanced at the rearview mirror again.

"The white sedan just pulled up behind us."

Chapter 3

Luke maneuvered in and out of traffic as he directed Julie to take his cell and call Detective Garcia. If this was Rob, he'd escalated to killing cops to get what he wanted, so murdering FBI wouldn't bother him.

The clue Rob had left earlier with the capitalized word resurfaced in Luke's thoughts. Nouns were capitalized. A noun could be a street name or a town. Luke thought about the word again—*Devil*. Proper nouns were capitalized, too. Could it be his last name?

Bluetooth picked up the call, and Garcia's voice boomed through the speakers. "What can I do for you?"

"I've picked up a tail. If he's not one of yours, I'm going to shake him."

"You should have a white unmarked sedan behind you to make sure you weren't being followed."

Luke glanced at the rearview mirror and caught the

quick flash of headlights. "Appreciate the extra eyes. Let me know if he sees anything, will you?"

"Absolutely. I'll text any information we get. So far, he says everything looks cool. We've been interviewing Ms. Davis's neighbors. No one saw anyone suspicious around her house. Didn't hear anything, either. We'll keep on it. Any information coming in from your guys at the Martin house?"

"No word from the team. The tech guys are working on her computer. Maybe they'll get lucky and we'll get an IP address."

"That would be like Christmas morning."

"Or like seeing the Tooth Fairy," Luke agreed. "You already know about the orange juice, right?"

"He take a drink by any chance?"

"Didn't get that lucky. The container was left out half-open."

"Looks like we might have a diabetic on our hands."

"My thoughts exactly. I sent you a snapshot of the note he left behind at Ms. Davis's place. You get a chance to check it out?"

"He sure seemed to like the word *Devil,* if his capitalizing it is anything to go by. Any possibility it's an honest mistake?"

"He's deliberate. He also thinks he's too smart for us. He's been right so far. I'm hoping his arrogance will be his downfall. Any nearby towns by the name of Devil?"

"Good question. I'll have my officers check. What about a last name? We could play around with the spelling and see what comes up."

"I thought about that, too. We'll have to investigate any and all Devils in the state, plus variations. See if there are any men in their early thirties in the family. Wouldn't hurt to check for street names in Dallas, too."

"Consider it done," Garcia said. "I'll keep you posted."

Luke said goodbye and ended the call. He and Garcia had mentally connected the first time they met. They thought alike and had mutual respect for one another. The detective was a good ally to have.

Luke glanced at Julie. She gripped her elbows. "We'll get a detailed report from the evidence response team soon. The suspect didn't get to follow his usual routine this time, so maybe he left something behind we can tag him with."

"Let's hope."

Luke needed more than optimism to find Rob.

A miracle would work.

Or just a good old-fashioned mistake on Rob's part.

Luke drove into the garage of his town house and parked. "My place isn't big. There's a decent kitchen, and coffee's always stocked."

She half smiled the way she did when she was nervous.

"Right. I forgot you don't drink coffee. Sorry, I don't have any tea."

"I drink coffee now. I only drink tea at night to help me sleep."

He cocked an eyebrow at her, remembering when he'd tried to get her to taste his and she had to hold her nose to get close. "Since when did you start drinking coffee?"

She shrugged. "I missed the smell."

He didn't know what the hell to do with that, so he took off his bloodstained pullover, discarded it and took her on a tour. He walked her through the downstairs, which had a similar layout as her place—shotgun style. "My sisters helped pick out the furniture. It's pretty basic."

"It's nice."

Why did those two words lift the heavy weight bearing down on his shoulders since the day he'd walked out? He decided to ignore it and move on.

"By the way, I thought FBI agents wore dark suits and starched white shirts."

He glanced down at his camo pants and black V-neck T-shirt. "Only the ones on TV. This is pretty standard-issue when we're combing through a crime scene."

"That where you were when they called you?"

He nodded. "I would've been by your place to talk to you tonight anyway."

Upstairs, he brought her to the guest room and stepped aside to let her lead the way. "This is where you'll sleep. I'm right next door if you need anything."

She swallowed hard, and he tried not to notice.

"I'm sure I'll be fine."

The fact that only a thin wall would separate them forced its way into his thoughts. "There's not much more than a bed in here, as you can see, but my family says it's comfortable."

"How are Meg and Lucy?"

"Fine. Meg just had a baby." It pleased him that she remembered his sisters.

Surprise widened Julie's amber eyes. "She's married?"

Being with Julie made the past few years fade away. He realized a lot had happened since they'd last spoken. "She's all grown up now with a family of her own."

"Did she have a boy or girl?"

"A boy."

"Another fine Campbell man," she noted. The pride in her tone caused Luke's chest to swell.

"He's an Evans, but, yeah, he'll always have Campbell blood running through him." He absently rubbed the scruff on his face. "He already acts like one of us. He's taken over their lives."

"Then she married Riley." A melancholy look overtook her otherwise-exhausted expression. "I wish I could've been there. Your sisters were always kind to me. I can't even imagine your gran's reaction to the news. She must be so proud."

"She's beside herself, all right. You know how she is. We had a big barbecue to celebrate the day he came into the world." He smiled, and a little bit of the tension from the day subsided.

"Mind if I ask his name?" She sat on the edge of the bed, folded her hands in her lap and beamed up at him.

"Henry, but we call him Hitch for the way he hitched a ride in all of our hearts." For a second, time warped. There she sat on his guest bed, wearing the AC/DC T-shirt she'd stolen from him. She'd claimed he'd broken it in for her. Conversation was easy, just like old times. He leaned against the doorjamb. Luke forgot how much he missed talking to his wife. *Ex-wife,* a little voice inside his head corrected.

As much as he wanted to stay on memory lane a little longer, he couldn't afford to get sidetracked for so many more reasons than just this case. "I should check in and see what the team has come up with. I'll be downstairs if you need anything."

Her chest deflated. "Okay."

The image of Julie on his bed in his nightshirt stirred

an inappropriate sexual reaction. Luke changed his plan and headed to the shower.

The blasting cool water went straight to his throbbing midsection. He folded his arms above his head and braced himself against the wall, allowing water to cascade down his back. He closed his eyes and concentrated on the case.

A distraction right now was about the worst thing. He needed to keep a clear head and his thoughts off those long silky legs of hers. Of course, his body screamed accomplishing that feat would be easier said than done with her under the same roof.

A serial killer wanted to stop her heart from beating, he reminded himself.

He let the thought sit for a minute, bearing the full weight of the returning rock.

The shower helped him refocus. Luke toweled off and threw on boxer shorts and a T-shirt.

Downstairs, he made a sandwich and then booted up his laptop. Skimming through two hundred–plus emails, he took a bite and chewed.

The first email he opened was from the leader of the evidence response team. Preliminary data didn't give them much to work with, other than the orange juice. They'd combed the place in a grid, as per standard operating procedure. Nothing stood out. Didn't seem to help that he hadn't had time to spread bleach everywhere, and especially on the victim. They'd pulled carpet fibers anyway. They'd taken photographs and diagrammed the scene. If they found anything useful, Luke would be the first to know, the team leader promised.

Luke scanned emails for Garcia's name or anything from tech.

Nothing yet on either count.

His cell phone buzzed. He moved to the table and retrieved it.

There were eight texts. They must've come in while he was in the shower. He scrolled through them and stopped at Garcia.

His message said there were no cities or residents named Devil in the state of Texas. But there were twenty-four people in Texas with the last name Devel.

Luke texted Garcia. Excellent. We can split the list and start from there.

Garcia pinged back immediately. I'll email the names and addresses.

Luke replied. I'll take the bottom half.

He thumbed through the rest of his messages. Most were from his family. There was a new picture of Hitch. A pain hit hard and fast looking at the little boy's round cheeks and toothless smile. For a split second, Luke wondered if his and Julie's baby would look like his nephew.

Shaking off the thought, the ache in his chest, he moved to his laptop.

In the system, he pulled up the email from Garcia and scanned all twelve names. He printed the list. Three were female. He'd pay them a visit anyway in case one had a brother, husband or father sharing the name. He put a question mark by their names.

One Devel was dead. He crossed out that entry. Eight names drew more interesting possibilities. Two weren't far. They lived in Addison and Dallas. The other names came from Austin, San Antonio and Houston. He could drive a circle. It would take only a couple of days max to investigate everyone on his list.

They'd start tomorrow.

Since both of his brothers worked in law enforcement, a U.S. marshal and a Border Patrol agent, Luke sent the list to them, as well, asking for background checks, paying special attention to anyone in the medical field.

The stairs creaked and Julie stepped into the room. "Just wanted a glass of water. Hope that's okay."

"Help yourself." He motioned toward the kitchen. Being around her, especially at night, made him want things he shouldn't. He kept his gaze focused on the monitor, where it belonged.

She poured her drink. "Not sure if I can sleep just yet. Mind if I sit?"

"Not at all," he said, but his brain protested. If she knew how his body went on autopilot sex alert every time she was near, he wondered if she'd run. He also wondered if she still made that sexy little groan when he traced his finger behind the back of her knee.

She took a seat across the dining room table from him. "Find anything interesting?"

He glanced up and his heart squeezed. "Not yet. Garcia sent a list of names. We're going on a road trip tomorrow to investigate a list of people who have a last name spelled *D-e-v-e-l*."

"How'd you get that name?"

"From his note. He capitalized the name Devil. We ran variations and this is the best match."

"Sounds promising."

"Might not be anything." They were playing probabilities. The real reason the letter *d* had been written in uppercase could mean something else entirely. Yeah, a copycat. Or Rob could simply be playing with them, waving that big IQ like a you're-an-idiot flag.

She took a sip of water.

He didn't want to get her hopes up, considering they had little to go on. "We don't know if it'll lead anywhere just yet." He looked into her amber eyes and saw that the color had deepened, the way it did when he brushed his lips across hers. Damn.

What time was it?

He glanced at the clock, needing a reality check.

"It's well after midnight," she said, her voice almost a whisper.

"We need to get on the road early tomorrow. I was hoping we could leave by six."

She gasped. "In the morning?"

He chuckled. She'd never been an early bird. Then again, he wasn't, either, when he'd had the chance to lie in bed with her, hold her, kiss her. He could lose an entire day with her in his arms. Nothing else mattered but the two of them, being together. Hell, they'd missed more than a few meals in favor of staying in bed. The war broke him of needing sleep. Broke him of a lot of other things, too.

Or maybe just broke him.

She drained her glass. "Guess I'll head upstairs."

"You want to take something to read?" he asked, remembering how she'd said it helped after he'd been deployed.

The reference didn't go unnoticed by her, as evidenced by her half smile. "I'll be okay. Thanks, though. I didn't think you remembered any of that stuff."

How could he forget? She was all he had thought about when he was locked into that hole in enemy camp.

His gaze touched hers and electricity fired through him when their eyes met. His growing erection tightened at what else he recalled about her body. "It's no big deal."

Her smiled faded too quickly as she disappeared up the stairs. "Okay."

He silently cursed himself for hurting her.

No. It was important to put some emotional distance between them. He was sliding down that slippery slope of needing her more than air again. And he'd only disappoint her.

This time, he'd be selfless. He wouldn't drag her into his crazy world only to destroy her. No matter what it cost him personally.

An hour slipped by before he looked at the clock again. He'd mapped their route and caught up on a few emails.

Checking on Julie was for work, he told himself as he walked upstairs and stood outside her door.

A muffled scream pumped a shot of adrenaline through him.

He burst into the room. "Julie?"

Chapter 4

Luke shot through the door. "I'm here."

Julie sat bolt upright. Fear seized her lungs as the image of her client's slit throat stamped her thoughts.

Her heart raced, tears streamed, and she immediately did what she knew better than to—reached for Luke.

He was already there at her side, kneeling by the bed.

She folded into his arms, sobbing.

"You're safe. I got you," he soothed. He whispered more comforting words that wrapped around her like a warm blanket.

She pulled back. "I'm sorry. I had a bad dream. I'm fine now."

"You're drenched. Hold on." He hopped up and disappeared around the corner.

Water ran in the hall bathroom.

Returning with a cool wet hand towel, he pressed it

to her forehead as he sat on the edge of the bed. "This should help."

A shiver raced through her when his finger grazed her cheek. Her pulse sped up another notch.

"Better?"

She nodded. When did he get so good at comforting others?

Whenever it was, she was grateful he was there. Dealing with this by herself was unthinkable. Then she reminded herself that Luke was the one who'd walked out.

And yet, her body remembered his touch—the way his finger grazed the back of her knee, sending a sexual current rippling through her. Naturally her body would remember, react to him being this close. Didn't mean she wanted to peel her clothes off and let those strong arms wrap around her naked body.

Did it?

"I'll be okay." She took the hand towel from him and used it to cool the back of her neck. "What time is it?"

He retrieved his cell from the next room. "Two-thirty."

There were dark circles under his eyes. He rubbed the stubble on his chin.

"You haven't slept, have you?"

He shook his head and then stabbed his fingers through his curly hair. "Guess time got away from me. I mapped out our route for in the morning."

Even with his bloodshot eyes and stray locks, he was a beautiful man. He'd laugh at her if she said it out loud, but he was beautiful. "Can you survive on less than four hours of sleep?"

He bit back a yawn and smiled, revealing a peek at his dimples. "Yeah."

What would happen if she tried to rest again? The thought of closing her eyes didn't do good things to her imagination. The nightmare had felt so real. And yet, depending on Luke wasn't a good idea, either.

"You don't have to babysit me. I'll be okay," she said, more so trying to convince herself.

"You had a nightmare."

"I saw her...right before she... That image...her eyes...will haunt me the rest of my life."

"Wish I had some magic formula to make it all go away."

"Me, too."

"The old saying is true. Time helps. Gives perspective. Dulls the pain."

"So does a good shot of whiskey." She tried to make a joke. Lighten the mood. As it was, she would jump out of her skin if a bunny hopped out of the corner.

"Tried that, too. Doesn't work. Only makes it worse. Then you lose everything important to you." His voice was husky, low.

Was he talking about her?

"I don't run away from things that go bump in the night, Luke. I know how to stick around."

"That what you think I did? Run?"

She needed to get him out of the room because the pain in his words was a presence between them. He sounded vulnerable and she wanted to comfort him. *Her.* Comfort *him.* What a joke. He was the one who'd disappeared on her. He'd ended their marriage.

"Doesn't matter. It's history. I'll try to get some rest. If not, I'll read or something. Not like you being next to me will make much of a difference. I already know you'll leave when I need you most." She was trying to frustrate him into leaving her alone. Because, honestly, if he offered to curl up with her right then, she'd jump at the chance, which wasn't her brightest idea.

Instead of fighting back, he bent forward, clasped his hands together and rested his elbows on his knees. "I deserved that."

A knife through her heart couldn't have hurt any less than seeing the haunted look on his face. He'd been through hell in Iraq. Came home a wreck. But inside, he was always a good man.

She bit back a curse. "Luke, I'm sorry. I shouldn't have said that."

"It's okay." He didn't look at her. His gaze intensified on a patch of carpet at his feet. "I can't change the past, but I'm here now. I want to help. I don't mind keeping you company. You've been through the wringer today."

"I must look washed-out, too." The thought of him sticking around sounded a hundred warning bells inside her. And yet, it was Luke. *Her* Luke. The man who'd once made her chuck all her rules and live in the moment. Truth be known, it was the only time she'd truly felt alive.

"Not at all. You're beautiful."

Hearing him say those words made her body hum and her thighs warm. Did he see the sexual desire flushing her cheeks? "Can I keep the light on?"

"Of course you can." He repositioned himself on the bed next to her, stretched out his more than six-foot frame and linked his fingers behind his head. "Remember when scary movies used to keep you up half the night?"

"True. I always made you change the channel." She laughed, relieved at the break from her internal struggle.

"Because you didn't want the bad stuff to be the last thing on your mind before you went to sleep."

He remembered? Her heart squeezed. She had to remind herself not to get too enthusiastic. He might recall a few details from their past, but they wouldn't be together right now if a serial killer hadn't set his sights on her.

The bottom line? Luke had left and hadn't looked back.

"We could go downstairs and turn on the TV for a while." He took her hand in his. His was big and strong.

Thoughts of the two of them, up late, entwined on the couch eating pizza, popcorn and anything else that was in the kitchen after spending half the night making love assaulted her. Not a good time for that memory. Especially not with him this close—so close all she had to do was move a little bit to the right in order to touch him. "You need some sleep."

He repositioned on his side, facing her. "What I need can't be found with my eyes closed. They've been shut too long already."

Logical thought screamed for her to bolt, to get a grip on her out-of-control emotions—damn dangerous emotions that were on a runaway train aimed for a head-on collision. Because, for a second, it felt as though nothing had changed between them.

Time machines didn't exist.

There was only here and now.

"I wish it were that easy, Luke."

His hand came up to her chin and lifted her face until her eyes met his. "I'm not asking forgiveness. I'd be an idiot not to realize I'm too late. I would like a shot at friendship. Is there any chance you'd consider it?"

Her heart raced when he was this close, flooding her with doubts.

They'd jumped into a relationship with both feet first last time around. Hot, sexy feet. But feet first had turned into a nosedive toward unimaginable pain. She needed his protection and professional skill, so there was no way to get out of spending time with him. Could they take it slow and get to know each other? Her heart said no.

"I can try."

His smile shouldn't warm her and make her feel safe.

"Thank you." His low baritone goose bumped her arms. He leaned over and pressed a kiss to her forehead, not immediately pulling back.

Her pulse kicked up, and heat filled the small space between them. She could see his heartbeat at the base of his throat. The rapid rhythm matched hers.

"I want to stick around to help. Will you let me?"

She nodded ever so slightly.

He eased back to his position on his side, still facing her. "You should try to get some sleep."

"You, too," Julie said, her brilliant amber eyes wide. He missed everything about her—her musical laugh, the way her forehead wrinkled and lips pursed when she really concentrated, her compassion.

He'd been an idiot to let her go.

If he could go back and change the past, he would.

"Nah. I'll be all right." Her fear had ripped through him. "I'll stay here with you. If you don't mind."

"I would like that, actually."

He settled on top of the covers beside her as she curled up next to him.

If he were being honest, she was the one he thought

about at night. She was the reason he still couldn't sleep over at a girlfriend's house. She was the reason he kept his heart behind a wall. And he had no one to blame but himself.

He'd made the offer of friendship, praying like hell he could handle it.

Julie had been nothing but sweet to him when he'd returned from the war a wreck. And how did he repay her? He'd pushed her away and ruined the best thing that had ever happened to him.

Minutes ticked by after she closed her eyes.

Her breathing slowed. Rhythmic, steady breathing said she'd drifted into sleep.

Being next to her again made his heart ache in the worst possible way. He'd been off balance ever since he'd ended their relationship. He'd convinced himself she'd be better off without him. All he'd done was hurt her. It was the only call he could make at the time. He'd been broken. Sooner or later, she would've seen it, too, and then what? She'd do the same thing his father had done when life got tough—abandon him so fast that four years later his head would still be spinning. There were about a half-dozen people Luke could trust. And most of them shared his last name. Plus, what if he hadn't come back from his mental prison? He would have been dooming her to a miserable life, too.

The decision had seemed like the kindest one he could make under the circumstances. Except that he hadn't considered what it would do to him.

Walking away from her had nearly torn him apart.

Even today, he was only half a man.

Watching her sleep brought back a flood of memories. The few years that had passed since then shriveled.

Having her in his home made them disappear. He wasn't sure what was worse. That he'd been a jackass then or that he had her here but couldn't touch her. His fingers flexed and released. She had been better off without him.

He'd barely pulled himself out of the dark hole he'd fallen in when all but one of his brothers in arms had been ambushed, lined up and shot in front of him. Luke had lived. He'd wasted enough of his life cursing over that little twist of fate. Time to move on.

And now Julie was back in his life.

How many times in the past four years had he wanted to drive by their old place again? Hundreds? Thousands?

Hell, he avoided that entire section of Dallas unless he had no choice. Last thing he wanted was to bump into her at a gas station or store. Even though he always looked for her. Every time he had to be in their old neighborhood, he searched the faces of strangers. Hoped.

Figured living with the torment of never seeing her was his punishment for walking away. He'd never be good enough for her. Nor would he be able to give her what she deserved no matter how much his heart wanted to believe differently.

She made a little mewling sound in her sleep and burrowed into his side. Muscle memory had him hauling her against him, bringing her closer. She rolled onto her side and tangled her leg in his.

With her body pressed to him, rational thinking flew south. He didn't want to risk waking her by moving her, so he didn't. But with her leg wrapped around his and her full breasts against his body, he couldn't stop himself from growing hard. A few pieces of cloth kept them from touching skin to skin. Being this close to the woman he never stopped loving was worse than hell.

This new punishment was probably deserved, too. He let that thought carry him to sleep.

Luke woke, but didn't move. Julie was still asleep and he couldn't bring himself to rouse her. A deep-seated need to protect her drummed through him. Anger at Rob tore through Luke. His body went on full alert and his hands shook, similar to when he'd faced a stressful situation after the war.

"Luke, what's wrong?" Julie eased into a sitting position. The look on her face was a hard slap to reality.

"I'm okay."

"You most certainly are not." She folded her arms.

The old signs of PTSD hadn't reared their heads in two years. What was going on? Wasn't he over those?

This case, being close to Julie, had to be stirring up old feelings—feelings he didn't talk about with anyone. Even in therapy, he'd glossed over his pain. How did he begin to explain to Julie what had happened without reliving the whole experience in Iraq?

"Luke?" Her voice was unsteady. Worry lines bracketed her mouth. Her eyes pleaded with him to say something.

He eased to a sitting position and leaned back against the headrest, closing his eyes against the bright sun streaming through the window. There had been no need to close the blinds. He rarely had company. "What time is it?"

"Ten o'clock." Her voice was tentative, but she scooted next to him.

They were four hours past schedule. "My body started freaking out."

"Like before?" She wrapped her arms around him and put her head on his chest. "Your heart's beating so fast."

"Yeah." The urge to move lost to his need to hold Julie. His body still shook, but with her near, he could deal with it. With her snuggled against him, his world seemed right in ways he knew better than to trust.

She looked up at him with such compassion he almost decided talking was a bad idea. Except that he found he wanted to open up a little more.

"They got much worse. That's why I slept downstairs. I didn't want you to see my weakness."

"I hate what they did to you, Luke." She held tighter to him.

He encircled her in his arms, chastising himself for his momentary weakness. "What they did to my buddies was worse. At least I survived."

"Did you?" she asked quietly, the power of her words a physical presence in the room.

He guessed not. "I'm alive."

"Not the same thing as really living, is it?" Compassion was still in her eyes, but there was something else there, too. Desire?

Did she still want him?

"True. Which I haven't been doing a lot of without you." An impulse to lean forward and kiss her slammed into him. Her mouth was inches from his. *Way to wreck a friendship before it got started, Campbell.*

He'd wait.

If and when the right time presented itself, he'd test to see if she still moaned when he captured her earlobe between his teeth. Or if she still shuddered when he ran his lips across the nape of her neck. The thought of all the other places he'd kissed didn't help his painful erection, which couldn't be more inappropriate under the circumstances. With Rob, Luke couldn't afford to let his guard down for a second.

"I'm so sorry, Luke. I wish I'd known." She shifted her position and ran her flat palm up his back.

"Sweetheart, I wouldn't do that if you plan to get out of bed this morning."

"Oh." Her eyes widened, and she smiled a sexy, sleepy smile. "That wouldn't do either one of us any good."

"I don't know. I think I'd rather enjoy it." He smiled.

A pink flush contrasted with her porcelain skin. "Me, too," she admitted. "Which is definitely why we shouldn't."

Probably true. Being with Julie in bed was never the difficult part. His erection throbbed harder. "Can't blame a guy for missing you."

"You missed me?" The surprise in her voice twisted his gut.

"Of course I did," he said into her mass of inky hair before kissing her forehead. "Why wouldn't I?"

"It seemed so easy for you to walk away. Never look back. I just figured you were done."

That was what she thought?

How did he explain that he'd left because he couldn't watch the hurt and disappointment play out in her eyes? That he'd known in his heart he would only make things worse for her?

"It was my fault."

"You said that before." She rolled over and tossed the covers off. "We'd better get going."

What did he say wrong? Everything *was* his fault. She didn't do anything to deserve the way he'd treated her.

How did he explain that he was trying to protect her by leaving? Maybe she didn't understand his reasoning, on some level he could see that now, but he was thinking of her at the time. He'd made the best decision he could.

"I thought you didn't love me" came out in a whisper.

He hauled her over to him. "I left because I loved you too much to make you sit and watch me wallow until I pulled myself together. I wasn't sure I could after what had happened overseas."

She blinked up at him, her amber eyes reaching deep inside him. She was the only one who'd affected him like that. Damn that she looked sexy and vulnerable. Did it mean something that she still wore his old AC/DC T-shirt to bed?

She pushed off him and sat up. "Isn't that what families do? They stick around and help each other through rough patches. They don't walk out when things get tough. They stay together and work through problems."

"I already apologized. I don't know what else to say about it." There was no way to make her understand. Luke had always had to be tough. Especially after his father had ditched the family. His eldest brother, Nick, had carried most of the burden. Luke had pulled his own weight, doing whatever was necessary to protect their tight-knit family. One thing he hadn't done was dump his problems on others.

Campbell boys held their own.

"Walking out on someone who loves you is just cruel." The sadness and pain in her voice almost doubled him over. She folded her arms and gripped her elbows.

True. But walking away was still better than dragging her to the depths of hell alongside him. He still hadn't completely healed.

Before he could say anything else, she climbed off the bed and grabbed her clothes.

He didn't want to be selfish when it came to Julie. It hurt seeing her like this, but maybe it was best if they kept a little distance between them over the next few days or weeks until they wrapped this case.

Maybe the two of them together wasn't such a good thing. He had options. There were safe houses...

Luke's cell buzzed.

He picked up his phone and checked the text.

There was a picture of him and Julie on her steps from last night. His arm was around her. The photo was captioned Hope you enjoy watching her die.

Rob had been there.

Right now, Luke wouldn't have been able to think clearly if he couldn't see for himself that she was safe. Could he be there for her, protect her, and keep his heart out of it?

No choice.

Ravishing Rob wasn't forgiving. He'd set his sights on Julie.

Luke would do whatever it took to make sure Rob failed. Besides, rushing into another killing wasn't his typical style. Normally, he worked on his "projects" for weeks, sometimes months. Mistakes happened when people got in a hurry.

Could he make a slip?

Luke hoped so. He'd be right there to make the arrest. If he could get five minutes alone with the lowlife,

Luke would gladly check his badge and gun at the door. Rob wouldn't be anyone's problem once Luke was finished.

The guy was thorough. And he wouldn't stop until he had Julie's head.

Literally.

Chapter 5

"Were you on a call?" Julie walked into the master bedroom dressed and ready to go wearing a pair of jeans, beige boots and a cream-colored pullover sweater.

Luke stood near the bed. He had his hand in his pocket as he stared out the window. From his profile she could see that all color had drained from his face.

"What's wrong?" She froze.

"Had to update my boss."

"Everything okay?"

"Fine." He'd dressed in jeans and a black T-shirt. His muscles stretched and thinned as he walked toward her. The fabric pulled taut across his thighs as they flexed. He was the perfect mix of athleticism and grace.

"You're sure?" She stepped aside to let him pass.

"'Course," he said, and his voice was stiff. Hurt? How many times had she begged him to tell her what was going on before? He'd refused. And yet, this time he'd been different. He'd opened up to her a little and allowed her a peek inside. The idea of a friendship had seemed possible. So, what had suddenly changed?

All she wanted was an update on the case. What had his boss said?

Once again, Luke was holding back. Not letting her in. As much as she wanted to believe otherwise, nothing was different. Sure, he'd opened up a little. Her and Luke's relationship, trust, had inched forward. So, why was he reverting to his old ways? She could tell that whatever had gone down with his boss a few minutes ago was important.

What was that saying about teaching old dogs?

Luke's trick was to shut her out when he got emotional.

"Do you have eggs?" she asked, resigned.

He nodded as she followed him downstairs.

"We need to move to a safe house as quickly as possible." He stopped on the staircase and cocked his head sideways.

"Why can't we just stay here?" She wished they could plant themselves somewhere. His place was comfortable, and even though she didn't have anything here that belonged to her, oddly it felt like home. Their old town house had been foreign to her ever since he'd left. And yet, she couldn't bring herself to sell.

"I'm afraid not. It was late last night, so this was our best bet for sleep. I don't want to push it, though."

The wooden floors creaked downstairs.

Luke pulled his gun. His cell vibrated. He fished it out of his pocket and checked the screen.

A furtive glance toward her, followed by a narrowed

gaze focused on the bottom of the stairwell, and Julie knew something bad was about to happen.

"What did it say?" she whispered.

His movement slowed and became purposeful as he wedged himself in front of her and downstairs.

She put her hand on his shoulder. "Luke. Don't shut me out again."

He handed her his phone.

The text read Come down and make breakfast for all of us. I'm here. And that bitch you're with is one step closer to getting what she deserves.

Luke took his cell from her, peeling back her white-knuckle grip slowly. He fired off several texts before easing down the stairs, weapon drawn, motioning Julie to stay behind him.

She had every intention of being glue.

A knock at the front door made her jump.

Shuffling noises were heard as Luke hopped the last couple of stairs and rounded the corner.

Julie followed. The place looked clear, save for the back door being left open.

The doorbell rang several times.

Luke closed and locked the back door after checking the powder room and announcing, "Clear."

He moved to the front door and to a waiting officer, holding his badge in full view as he opened the door.

The officer greeted him and asked permission to come inside.

Luke nodded. They swept the area one more time for safety's sake as more squad cars arrived out front.

"Anything out of place, sir?"

"No. He managed to disarm my alarm, though, and leave out the back door before I could catch him."

"I'll write a report," the officer said. He spoke into his radio then turned his attention to Luke.

"You didn't see anything outside?"

"No, sir. I heard a noise around the side of the house, called it in and vacated my post to investigate. Everything looked fine."

"The noise must've spooked him." He thanked the officer and let him out, locking the door behind him.

"How'd he get inside?" She repressed the fear nipping at her.

"A skilled burglar can bypass even the best alarm systems. There will be more police protection around this place than we need for the next few hours, but it'll be safe for now."

Julie followed Luke as he moved toward the kitchen, reminding herself to breathe through her stress.

His broad back and strong shoulders were eye level as he walked in front of her. Did he know how difficult it was not to reach out to touch him? Get lost in him? Let him be her strength?

But she'd touched that stove once.

Had the burn marks to prove it.

Wasn't the definition of insanity repeating the same mistake over and over again but expecting a different result?

Besides, seeing the man who'd lit wildfires inside her brought back all sorts of raging memories. And the very real disappointment that he'd been her only failure. Luke had been her biggest regret. And that was playing tricks on her emotions. She'd been ready to move on before. Hadn't she?

Luke stopped and she bumped into his back. God help her, but it was like walking into a brick wall with a much better view. "Sorry about that. Wasn't paying attention. Step aside. I'm sure I can whip something up. What have you got in here other than eggs?"

She moved beside him and glanced around the kitchen.

"Sit." He pointed to a bar stool on the other side of the bar.

"What? You? Cook?"

"Try not to look so surprised."

The corners of his mouth turned up in a sexy little grin. His eyes told a different story. An emotion she couldn't quite put her finger on flickered behind his brown gaze. Worry? Fear?

"Okay. Fine. Let me see what you can do, big man." She perched on the seat.

Not five minutes later, she had a steaming cup of coffee in her hand. "Thank you, Mr. Campbell."

When she smiled after taking a sip, he shot her an I-told-you-so look.

She rolled her eyes. "Of course you can brew a pot. It's good. But I'm still waiting to be impressed with your culinary skills."

After experiencing his handiwork with an iron skillet, a handful of eggs and chopped veggies, she was too full to eat her words.

She put her hands up in the universal sign of surrender. "Okay. You got me. Where'd you learn to cook like that?"

"My sisters taught me. What can I say, I missed your cooking." He pulled a seat across the island from her and sat down with his own plate. "You really like it?"

"Not bad, Campbell." She leaned back in her seat and folded her arms after swallowing the last bite. Not wanting to get too comfortable in his home, she added, "Where are we heading today?"

"The first two stops are Addison and Dallas. We find something there, and we save ourselves a driving tour of Texas. Just give me a minute to finish eating and throw together an overnight bag. And you should bring your stuff, too. If we hit a dead end around here, we'll head to Austin next."

"Live-music capital of the world." Was he thinking the same thing she was? Their first weekend trip together had been to watch the bats under the Congress Avenue Bridge at sunset.

He nodded, picking up his plate.

"The least I can do is clean the dishes." She moved around the island to where he stood.

Luke didn't immediately move. Nor did she.

The air charged around them, electrified with sexual chemistry. She couldn't deny missing Luke. Or thinking about him. She'd dreamed about him more than she cared to admit in the past few years.

She cleared her dry throat.

He hesitated, then half smiled and walked away.

Was he thinking about all the times they'd abandoned breakfast dishes and made love on the kitchen counter? The island?

She could almost feel his strong hands around her hips, helping her move with him as he thrust deeper and deeper home.

Julie shook off the memory and turned on the faucet, trying not to think about the changes in Luke as she loaded the dishwasher.

He logged on to his laptop. His solemn expression had returned. "The crime scene was clear except for a print in the yard. The team's running analysis on the type of shoe to see if we can find anything there."

"Doesn't sound like they have much to work with."

"Unfortunately, no. I'd hoped for more this time around." He stood and motioned toward the garage door. "The print is unusual. Might give us something else to go on."

Julie followed him and buckled in. "How many people has he…?"

"Six so far."

"All women?" she asked, but figured she already knew the answer.

"Yes."

"And what he did to her…to my client… Does he do that to all his victims?"

"Pretty much." Luke backed out of the garage, watching every movement around them. "Usually worse."

He cut their heads off? A rock sat in Julie's stomach.

She sat quietly for the rest of the twenty-minute drive. As usual, I-635 was a parking lot, gearing up for the lunch rush.

He exited onto the Dallas North Tollway, then took Beltline to Addison Road. "The first name on the list lives on Quorum Drive."

"I remember when these apartments were being built. Thought this area was for young professionals."

"Our guy is smart. Profile says he's probably educated and most likely in his early thirties."

A chill gripped her spine. "Sounds like the kind of person I could walk down the street next to and never realize he's a monster."

"That's what makes guys like him so hard to track. We catch killers with a low IQ quickly."

"So, he could be young, attractive and rich?"

"Yes."

"Then why? Why would someone who has it all need to do…that…to women? Is he crazy?"

"No. Believe it or not, he's not crazy. To people like you and me he seems that way. His actions are calculated, justified in his twisted mind. This guy enjoys researching 'projects,' as he calls them. Once he identifies his mark, he studies her. Learns her daily patterns. We have at least two cases where we know he hacked into their computers."

"Doesn't that leave a cybertrail?"

"He's not stupid. Every IP we follow leads us to a dead end. So far, he's been a step ahead. But he's arrogant."

"With me, in my case, it's different. Isn't it? I wasn't on his radar before."

"No."

She sucked in a burst of air. "Then why me?"

"You fit his M.O. He targets women between the ages of twenty-five to twenty-seven with black hair. Plus, you may have seen him and you're connected to me." Luke's hand covered hers. "He'll make a mistake and we'll be right there to catch him. He doesn't normally work like this, and that's a good thing. He's moving too fast. I'm not going to let him get to you. That's why you're here with me. I'm keeping you right by my side, where I can watch you at all times."

"I'm glad it's you and not some stranger." She smiled weakly. "No way would someone else care this much."

Guilt or whatever it was that made Luke want to give her life back didn't matter. Her safety in exchange for him being able to walk away with a clean conscience didn't seem like a bad trade.

But could she really trust him? He wasn't the first person who'd been emotionally unavailable. Hadn't her father primed her for men like Luke? Except that she'd believed he was different, had broken all her rules for him, and then he'd shut her out just like her father always had.

Freud would've had a field day.

A little piece of her protested, saying that Luke had been different. The part of her that wanted to believe in him no matter what logical evidence was presented against it. But then, emotions weren't ruled by reason.

Luke pulled into an off-street parking spot and cut the ignition. He double-checked the address on his phone. "Stick behind me."

She did.

Being with Luke brought a dangerous sense of comfort.

Luke held the door open and waited for Julie to climb out of the cab. She deserved to know what she was up against, so he'd shared case information. Her reaction left him wondering if that had been such a good idea. The part about Luke fearing for her life he'd keep close to his chest.

Luke's hands fisted.

The deranged jerk wouldn't get to her. Not as long as Luke was alive. Period.

Intel said the person in this building wasn't likely the one Luke was searching for. Chad Devel was twenty-six years old. He worked as a sous chef in a nearby trendy restaurant and had had three loud-music complaints at this address in the past six months. He'd been pulled over twice and hauled in for suspicion of driving while intoxicated. He'd pleaded out once. The other DWI case was pending.

Not exactly the kind of guy concerned with flying under the radar.

"Which building?" Julie asked. Her voice still sounded sweet to him, like waking up late on a Saturday morning in a cabin in the woods.

A quick glance at his phone and he pointed to the one on the right. "We're looking for apartment number one hundred fifty."

He'd spotted it as he'd said it. "There. Ground floor."

"Looks pricey."

"Would take someone with a good job to afford a place like this."

"Maybe even with a college degree?" She looked at him intently with those amber eyes. "Do sous chefs normally have degrees?"

"Sometimes." Luke palmed his badge and knocked on the door. Since Chad seemed to enjoy partying at night, he'd most likely still be asleep.

No one answered.

The next knocks sounded off louder, more urgently. "Mr. Devel. Open up."

"Okay, okay" came through the door.

It swung open.

A young guy with curly hair stood at the opened door. He blinked against the bright sun and shielded his eyes with his forearm. His gaze moved from Luke to Julie. "What do you want?"

"Are you Chad Devel?"

The young guy looked as if he'd just stepped out of

an Abercrombie & Fitch commercial. He had on boxer shorts and no shirt. He was tall, at least six feet, with a lean runner's build. His sandy-blond hair looked windswept, as if he'd just gotten off a yacht. He rubbed his blue eyes and bit back a yawn.

Luke flashed his badge. "I'm Special Agent Campbell. May we come in?"

Surprise widened the young guy's gaze as he stood there stunned. Typical reaction.

"You didn't answer either of my questions."

"Oh. Right. Yes, I'm Chad. I haven't done anything wrong. My court date isn't until—"

"Where were you the night before last, Mr. Devel?" On first appraisal, this kid looked as though he'd grown up with too much money and free time. Yet, he had a job. Maybe Daddy had cut him off?

"Work."

Easy enough to verify. "And that is where?"

"DeBleu on Beltline close to Midway. Why?"

"May we come inside?" Luke asked again. He'd like the chance to look around. Make certain he didn't need to circle back to this guy later.

"Um, sure." The door swung open wide. "The place is a mess. Had a few friends over last night after work."

Luke stepped inside, motioning Julie to follow. "Can your boss corroborate your story?"

"Yeah. He was there. I worked with Tony and Angie, too. They can tell you where I was. They were here last night. I can give you their phone numbers if you want to check."

Luke pulled out his phone and took the information. The guy didn't fit the profile for Rob, but Luke didn't plan on taking any chances with this case.

Besides, something about Chad had Luke's radar up.

Chad's heartbeat at the base of his throat beat too rapidly. Not exactly probable cause for an arrest, but Luke didn't like it. He'd lean on him a little bit. See if he could fish any information out. He handed Chad a piece of paper and a pen. "Write your name."

He complied.

Luke studied the page. The handwriting didn't match Rob's note, which could be on purpose. Most serial killers didn't warn their victims in advance. Rob was no exception. This was all a big game to the bastard. "Where'd you go to college?"

"Here, locally. Dropped out after a couple semesters."

"Your dad work in the medical field?"

"No."

"What did you study?"

Chad's dark eyebrows knitted. "Finance. Why?"

The apartment was small but upscale. Luke could see to the back door from where he stood in the living room. There were hardwood floors, contemporary furnishings. Ansel Adams black-and-white photos hung on the walls. There were no signs of the souvenirs Rob liked to take from his victims, but that didn't mean he would keep them at his house or out in the open. Empty imported-beer bottles lined the glass coffee table. Sofa cushions were strewn around. "Looks like you had a good time."

"We did. Didn't get much sleep." Chad's gaze darted around.

Half of an unrolled cigar lay open on the glass coffee table, a common place to hide weed. Pot was small-time compared to what Luke was used to seeing. Could Chad be on heavy drugs? K2?

Possibly.

Three years on the job had Luke's interest piqued. While he wasn't there to pop the guy for a nickel bag, Luke didn't plan to share.

Chad needed to sweat, and by the looks of him, he was.

Luke moved to the coffee table, picked up the cigar and rolled it under his nose. "Cuban?"

"No, sir. Those are illegal. That one's from Venezuela." Chad shifted his weight to his other foot. A few seconds later, he did it again.

Luke focused on Chad.

"You like to hunt?"

"Not really. My dad forces us to go on a trip once a year." Chad kept chancing a look toward Julie. Luke didn't like the way Chad looked at her. Then again, after Rob's direct threat this morning, Luke was on high alert.

"Your dad live around here?"

"No, sir. California."

There was another point worth considering. Rob knew what Julie looked like. Chad didn't have a clue when he saw her. Luke had been careful to gauge the guy's reaction to her. There would have been some hint of recognition. Pupils dilated. A twitch.

Chad hadn't so much as lifted a thick brow. "You have any medical conditions?"

"No, sir. Why?"

"You don't take medicine?"

"No."

"Mind if I check your cabinets?"

"Go ahead."

Luke motioned for Julie to stay by the door as he moved to the open-concept kitchen and flipped through cabinets and drawers. No medicine bottles or telltale syringes were present. The bathroom was across the living room. The door was open to the main space. He checked the medicine chest before returning.

"Do you have any relatives in the area?"

"My mom lives in Dallas."

"That it?"

"Yeah…um…no. Wait a minute. I have a half brother, if he counts. My parents divorced when I was a kid. My dad moved out of state with his second wife. They had a kid. Got a text from him last month saying he'd moved here."

Chad's age pushed the boundaries of Rob's profile. His half brother would be even younger. "Must be nice to have family in town."

"Not really. We aren't close. He's flaky."

"That's tough when families split. You two didn't grow up together?"

Chad nearly choked. "Not on my mother's life would she stand for that."

"How come?"

"This woman and my dad had been having an affair since before I was born. Rick, my half brother, is four years older than me."

This put him at the exact age of the profile, which meant nothing if the guy was in California the whole time. Julie's eyes widened. She caught on to it, too.

If the brother had just moved here, he wouldn't show up in any databases yet. "Those hunting trips you mentioned."

"Yeah?"

"Your brother into them?"

"He likes them a hell of a lot more than I do. Why?"

"Do you have contact information for Rick? I'd like to speak to him."

"Um, yeah. I think. It would be on my phone. Hold on." Chad moved to the bar separating the living space from the kitchen and started shifting stacks of junk. Mail, papers, books were tossed around.

Couch cushions were next. He checked behind each one. "Oh, wait. I know where it is."

Chad disappeared into the bathroom, returning a moment later holding up a pair of jeans. He fished in the front pocket and produced his cell. Another few seconds of scrolling through text messages and he stopped on a name. He tilted the screen toward Luke. The name read Rick Camden.

"That's your half brother?"

"Yeah." Chad rolled his eyes and tossed his hair back. "His mom didn't want to give them away by naming him after my father. Turns out, the sleazy bitch worked at my dad's office."

"You have an address?"

"No. Sorry. I haven't even seen him."

The women Rob chose were between the ages of twenty-five and twenty-seven. All had black hair. Had Dad's sleeping around caused Chad or his mother to resent women?

Interesting theory. Luke made a mental note to check into Chad's mother's background, too. Female serial killers might be rare, but the few who crossed the line were vicious. Time to find out if the bloodline could use some bleach.

Of course, that didn't explain the male voice who'd phoned Luke before. Although, she might be *that* crafty. "Doesn't sound like the family recovered once their secret came out in the open." Luke could relate to the bitterness he saw in Chad's eyes at his father's abandonment. He also knew that holding on to anger was like drinking poison and expecting it to kill someone else.

Chad shook his head. "We don't exactly get together for holidays."

Luke took note of Rick's information. "This guy grew up in California?"

"Uh-huh."

The way Rob studied his intended victims didn't mesh logistically with someone who lived out of state. But with money like theirs, he could travel back and forth. Even so, Luke would follow up. He'd become the best because he was thorough.

"What about your brother?"

"Half brother," Chad corrected.

"Sorry. He have any medical conditions you know about?"

"Nah. Not to my knowledge. But then, I wouldn't really know."

"You look like your mom or your dad?"

"My mom."

"You have a picture of her?" He needed to see if Chad's mother had black hair.

Chad produced a photo on his cell phone. The image of him and his mother showed their family resemblance.

"What about Rick's mom? She still alive?"

"Yeah. She's pretty, I guess. She's thin. Has black hair."

Interviewing Rick just became a priority.

"We'll be in contact should we have any more questions," Luke said as he made a move toward the door.

"Can you tell me what this is about, at least?"

"Murder." Luke let the word hang in the air.

The guy shook as if he might unravel. Rob was so detached he'd most likely be calm, no matter what. He didn't see what he did to women as bad. In his eyes, killing them was justified.

"Look, I'm not perfect. I like to party. But I would never hurt anyone on purpose."

With his tanned face and Kennedy family–like good looks, Luke figured it wouldn't be hard to find women who wanted to party with Chad.

"Keep it that way," he said as he opened the door for Julie.

One down. Seven to go. Rick was a better fit to the profile. Too bad he hadn't lived in Texas over the past two years.

"I will, sir."

Based on the guy's fearful expression, he wouldn't be so much as jaywalking anytime soon. Chad knew how to throw a party. Was he a killer?

Luke followed Julie back to the truck with the ever-present feeling of eyes on them. He matched her stride and possessively put his hand low on her back.

A visual scan revealed nothing suspect. Chad's door was closed.

So, what was with the creepy feeling?

Chapter 6

Julie wasn't sure what to expect if she saw a killer face-to-face. Would she even know?

"You were tense in there," she said to Luke on the short walk to the truck.

"I don't like his half brother. I can't ignore the link to the Devel name. His age matches the profile. He likes to hunt. His mother has black hair. We'll know more once we talk to him." He paused for a couple of beats. "The only problem is, the killings are happening in the Dallas–Fort Worth Metroplex, and he's supposedly been in California."

She climbed into the cab of the truck and clicked on her seat belt. "Chad said his half brother doesn't have any medical problems. Isn't your guy supposed to be a diabetic?"

"Could be. Then again, he might've just been thirsty."

She had picked up on that. Luke's fingers gripped the steering wheel so tightly, they turned white.

He palmed his cell and punched in Rick's number.

"Interesting."

"What is it?"

"The number's bad. It's been disconnected."

"Does that mean he left town? His brother said he wasn't stable."

"Could be. I'll have Nick check into it." He sent a text to his brother asking for any information he could dig up about Rick Camden. "Or Chad gave us a fake number."

"He seemed like a typical twenty-year-old to me." She shrugged. "If it turns out he's the killer, I wouldn't be any good at your job."

"He could hold a grudge against his stepmother for ruining his family. Some serial killers are charming and popular, and they can start at any age."

"Oh." That last bit of information sat hard on her stomach. "He was good-looking. A woman might never know who she was dealing with until it was too late."

"That's Rob's M.O." Luke started the engine, pulled out of the parking lot and made his way back onto the Tollway.

"So he calls himself Ravishing Rob?"

"Captivates then decapitates."

A wave of nausea slammed into her as Ms. Martin's face flashed through her mind. Julie bent forward to stave off the bile rising in her throat. She'd stopped him from cutting off her client's head, which hardly seemed like a consolation under the circumstances. And now he wanted hers. "What kind of monster does that to people?"

"I'm sorry. That was too much information."

She dragged in a breath. "No. It's good. I need to hear everything. Believe me, there are moments when I just don't want to know. But I have to be prepared, right?"

"Yes, but you can do this in doses. If this is more than you can handle, I can drop you at the station during the day while I investigate. You'll be safe there."

How did she tell him there was nowhere she'd rather be than with him? That she only felt truly safe by his side? "No. I'm fine. I knew this would be hard. I have to toughen up and stay informed. This might be difficult, but it's important, and I can't close myself off to all the bad things in the world. That could get me killed someday. Plus, what if you don't get back tonight? Where would that leave me?"

"Right now, let's think about something else." His gaze stayed focused on the road in front of him as he moved the pickup through traffic.

"I like it when you include me. I mean, you didn't for so long. This is a lot to process, believe me, but I'd rather know."

"And I'd rather protect you from the truth." His tone was solemn. Regret?

Did he mean now or before? Both?

"Can I ask a question?"

He nodded.

"What happened to you in Iraq?"

"War." His gaze intensified on the stretch of road in front of him. His hands gripped the wheel tighter.

"I know you went overseas, but I mean, you didn't talk about it when you came home. The guys you served with were like brothers…"

His nod was almost imperceptible.

Whatever happened must've been pretty bad. After

all these years, he still couldn't talk about it. Not even after all they'd been through in the past twenty-four hours. Maybe he would never be able to share. "Whatever it was, I'm sorry."

"I hope you don't think any of what happened between us was your fault."

"It takes two people to wreck a marriage."

"No. It doesn't. It takes two people to make a good marriage. Only one to destroy it."

"If only I'd—"

He pulled the truck off the Tollway and into a hotel parking lot where he parked.

The force of his stare when he turned to face her threw her.

"Believe me when I say you did nothing wrong."

Hot tears of frustration pricked the backs of her eyes. "If that were true, we'd still be married and none of this would be happening."

"I repeat, none of what happened to us was your fault." The intensity of his gaze matched the determination in his clenched jaw.

The words were like bullets through her heart. No matter what he said, it wouldn't change the fact she was a failure. Her father had drilled it into her head that Davises didn't give up. Yet, she had. "How can you say that? It takes two people to kill a relationship, Luke. If I'd been a better wife, you would've been able to confide in me. You wouldn't have walked out."

"I take full responsibility."

"They teach you that in counseling? That it was all your fault?"

"No" came out through thinned lips.

"Why, Luke? Why'd you walk out?" Her emotions

were taking over, and she knew she shouldn't ask the question. But she had. Well, she'd said it. Couldn't take her words back now. Everything happening around her made her realize just how fragile life really was. One minute, she thought she was starting to figure out her next move and get comfortable in life, and then everything changed just like before.

"Because I was broken, dammit. I came back damaged. They were killed. All of them." He hung his head low.

The truth crushed down on her rib cage, making it hurt to even breathe. Based on his expression, he seemed as devastated as she felt.

"We were ambushed."

Her heart ached for him. She couldn't imagine what that would do to a person. And yet a little piece of her heart filled with hope. He was finally talking about the past. Telling her something important.

"It was my fault."

She put her hand on his arm, ignoring the pulses of electricity she'd come to expect whenever they touched. "Couldn't have been."

He got quiet.

"I wish I could've been there for you, Luke." She couldn't stop the sieve now that it had opened.

"You were perfect. I wasn't. It was my fault. Everything. I hurt you and I couldn't keep going like that. You didn't deserve to be treated like that."

"I was expendable. You must've realized we'd made a mistake. You didn't want me anymore. You left." Tears streamed down her cheeks.

He brought his hand up and brushed them away, only glancing over at her for a second then quickly shifting back to the empty parking spot in front of them. "Do you want to know how much I wanted you back then? How much I still want you?"

She nodded.

His gaze met hers as the space between them disappeared faster than she could blink.

He leaned into her and kissed her, hard, bruising, hungry.

Luke expected Julie to pull back or push him away. Slap him. She didn't.

When her hands came up and her fingers tunneled into his hair, urging him even closer, he battled every instinct he had to lay the seat down and unleash all the primal instincts that had built up in the years since he'd been gone. He was already hard.

He deepened the kiss. She tasted like honey and coffee with just a little bit of spearmint left over from brushing her teeth this morning.

Her lips moved against his, and he swallowed her soft moan. Awareness zinged through his body, wiring his muscles even tighter.

He thrust his tongue in her mouth, and she met his every stroke.

A niggle of conscience ate at his gut.

Her nerves were fried. She'd been through hell. She was reaching out to him for comfort…and he was crossing the line.

Oh, hell. This was one of those rare times he wished he could set aside what was right for what was right *now*.

The hurt expression on her face a few minutes ago would haunt his dreams.

He shivered then pulled back. "I can't do this."

The back of her hand came up to her swollen, pink lips. Her breathing was heavy but she didn't speak. Her gaze trained out the window ahead of her, as though she was trying to make sense of…this.

He hated hurting her again.

What was broken in him that made him assume everyone would turn their backs on him eventually?

His father?

Luke couldn't deny having his old man walk out before Luke was old enough to say the guy's name had damaged him. His family tree left leaves of betrayal scattered around the earth, which only proved to Luke that he couldn't trust his instincts when it came to love.

Then there was his first love, Chloe. The day she'd bolted was still fresh in his mind. The conversation as vivid today as it had been when they'd had it. With no money to go to college, he'd decided to join the military first. Believing what he had with Chloe was real, he'd shared his plans to save money so they could get married someday. But first, he needed to help his family get out of debt.

She didn't respond well to the fact he needed to help out back home, saying she'd expected to come first in his life. That she'd pouted had caught him off guard.

Chloe demanded he change his plans and join her at the state school she'd planned to attend in the fall. Her look of disappointment when he'd balked was still stamped in Luke's mind. An only child to wealthy parents, Chloe was used to getting everything her way.

But Luke had responsibilities. Commitments. His family had been everything to him and there was no way he'd turn his back on them.

When she couldn't convince him otherwise, she broke

it off, but not before she let him know just how much he'd hurt her.

Deep down, he'd realized what he'd had with her was puppy love. Yet, it didn't stop him from licking his wounds from her betrayal or closing off another little piece of his heart to the world.

Didn't people always bolt when life got serious?

It wasn't that much longer after that when he'd met Julie, fallen hard and figured out what real love was. He'd been able to trust it while times were good. But when he came home a mess and saw disappointment in her eyes…he'd assumed she'd do what everyone else had. Walk away.

He'd preempted.

Ringtones broke through his heavy thoughts. He pulled out his cell and checked the screen. His brother Nick was calling. Good. "Did you find anything for me on those background checks?"

"Nothing helpful, I'm afraid. Most of the men on the list are too old. None had medical issues. The only person who comes close to fitting is Chad Devel, who doesn't fit your profile."

"Just left his place. Did you find anything on his half brother?"

"Nothing yet."

"His brother said he just moved to the area a month ago from California."

"And he has no idea where he lives?"

"That's what he says. Doesn't seem to be any love lost between them. The family was split by an affair. Get this—Rick's mother has black hair."

"Not exactly a saw with blood on it."

"True. I'll take any lead I can get in this case," he

said wearily. "Dig around a little? See what you come up with? And will you check into his mother, too?"

"Will do. I'll be in touch."

Luke ended the call as Julie touched his arm. "What were you thinking about before?"

"Nothing," he lied, glancing around to get his bearings and register his thoughts firmly in the present. He'd hoped for something interesting to come out of the background checks. He repositioned as he scanned the area, careful to watch for anyone who might be trying to surprise them, ignoring the heat radiating up his arm from her touch. Satisfied they were safe, he settled into his seat and rubbed the scruff on his chin. "I came back a mess. You know that already. What you didn't know is that I was a POW."

"I'm so sorry, Luke." Tears brimmed in her eyes.

An overwhelming urge to lean over and capture those pink lips again assaulted him. As much as he wanted to kiss away her tears, hear her say his name over and over again when she hit the heights of sexual desire, he refused to let his hormones rule. "Beatings and starvation were a couple of their favorite forms of torture. But that just scratched the surface. They saved the worst for later."

And now she knew more than his family and the U.S. government put together. Could he tell her the rest even if he wanted to? He doubted it.

Thinking about it shot his anger level to red-hot alert. The psychiatrist had pushed him to open up and discuss his time in enemy camp. He couldn't. Not even with a trained professional. This was different. He felt less exposed with Julie.

"Did all this have anything to do with the award you hid?"

"You found that?" There'd never been any mention of it before. But then, he hadn't exactly been easy to talk to back then.

She nodded. "I didn't open it, though. I promise."

"Didn't feel like I deserved a medal for living."

Her amber eyes filled with remorse and tears and maybe just a little bit of hope.

There was no fantasy she'd take him back. And yet, for whatever crazy reason, a little piece of the armor he'd secured around his heart cracked.

"You're a survivor, Luke. Not many people can say that."

"No one deserves a medal because they kept breathing." Or for not being there for his squad when they needed him. For all intents and purposes, he'd abandoned them. Just like his own father had abandoned him. How could he live with himself? He'd lived the pain firsthand, so to inflict it on others, willingly or not, was more than he could bear.

She paused, her forehead wrinkling in the way it did when she was concentrating. "You came back so thin. And you'd stopped talking to everyone. Me, your family. You changed so much I almost didn't recognize you."

"There was nothing but anger and hurt inside me. I wanted to lash out. Fight something. Except, there you were. You represented everything good in my life. One look and I knew I didn't deserve you—would never be good enough for you."

He expected anger when he glanced at her to see if there was any possibility she could understand where he was coming from. In Luke's life, he'd learned when things got tough, people left. Instead, Julie gave him compassion.

"That's just not true, Luke. You didn't have to go through that alone."

She touched his hand. Electricity and warmth moved through him, spreading from the point of contact.

Julie. *His Julie.*

He'd asked himself a thousand times what he'd done to deserve her. Even for the short time she'd belonged to him. Never could come up with an answer.

"I didn't know how to open up. Not exactly a Campbell trait. We held our family together by taking care of things, not by moving our mouths."

"I remember how worried they were about you. Especially Gran."

"I got through it eventually." Problem was, when he came up on the other side of that dark hole he'd been in, Julie was gone. He'd pushed her away and didn't have the first idea of how to get her back. Didn't figure he could. He assumed most ships that sailed didn't come back to shore. "For what it's worth, I'm sorry."

"I know."

Luke scanned the lot. His gaze stopped at a sedan parked under the hotel canopy.

"Everything okay?"

He shot a glance toward Julie. Her brow was arched, her forehead wrinkled.

"Not sure yet."

The tension radiating from her body filled the air thickly, but she held her head high.

Why did that make him proud? He had no right to feel anything when it came to Julie.

Tell that to his body. To his heart.

He put the gearshift in Drive and eased toward the car. As he neared, the gray sedan snaked between several cars and sped off. Luke tried to navigate in the same traffic but his truck was too big.

"That car?" She pointed to the sedan.

"Yeah. There's something not right. I can feel it. Let's check it out." He put his pickup in Reverse and made a big circle around the check-in lane under the canopy of the grand hotel.

The car was gone.

Luke hooked a right turn out of the parking lot. People in a hurry didn't wait for lights to change green. They always turned right, and this guy had been in a rush.

A phone call to his boss about Rick and his mother would have to wait. Garcia needed an update, too. Luke made a mental note to do it later and moved on while he scanned vehicles.

Julie's quiet demeanor told him all he needed to know about how she was processing the events. When she was truly scared, she got real still. Fear or not, she never backed down. It was one of the many qualities he admired about her.

Two more right turns and he was on the service road to the Tollway. If the guy hit the on-ramp, it'd be all over. He could disappear into the myriad cars snaking down the road.

If Luke had been able to see a license plate, even a partial, he could call Detective Garcia and have the jerk's home address in ten minutes or less.

"There. Over there. Do you see him?" Julie's voice rose in a mix of adrenaline and fear. "Is that him?"

Luke maneuvered closer to the gray sedan. His left

hand was planted firmly on the steering wheel, his right gripping his weapon. "Might be. Let's get a closer look."

The car made a quick left before he could get a visual on the driver.

At least half a dozen cars separated them.

Luke swerved in traffic and sped up. An SUV blocked his view.

Horns honked as he pushed in between cars and cut off others. "If you get a good visual, call out the license plate."

"Okay." Julie pulled her cell from her purse and repositioned in her seat, craning her neck to get a better look.

She had to be scared half to death. The sedan stayed in sight just enough to keep Luke on its tail. Although he'd love to get the license plate, it could be a fake. Whoever was driving seemed to know what he was doing, which brought him back to a point he hadn't wanted to consider but had been eating at the back of his mind all day. The killer had uncanny access to information, which he knew how to use. Another troublesome fact: the man sure knew how to hunt someone.

Even though Rick Camden was an interesting lead, Luke had to consider other possibilities, including the unthinkable. Could Rob work in law enforcement? The officer who'd appeared on the scene first at Julie's town house had disappeared a little too quickly. Was it possible that Luke stared Rob in the face and didn't know it? There had been no sirens, no squad car.

Had Rob gotten away with the crime he'd committed in the alley because he wore a uniform? A chill gripped Luke's spine.

A law-enforcement officer going rogue was one of the

worst possible scenarios. A man trained to kill wasn't a good person to have hunting Julie.

Of course, the guy wouldn't have to be currently on the force. He could be disgruntled, disillusioned, or might have been kicked off. Another possibility was that he might've flunked out of the academy and enjoyed playing cop. Of course, the more likely scenario involved someone who worked in the medical field. Even so, Luke didn't want to rule anything out.

The bastard had somehow gotten Luke's home address. He already had his cell number.

What else did Rob know?

Chapter 7

"He's gone." Luke sighed sharply. The car he'd been following had disappeared.

"I wish I could've gotten at least a partial plate." Julie gripped her seat belt where it crossed her chest and leaned against the headrest. She sat silent for a long moment. Her forehead creased the way it did when she was concentrating, and her lips compressed into a thin line.

He could tell she was having trouble processing what had just happened. She needed a distraction. "We should think about eating lunch."

"How about that barbecue place at Preston and LBJ?" She blinked her eyes open.

How could he forget? It was their favorite. "Sounds good. Let's check it out."

"Luke."

"Yeah."

"Thanks for telling me what you did in the parking lot before. It helps."

"It was true." Their earlier conversation, being able to tell her that everything had been his fault, had lightened what otherwise would've been a horrendous mood on a screwed-up day. And that shocked him.

Wasn't like him to get all talky and share his feelings with anyone. Even more surprising was that he'd felt better afterward. As if the boulder that had been sitting on his chest since he'd left Julie had dislodged. Still there, but less pressure weighing down on him. Not much else was going his way today and he sure didn't like the feeling of always chasing behind Rob. The cold-hearted killer was always a step ahead. Bright guy.

But that she'd believed she was a failure because of their broken marriage pierced right through him. None of it had been her fault. For what it was worth, he'd go back and change everything if he could. But life didn't give do-overs. Luke figured all he could do was move forward and not repeat his mistakes.

Within ten minutes, he'd parked in the busy lot. "Doesn't look like they're hurting for business."

"Nope."

He opened Julie's door and then followed her inside. They got in line and stood in silence, contemplating the menu. After all that had happened, he was glad she had an appetite at all.

Julie took in a deep breath. "I haven't been here in a long time. Still smells the same."

The Barbecue Shack brought back a flood of good memories. "Just like Sunday afternoons at Gran's ranch."

"My mouth is already watering." She turned to face

him, smiling. "You guys used to smoke a brisket in the slow cooker all day."

"The food was ready when the sun kissed the horizon."

"Remember all those evenings in the barn after supper?" Her cheeks flushed a soft pink.

"Some of the best nights of my life."

"You come here a lot? You know, since we…"

"No. Not since us."

He put his hand on the small of her back, urging her as the line moved forward. Touching Julie felt as natural as waking up in the morning.

Nothing in his world had been right in a long time.

"Being here, together, seems a lot like old times, doesn't it?" She turned and pushed up on her tiptoes, planting a kiss on his cheek.

Blood roared in his ears and his heartbeat thundered in his chest. "Yeah. It's nice."

"I like being friends, Luke." Her gaze lingered on his.

"Me, too." Before he could find a good reason not to, his arms encircled her waist. With her body flush to his, more than his heart grew warm. "It's been too long."

"Agreed." She smiled up at him.

He pressed his forehead to hers and released a slow breath.

They both stood rooted, for a long moment, breathing each other in.

Then she turned and took another step forward as the line moved. Her hand reached back and found his.

He twined their fingers and hauled her against him. Her sweet round bottom in a perfectly fitted pair of jeans pressed against him. His control faltered.

He breathed in. The scent of her shampoo, coconut and pineapple, filled his senses.

The line moved another couple of steps forward.

Luke didn't want to budge. He wanted to stay rooted to his spot, with Julie, and forget everything else. The past. The craziness. The now.

The couple in front of them moved. He and Julie were up next to order. She leaned into him a little more.

Too soon, the line cleared, and it was their turn. She stepped aside, moving elbow to elbow.

"The usual?" he asked.

She nodded, reaching inside her purse.

He frowned. "Two plates of brisket."

Glancing at her, he added, "And lunch is on me."

The attendant nodded. "Drinks?"

Luke confirmed.

The young guy stuck out two cups.

Julie took them as Luke paid.

Yeah. This felt a lot like old times. They were damn good times, too. He wasn't kidding when he'd said those months with her was the best time of his life. He'd just been too stubborn and too young to realize letting her go would almost kill him.

"What do you want to drink?"

"Surprise me."

Luke piled mashed potatoes and beans on their plates as she manned the drinks stand. They got their usual booth in the corner.

And for a second, life didn't feel as if it was tilted, slowly spinning off its axis.

The moment wouldn't last.

This case would be over as soon as Luke found Rob. And he would find the SOB. Julie would return to her normal life. To Herb. And Luke would settle into his routine again.

Even though letting her go had almost killed him, he'd survived, hadn't he?

Because suddenly, the thought of trying to live without Julie was a sucker punch and he couldn't breathe.

Shake it off.

He slid onto the wooden bench across from her.

Every bit of him wanted to move across the table and snuggle in beside her, but he needed to keep his head clear.

A few bites into his meal, his cell buzzed. He fished it out of his pocket. The name on the screen read Bill Hightower.

What was the local newscaster doing calling Luke?

"Campbell here."

"Sir, this is—"

"I know who this is. Can you advise me of the nature of the call?"

"Something showed up in a studio here at the TV station that I think you'll be interested in seeing."

"Mind giving me a hint?"

"It's a message. A note for you. From a guy who calls himself Ravishing Rob."

"Did you touch it?"

"I'm afraid so. No one knew what we had at first."

The original prints might've been damaged. Luke bit back a curse. "Who discovered it?"

"One of my producers." The normally even-toned newscaster sounded a little rattled.

"Keep it somewhere safe. Don't touch it. I'll be there in ten minutes." Luke motioned for Julie to finish eating as he ended the call.

"Who was that?"

"A TV reporter. Said he has a message from Rob."

"That where we're headed?" She'd already grabbed her purse and was sliding out of the booth.

"I need to take a look at the evidence. I want to know where Rob left it. Check the area. Talk to the staff. Maybe someone saw something. We'll head to Austin afterward if we can't get an address on Camden. Since we're getting a late start, we'll plan to stay over." The thought of spending the night with Julie in a hotel room didn't do good things to Luke's libido.

"Okay."

"Obviously, my place has been compromised."

"Understood."

On their way out, Luke phoned his boss about Rick and updated him on the gray late-model sedan, too. His next call was to his older brother, Nick, but he didn't pick up.

On the walk to his truck, Julie slipped her hand in his. Friends? Could he limit their relationship? She felt a lot like home.

The drive downtown to the TV station took longer than he'd expected. Traffic was heavy, which doubled his time.

There was no close parking, so Luke parked in a nearby garage and opened the door for Julie. She made no move to hold his hand again. His mind was elsewhere, and she seemed to understand why.

Even though he'd stopped talking, he hoped she understood this was different. He was still available. This was focus, not completely shutting her out.

Their silence was warm and companionable as they walked the street filled with luxury hotels and apartments. This urban area was like so many, one block up-scale, the next graffiti-covered walls and empty beer cans lined the streets.

Workers huddled near doors, smoking.

An argument broke out a few feet in front of them between two men in suits. Fists flew and the crowd parted, creating a circle around the action.

Luke shot Julie a look before jogging toward the pair. "Break it up. I'm Special Agent Campbell, and I don't want to have to arrest either of you."

He tapped the badge on his waistband.

The younger man took a step back and touched his lip. Drops of blood trickled down his chin. "He busted my lip. He wasn't supposed to do that."

He made a move toward the other guy. Luke stepped in between them, his palm flat against Young Guy's chest.

"What do you mean he wasn't *supposed* to do that?"

"Some dude paid us three hundred dollars each to pretend like we were fighting."

A diversion? Luke glanced toward where he'd left Julie.

She was gone.

A loud scream split the air.

"Julie." Damn that he'd allowed himself a moment of distraction. She might pay for his mistake with her life. The feeling of guilt and shame washed over him as his body trembled. The all-too-familiar feelings rushed him.

Luke pushed through the crowd toward the sound of the scream. Where was Julie?

He bolted through the bodies surrounding him. There was no sign of her.

His brain couldn't wrap around the fact Rob had her.

Thinking about what he would do with her sent an icy chill down Luke's spine.

They couldn't have gotten far.

Worst-case scenarios drilled Luke's thoughts as he searched the street, running. Rob could have stuffed her into a waiting car.

The air thinned around Luke.

In that case, the bastard could already be on the highway heading almost anywhere. Luke cursed. If that was true, it could be game over.

Luke rounded the corner and stopped the first person he saw. "Did you see a woman with black hair come this way with a man?"

The person shook their head. "Sorry."

Anger coursed through Luke. This could not be happening. Period. He'd kept Julie next to him for a reason. Helplessness rolled through him in waves. He refused to acknowledge it. Instead, he rushed to the next person, who was on her cell, and asked the same question while flashing his badge.

She nodded and pointed south. "I'm on hold with the police. I saw a man dragging a woman that way. Couldn't get a good look at her. She was struggling."

"Stay on the phone with the police. Tell them everything you just told me," Luke instructed her as he bolted south, maintaining eye contact to ensure the woman understood.

"Okay. I will." Her voice rose from adrenaline.

"Tell them Special Agent Campbell needs backup." Luke broke into a dead run. His tremors returned. He couldn't even consider the possibility of not finding Julie. *Another few minutes, Rob gets her to a secure location, and it's over.*

Luke stopped at the intersection, glancing left then right. Nothing. She couldn't be gone.

This case was bringing back more of the past than his relationship with his ex.

A hand covered Julie's mouth. She tried to bite it. Couldn't. He must've anticipated the move.

She jabbed her elbow back, connecting with his rib cage.

Her attacker swore. He dropped his hand to force her arms behind her back.

She finally broke free enough to scream again, praying Luke would be able to track her location. Had Rob dragged her too far? Had Luke realized she was gone yet?

Luke was good at his job. He would come, she reassured herself.

The next thing she knew, a bag or some kind of cloth material covered her head, and she was being dragged again. She kicked, wriggled and struggled against the viselike grip around her hands—hands that had been shoved behind her back.

She managed another scream before she was dropped and concrete slammed into her. Her head cracked against the unforgiving sidewalk.

He swore again, and then he was gone.

With her hands freed, she pulled off the covering in time to see Luke coming at a full run toward her. She pushed up to a sitting position as he stopped in front of her and dropped to his knees.

The haunted look on his face sent chills up her back.

"You all right?" He scanned the area.

"I'm fine. Go."

He took off in the direction she'd heard footsteps, hesitated, then circled back. "Might be playing into his hands by chasing him. He caught us off guard. I won't let it happen twice."

A small crowd had gathered around her.

Julie stood and shook off the shock. "Someone had to have seen him." She looked around. "Did any of you see what happened to me?"

A Hispanic male wearing a uniform stepped forward. "I was watching the fight. Then I heard a scream and turned to look over here, but by that time all I saw was the back of a man. He was taller than me. About this big." He held his hand up to indicate close to Luke's height.

"Around six feet?"

A few heads nodded in the crowd.

"Yeah. That seems about right. He looked like he might be a runner. Slim but athletic. A few inches shorter than you, maybe." He shrugged. "I couldn't see much more than that."

Luke thanked him, very aware of the fact that the height given matched that of the uniformed officer who'd shown up at Julie's place. "Did anyone else see the guy?"

Shoulders shrugged. A woman confirmed, "I think that's a pretty good description. His back was turned, so I didn't get a look at his face."

After thanking the group, Luke turned to Julie. "I need to talk to the people who distracted us."

They jogged back to the spot of the earlier altercation. A pair of officers were interviewing the men who'd been involved in the fake fight.

Luke introduced himself, then turned to the older guy in a suit. "Tell me about the person who paid you."

"He was wearing a hoodie and sunglasses, but I could see that he had dark hair."

The young guy nodded in agreement.

"And you didn't think anything was wrong with the picture when he offered you money to fight?" Luke shot a heated look at them.

"Sure I did. At first. I said no," the young guy piped up.

"What changed your mind?"

"He seemed like a nice guy. Said he was playing a prank on his roommate. That it was his birthday. We weren't actually supposed to throw punches." He sneered at the older guy.

"And you believed him?"

"Honestly, I thought I was on one of those TV prank shows at first. Then I thought, what could it hurt?" The young guy shrugged. Looking toward the uniformed officer, he asked, "Am I under arrest?"

The officer shot a glance toward Luke.

"No," Luke said. "But give your information to this officer for his report. If we need to talk to you again, we'll be in touch." He hesitated. "And the next time someone asks you for a favor, I'd suggest you both walk away."

"You bet I will," the young man said.

Luke clamped his hand around Julie's, gripping her tightly. "Let's check in at the TV station."

Another block and they stood in front of American Airlines Stadium. Luke located the glass doors at the entrance to the station and guided them toward the door. Julie's body still shook from adrenaline and fear, and she noticed a tremble in Luke's hand, too.

The big and brave Luke had never seemed quite

so vulnerable to her before. Even when he came back from the war, he seemed more angry than anything else. Afraid? No.

He stopped at the door and turned to her. "You okay?"

"Yeah. I'd be lying if I didn't admit to being shaken up, but I'm fine."

"That's my girl." He pressed a kiss to her forehead. "I can drop you off at the police station if you want out. You'd be safe there." His gaze bored deeply into hers. His brown eyes filled with worry and what looked a lot like fear.

"As long as I'm with you, I'll be all right," she reassured him.

"But he got…to…you." His voice broke on the last word.

"And you saved me, Luke."

He took in a sharp breath. "Not good enough. You're sure you want to go through with this? I can take you back to the ranch. There's enough law enforcement crawling in and out of there on a daily basis to ensure your safety. I know Gran would like to see you again."

"Me, too. As soon as all this is cleared, I'd like to go out for a visit. I miss her." The warmth in his gaze nearly knocked her back a step.

This time he planted a kiss on her lips before leading her into the news studio.

The receptionist was a cute and perky brunette. She asked them to wait while she paged the newscaster. An armed guard stood sentinel behind her, nodding toward Luke.

Julie immediately recognized Bill Hightower the second he stepped into the lobby. He was shorter in person than he looked on TV. Blond hair, blue eyes and a million-dollar smile with perfectly straight white teeth. He looked to be in his mid- to late-thirties. He had a crisp, new-car-salesman look about him. Suit on, he was polished and ready for the camera.

His hand jutted out in front of Luke, who accepted the shake without a lot of enthusiasm. For whatever reason, Luke didn't seem to care much for this person.

"I wish you were here under different circumstances." Bill's lips curled down in a frown. His brow furrowed.

Julie had to give it to him—he could sell his words. Maybe a bit too perfectly?

"As do we," Luke said, not appearing affected or impressed by the newscaster's plastic concern.

"It's a pleasure to meet you, Special Agent Campbell. You already know I've been wanting an interview with you for months. I understand you're here for a different reason, but while I have you, I wonder if you'd consider answering a few questions?"

"Call me Luke." He paused. The muscle in his jaw ticked. "You said on the phone that you have something for me."

"Yes. I do," he stalled.

"Then, if you don't mind, I'd like to see it."

The reporter turned his attention toward Julie and put on a charming smile. "And you are?"

"Julie Davis."

Luke stepped in between them, drawing the reporter's blue-eyed gaze. "If we could see the message, we'll get out of your way. I'm sure you're busy and I'd hate to be underfoot."

"No trouble at all."

"Is it here at the front?" Luke pressed.

"No. Follow me." Bill led them down the hall to his

office, stopping at the door. He motioned toward a pair of leather chairs as he perched on his desk. "Any chance this is actually from the serial killer you've been following?"

"You know I can't comment on an ongoing investigation." Luke parted his feet in an athletic stance and folded his arms. He'd be intimidating to most men, standing at his full six-foot-one height.

Bill seemed to dismiss the threat. "Then it *is* part of the investigation?"

"I haven't seen the message yet." Luke cracked a smile meant to ease the tension.

"Would you both mind holding on for a minute?"

Luke said he didn't, but his expression told another story. Julie knew him inside and out. She doubted the reporter picked up on Luke's frustration. She could see that he was growing increasingly annoyed.

The reporter disappeared, returning a few moments later with a tentative smile. Was he nervous?

Julie certainly understood the newscaster's trepidation. Rob was a monster. And a desperate one at that. Or was there something else going on?

A shiver raced up her spine thinking about how close she'd just come to being dragged to some random place in that psycho's clutches. Trapped. Icy fingers closed around her heart and squeezed at the memory.

She blew out a breath. Her quick thinking had most likely saved her life. Fighting had worked. No matter what else Rob tried to do, she wouldn't be an easy target. Julie planned to fight.

She already knew what would happen if he got her to another location. He'd been so close moments before. Just thinking about it made her skin sting like a thousand fire-ant bites. She shivered, remembering that the best way to escape a sicko was not to let him take you to a second site. Thank God Luke arrived when he had. She couldn't remember where, but she'd read that an abductor all but assured no possibility of escape if he could get his victim to a different spot where it would be harder to break free.

If she'd had to force the man to snap her neck on the street corner, she would not give him the satisfaction of performing his ritual murder on her.

She was not one of his *projects*.

Bill returned, easing onto his desk, and used a nail clipper to pick up a piece of paper and a hair ribbon.

If the items had been there all along, why did Bill disappear down the hall pretending to go get them?

"It's probably too late, but I secured these from Hair and Makeup on the off chance his print is still there."

Wasn't he being helpful?

Luke eyed the reporter suspiciously, took a small paper bag from his back pocket and nodded. "Much appreciated."

He examined the paper. Deep frown lines bracketed his mouth.

Julie moved closer to get a look.

On the handwritten note was printed "I could be anywhere. Even here. The Devil's in the details, but rest assured, the body count is about to rise."

Chapter 8

Another cold chill trickled down Julie's spine as she glanced around. He could be anywhere. Even there. Watching.

Bill clasped his hands and leaned forward. "The note isn't signed. Is this actually a message from Ravishing Rob?"

"No comment." Luke's tone was cold. His temper was on a short leash.

"So you're not denying it?" the reporter pressed.

"No comment." Luke closed the paper bag. "Where did you find this?

"I didn't."

Luke ate the real estate between them with a couple of quick strides. His hand fisted when he stood over the man who cowered on his desk. "Look. You want to play games with me? Is that your best move right now, Mr.

Hightower? You want to spend the night in jail for obstructing an ongoing investigation?"

"No."

A soft knock at the door turned them around. A small woman stood behind them, holding a white piece of paper with a scribble on it.

Bill motioned for her to come in. After handing him the note, she immediately excused herself and disappeared down the hall without making eye contact with Julie or Luke. That couldn't be a good sign.

"One of my producers discovered them taped to a camera lens." Bill sounded distracted. Whatever she'd handed him got his full attention.

"Which one?" Luke took a step back.

"In the studio."

"I thought the newsroom was secure."

"It's supposed to be."

"How'd the note get there?"

"No one saw anyone come in." Bill shrugged. "I have a few questions for you. Unless you plan to get in my face again."

"You didn't answer mine."

"Funny. You didn't respond to my request for an interview last month. Or the one before that. Or the one before that. Can you give us any idea of Rob's profile? People deserve to know. Otherwise, you're allowing a killer to walk around invisible."

"I'd like to speak to the person who found the note."

Bill didn't make a move. "There are no killers here. I have no reason to believe the person who left this note is an employee of the station."

"That's not your call to make." The pieces fit together. Someone had left the note knowing the person who found it would call the agent in charge of the investigation, who happened to have the killer's new target in protective custody.

The newscaster didn't budge.

"You don't want to talk here? We can head to Lew Sterrett Justice Center if you think everyone would be more comfortable having a conversation there." Luke's steel gaze centered on Bill.

"Fine. The guy who found the note is a producer on the morning show. His name is Lowell Duncan." Bill loosened his tie, then pushed a buzzer on the phone and asked to see Duncan.

Not five minutes later, a sloppily dressed man in his mid-forties stood at the door. Didn't fit the description of the killer Luke had described, but then, he'd also said it could be almost anyone.

One glance toward Luke told her he was sizing this guy up.

"Come in, Lowell," Bill said sharply.

It was clear the two didn't have a warm-and-fuzzy relationship.

"Sir."

Bill gestured toward Luke. "Special Agent Campbell would like a word with you."

Lowell turned. "Yes, sir. I'm guessing this is about the note I found."

"It is. I appreciate your time. You must be busy keeping this place in line." Luke extended his hand to Lowell. The man smiled and took the hand being offered.

Lowell's tense expression softened as he nodded.

"Can you show me where you found the note?"

"Sure." Lowell turned and backtracked down the hall toward the studio.

Julie stayed close to Luke as they walked down the hall. The room where the morning show was taped was smaller than she'd anticipated. Three walls of windows didn't afford a lot of privacy, either.

Lowell stopped at the threshold. "There's a live broadcast going. But I can point to the camera."

He motioned toward the one positioned front and center, aimed toward the newscaster. "It was here when I came on this morning at four o'clock to work *Good Morning Sun*." Lowell shoved his hands in his pockets and balanced on the balls of his feet.

"Which entrance do you use to get to work?"

"The one in the alley."

"Did you see anyone around this morning on your way in to work? Anyone hanging around back there?"

"No. Nothing out of the ordinary."

"What about inside the studio? Was anything else unusual delivered or did you see anyone who didn't belong?"

"Nothing out of place. I checked everything. It's part of my morning ritual. The fools on my crew like to mess with me. I never know what's going to happen when I unscrew a lid anymore." He held his hands up, palms out.

"But you didn't call it in until much later? What made you hold on to it?"

"I'm sorry about that. Thought it was a trick at first."

Luke nodded his understanding. Julie figured growing up with a couple of brothers, he could relate.

"What made you decide to call it in?"

"No one claimed responsibility by the end of the show." He glanced from Luke to Julie and seemed to realize neither of them knew when that was. "It's over at ten o'clock."

Luke glanced at his watch. "Does someone always come forward by now? When they play a practical joke?"

Lowell half smiled. "Seems to be half the fun for these buffoons. Getting away with it is the first kick. Laughing about it when it's over comes in a close second. None of the guys even knew it was there."

"How many work on the show?"

"Three full-timers. I've got one intern."

"Are they here by any chance?"

"Nah. They left a few hours ago after the wrap."

Luke cocked an eyebrow.

"I have them come in my office and we talk about what worked, what didn't. See what we can improve for next time." Lowell had a genuine quality to him. Julie figured he'd make a good boss. Heck, a good person. She wasn't so sure about Bill Hightower.

"I'll need to follow up with them," Luke said. "Can I have a list of names?"

"Sure." Lowell rubbed the scrub on his chin. You need me to round them up? I can call them in if you'd like."

"No. Thank you. I'll swing by in the morning."

"I'll put your name on the list. Feel free to watch the show."

"Will do." Luke smiled. His laid-back expression told Julie he believed Lowell. "Do you always come in at four?"

"Usually. Not much traffic to contend with at that hour, so I'm generally right on time. Maybe a little early some days."

"And you're sure there was nothing different about this morning?"

"Nope. No, sir." He paused as if to take a moment to check his thoughts. "I started to rip it up and toss it in the can, but then Mr. Hightower showed up. I told him what had happened, and he asked to see the note."

"He gets here around ten to do the lunch news?"

"Has to. It's in his contract." Lowell froze as if he'd said something wrong. "I'm sure he would anyway."

Luke nodded. "Then what happened?"

"Next thing I know, I'm being asked to talk to you."

"I appreciate your time, Lowell. Is there an easy way to reach you if I have more questions?"

"I'm almost always here at the station. My house is a few blocks away. I can give you my cell. But the receptionist keeps me on a short leash." He chuckled. "The station always knows where to find me."

Bill reappeared as Luke made a move toward the lobby. Bill's gaze trained on Julie. "Tell me, Agent Campbell, is it ethical for you to work on a case involving your ex-wife?"

The two men locked eyes.

Luke's eyes flashed fire. "Thank you for your time."

Bill must've realized his story was about to walk out the door. He stood in between them and the exit. "I can keep a secret if it's for a good reason."

"You sure you want to do that?" Luke turned to the reporter and took a menacing step forward, poking his finger in Bill's chest. "Threaten me?"

"I—uh—"

"That really your best move?"

"No, sir."

"Good. I'll be back and I expect your full cooperation. Understood?"

Bill nodded slowly.

Luke twined his and Julie's fingers and stalked toward the exit.

The reporter stayed rooted to his spot. Smart move.

"That guy was a jerk. What the heck's going on with him?" she asked when they were out in the fresh air again.

"Maybe he's just a jerk wanting an exclusive." Luke held tight to her hand.

"Where to next? Austin?"

Luke already had his phone out of his pocket. He let go of her hand long enough to make a call. His first was to Detective Garcia to update him on all that had happened. The next was to his boss. He finished the call as they located the truck. "No. That trip's on hold for the time being. We need to drop off the evidence at the lab before we do anything else. They grab a print and there's no road trip necessary. We'll find our guy."

"How about after that?"

"I realized we have one more location in Addison. One in Dallas. Then we'll think about hitting the road. The team should be able to lift prints quickly if there's anything to work with on that piece of paper. And we know Rob's here."

Luke started the engine and snaked out of the parking garage, glancing in his rearview mirror.

"What is it?"

"Either someone at the station is involved, or Rob planted the note to make sure we went there." The anger in his tone nearly took her breath away.

"So he could get us out in public? It's not like we're hiding. We've been in plain sight all day."

"True, but he didn't know where we were before. And he ambushed us. He might have been trying to flush us out all along by bringing us to the station. He could've been there hiding since this morning." Luke's jaw ticked. "Or it's possible Hightower faked the note."

"Why would he do that?"

"He's been after me for an interview for months. He could've set up the scenario in an attempt to get me to the station. And our guy could've been following us, waiting for a chance to snatch you."

"A reporter wouldn't resort to this, would he? Isn't that a crime?" Was that why Luke had such a bitter response to Bill Hightower? Or had he just had bad experiences with reporters in general? There was something about their interaction that had Julie wondering what else was between the two of them.

And those last words, the ones about her and Luke. Could Hightower cause problems for Luke at work?

"He did an investigative report on the FBI and tried to dig into my past to expose me, questioning whether or not I could do my job. And, yes, it's a crime."

"I don't remember reading anything in the news about you. What a jerk. I'm so sorry someone would do that."

"He didn't succeed. My boss struck a deal with him so he wouldn't run his story. He kept it quiet in exchange for information."

"Your boss must think a lot of you to do that."

"We take care of our own."

"What he did doesn't seem ethical."

"Believe me, reporters have stepped over the line more than once to get a story. And this guy is no exception." Luke's cell buzzed. He glanced at the screen and then locked eyes with Julie.

"Or maybe this whole thing has been a wild-goose chase meant to distract us so Rob could kill again."

Chapter 9

"Oh. God. No. What happened?" Julie fought the panic closing her windpipe.

"We're heading north. The house of a twenty-seven-year-old woman is being broken into. A neighbor called in a suspicious-person report. The guy's wearing a hoodie and sunglasses." He hit the gas pedal and sped out of the parking structure.

Julie sat perfectly still, watching as Luke punched data into his laptop at every red light on the road heading north. He'd avoided taking the Tollway since there was a wreck reported, instead opting for a straight shot up Preston Road.

Driving to Plano took less than ten minutes.

Another few minutes that ticked by like years, and they pulled in front of a large two-story brick house. The lawns were neatly manicured in the suburb—a safe place with good schools where bad things weren't supposed to happen. Julie realized heinous crimes could occur anywhere. Recent events had taught her if someone fixated on her there wasn't much anyone could do to stop him. Even a skilled FBI agent like Luke could barely keep her safe.

"Keep close to me." The rich timbre in Luke's voice softened his command.

He parked in front of the residence and palmed his weapon, leading with his gun.

Luke approached the house cautiously. The front door was unlocked, so he turned the knob slowly and shot Julie a look. The overwhelming smell of bleach assaulted her as she stepped inside the door behind him.

Step by step, she followed him into the living area. A glance to the right nearly knocked Julie off her feet. She stumbled backward the moment her eyes made contact with the victim.

The woman's body had been neatly arranged on the couch. Some blood was splattered, but there was surprisingly little. Bleach had been poured on her clothing. But the severed head made Julie's stomach twist, nearly doubling her over. Bile burned the back of her throat, and she tasted vomit.

Luke tucked her behind him, cursing. His massive shoulder blocked most of her view.

The only thing holding her together was Luke. She heard him whisper an apology as he continued through the house, checking behind every door, in each room, every closet.

Sirens wailed in the distance, roaring toward them. Luke had notified local police he was inside the house.

Moments later, lights blared from the street. Luke

palmed his badge and met the officers in the yard, tightening his grip on Julie's hand.

"The house is clear," he said to the nearest officer. He relayed other information as Julie stood there, stunned.

The officer thanked Luke and headed toward the front door.

Thinking about what was inside sent a wave of nausea rippling through Julie. "What does he do with the... head?"

"He takes special care with cleaning it," he said in a low voice. "Always puts it in a different place after he chops some hair off. Like a twisted game of hide-and-seek. It's his signature."

"He takes a piece of their hair? What does he do with it?" Julie could scarcely contain her horror.

The answer hit her fast and hard. "He's making a human wig, isn't he?"

Luke didn't answer. Didn't have to. Julie could see from his expression she was right. "This was him, then. I could tell she had black hair."

"Looks like it."

"When did he...?"

"Not long ago."

"How do you know?"

"Normally, we can tell by the blood. When the heart stops, it pools inside the body, so in her position, it was at her feet and ankles."

"You saw that?"

He nodded, his gaze intent on her.

"One look at her and I froze," Julie said. "The bleach. You mentioned that before." She wrinkled her nose involuntarily. "Why does he use it?"

"Makes forensic evidence harder to find, for one. Not

impossible, but difficult. Even so, I think it goes deeper than that. He sees these women as unclean, which is how he justifies his actions."

"So, he's cleansing them?"

Luke nodded. "And then punishing them."

Julie trained her gaze on the ground, unable to keep the tears from her eyes or hold her composure. Her stomach revolted.

Before she realized what was happening, his hand was low on her back, ushering her toward the truck.

The chilly breeze was a welcome respite on her warm cheeks. She stepped on the curb just in time for the first heave.

Luke held her hair off her face and whispered words of comfort.

Embarrassment edged in as her heaves became productive. "I'm sorry."

"Don't be."

Looking at him now, he was different but stronger. Could she continue to let him be her strength?

Even after all they'd been through?

When she really thought about it, she had a habit of being with men who shut themselves off emotionally.

Her father had never been there for her. Not even when her mother died. Julie had been a little girl. She remembered the day vividly. It was the first day of kindergarten. She knew her mother had been sick, but no one had prepared her for the fact her mom might die.

Coming home to the news had made her close herself off, too.

Especially when her father hugged her once, then told her they had to get tight and move on.

Most of her childhood memories had faded, but Julie

knew exactly the last time she was hugged by both of her parents that first day of school. Julie hadn't understood the tears her mom shed that morning. She thought they had been for the fact she was going to school.

Little did she know her mom would be gone by the time she got home.

Julie hated first days.

From that day forward, she'd get sick in the pit of her stomach at all firsts. And especially when summer ended and school started again.

Her mother had been the soft, emotional one. Her father had been all about self-discipline and order. Physically, he was always present, but emotionally? Butch Davis didn't do emotions.

Instead of tucking her into bed at night, he had morning inspections. By the second week of school, Julie had learned how to make her own bed and pass muster.

That first night, he took down all the pictures of her mother and neatly packed them away in boxes, storing them in the attic. He never went up there again. Not even when they moved two years later.

The worst part of the whole ordeal was that he never talked about her mother. Ever. It was as if she'd never existed to him. And Julie knew on instinct she wasn't supposed to talk about her mother, either. He'd remarried before the first anniversary of her death.

There were no complaints about her stepmother. She was a nice woman who cleaned when she got nervous. Supper was on time every day. Six o'clock. Very little real conversation was ever had at the dinner table or anywhere else, for that matter.

Was that why Julie was so lost when it came to talking about her own feelings? Why she couldn't for the life of her find the words to help Luke when he was drowning emotionally after Iraq?

Deep down inside, she knew her father had done the best he could. He'd dealt with what life had thrown at him the only way he knew how. She didn't hate him for her childhood. He'd provided all the basic necessities of a roof over her head and food in her stomach. His way of dealing with emotion had been to shut down and ignore it. He'd developed heart disease in his fifties and joined her mother the same year she'd met Luke.

And yet, the Luke she'd met was nothing like her father. Maybe that was the big draw at first?

No one understood her better than Luke. No one made her laugh like Luke. No one caused her body to soar like Luke.

Theirs was a bond so strong, Julie had thought it to be unbreakable. And that was why she'd trashed every one of her rules and married him a month after they'd met. This kind of connection came along once in a lifetime, she'd reasoned. What they had was real and no one could take it away, she'd told herself.

She'd made herself a promise a long time ago that if she should ever get married and have a family of her own, she'd hug them every day. They would know how very much they meant to her every minute. Because life had taught Julie at an early age those she loved could be taken away in an instant.

She had no plans to waste hers by leaving those she loved wondering about her feelings. This was the relationship she'd thought she had with Luke.

And hadn't she?

Then he'd shipped off. She hadn't recognized the man who came home to her.

Determination forced her to stay in the relationship even after he'd quit. She'd thought surely she could bring him back. Their love could move mountains.

"I know this is hard," he soothed, snapping her mind back to the present—a place she was no longer convinced she wanted to be.

Besides, sure Luke was there for her now, but how long before the wire tripped again and he went all emotional desert on her?

She'd been naive the first time she'd fallen for him. Lucky for her, experience was a good teacher.

"Dammit, Luke. I'm fine."

The fact she swore didn't mean good things. Luke also didn't like her sharp tone, because it signaled she was overwhelmed.

Of course she was. She wasn't the first person who'd had a visceral reaction to her first crime scene. Technically, it was her second, but she'd been in shock during the first, so it wasn't the same. Her mind was fully aware this time. Processing every sight, smell, sound. Taking everything in.

"We don't have to be here," he soothed.

"I don't want to get in the way of your case. You need to investigate. I can handle this."

"My team will be here to process the scene. The sergeant looks like he has everything under control until then. Nothing says we have to stay." He thumbed away a tear rolling down her cheek.

"I'm in the way."

"No. You're right where you need to be."

She looked up at him with those amber eyes—eyes filled with pain—and his heart squeezed. Another chink in his armor obliterated. Spending time together was a mistake. All his good memories came crashing down, suffocating him at the thought of walking away from her again.

If there was another place to stash her, somewhere far away from him, he would do it.

The reality? He was her best hope.

He'd already thought about sending her to Europe or Mexico to hide. Hell, he'd pay for the trip out of his own pocket if it would do any good.

Rob wanted Julie. He would go to the ends of the earth to find her. He seemed to know where they were at every step. Had he gotten close enough to bug Luke's truck?

The guy had skills.

Too bad he was on the other side of the law. Luke could use someone with Rob's abilities, if not his morals, on his team.

Not happening. The guy was a cold-blooded killer. Another woman was dead because Luke couldn't get a step ahead of Rob.

Shame and guilt ate away at Luke's stomach lining.

"Luke."

"Yeah."

Those eyes pierced through him. "Get me out of here."

She'd seen enough for one day. He wanted to give her one night of peace.

By the time they reached his truck, his team had texted their location. They were a couple of blocks away. They'd be there in less than five minutes.

Luke checked for a device under his truck and then under the hood. He didn't find anything, which didn't mean much. Gadgets were so small these days they were virtually undetectable. He made a mental note and moved on.

He'd most likely cross paths with his team on the way out of the neighborhood because he needed to stay put for a minute and update the file.

Luke keyed in information before starting the truck and pulling away.

The signature on this killing was Rob's. But the timing was off. Why so soon? What did this murder have to do with Julie?

If Rob was trying to flush them out, he had. He'd been dictating their movements all day, Luke realized.

"Are you thirsty?"

"I could use some water," Julie said, staring out the front window. Her color was slowly returning.

Luke pulled into the first convenience store he could find.

"I need a bathroom, if that's okay," Julie said.

He led her to the back of the place and stood guard at the door.

Five minutes later, he knocked. "Everything okay in there?"

"I'm almost done. I'll be out in a minute."

Another couple of uncomfortable minutes and she came out. She'd pulled her hair back in a ponytail and, from the looks of it, had splashed water on her face.

"Better?"

"I had to get that taste out of my mouth. Luckily, I always keep a travel toothbrush and toothpaste in my purse."

Jealousy flashed through him with the speed of a lightning bolt. Why did she keep those items close at hand? Logic told him it was in case she slept over at her boyfriend's.

Luke walked to the drinks case and pulled two bottled waters.

He had no business knowing why she kept those items in her bag. Anything outside of this case was none of his business. So why did a voice in the back of his head say, *She's mine?*

Julie wasn't *his* anymore. No matter how much it felt like old times being near her. And not just any times, but the good times. He had a life apart from her. She had a boyfriend.

He let silence sit between them as he paid for their water. She followed him to the truck, where he opened her door for her.

Luke made a move to close the door but stopped.

A question was eating away at him.

Before he let this—whatever this was—go any further between the two of them, he had to know.

"Is it serious between you two?"

Chapter 10

"What?" The question caught her off guard. How did Julie tell Luke that his memory was enough to stop her from being able to get close to any other man?

Should she tell him?

What could she possibly accomplish by pouring her soul out to the one man who'd stomped on her heart? Not to mention the fact that if a serial killer hadn't brought Luke to her doorstep, they wouldn't be speaking right now. If he'd come on his own terms, she could trust his feelings. But this? No.

"We've known each other for a while."

"Oh."

She steeled herself against the pain in his voice. Her heart begged her to tell him the truth. Herb was barely in the picture right now. No man before or since Luke had broken through her walls. He was her kryptonite.

Was that such a good thing?

He'd walked out once without looking back. What would stop him from doing it again?

Neither one seemed to feel like talking on the road. Julie didn't. Not after what she'd seen. Then there were her mixed-up feelings for Luke to contend with. Being with him was the first time she'd felt home in years—ever. And yet, her mind couldn't wrap around making the same mistake twice. What was that old saying? *Fool me once, shame on you. Fool me twice, shame on me.* Sure it was a cliché, but it worked for her.

She closed her eyes and leaned her head against the headrest. Images assaulted her. She rubbed her eyes and then opened them.

Luke pulled into a parking garage, found a spot and then cut the engine. "What is it, Julie?"

"This. My life. It's so screwed up that I can't begin to sort through it." She wasn't just talking about Rob, but she didn't want Luke to know. She wasn't ready to discuss their relationship—a relationship that confused her as much as comforted her. "Where are we?"

"Safe house." He hopped out and was at her side before she could reach for the door handle. His lips were curved in a frown. His disposition had shifted to dark and moody.

Was he still bothered by her admission? False or not, she'd done her best to sell it.

The parking garage was active. Well-dressed couples held hands, walking toward either the elevator or the stairs.

"Where are we?"

"There are condos above the shops on this street. This garage will conceal my truck."

"It's busy here. Is it safe to get out?"

"We'll blend in." He placed his hand on the small of her back and electricity shot through her. Unfair that his touch could heat her body so easily.

They moved to the street and into the crowd of forty-somethings as they made their way down the tree-lined road. There were plenty of couples, but single people were abundant, too. Small groups of women looked as if they were out for girls' night. Pairs of men were on the hunt. The place was bustling with restaurants and shops.

"What time is it?" Julie had barely noticed that it had become dark outside. Her nerves were stretched thin from the day's events. Images from the crime scene would haunt her for the rest of her life. She wondered if she'd ever be able to close her eyes again without seeing those horrible crimes relived in her nightmares.

"Eight-thirty." He led her to an elevator, pushed the button and waited. "I'll pick up something for supper once we're settled."

She hadn't eaten since lunch, which had been interrupted. Seriously doubted she could now. "I'm not hungry."

"I know. But you need to get something in your stomach. There's a deli on the corner. They make a great panini and tomato soup." His words were crisp and held a sharp edge, which was probably a good thing. Was he still thinking about what she'd said? Good. Because one touch and he'd melt her resolve.

"I'll try."

The elevator doors opened, closed. They stopped on the fifth floor.

Julie followed Luke down the hallway, feeling the weight of the day in every step.

"I called ahead and had someone bring clothing. You want to jump into the shower while I get food?"

"No." How did she tell him? Admit her vulnerability? Should she come straight out with it? "I...I'm scared, Luke."

His arm encircled her waist as they walked down the hallway. "You know I'm not going to let anything happen to you, right."

It wasn't a question.

She nodded as his arm tightened around her, sending currents of electricity pulsing through her body.

He stopped in front of the door, leaned over and then pressed a kiss into her hair. She leaned into him as he worked the key.

The first thing she noticed when she walked across the threshold was how beautiful and plush the apartment was. The feminine decor was tastefully done. This was clearly not a bachelor pad. She wasn't exactly sure why she thought it would be. "Who provides these places?"

"Nice, isn't it?"

"'Gorgeous' is more like it. Surely this doesn't belong to the government." One look at the hand-scraped hardwood floors and high-end appliances in the open-concept kitchen and she could tell this most certainly was not something Uncle Sam would provide. The sky was clear and she could see lights all the way from downtown Dallas.

"It serves a purpose. Make yourself comfortable." He went to the kitchen cabinet and pulled out two glasses, then retrieved a bottled water from the fridge. He seemed to know his way around rather well.

Had she even known him before he'd left for duty? She believed she had, but she'd been wrong about so much in their life together. She'd also been naive enough to think they could get through anything as long as they were together.

Look how that had turned out.

Julie leaned into the sofa, half listening to Luke call in their dinner order. She heard him end the call as the sound of his footsteps drew closer.

"One of the officers downstairs volunteered to pick up our food."

She smiled, trying to erase the horrible images from her mind. "You want to walk downstairs with me to get it?"

"No. I'll wait here."

"Then keep this with you." He placed a small handgun on the coffee table. "You remember what I taught you about shooting?"

She remembered a lot of things. And that was most likely her biggest problem now. "Yes."

"Okay. The safety's on. There are officers stationed around the building. Don't answer the door for anyone. You can reach me on my cell. I won't be long." He walked right to her, planted a firm kiss on her lips and then locked the door behind him.

Julie hugged a throw pillow to her chest.

Her cell buzzed. She retrieved it from her purse. Luke had sent a text checking on her. She let him know she was fine and then turned on the gas fireplace.

Sleep would come about as easily as snow in a Texas summer, but fatigue was catching up with her, so she leaned back and closed her eyes.

The image of her client and the innocent woman from earlier had stamped her thoughts.

Sobs broke free before she could suppress them. Tears flooded her eyes.

The doorknob turned. She palmed the gun and held her breath until she saw Luke's face. His presence brought a sense of warmth and calm over her.

He locked the door, set the food on the coffee table and dropped to his knees in front of her. "You're shaking."

She folded into his arms.

Before she could stop herself, her fingers mapped the strong muscles in his back. His hands were on her, then circled around her head, pulling her toward home.

He kissed her with a tenderness that caused a flutter in her stomach.

She wanted to erase the images from her mind, lose herself in the moment and forget about real life where people were hurt and Luke had been with other women.

He deepened the kiss and all rational thought flew out of her mind. One word overtook all others. "More."

Julie rose from the sofa onto bent knees. She gripped the hemline of her shirt and pulled it over her head in one motion. All Luke could see was the flesh-colored lacy bra covering her full pert breasts.

"You're even sexier than I remember." He made a move to get up, to reduce the space between them.

Her hands gripped his shoulders before pushing him down. "You, stay right there."

Surrender never felt this much like heaven.

Her jeans hit the floor next and, glory of all glories, Luke's eyes feasted on the matching silk panties. He was already hard, and she seemed prepared to make this end before it began with the way her fingers lingered on the strap of her bra.

"Luke?"

"Yeah."

"I have to ask you a serious question before anything…before *this* can happen."

"You can have whatever you want." He held out his arms. "Take it."

She pushed him down to the floor and straddled him. "All kidding aside."

His body craved to be inside her so badly, he shook. He hoped like hell she was about to ask for more than one night. He'd promised himself a thousand times if he was ever lucky enough to get her back in his bed, he had no intention of letting her out.

"What is it?"

"Do you want me?"

"That's not a serious question."

Her amber eyes bored into him.

"Luke."

"Yeah."

"Do you want me?"

"What kind of question is that? Of course I want you. Do you see what you're doing to me?" He glanced down at his painfully stiff erection.

"I mean, *really* want me." She grabbed his wrists and pulled them above his head.

He looked into her eyes—eyes that possessed kindness, compassion and fire—everything he wanted in a woman. "More than I can ever say. More than you'll ever know. More than I'll ever deserve."

He broke free from her grasp. "I think it's pretty obvious I want this." He picked her up and took her to the bedroom, placing her on top of the duvet. He let his fingertip graze the vee between her breasts. "And this." His finger trailed down her belly to the waistline of her silk panties.

Her stomach quivered and a soft gasp drew from her lips.

He let his eyes take her in for a long moment before trailing his finger across her belly to her hip, making a line up her side. "And this."

"I missed how you fit me physically in every possible way. You have no idea how badly I want to wedge myself in between your thighs and thrust my way home again."

She started to speak but her words caught.

"But you know what?"

Her long dark lashes screened her eyes, but her face was flush with arousal. She shook her head.

"I miss this most of all." He pressed his finger to her forehead. "I miss the way you think. Your wit. How you know exactly what to say to make me laugh when I should be serious."

She restraddled him and then leaned down far enough to press her lips to his.

"I miss those, too."

She slowly pushed up to her knees, her gaze locked onto his the entire time.

Her body was grace and poetry in motion, and Luke couldn't help but stop to appreciate her movements. Yeah, she was sexy as all get-out, but she was so much more. He struggled for the words, the context, but sex with her was like rising to a whole new plane.

No one left him with the same feeling after as Julie had. Everyone else had met a physical need, and that was it.

He'd never known to expect more from a physical act.

She unhitched the silk bra she wore and tossed it to the side in one sweeping motion, releasing her ample breasts and pink nipples.

"You're beautiful." Luke made a move to touch her again, but she shoved him back down.

"Not yet."

"Keep this up and this'll be over before it begins," he half joked. Sex wasn't something he'd indulged in for a long time. The couple of women he'd been with after Julie had left him feeling hollow afterward. He figured he needed more time.

"I happen to know you have incredible stamina, Campbell." Her low, sexy voice rolled over him.

He pressed his palm on her belly. "Confession."

She looked at him.

"It's been a long time."

Her gaze widened.

"Surprised?"

"A guy like you could have pretty much anyone he wanted. I just figured—"

"Wrong. You figured wrong," he parroted, stroking her hip. "I didn't want anyone else."

The thought of someone else touching her could eat away his stomach lining, which was totally unfair. He wouldn't ask if she'd been with another man, with Herb.

She stared at him for a long moment. Her forehead wrinkled in that adorable way when she concentrated. "Confession."

The last thing he could stand hearing about would be her and another man. But he owed it to her to listen. After all, she never would've been with anyone else if he hadn't been such a jerk before. "You can tell me anything."

"I haven't been with anyone. Not since you."

"No one?" he repeated. His heart nearly burst out of his chest, filling with something that felt a lot like love. "Then it's been too long."

He tugged her down and wheeled her around, her breasts flush with his chest. He wasn't sure who managed to get her silk panties off, him or her, but he felt her sweet heat against his erection. Their hands and arms were a tangle, as were their legs as he moved in between the vee of her legs.

She arched her back as he drew figure eights on her sweet heat.

Her hand gripped his swollen erection.

Skin that was softer than silk pressed against him as she guided him inside her moist heat. One thrust and he was in deep. *Home.*

One hand continued working her mound and his other palmed her breast, all while he spread kisses along the nape of her neck. Sucking. Biting.

A low, sexy moan escaped as he rolled her nipple in between his fingers, moving from one to the other, tugging and pulling as she moved her hips in rhythm with his.

Luke nearly exploded when he sensed her climax was near.

She moaned and rocked and whispered his name until he felt her muscles contracting around his length, and then he felt her burst into a thousand flecks of light.

Her rhythm didn't change as she coaxed him toward the same blissful release.

He thrust deeper and deeper as she flowered to take him in.

He groaned, low and feral, as complete rapture neared, every sense heightened.

Her sweet heat ground on his sex as he gripped her hips with both hands and pushed deeper until he detonated. Explosions rocked through him in the release only Julie could give him. His body tingled and pulsed afterward.

Heaving, he rolled over onto his back.

She turned to face him and settled into the crook of his arm.

He looked deep into her eyes and found everything he'd been missing for the past few years. And yet, now was not the right time for a distraction.

They'd taken the relationship well past friendship and he couldn't remember the last time he'd been this happy, but keeping her safe had to be his priority. "I didn't think I'd get this chance again. To be with you like this." He wanted to tell her he loved her, but he wasn't sure she was ready to hear the words any more than he could promise everything would work out differently this time. He didn't want to scare her away. Everything inside him said she felt the same way. He didn't need to hear the words. Yet. "I'm happy."

She blinked up at him, and he realized he was holding his breath.

The smile she gave him would have kept them warm through a blizzard. "Me, too."

All Luke's internal warning bells sounded. He was in deep with no way out. Hurting her again would kill him. But could he give her everything she deserved?

Chapter 11

Julie nuzzled into Luke's side, where she reminded herself not to get too comfortable. Everything could change in an instant. Not that she needed the fact brought to her attention, especially with Rob a step ahead of them. Even a strong, capable man like Luke might not be able to keep the determined killer away.

"What are you thinking?" Luke kissed her forehead.

"About how much I missed this," she lied.

"Your eye twitched. You never were a good liar."

"This is nice. Us talking like this. I missed this."

"Me, too. You have no idea how much." His voice was low and had a gravel-like quality. He moved to face her, hauling her body flush with his and smiling a dry crack of a smile—his trademark. Those sharp brown eyes were all glittery with need. "You know what else would be 'nice'?" He pressed his erection to the inside of her thigh, sending heat to her feminine parts. His breath warmed her neck as he moved to her ear and whispered, "I can't get enough of you."

They made love slowly this time, savoring every inch of each other, as if both knew their time together could end in a flash.

A very real threat stalked her, determined as a pit bull.

And she'd learned the hard way there were no guarantees when it came to her and Luke.

He kissed her again before mumbling something about food. He disappeared down the hall, returning a minute later with plates balanced on his arms.

As they ate, he paused long enough to pepper kisses on her forehead, her nose, her chin. She surprised herself by getting a solid meal inside her.

Afterward, she fell into a deep sleep with her arms and legs entwined with Luke's.

The next morning, Julie blinked her eyes open.

She'd slept a solid eight. The bed was cold in the space Luke had occupied. She glanced around the room. His jeans were gone, but his shirt was crumpled on the floor.

Julie laid her head back on the pillow. The thought of her and Luke back together brought warmth and light into her heart. Would it last?

Clanking noises in the kitchen confirmed his presence in the apartment.

"Luke?"

"Be there in a minute. Don't move." He strolled in a moment later wearing jeans and a serious expression, holding two cups of coffee.

"Everything all right?"

"Yeah. Fine."

But was it? Something was on his mind. He was holding back. If they were going to think about having a relationship, this wouldn't cut it. She needed coffee to clear
her head first. Then she had every intention of confront-
ing Luke. She sat up and took the hot brew. *Heaven.*

Luke's cell buzzed before she could properly thank
him.

He fished it from his pocket. "What's up?"

He said a few uh-huhs into the receiver before setting the phone down.

"What was that all about?"

"First things first." He leaned forward and pressed
a kiss to her lips.

His breath smelled like a mix of peppermint toothpaste and coffee. Her new favorite combination. "What's
going on?"

"My boss wants me to check out the news." He pulled
a remote control from the bedside table and clicked on
the thirty-two-inch flat-screen mounted on the wall.

Julie ignored the obvious reason he'd known it was
there. He'd taken others here, maybe even women. A
stab of jealousy pierced low in her belly. She refocused
as Bill Hightower's face covered the screen. Below him
was a ticker tape that read *Serial killer strikes again.
Has the FBI been compromised?*

Hightower went on to talk about Luke guarding his
ex-wife at the cost of taxpayers.

Luke picked up the phone and held it to his ear. He
clenched his back teeth as he listened.

"I'm not leaving the case," he finally said.

He was silent for another long moment as though
hearing out an argument.

"I know what he said, but I'm not handing her off to

someone else." More beats of silence. "What would you do if this was your wife?"

The sound of the last word as it rolled off Luke's tongue sent tingles through her. She scooted closer to him and rested her cheek on his strong back.

"Take me off the case and you might as well kick me out of the Bureau. By giving away my relationship with Julie, he just made killing her more of a game for Rob."

Had Luke seen this possibility coming?

"I understand. Do what you need to do." He ended the call.

"Everything okay?" she asked as she took another sip of coffee.

"Yeah."

"Sounded like you got in trouble with your boss."

"No. He said what he needed to say."

"Is he taking you off the case?"

"No. It's fine. He trusts me."

"Luke, you're not telling me something." She sat up and faced the opposite wall.

He pulled her closer to him again without managing to spill a drop of her coffee. "That's better."

She couldn't argue being close to Luke was nice.

The look he gave her nearly stopped her heart. His gaze intensified. "Last night changed things between us, right?"

She nodded. "It did for me."

"Good."

Julie needed more time to process exactly how much things had changed, but this was a start. Could she trust it? Her logical mind said no even as her heart begged to disagree. "Maybe we got married too soon back then."

The hurt in his brown eyes nearly knocked her back. "It wasn't too soon for me. Was it for you?"

She didn't immediately answer.

"Do you regret marrying me?" His gaze didn't waver.

"No. It's not that. I was just thinking if we'd met now instead of then, maybe things would be different."

"I regret a whole lot of things. None of them have anything to do with the time I spent with you, Julie. You were the only thing I thought about when they captured me. Thinking about you kept me going no matter how hard they beat me or what else they did."

Pain serrated her heart at thinking about what he'd been forced to endure. No wonder all he wanted to do was close up and forget everything that had happened when he'd finally made it back home. "I'm sorry, Luke. I had no idea."

"How could you when I shut you out?"

"I just wish I could've been more comfort. If I'd known, maybe there was something I could've done to ease the pain."

He kissed her. Hard, then sweet. "I was an idiot. I blamed myself for everything that happened overseas. The shrink said I had signs of PTSD. I thought if you knew how weak I was, you'd leave me."

"Luke, I would never—"

"I know that now. It was in my head then. You didn't walk away. Not even when I pushed you."

Those beautiful brown eyes of his caused her stomach to free-fall. "Then why'd you force me to?"

"Every time you looked at me with pity in your eyes, I felt like less of a man. I came back broken...." Speaking the words looked as though they might kill him. His voice had gone rough. "No one could've convinced me I was worthy of being with you—you were sunshine and happiness and all those things I didn't know how to get back to. If I allowed myself to be happy, it seemed totally unfair to the men I lost."

"But it wasn't your fault. None of what happened to you was. Or them." She kissed him.

"They beat me, starved me, and that was okay. I was trained to handle physical abuse. It was nothing. Men died because of my decision." His voice cracked. "Jared was the baby. I was supposed to bring him home safe. What did I do? Got him killed."

"You wouldn't have done that on purpose."

"It was my fault we were in the situation in the first place. I take that to my grave. We were sent into a red zone. Command couldn't give us much detail about what we were walking into. By their best estimates, we had a little time before the enemy arrived." He paused, taking a deep breath. "We were in formation. Ready. Everything was cool. Then I saw something to my right I couldn't ignore. The area was supposed to be civilian free, but there was this little kid heading straight into the line of fire. I knew it was about to be a bloodbath. I'd killed plenty of men by then. But I couldn't sit back and watch this innocent kid die. I thought I had more time before the enemy arrived. I made the decision to move without proper intel." He turned his face away from her.

"Oh, Luke." Tears welled, but she held them at bay. "Look at me."

Slowly, he did.

"You were trying to save a child." She kissed his eyelids, his forehead. "I'm so sorry."

He was opening up and talking about something real,

allowing her to share in his pain—pain that was still raw after all these years.

Maybe they could go back. Correct past mistakes. Maybe she could trust that what was happening between them was real and could last this time.

Or was history the best predictor of the future?

Luke had never spoken about the details of the day he was captured and Jared was killed. Not to his counselor. Not to his family. Not to anyone. "As soon as I grabbed the kid, I ran toward the tree line. All hell broke loose. I got shot before I made it to cover. Jared came running out, firing his weapon wildly. The guys came after him. I'd told them to leave me no matter what happened. They didn't. I should've known better because I would've done the same thing."

"Oh, baby, it wasn't your fault. You didn't have to go through that alone," Julie said.

Her words soothed his aching heart. He'd kept those feelings bottled up for so long, he felt as if he might explode some days. Time healed physical wounds—he had proof on his thigh where the bullet had penetrated him—but emotional scars were a totally different story. Did they ever really heal?

She whispered a few more words that brought a sense of calm over him. For the first time in a long time, he felt the dagger that had been stabbed through his heart had loosened. The constant hollow feeling in his chest was beginning to fill with hope and light. Surprisingly, it didn't feel like a betrayal.

Her breath on his skin as she whispered soothing words brought him back to life.

Julie brought him back to life.

He took her in his arms, pulled her tightly into his chest and released tears of anger and frustration that had been bottled inside him far too long. "Losing my friends made me want to die, but losing Jared…that was the worst. That's why I couldn't talk about him."

"I'm glad you told me, Luke."

He turned away, the familiar feeling of shame washing over him. Luke Campbell didn't cry. Besides, if he looked into her eyes, would he see pity there? He wouldn't be able to stand it if he'd let her down, too.

"Look at me."

Was it confirmation that had him needing to see her? Wiping away the moisture that had gathered under his eyes, he turned and faced her.

Her gaze was steady, reassuring and filled with compassion, not pity. "It's not weakness that makes you feel emotion, Luke Campbell."

"You didn't grow up with brothers," he mumbled, half joking, trying to lighten the mood. Although he'd never cried in front of his brothers, he knew deep down inside that they wouldn't fault him for it. The Campbell family always had each other's backs. Trusting outside of their circle was the difficult part. Luke thought about the soldier he'd helped train who never came home. Luke had nearly died overseas. The torture he'd endured felt like just deserts. But Luke had survived a bullet wound and weeks in enemy camp. He'd lived despite the odds. He finally picked himself up, decided to come home and waited until he could escape. And yet, there wasn't a day that went by he wouldn't exchange his life for any one of the men he'd fought alongside.

Luke had spent a year in counseling before he could round up the courage to visit Jared's parents in Spokane,

Washington. He drove his truck from the family ranch. The closer he got, the heavier his arms felt.

"The people who tortured you were savage. Being sad or hurt because you had to watch people you love die doesn't make you weak. Compassion separates good people from bad," she said, cutting into Luke's heavy thoughts. "Think that monster chasing us cares about the lives he wrecks? Ignoring your pain and not facing it makes it grow into a beast."

There was truth in her words and they resonated with Luke. "Guess I never thought of it that way. I thought I had to be the strong one. Hold everything inside."

"Well, you don't. I'm here for you, Luke. You can't always go around protecting me and disappearing. I wanted to be there for you before."

"What about now?" He arched a brow and tried his level best not to reveal how much her answer mattered to him.

"How could I not? My feelings for you haven't changed, but I have."

"Because of me."

"No matter what happens between us, I will always be there for you as a friend."

Hurt darkened his brown eyes, but he blinked it away, kissing her pulse at the base of her neck. He smoothed his palm over her flat belly. "Have I told you how much I like this?"

"Yes."

"Or how beautiful you are first thing in the morning?"

His lips brushed the soft skin of her throat, leading to her pink lips.

"Yes."

"Or how seeing you in my old AC/DC shirt nearly drove me wild the other night?"

"That one I haven't heard."

"It did." He nibbled her earlobe.

"Do you forgive yourself yet?"

"I'm a work in progress." He palmed her breast. Her nipple pebbled in his hand.

Her fingers tunneled into his hair, and she gently pulled a fistful.

He pressed his forehead to hers. "So, where does that leave us exactly?"

"I don't know yet." She paused a beat. "We're a work in progress."

"Sounds fair." He could live with that.

The sounds of his cell vibrating cut into the moment. He glanced at the screen. Jenny from his forensic evidence team was on the line. "I better take this." He kissed her again. On the lips this time. The taste of coffee lingered on her mouth.

"Sorry it's taken so long to get back to you, but we have a match on the shoe print," Jenny said.

"Great. What did you find?"

"This particular shoe isn't cheap. It's handcrafted by—get this—an old man who lives in a small village in Italy. They don't sell a lot because each pair costs over a thousand dollars."

"Not something many men would spend money on." Which didn't exactly rule Rick out, or Chad, for that matter. Luke made a mental note to circle back around to Chad. The phone number he'd given Luke for his stepbrother had turned out to be a dead end.

Was Chad covering for his half brother?

He didn't appear to like Rick. But appearances

weren't everything. And blood was blood. Maybe the two were closer than Chad had let on.

More questions that needed answers entered Luke's mind. He needed to interview the young guy's coworkers. See if he could dig up more about the relationship between him and his sibling. "So, what you're saying is whoever owns this shoe has serious funds?"

"Exactly. You didn't find anything missing from the crime scene this time, did you?"

"No. He must not've had time. The trinkets he really likes to take can't be bought. This guy likes hair and scalp."

"We knew that much." Most ritual killers held on to whatever piece of their victim they'd taken in order to relive the event for weeks, months.

"On the shoes, not many people can afford these babies. Fine Italian leather. Good news for us is they leave a specific impression."

"I'd like to see for myself. Maybe I need to dust off my passport." Disappearing and taking Julie with him had crossed Luke's mind more than once. He needed a minute to sort through all the information he'd gained in the past forty-eight hours.

A chortle came across the line. "You wish. The boss isn't sending you to Italy to check on shoes."

Luke thanked her and ended the call.

He'd especially considered going on the run with Julie until this whole mess blew over and Rob was behind bars. Problem was, Luke was the FBI's best chance at catching Rob. And there were already too many innocent women being butchered in the meantime. Now that this had become personal, the body count was rising.

Rob had promised more. In his haste, he would make a mistake. He had to.

Julie had disappeared into the bathroom, returning wearing nothing more than one of his T-shirts and her underwear.

He pulled her onto his lap and kissed the back of her neck.

Luke had a problem. Protocol said he should leave her at the safe house, guarded. Yet, Rob had tricked Luke before and almost got away with abducting her. He couldn't risk that happening twice. Keeping her with him was the only option.

"We have a serious problem to take care of before we leave," he said to her.

She turned enough for him to see her brow furrowed. "What is it, Luke?"

He spun her around to face him and then kissed her. She tasted minty and like dark-roasted coffee. "I can't get enough of you."

Julie broke into a laugh as she lowered her hand to his already straining erection. "Is that so?"

He nodded, groaning as her fingers curled around his shaft and gently squeezed.

"Good. Because I'm not done with you, either."

Chapter 12

Luke had reluctantly finished dressing and kissed Julie again before moving into the living room to check his laptop.

He'd received an email from Nick stating that the background check on Chad's mother came up clean. In fact, he and his mother had been on vacation together during one of the murders. Nick was still digging around to find an address for Rick.

Luke glanced up from the screen, and his heart flipped when he saw her. She looked as beautiful as ever. No, more. Her hair was pulled back in a ponytail. A few loose strands framed her face. Her body was amazing. He already knew he'd never get enough of exploring her sensual curves. He logged off before that body of hers got him going again. "Ready?"

She nodded.

He led her to the elevator and then the truck. Backup was all around them, and yet an uneasy feeling still sat in his stomach like bad food.

Of course, every time he walked out the door with Julie he disliked the feeling of being exposed. With one hand on her back and the other ready to grip his weapon, he kept a watchful eye on everyone who passed by.

Rob had succeeded in making Luke paranoid. But the stakes had never been higher. The thought of what Rob would do to Julie if he got his hands on her... Luke couldn't go there.

A visual scan of the garage yielded nothing.

One of his guys stood in the corner, smoking. He had arm-sleeve tattoos and wore a rock-band T-shirt with ripped jeans. Luke glanced at him for confirmation. The undercover agent popped his chin, giving the all-clear sign.

The restaurant would be easy enough to find using GPS. Upscale places like the DeBleu usually required their waiters to show up at lunch to taste the evening's specials and prepare their stations, so if Luke was lucky the staff would be there.

Traffic was light enough to make it to Addison in twenty minutes. For most of the ride, he filled Julie in on the shoe print left at the crime scene and the news he'd received from his brother. After parking and scanning the lot, Luke double-checked the notes he'd made on his phone.

Inside, a man wearing a long white apron greeted them. "I'm sorry. We're not open for lunch."

"We're not here for food." Luke flashed his badge and introduced himself. "I'd appreciate a moment of your time."

A look of shock crossed the guy's blond features. He introduced himself as Stephen before saying, "Of course."

"I'd like to speak to you about Chad Devel. Is he here by any chance?"

"Afraid not. He's not on the schedule tonight. Why? Did he do something wrong?"

"No." Luke smiled to ease the guy's tension. "I was hoping to ask him a few routine questions while I was here. Did he work on the night of the twenty-second?"

"Let's see. I worked that night. It was a Thursday. Decent night for tips." He glanced right as he recalled the date. "Yeah, he was here."

"Can you verify he was here the entire evening?"

"Yes. We give twenty minutes for dinner break, so he was here all night."

"Doesn't seem like much time to eat."

"I've found if I give longer, they disappear and don't always come back. Twenty minutes is enough time to eat. They put their order in before break, and when it comes up, they hit the back room," he said defensively.

Luke nodded as if he understood, to gain sympathy. "Is Chad a good sous chef?"

"He took a while to train, but once he got the hang of it, he's done all right," Stephen said.

"I hate to ask this question, but is he trustworthy?" Luke figured he'd get more information if he buddied up with Stephen.

"He wouldn't still work here if he wasn't."

"This is a beautiful place," Julie said.

Pride flashed behind Stephen's eyes as he looked at Luke. "You should bring her back for dinner sometime. On me."

"I appreciate it. I'll keep that in mind." Luke paused for effect. "Mind if I speak with a couple of your employees while I'm here?"

"Sure. Which ones?" Being treated with respect seemed to be the trick to getting Stephen to open up.

"Tony and Angie. Are they around by any chance?"

"Unfortunately, only one still works here. Angie quit last night in the middle of her shift."

"Sounds like she left you in the lurch."

"You wouldn't believe. I got it covered, but what a disaster."

"I can only imagine. These kids have no idea what real responsibility is like."

Stephen gave a nod of approval for the solidarity.

"Do you happen to have a good address for Tony?"

"Sure. Give me a minute, and I'll check employee records." The man made a move toward the kitchen but stopped and turned. "Would either of you like a cup of coffee? Tea?"

Luke glanced toward Julie, who smiled and shook her head.

"We're okay. Thanks."

Satisfied, Stephen disappeared toward the sounds of clanking pans.

Quick surveillance of the restaurant showed nothing unusual. Luke hadn't expected to find anything out of the ordinary, but experience had taught him he could never be sure when a case was about to break wide open. And they usually did so in an instant. Gut instinct was honed from years of experience. And his rarely failed.

He moved to block more of Julie with his large frame as they waited for Stephen to return.

The blond manager exploded from the kitchen with a piece of paper in his hands. "I'm sorry."

Luke's body went on full alert—ready for whatever was about to come his way. His hand instinctively went to the handle of his gun resting on his hip.

"It seems word got out you were here interrogating me. Tony ran out the back door." He jogged toward them and stuck out the piece of paper.

The roar of a motorcycle engine sounded from the parking lot. Luke muttered a curse and turned tail after taking the address.

"Thanks for the information," he said out of the side of his mouth with a dry smile. "And if I were interrogating you, you'd know it."

He winked, motioning Julie to follow.

Camera phone ready, he snapped a pic of the motorcycle as it turned right out of the parking lot. He sent the photo to Detective Garcia.

The guy's address was on the sheet of paper. If it was legit, then Luke would wait for him at his house. Running was never a sign of innocence. This guy was doing something wrong. Luke needed to figure out what.

From the parking lot to Tony's apartment was a three-minute ride. Luke didn't figure the guy would be stupid enough to go home, but that was exactly what he'd done. The motorcycle sat in the parking lot near the address the restaurant manager had provided.

Either this guy was small-time or just stupid. Luke's experience had taught him to reserve judgment until he spoke to someone.

The two-story stucco apartment building had roughly thirty units total.

Tony's was on the second floor.

"I want you so close I can feel your breath," he said to Julie.

She nodded, her wide amber eyes signaling her fear.

"We'll be fine," he reassured her, then ascended the concrete-and-metal stairs at the end of the building.

"You don't think it's him?"

"No. Something's up. But I don't think it's Rob. Believe me, we wouldn't be going in without backup if I thought for a second he'd be here, but this guy's scared, and I need to find out what he's hiding."

She was so close he could hear her blow out a breath behind him. His reassurance seemed to ease her tension a notch below panic. Good. He liked being able to calm her fears.

Besides, what he'd said was absolute gospel. He'd never knowingly face down Rob with her present and without any reinforcements. There was a slight possibility that Rob was working with someone else. If not directly, then someone could be covering his tracks. That someone could be his brother or Chad's friends. The circumstantial evidence against Rick was mounting. A rich dad might do anything to shield his son. Especially if the boy had been abused. But the fact Rick grew up in California worked against them logistically, Luke thought as he rapped on the door. "FBI. Open up."

Silence.

"Open up or I'll break down the door. Either way, we're going to talk. Your choice." Luke didn't have a warrant, so there was no way he would force entry. But the guy behind the door didn't know that. It was a gamble.

The door swung open.

Taking a risk paid off.

A twentysomething guy stood there, wide-eyed. His hand trembled on the knob. "Can I help you?"

"I'm Special Agent Campbell, and I'd like to ask you a few questions."

"Okay." His five-foot-ten frame blocked the opening.

"May we come in?"

"No, sir." The guy's voice shook, too.

"I'm not here to bust you. I need answers. As long as you cooperate, we're good." He intentionally used a calm tone.

"Okay. Did I do something wrong?" The door didn't budge.

"Not that I know of. At least, not yet. Obstructing an ongoing murder investigation is a serious charge."

"Holy crap." He shook his head. "I didn't kill anyone."

"I know you didn't." Luke paused to give the young man a minute to think. "But you might be able to stop a crime."

The guy glanced around. "Can't you ask me right here?"

"There anything inside I need to be worried about?"

"No."

"Are you lying to me?"

"No, sir."

"Then why are you afraid to open the door?"

"I'm not, sir." He glanced around nervously and cracked the door. "Is that good?"

"Better." Luke felt more comfortable being able to see inside. "Do you know Chad Devel?"

"Yes." A mix of relief and apprehension played across his features. "He's a buddy of mine from work."

"You two close?"

"Somewhat. Why? Is he okay?" Concern knitted his

dark bushy eyebrows together. He was another one who looked as if he'd stepped off an Abercrombie & Fitch ad. Tall, thin, with thick hair and a sullen look on his face.

"Everything's fine. We're trying to make sure it stays that way."

"Is someone after him?" He scrubbed his hands across the light stubble on his chin.

"Do you know his brother?"

"Rick? Yeah, sure. Haven't seen him in a while, though. He hasn't been coming around to Chad's place."

Interesting. Chad had given them the impression he didn't hang out with his brother.

Guess he'd lied. Luke didn't like liars. "When's the last time you saw him at his brother's?"

"Been a couple of months. Why? Did Rick do something wrong?"

That put him in the Metroplex for a few of the killings. "No. You expecting him to?"

The guy wiped his palms down the front of his pants. "He seems the type. I mean, he hangs around with us but doesn't party. Doesn't say much, either. He's sort of creepy."

"Couldn't he just be straitlaced?"

"That's what I thought at first, too. But then he showed up one night—one look at him and I could tell he was on something."

"Drugs?"

Tony nodded. "Except Chad swore his brother didn't partake, you know."

Luke didn't, but he nodded anyway. "I didn't think Rick lived around here."

"Yeah. He's got a place near Chad."

"Addison Circle?"

Tony nodded. "I've never been to his place, though."

"I didn't realize the two of them were so close."

"Chad's kind of protective of him. Feels sorry for him. Said he had a bad childhood or something."

"Their dad?"

"Nah. His mom. She's some kind of freak, from what Chad says. He doesn't really like his brother. He pities the guy."

Luke didn't see that one coming. Rick fit the profile. His age was on the money. Learning he had an estranged mother made Luke wonder if that had anything to do with the bleach. He cleansed his "projects" then tortured them. This was one angry and twisted guy. Of course, abuse did bad things to a kid's brain. He certainly had the income to be able to afford expensive Italian shoes, or they could've been a present.

He exchanged a look with Julie. She was clearly thinking the same thing.

Except Luke's killer knew the area well. "How long has his brother been living here?"

"On and off for a year, I think."

"Where else does he live?"

"He goes back and forth between here and California now that he got kicked out of medical school."

Luke practically had the wind knocked out of him.

Rob cut his victims with medical precision. Rick had been in medical school? He'd have access to the kind of tools Rob used. "How long did you say he's been here?"

"This time? A year."

"What do you mean by 'this time'?"

"Oh. He came here for high school. His dad shipped him off to an all-male boarding school to get him away from his mother or something. Sent him to Dallas so he'd be close to Chad."

Spending his high-school years here would definitely give him insight into the area. "You have Rick's address?"

"No. Like I said, I've never been to his place. I just know it's close to Chad's."

"You planning on leaving the area anytime soon?"

"No, sir."

"Good. I expect to be able to find you if I have more questions."

"Yes, sir."

"And if you run from me next time, I'll haul your butt to jail. Understood?"

"Yes, sir."

Luke led Julie out the door.

"Chad wasn't exactly honest with us yesterday, was he?" she asked in a whisper.

"Nope."

"We find him and we get our killer, don't we?" Her tone was like a line that had been pulled so taut, it was about to break.

"Looks that way," he said calmly.

"So are we heading to Chad's place?" Her voice hitched on the last word.

"No."

"Why not?" She whirled on him.

"I told you that I wouldn't risk your safety. We can't go back alone." He urged her to keep walking. Truth was, Rob could be watching them right now.

Reality dawned on her as her eyes widened. "Oh. Right. *He* could be there."

Luke followed her down the stairs and to the truck.

He opened her door for her and helped her in. "He's near. And I'd venture to guess either he or Chad drives a gray sedan."

She gasped as she buckled her seat belt. "The car that followed us?"

"I didn't believe it was a coincidence then. And I sure don't now." Luke took his seat on the driver's side and scanned the lot. "I need to find a good place for you to hide while I pay our friend another visit."

Her hand on his arm normally brought heat where she touched. This time was different. He could feel her shaking. The idea of being away from her didn't do good things to the acid already churning in his gut. On balance, there was no other choice. Under the circumstances, there was only one option he could consider. Luke fished his cell from his pocket and tapped on his brother-in-law's name in his contacts. "Riley, are you on shift right now?"

"Yes, but I can break for lunch anytime. What's up?"

"I need a favor."

"Anything."

Luke picked a meeting spot halfway between them, which was fifteen minutes away, and ended the call. He turned to Julie as he started the ignition. "You okay with hanging out with Riley for a while?"

"Of course. It'll be good to see him." Her eyes told him a different story.

"What is it?"

"Nothing." She bit her bottom lip.

Lying?

"You know I'm going to be fine." He glanced in her direction as he pulled out of the parking lot and headed north. They'd agreed on a spot at the border where Plano met Dallas on the Tollway.

She didn't respond.

"I don't take unnecessary risks."

"I know," she said quietly. "This guy is…bad."

"I've dealt with worse," he said, trying his best to sound convincing. Luke meandered onto the Tollway and headed north. He took the Parker Road exit and pulled into the strip shopping center. He hadn't noticed the voice mail registered on his phone. Luke listened to the message from Nick, confirming what he'd just learned—Rick Camden had flunked out of medical school. Nick was working on getting a current address. Luke hit the end button and stuffed the phone in his pocket.

Riley waited in his squad car.

"Give me a minute to get Riley up to speed, okay?" he asked Julie.

She nodded.

He didn't like how quiet she was being, especially since seeing the concern in her eyes.

With his hand on the door handle, he paused. "You know I'm coming back to get you in an hour, right?"

It was then he noticed the tears that had been welling in her eyes. He came around to her side of the truck and pulled her into his arms. She burrowed into his chest, trembling. "Be careful."

"I'll be fine."

He lifted her chin until her gaze met his. He thumbed away her tears. "Look at me. I promise I'll be back in an hour or two. You're not getting rid of me that easy." He winked.

Her nod was tentative.

"I give you my word." He paused for emphasis. "You believe me, right?"

"Yes." Her chin lifted a little higher.

"That's my girl."

He tucked her into the passenger seat of Riley's SUV, the standard issue for patrol in Plano, and asked his brother-in-law to step out for a minute.

Riley did.

"You need a heads-up on this one. This guy's the worst."

"I've been watching the bulletins. Plus, we got information at briefing. We have a lot of eyes looking for him."

"Then you know what he's capable of."

Riley nodded, an ominous look settling over his features.

"Keep her safe." Luke didn't like leaving her, not even with one of the few men he'd trust with his own life. "And be careful. This guy doesn't care about the badge you're wearing. Won't stop him."

"Got it. You, too. Your sister would kill me if anything happened to you on my watch." Riley's attempt at humor succeeded in lightening the somber mood.

Luke couldn't help but crack a smile. "I wouldn't want to be on the wrong side of a postpartum woman like Meg."

"Good thing I love her."

Luke had already started toward his truck.

"Watch your back, man," Riley said.

Luke waved, turned to circle around the vehicle and give Julie another kiss goodbye. "I'll see you after lunch. Save me a taco."

Chapter 13

"It's great to see you again, Riley." Julie tried to distract herself from the fact that Luke was about to face down a ruthless killer. *Possibly* face down, she corrected. After all, the guy might not be home. And, although the evidence was condemning, there was no guarantee they were on the right track. Plus, he was going to see Chad, not Rick.

Her nerves were bundled tight. She feared they'd snap if someone so much as said boo.

"You, too," Riley said.

"Congratulations on two fronts. Getting married and I heard you're a new dad. I bet he's beautiful." Any other time she'd be interested in hearing all the details about the boy's birth and first few weeks in the world, but all she could focus on now was Luke's safety.

"He is. Keeping us on our toes." Riley smiled as he

cut across the lot and parked in front of the Tex-Mex restaurant she remembered was his favorite.

"I haven't been here in ages. I miss the food."

"It's almost a sin to live anywhere near here and not visit Eduardo's."

She smiled at his visible display of outrage. "How's Meg?"

"Good. Becoming a mother suits her."

Julie got out of the SUV and met him around the front of the hood. She couldn't help but check out the people around her warily. Would there ever come a time when she didn't fear someone was watching? Riley stared at her, one hand on the butt of his gun. "Everything okay?"

"Yeah. It's just I always feel like he's close." She shivered.

"You've been through a lot. I can't blame you for being spooked. You want to go somewhere else to eat? Meg's home. I can take you there."

"And make you miss out on Eduardo's enchiladas? Are you crazy?" She tried to shake off the feeling. "Besides, I don't want to get in the way of Meg bonding with her new baby. And I want to hear about Hitch."

Riley followed her inside. As they waited for a table, he leaned toward her and whispered, "Three of my fellow officers are outside."

"I didn't see anyone else." And she'd looked carefully.

"Exactly. They're in plain clothes. Out of sight. But they're there. I called in a few favors after my conversation with Luke."

The hostess greeted them and led them toward their table in between no less than four tables full of uniformed officers from Dallas and Richardson. She guessed it was true what they said about law enforcement sticking together.

She smiled. "More favors?"

He nodded as he took his seat. "Couldn't have Luke worrying about you while he did his job, now, could I?"

Julie let out her breath, realizing for the first time her fingers had been practically clamped together in a death grip. "Thank you."

"He called in for backup. You know that, right?" Riley said, his tone serious.

"I hadn't thought of it, but you're right. Of course he would do that."

"You're safe. He's doing his job. And he's the best. He's survived much worse. A jerk like Rob isn't going to get the best of Luke."

"You're right again." She wished she shared his confidence. Fear of losing Luke rippled through her. If not by Rob's hands, then by some trigger that made Luke shut down again. She didn't want to admit to herself how deeply her feelings ran. She'd sworn no one would have that kind of power over her again. Her feelings for him were resurfacing, but that didn't mean things would magically work out this time.

The waiter came to take their orders. He placed a bowl of chips and salsa on the table.

Riley picked up a chip and dipped it in the salsa. "You okay?"

"I guess. Everything's happening so fast. This guy. He's everywhere but nowhere."

"Everyone's looking for him."

"Between that and being this close to Luke again, I'm confused. Scared."

"He hasn't been the same for the past four years."

"But he picked up his life and moved on. I know he's dated other people."

"After a few years we tried to set him up. Lucy had a friend on the force she thought might help bring him out of his funk."

A jealous twinge fired through her.

"Didn't work. He wouldn't…didn't… She liked him, but they ended up friends. The relationship was purely platonic."

"I'm sure there were others." She didn't lift her gaze to meet his. Instead, she toyed with the chip in her fingers.

"True. Over time. I heard."

"You didn't meet them?"

"No. He never brought them to the ranch."

Her heavy heart filled with light.

Food arrived.

They smiled at the waiter and thanked him.

"Thanks for telling me that." It didn't solve all their problems, but it did ease the sting of how easy it seemed for him to walk away before.

"I just hate to see two people who fit so well together go through what you two have."

"When did you become such a hopeless romantic?"

"Having a baby has weakened me," he joked. He pulled his phone from his shirt pocket and opened a picture then handed it to her.

"Is that him?" Hitch had the Campbell family's dark hair. Brown eyes. Dimpled smile. If her heart could've melted in her chest right then and there, it would've.

Riley practically beamed.

Julie smiled back at him. "One look at that angel's face and I can see why you changed."

She handed the phone to him, took a chip, dipped it in salsa and leaned closer. "Thank you for telling me what you did before. About me and Luke. It helps. But now I'd like to hear more about that beautiful wife and boy of yours."

Luke had called for backup on his way south on the Tollway. Chad wasn't at work. With it being midday, Luke figured there was a good chance the guy was still asleep. He already knew Chad liked to party on his days off.

A squad car was already parked in the lot when Luke arrived. He thanked the SWAT officers and led the way to Chad's place.

Three raps on the door, and he yelled, "FBI. Open up."

Noises came from the other side of the door. Did Chad have company? Rick wouldn't go down easy.

"Might be hot," he told the pair of SWAT officers flanking him.

They stepped aside, following his lead.

He pounded the door with his fist this time. "I hear you in there, Chad. Open up."

A minute later, the door flew open. Chad stood there in his boxer shorts. A young woman, barely clothed, curled up on the couch, hugging a pillow.

"What can I do for you?"

Luke stepped inside and grabbed Chad by the neck, slamming his back against the door. "You lied to me."

Chad shook his head, wincing.

The girl screamed.

"You want to start all over, and tell me the truth this time?"

Chad shook his head. His face turned blood red. "Lawyer."

"Innocent people don't need lawyers, Chad." Luke loosened his grip enough for Chad to speak.

"Dude, I don't know what you're talking about."

"You told me you didn't know where Rick was. Is he here right now?"

Chad shook his head.

"You better not be lying to me. Mind if the officers double-check?"

"Go ahead. I swear he isn't here."

The officers split up, guns leveled.

"Why did you lie to me, Chad?" Luke gripped the guy's neck a little tighter.

"Who told you I lied?"

"I visited your job and asked a few questions. You and Rick are close, aren't you? What? Didn't you think I'd check up on your story?"

Chad shook his head, gasping for air.

Luke eased up enough for Chad to breathe.

"Stop. You're hurting him," the girl pleaded, hugging the pillow tighter.

"You want a trip downtown?" Luke didn't move his arm from across Chad's chest and neck, but he glanced at her.

"No."

"No, what?"

"No, sir."

"Then stay put and keep quiet." Luke turned his attention back to Chad, keeping the girl in his peripheral view. "Your brother have a medical problem?"

"He's diabetic."

Luke bit back a curse.

"Clear," one of the officers said.

The other repeated the word a few minutes later. They returned to the living room at the same time. One held up a shoe with a gloved hand.

"This the item you're looking for, Special Agent Campbell?"

Luke examined the shoe without touching it, keeping one elbow on Chad's chest. "This is it." He leveled his gaze at Chad.

"What does my shoe have to do with anything?"

"Still playing stupid, Chad?"

"I seriously don't know what you're talking about."

"This your shoe?"

"Yes."

"Then you just bought yourself a trip downtown." Luke turned to the officers. "Gentlemen."

"Hold on a sec. What's going on?" The young man looked genuinely confused.

Luke had to give it to Chad: the guy played stupid to an art form. Either that or he really was in the dark about his half brother's illegal activity.

"This shoe is rare, isn't it, Chad?"

"Yeah. So what?"

"This print was found at the scene of two murders."

The color drained from Chad's face.

"Gruesome murders. Someone's chopping up women with a surgical saw." Luke loosened his grip so Chad wouldn't pass out. Instead, he sank to the floor.

"My dad gave me those shoes for Christmas three years ago."

"Let me guess—he gave your brother the same pair."

"Half brother."

"So I'm reminded."

"And the answer is yes." Sitting on the floor, Chad looked small and devastated. Both hands gripped his head as he leaned his face toward his knees.

"You've been covering for your half brother, haven't you?"

"Yeah, because I feel sorry for the guy."

"Why?"

"His mom is crazy. The only reason Dad left my mom for her was because he didn't want Rick growing up alone. I suspected she did cruel...*things*...to him, but he never talked about it."

"What things?"

Tears spilled onto his cheeks. "I don't know. Torture, I guess. He'd show up with bruises all over his body. Dad would send him here because he couldn't go back to school looking like that. Even as a kid I knew he didn't get them from playing. He wasn't into sports, either. He was pretty brainy. He'd sit in the corner of my room and rock his head back and forth. Sometimes, it'd take days for him to acknowledge me. Whatever Bev did to him was awful. His mom was a twisted bitch."

"That why he soaks his victim's clothes in bleach?"

Chad dry heaved. "I'm sorry. I didn't know. According to my mom, Bev threatened to ruin my dad's reputation and that's why he left us. She manipulated and blackmailed him. I can only imagine what else she did to Rick."

"Or cuts out pieces of their hair and scalps?"

"I would've turned him in myself if I'd…"

Luke bent down to Chad's level. "Where does he live?"

Chad stood, moved in front of the door and pointed

to a building across the parking lot. "Right there. Number two hundred and two."

"You listen to me carefully. Your sick bastard of a brother is after someone I love. You run into him, you better tell him this for me. He just made this personal. I'll see him in hell before I let him hurt the people I care about."

Chad nodded slowly.

Luke lowered his voice when he said, "You see him? Tell him he's not the only one who can play games."

He turned toward the officers. "Anything worth running him downtown for here?"

They shook their heads. "If he had anything, he got rid of it before he let us in."

"Mind taking his statement and filing the report?"

"Not at all," one of the officers replied.

"I owe you one." Luke needed to get out of there.

An ominous feeling had settled over him, and all he could think about was getting to Julie.

Chapter 14

Luke updated his report, put out a BOLO—a Be On the Lookout alert—and entered Rick's address into the system with a request for a warrant to search the premises. If all went well, he'd be back at Rick's in an hour, and Julie would be safe. Heck, as long as he was wishing, Rick would be locked up before she finished lunch.

Before Luke left the parking lot, he rounded up the pair of officers and headed toward the apartment across the lot. He rapped on the door several times and listened. No one answered, and the place was dead quiet. Knowing the way this guy operated, he'd watched the events unfold at his half brother's and was long gone.

No answer. No warrant. They'd have to come back.

After thanking the officers, Luke hopped on the Tollway and headed toward Plano.

Seeing a half-dozen officers surround Julie when he

arrived at the restaurant lowered his blood pressure to a reasonable level.

Her face lit up when he walked into the room, and his muscles relaxed another notch.

"How'd it go?" She threw her arms open and turned her face to the side slightly.

He'd already seen the tears of relief. He held her until she stopped shaking and kissed the top of her head.

The waiter interrupted, taking Luke's order before disappearing into the kitchen.

Julie took a seat next to him as he turned his attention toward Riley. "I owe you one, man."

"I'll start a tab," he joked, no doubt an attempt to lighten the mood.

Luke smiled his gratitude. "We need a new place to stay. Think you can help out with that?" Staying on the move was their best chance.

"I know of a place. I'd like to keep you inside my city limits. You good with that?"

"Absolutely." Luke figured the best place for them was close to family in case he needed a quick place to stash Julie. Besides, with half of Plano P.D. watching out for them, he'd sleep better at night.

"Find anything useful on your shopping trip?" Riley glanced around, using code on the off chance someone was listening.

Luke nodded. "Wasn't bad. Call you later with the details?"

"Sure. Sounds like you identified what you were looking for."

"It's him. No doubt in my mind."

Officers stood, one by one, and gave a nod toward Riley's table.

Luke shook their hands. After eating and thanking his brother-in-law again, Luke helped Julie into the truck and waved goodbye.

"I'll get back to you with the address we talked about," Riley shouted before he drove off.

Before Luke could put the truck in Drive, he got the text he'd been hoping for. "I have a warrant to search Rick's place. We're heading back to Addison."

Julie's gaze widened. "You found out where he lives?"

"Yeah. And it's right across the parking lot from Chad. I've requested uniformed officers to assist. There'll be plenty of backup. Plus, I already know he's not there."

"How can you be sure?"

"He's too smart, for one. He knows we're onto him. Plus, with the location of his place across from Chad's, he's been watching everything that goes on at his brother's. Chad's most likely telling his brother all about our conversation. The shoe print found at the scene of the murders belongs to a shoe given to Rick for Christmas three years ago, according to his brother."

"Is it safe?"

"I don't know what we'll find at his place, maybe nothing, but I'm one hundred percent certain he won't be there. If I had any doubt, I wouldn't bring you." He glanced at her as he navigated the truck out of the parking lot and headed toward the on-ramp. "You good with this? I can always drop you at the station until we're done."

"No," she said quickly. "I want to go with you. It was agony being in the restaurant without you. Not knowing if something had happened... I'd rather be there."

Luke knew exactly how she felt. Even with officers

surrounding her the entire time he was away, he'd had an uneasy feeling. Rick was *that* cunning.

His phone chirped, indicating a text had arrived. Luke retrieved his cell from his pocket and handed it to Julie.

She studied the screen. "It's an address from Riley."

"Looks like we have a place to stay tonight."

"I guess there's no chance we can go back to where we were before?" She sounded resigned to be on the run.

"It's best to stay on the move. That's the only way to keep ahead of Rick. Besides, I don't want to jeopardize my friends any more than I have to." The situation was no doubt wearing her down. She seemed determined to keep fighting and hold her own. Her innate survival instincts would help keep her alive.

Problem was, this case was escalating fast. Too fast.

They arrived back at Rick's apartment before the police. Luke parked the truck and palmed his weapon. He surveyed the parking lot for a gray sedan but found nothing matching the description.

"What did you find out from Chad?"

"It's him. Rick is our guy. In addition to the shoe match, Chad also confirmed his brother is diabetic."

"The orange juice that was left out at my client's house."

"Exactly. Plus, there's a history of mental instability in the family."

"His dad?"

"Mom. The reason Dad left Chad's mom to be with the other woman was because he didn't trust her to be alone with his son. Sounds like she held Rick over his head, too. If news of that got out, it could threaten his professional reputation."

"Sounds bad. What kind of person would hurt their own child?"

"Might explain why Rob chops off his victims' heads. He's trying to make his mother pay."

Color drained from Julie's face. "That's so sad."

"Chad believes there was torture involved, but he didn't talk specifics."

"It's awful what human beings can do to one another."

"Not all kinds of love is good." Luke's had been poison when he'd returned from active duty. Or so he'd thought at the time. Took him a year and visits with a counselor to acknowledge he had the classic signs of post-traumatic stress disorder. The same shame he felt at not being able to save his brothers in arms resurfaced every time he heard Rick killed another innocent victim. Every part of Luke wanted to shut down again with the news. The past two years had been like reliving those early months all over again. Except now that he had Julie in his life again, he had even more to fight for to stay grounded and not let the situation get the best of him.

A dull ache pounded between his temples—a searing headache threatened. He remembered the killer ones he'd had four years ago. They'd almost split his head in two.

Other PTSD signs were returning, too.

Luke shoved them down deep. He had to catch Rick or risk losing everything again.

A pair of squad cars parked in front of Luke's truck. He was informed the SWAT team would be arriving to assist.

"He's clever, so don't expect much," he warned the officers. "We might find a shoe match to crime scenes." He showed them the picture.

A minivan pulled up, the doors opened and a team

of SWAT officers spilled out. Luke greeted them and pointed toward Rick's door. "Where can she stay while we check things out?"

"In the squad car with Officer Haines," Officer Melton said.

The SWAT officers took position with the Hammer—the key to the city known for its ability to open all doors.

"One…two…three…" The officer who'd identified himself as the supervisor swung the Hammer, bursting through the lock. The door flew open.

One officer went right. One went left. The third took the middle. The officer with the Hammer held position at the door.

Not three minutes later, the supervisor gave the all clear.

Luke strode inside.

The place had a few pieces of modern furniture with a forty-two-inch flat-screen mounted on the wall. Since the space was open concept, Luke could see through to the kitchen with its stainless-steel appliances and granite countertops. In the bedroom, clothes were strewn and cabinets already half-empty. Clearly, Rick had made a hasty exit. Luke bit back a curse. He was so close he could almost feel the guy's presence still in the room. It was pure evil—not that he believed in that.

Besides, even if Rick were the devil incarnate, he'd still spend the rest of his days behind bars just like every other heinous criminal. If found guilty of multiple murders, he might just land an express ticket to death row, where he would be executed.

Luke turned the place over in twenty minutes while SWAT kept a close watch on the door and windows. There wasn't much to see except several cartons of orange juice in the fridge and empty bottles of insulin in the bathroom trash can. Proof he was a diabetic, but not necessarily a murderer. The empty bottles of hair-bonding glue in the trash were far more damning.

Maybe his evidence response team could find hair fibers linking Rick to one of the victims?

Luke updated the SWAT officers and called it in.

With Chad's statement, Rick qualified as a person of interest. It was enough to detain him for questioning. But if Luke had found something more concrete, even a drop of a victim's blood on Rick's clothing, he would feel better. Luke figured the guy would be smart enough to keep his tools somewhere else. But where? Surely not in his car.

The headache that had started in the car raged, causing a burning sensation in the backs of Luke's eyes.

A SWAT officer's body stiffened. "I see a guy who fits the description of the suspect watching us from across the parking lot. He's wearing a cobalt-blue sweatshirt and jeans."

Luke muttered a curse as he tore through the door, giving chase. He heard an officer say he would follow. Luke's full attention zeroed in on Sweatshirt.

The second Luke's foot hit concrete, Sweatshirt bolted. This was the closest Luke had been to the deranged killer. He could feel in his bones that this was Rick. A quick shot of adrenaline pulsed through him, powering his legs forward like rockets.

Rick disappeared in between buildings two hundred yards in front of Luke, but he kept pushing anyway. This might be his only hope of catching the bastard before he hurt someone else.

Anger and frustration coursed through Luke as he

reached the buildings. He had to take a guess on the direction Rick went. His odds were fifty-fifty, and they were the best he'd had since this whole journey began two years ago. Luke didn't like it. He could not risk losing the guy this time.

"I'll take right," Luke shouted to the officer following without looking back. Acknowledgment came a second later through labored breaths.

Pushing forward, Luke ran until his sides cramped, his thighs burned and his lungs felt as if they might explode.

Shelving the pain, he ran some more.

He'd lost visual contact with Sweatshirt. The situation was becoming more hopeless by the second. A wave of desperation crashed through him. Then he saw something. A glimpse of cobalt blue sticking out from behind a car.

Luke charged toward it.

The piece of sweatshirt disappeared before Luke could get within twenty yards.

At least he was back on track.

The guy wasn't going to get far, if Luke had anything to say about it. He zigzagged through cars, pushing his body to the limit.

No way was Rick in better physical condition than Luke. If he could get close, he had no doubt he could overpower the guy or outrun him. All the advantage had gone to Rick so far. That was about to change. Luke knew who the bastard was, and so would the rest of the world as soon as Luke called Bill Hightower.

Heck, give him five minutes alone with the piece of human garbage and he'd do more than talk a confession out of him. He'd break him. Another five without the badge, and the man wouldn't walk out alive.

Another turn and Luke was closing in on him. He clenched his fists with the need to get his hands around the guy's neck.

Less than half a city block away, Luke pushed his legs further. Closing in at this speed, he'd be on top of Rick in a matter of minutes.

Before Luke could close the last bit of gap between them, Rick disappeared into a small crowd. There was a barbershop and a travel agency side by side at the place Luke had lost visual contact. After checking through the windows of both, it was clear from the commotion that Sweatshirt had ducked into the first.

A few seconds later, Luke burst through the doors of the barbershop. The few men inside looked startled.

"FBI." He flashed his badge. "There was a man who just ran through here."

Heads nodded confirmation.

"Where'd he go?"

Several men pointed toward what looked like a stockroom.

"Any employees in there I need to know about?" He drew his gun, leveled it.

"No. Everyone's out here," one of the employees said, already heading toward the front door.

"Where does that lead?" Luke asked as he stalked toward the back room.

"The alley."

Luke's hopes the place was sealed were dashed. "Everyone outside until someone with a badge tells you it's clear. Got it?" Luke muttered a curse and hauled himself toward the stockroom.

The door was open. He surveyed the room before entering. Even though it had been staged to look as if Rick had run out the back, he could be anywhere, ready to strike.

Luke took measured steps forward, keenly aware of the fact his guy might be getting away.

Underestimating Rick, believing the obvious, had gotten an officer killed already.

By the time Luke reached the alley, there was no sign of Rick. Didn't stop Luke from verifying what his eyes had already shown him. He doubled back and checked the stockroom one more time as he moved through it again. Luke slammed his fist against the wall and released a string of swearwords.

He pulled his composure together as he walked out front. "Everything's safe. Go inside and lock the doors."

"Thank you." The look of relief on the guy's face was fleeting as he scurried toward the stockroom.

Luke took a minute to get his bearings before making his way to the apartment.

Julie sat in the car of one of the SWAT officers.

"He knows the area well," Luke said to the supervisor, still heaving, trying to fill his lungs with air. Sweat rolled down his neck.

"We sent a couple of guys to back you up. They didn't get anywhere, either. We'll stick around until your team shows up to process the place."

After shaking his hand and thanking him for his help, Luke walked Julie to the truck. He'd been so close to catching Rick. Anger railed through him. His hands shook. Head pounded.

If anyone else was hurt, how could he ever forgive himself?

A jolt of shame washed through him, and his body trembled.

"Luke? What's wrong?" Concern wrinkled Julie's forehead.

"Headache." He couldn't help but feel responsible for the deaths of the women so far. How the heck did he open up and talk about that? If he'd caught Rick two years ago, more than half a dozen lives would've been saved. Not to mention Julie wouldn't be in this mess.

The tremors started again as his headache dulled.

Fury ate at his gut as he fought the signs of PTSD overwhelming him.

Chapter 15

Luke checked outside the window onto the street. An officer was stationed in front of the house. Everything looked fine. And yet, everything felt off. Why?

"This case," he said under his breath. There was a chill in the air and his warning systems had been tripped. Then again, his internal alarms had been firing rapidly ever since he'd chased Rick.

The small two-story in historic Plano was a good cover, he repeated silently for the hundredth time. One of Riley's friends would be driving past every ten minutes or so, in addition to the marked car on the street.

Luke prayed it would be enough.

He distracted himself by moving to the kitchen and fixing a light dinner of soup and BLTs for him and Julie, placing the meal on the island.

Julie descended the stairs. So beautiful. Her hair was

still wet from the shower. Water beaded and rolled down her neck where he'd left a few love bites the night before. If anyone could keep him planted in reality, it was her.

"Feels so good to be clean," she said, taking a seat next to him.

"I can think of a few reasons to be dirty." He leaned toward her, touching elbows. The point of contact still spread heat through his arm. He'd never get tired of her.

A distant sound scarcely registered. Luke stiffened as he glanced toward the street. He raised his head as he scooped her up and instinctively headed for cover.

Tucking her behind the sofa, he set her down gently on the wooden floor. "Stay here until I say different."

Sounds of shouting rose from out front. A scuffle?

Before Luke could get to the window, the crack of a bullet split the air.

Luke immediately jumped into action, pulling his handgun from the waistband of his jeans and placing it in her palm. "Anyone you don't recognize comes through the door, aim and shoot. Ask questions later."

Her eyes were fearful, but she nodded, gripping the handle.

"And call 911. I'm heading out the back. Then I'll slip around the side. Find a safe spot and hide." Luke palmed his own weapon as he moved out the door and motioned for her to lock it behind him.

The porch lamp was on, lighting a small circle around the backyard. He didn't breathe easier until he heard the snick of the lock behind him. Back against the wall, he moved toward the street in the darkness.

The front-porch light was off and the street wasn't well lit. It would take a moment for his eyes to adjust to the pitch black surrounding him.

Luke moved to the black-and-white parked at the curb. No movement inside was not a good sign. He got close enough to see that the officer was slumped over. Luke released a string of curse words under his breath.

A flashback to the war assaulted him. *He watched helplessly as one of his best buddies was shot execution style.*

Luke raged against the memory. This was not Iraq. He was in Plano now, chasing a killer.

Fighting the instinct to run to the injured man, Luke realized how vulnerable it would make him. How exposed Julie would be if anything happened to him.

Circling back, Luke texted his boss. Confirmation came quickly. More uniforms were on their way.

Rob was cunning. Luke had to give it to him. He was a determined killer.

But what the killer hadn't estimated was Luke's determination to stop him. He'd rather die than allow anything to happen to Julie. The thought of losing her again or, worse yet, having her taken from him detonated explosions of fire in his chest.

Running as fast as his legs would carry him, he reached the back door and knocked softly, not wanting to draw unwanted attention to himself. He pressed his back against the door and leveled his weapon, ready for an attack from the yard.

Anyone tried to cross that grass, Luke would be ready.

His chest squeezed when Julie didn't answer.

"Julie," he whispered, ever watchful of the threat around him. He'd break the door down in a heartbeat.

He knocked again. Still no answer.

Luke spun around and thrust his boot against the

sweet spot in the door. It popped open. He wanted to scream her name but knew better.

Easing inside the kitchen, he crouched below the window line and moved through the space. One by one, he opened every door, checking for any sign of her.

The first floor was clear. Luke ascended the stairs, checking doors as he moved stealthily down the hallway toward the bedrooms.

The hall bath was empty, as were two secondary bedrooms.

A clank sounded downstairs.

Every instinct inside him said Rick was in the house. Luke bit back another urge to call for Julie. He had to find her—now.

And he had to do it quietly.

He eased across the hardwood flooring, stepping around the places where the wood creaked, silently cursing Rick.

Tension pulled his shoulder blades taut. Where was she?

Where would she hide? Luke managed to make it to the walk-in closet in the master bedroom without making a sound.

However, someone was moving up the stairs and not being nearly as quiet. Rick? A cop?

Luke couldn't say for sure. All he could think about was getting to Julie. If she was still here. And that was a big *if*.

His grip on his handgun could crack concrete.

The door to the closet was ajar. The light off. Inside, there were two racks of clothing on either side. The back wall was made of deep shelving.

"Julie," he whispered.

A figure moved to his right.

Before he could get a good look, he had a body pinned against the wall and a hand over their mouth.

As soon as the body was flush with his, he realized Julie was in his arms, safe. He removed his hand.

"Is he here?" she whispered, rocketing into his arms.

"Someone's coming up the stairs. Don't figure we should wait to find out who." He tucked her behind his back and, weapon drawn, exited the closet.

A noise from the hall indicated that option was closed off.

They had two choices. Hide in the master bathroom and ambush the intruder and shoot at the first sign of movement. Or they could climb out the windows and get the hell out of there.

He double-checked that Julie was still armed, motioned for her to keep her eyes glued to the door and cranked open the pane in the historic house.

There should be just enough room for Julie to slip out. The opening might not be big enough for Luke, but he could cover her until she could get to safety.

Luke touched Julie's arm to get her attention. The ledge was skinny, but she could scale it as long as she didn't look down. This wasn't the time to think about the fact she was afraid of heights.

Her wide eyes stared for a moment before she inhaled a deep breath, tucked the gun in the waistband of her jeans and climbed onto the ledge.

Luke kept his back to the window, facing the door. If Rob walked in, he'd be in for a surprise.

Daring a glance out the window a few minutes—minutes that ticked by like hours—later, he could see that she was safely on the ground, her weapon drawn just as he'd instructed. Pride swelled in his chest.

With Luke being significantly bigger than her, he'd have a much harder time squeezing his big frame through the opening.

As he jimmied his way outside, a noise in the hallway got his heart pumping. Right about that time, he realized he couldn't make forward progress. He tried to reposition so he could shift his weight toward the room and go back but understood pretty quickly he was wedged in too well. In other words, stuck. Adrenaline kicking into high gear, Luke settled into the space half inside the room and half out and leveled his weapon toward the hallway.

"Special Agent Campbell?"

Ice gripped Luke's chest and lowered his core temperature in the split second when he heard the voice. He knew instantly whom it belonged to. Rob.

Was he about to show his face? Finally reveal himself? That would make Luke's job a helluva lot easier. "You're welcome to come in. I seriously doubt you'll like what you find in here."

A figure lurked just beside the door frame.

Luke took aim but couldn't get off a good round. If he could get a clean shot, he wouldn't hesitate to take it. If not, he wouldn't risk his bullet passing through Sheetrock and into an unintended target.

Rob's eardrum-piercing chuckle split the air.

"You think that's funny? Why not go man-to-man for a change instead of creeping around, preying on innocent women?"

"I doubt you'd understand." Rob's voice was high-pitched, agitated.

Had Luke hit a nerve? Think he cared? Think again.

If the monster showed himself, Luke was ready, which was exactly the reason he knew Rob wouldn't bite. He was an opportunist. Like a vulture, he waited until his prey was too vulnerable to fight back.

The barrel of a shotgun poked into the room.

If Luke repositioned now, could he get a better angle? "You want to kill me in cold blood?"

No answer.

"What? You can't talk all of a sudden? We both know that's not usually your problem, now, is it?" Just a little more to the left. Luke leaned, the window frame blocking his view. "Normally, you're a regular Chatty Cathy. And just as ignorant. Like your mother."

Luke was goading Rob on purpose, trying to see if he could throw him off his game. All Luke needed was one little slip. He was right there. So close Luke could hear the SOB breathe.

If he squeezed the trigger, moved his finger a fraction of an inch, Rob might just drop to the floor. But Luke was responsible for every bullet he discharged and he couldn't risk one going astray. There were too many innocent lives around and his bullet would easily pierce these walls.

"You think you can outsmart me, don't you, Special Agent Campbell?" The voice was somber. Depressed? Did Rob suffer from depression? "You don't understand anything about me or my family."

"No. I don't. Afraid I don't speak ignorant, either."

"I can assure you that your insults won't get you where you'd like to go." Rob's high-pitched chortle belied his words. The controlled anger in his tone said otherwise.

"Let me ask you something, *Rick*. Why not fight me? You know, one-on-one? Instead of always sneaking in the shadows. Hurting people who have done nothing to you." Luke paused, hoping for confirmation.

A choked laugh escaped. "That's where you're wrong. These women are far from innocent. And if I wanted to fight a man, I'd choose a more worthy adversary than you." Rick didn't deny the fact he was Rob.

The floor creaked in the hallway. Rick was on the move, heading the wrong direction.

Luke knew Rick was already gone but needed a visual to confirm. Of course, if he wedged himself back inside the bedroom that would give Rick time to get to Julie on the lawn.

Stuck in the pane, Luke couldn't move another inch, leaving Julie unprotected. Did Rick realize that, too?

"Keep your gun ready and shoot anyone who comes out that front door or around the side of the building, Julie." He hoped she heard him.

Luke patiently worked his way through the window, keeping one eye on the room and his hand secured around the butt of his Glock. He managed to squeeze through the opening and shimmy the rest of the way out the window.

He dropped to the ground, scanned the perimeter and motioned for Julie to follow him around the side of the building.

Her hand visibly shook, but to her credit, she held the gun and her composure intact. *That's my girl.*

On Luke's way to the front of the house, he made a call to his boss to provide an update. Backup was a block away. By the time he reached the streets, he knew in his gut that Rob was gone.

Frustration flooded him. Sirens wailed toward him as he conducted a thorough search of the perimeter just to be sure.

He gave a statement to the uniformed officer who arrived on the scene. The officer who'd been stationed on the street was confirmed dead.

With a heavy chest, Luke walked Julie to his truck.

"We have to move. Find another safe house. Or, better yet, just stay on the road."

Julie fastened her seat belt. "How can he be behind us every step? How can he anticipate our moves?"

"He's cunning."

If Rick knew where Luke lived, he'd also know what he drove. Then he remembered that Rick had been on their tail ever since they'd left the TV station. Everything snapped into place. His head pounded.

"Hold on." Luke popped out of the driver's seat.

"What is it, Luke?"

He examined the bottom of the truck again, running his hand along the boards. Nothing. He popped the hood next and checked every part. The filter. The engine. He ran his hand along the drivetrain and released a string of curse words. "Guy figured out what I was driving. He put a tracker on us."

"So he's been following our movements ever since the TV station?"

"Guess he figured he needed insurance in case you got away. We played right into his hands." Luke removed the device and palmed it. "Now the question is, what do we do with this?"

"Toss it?"

"Not unless I want him to know I found it. No. This is too valuable. And our first real break. He doesn't realize we've made the discovery." Luke tucked the small piece of metal in his front jeans' pocket.

"No, Luke. Turn it in. Get rid of it." Her body visibly shuddered. "Won't your boss know what to do with it? Maybe he can destroy it. Send it to the bottom of the Trinity River."

"Don't worry about it. I know exactly what to do." Luke had a plan. He'd lead the bastard away from her.

Julie didn't know what Luke intended to do with that device, but she had a bad feeling he had no inclination to clue her in. Or was it just a bad feeling in general? Probably a little bit of both. Being close to a murderer moments ago had her skin crawling.

Then again, there wasn't much about this situation that she liked. Worse yet, he'd shut down again, cut her out. The gleam in his eyes said he had an idea. The determined set to his jaw said he didn't intend to share, either.

There was so much about him now that was different than before. She'd never felt closer to him in so many ways. And yet, even though her heart wanted to believe this was different, how could it be? Not if he continued to shut her out at critical times.

A feeling of stupidity washed over her.

Wasn't past behavior the best predictor of future actions? And yet, hadn't she clung to the slim hope this time would be different? That he'd changed?

Was that even possible?

Didn't she read somewhere that behavior was the hardest thing to change? Even if someone wanted to?

There were signs of his PTSD returning, too. The headaches. The sleepless nights. The night sweats.

At least he was talking this time, a little voice reminded her. Not completely shutting her out like before.

Yeah. She guessed that was true.

And yet, he wasn't opening up about what he planned to do with that device.

"Luke, talk to me. Please."

He maneuvered onto the on-ramp of Interstate 75. "Everything will be okay. We're making progress, Julie."

Adrenaline caused his hands to shake on the wheel.

Julie had sat by idly before, but she refused to do it now. If she'd learned one thing, it was that she had to fight for what she loved. "Don't shut me out, Luke. Don't you dare shut me out."

He must've realized the implication of what she said because he immediately exited the highway and parked in a retail lot. "I wouldn't do that to you, Julie."

"You are. I see what's going on, Luke. It's happening again."

"No. It's not. This is different. I need you to trust that I know what I'm doing." He held her gaze as he leaned toward her and captured her face in his hands. "I love you. Nothing is going to change that."

"Look what this is doing to you, Luke."

"I'll do whatever it takes to protect you. That much is true. This case has been hell." The weariness in his eyes made her ache.

"I need to know you're not going to disappear on me again."

"You have my word."

If only she could be certain. "You know I love you."

"Then believe in me. This is different."

"How? You can't sleep. You're having nightmares again. What's different this time?"

"I know what's at stake. I have you to talk to. And I have been telling you as much as I can."

She couldn't deny he was including her for the most part. "But you're hiding something now."

She steadied herself for the lie.

"You're right."

If she hadn't been sitting, his admission would've knocked her off balance. "Then how is this different? Give me something to hang on to."

"I know what I'm doing now. I can't tell you every-thing, but as soon as this is over, I will. You have no idea how much I need you."

She held on to his gaze.

"But you can't tell me anything else?"

"Not yet. I need to know you have faith in me."

She answered with a kiss and a silent prayer he'd come back alive.

Chapter 16

Luke figured his best chance to draw Rick out was to use himself as bait. He'd drop Julie off with Detective Garcia and park himself somewhere. But where?

His first choice would be an open place like the Katy Trail. SWAT could easily hide in the nearby trees and cover the perimeter. Or if he used the Nature Preserve in Plano, then snipers could surround the parking lot. When Rick so much as stepped out of his vehicle, he'd be arrested or shot. Problem solved.

But that wasn't the case here. Rick would realize something was off in an instant. Luke would not take Julie to a park randomly in the middle of the day. A restaurant wouldn't work, either. Too public. Rick had already proved he'd kill innocent people if it meant gaining his freedom.

A motel? Nope. Where else? Luke navigated back onto the highway. "I need to investigate a lead."

"I already know the answer to this question, but I'm going to ask anyway. You mean by yourself?"

"Yes."

"And you don't plan to tell me where you're going or who you're investigating?"

"No."

"Is it too dangerous for me to come?"

"Yes." Was he closing himself off to her? He didn't think so. The only reason he didn't tell her was he didn't want to compromise her.

Hold on.

Was that true?

Or was he falling down that hole again, taking on everything himself? Not allowing her to share in his pain? His hurt?

Keeping his emotions bottled up under the guise he was protecting her?

Luke took a deep breath and kept his focus on the road. "I plan to see if I can draw him out using the tracking device I found on the truck."

He prepared himself for the fallout, expecting her to protest that the mission was too dangerous.

"Where do you plan for all this to happen?"

"Haven't decided that part yet."

He didn't need to look at her to know she was assessing him. She studied him for a long moment.

"What about that ranch in McKinney? It's isolated enough to keep people safe, but other officers could hide in the brush." There was no anger in her voice. Concern and caring were the only notes he detected.

"That was my next thought, too." Luke needed to quit underestimating her. She'd proved she could handle just about anything thrown her way. It was time he acknowledged it. "Grab the phone out of my pocket and dial Detective Garcia's number."

She did.

"Place the call on speaker."

Garcia answered on the second ring.

Luke identified himself. "You're on speaker, Detective. Julie Davis is on the line, as well. I need a favor."

"Name it. This have anything to do with our serial killer?"

"He's my only concern right now. I need more people and a personal guarantee."

"Done."

Luke filled the detective in on the plan to draw out Rick and the location. "One more thing. I want to keep Jul—the victim—out of sight. Here's where the personal guarantee comes into play. You're the only one I trust to keep her safe until I get back."

"I won't take my eyes off her, man."

"Appreciate it."

"Where should we meet?"

"Knox and Henderson." He'd feel a lot safer if she were in Dallas, far away, when he trapped Rick in McKinney.

"Will do. See you in ten minutes."

Julie ended the call and sat quietly on the ride to the meeting point. They beat Garcia, so Luke parked and waited.

He wished he knew what she was thinking. "Scared?"

"For you."

"Don't be. This is my job. Believe it or not, I'm pretty good at it." He cracked a smile, trying to ease the tension.

"I know. It's just…"

"What?"

"I don't want to lose you again." A few tears fell.

"You won't. Besides, I'm not the one he wants."

"He's already killed two officers who got in his way."

She had a point. He could sugarcoat this all day, but that wasn't exactly being fair to her. "Look. There are dangers to my job. Not just this case. This is what I do, who I am, and I need to know you can handle it."

"I did all right before…" She blew out a breath. "It's you I'm worried about."

He resisted the urge to curse. She was right. She hadn't tried to stop him from doing his job. This was who he was. He was the one who'd come home and proved he couldn't handle it. She'd been more than willing to stick around and help him through what he was experiencing.

He captured her hand in his and brought her fingers to his lips, kissing the tips of each one. Promises sat heavy. He wanted to be able to tell her everything would be okay, but she deserved proof. "You're right."

This wasn't the time for talk. He needed to show her that he could come back from anything life threw at them and still be himself. How did he tell her there wasn't anything Rick or anyone else could do to him personally that would affect him? The only thing that could hurt him was if Rick got to her.

He unhooked her seat belt and pulled her next to him. "I'm stronger because of you."

Julie looked him straight in the eye. "You come back to me in one piece as soon as this is done."

"You have my word." And he meant it.

He kissed her, hard. Needing to remember the way she tasted, just in case things didn't go as planned.

Detective Garcia pulled alongside them.

"Be safe," Julie said before switching cars.

"Keep a close eye on her for me," he said to Garcia.

"Won't let her out of my sight."

"Thank you." They exchanged a few details about the meet-up location and where Garcia planned to take her. "Call me if anything changes. And if—"

"You just worry about keeping metal out of your own butt," Garcia said. "I'll protect her."

Luke nodded his thanks, put the truck in Drive and navigated out of the lot.

A half hour later, he parked at the McKinney safe house. It sat on an acre of land in northern Collin County. The location was perfect. It'd be impossible for anyone to drive up or get close with a vehicle unnoticed. ATVs and motorcycles were too noisy to use.

Normally, ops took weeks to plan where intel was gathered and scenarios ran through dozens of times before executing. But a small window of opportunity existed here. Luke had no plans to waste any possible advantage he could squeeze out of this.

The house was considered as part of a suburb but the neighbors were far enough away to keep them out of danger. Before Luke arrived, he'd picked up enough supplies to last the night. The place had a male quality to the decor, meaning there wasn't much furniture except what was absolutely necessary. A slipcovered couch and a TV tray for an end table were in the living room. The small dining nook had a table with four chairs. They all matched but looked like relics from the seventies. Especially the wallpaper in the kitchen. Those hues of green and yellow had seen better days.

There was no TV. Today, the place would've been described as open-concept living, dining, kitchen with one bedroom off the living room, but Luke suspected when it was built, the place would've been described as quaint.

If Luke put a kitchen chair in the middle of the open-concept space and opened the door to the bedroom and bathroom, he could see every possible entry point into the place.

He moved to the bedroom and, using the key he'd been given when he used the place last month, unlocked the safe. He pulled an AR-15 and loaded a magazine of silver-tip bullets into the clip. He closed the door, slid the key into his back pocket and pulled a chair into the middle of the room.

Even though he couldn't see any of the SWAT officers, he knew they were there, watching. If something happened to Luke, they still had more than a good chance of capturing Rick. Either way, Julie would be safe.

Of course, Luke's plan involved capturing the bad guy and returning in good health to spend a considerable amount of time with the woman he loved. Preferably naked. If he had anything to say about it, spending the rest of his life with Julie would be a good place to start.

Now all he had to do was sit and wait.

Julie clicked off her seat belt and followed Detective Garcia into the small ranch-style house.

"I'd like you to meet my wife, Pilar." The woman he referred to was a couple of inches shorter than Julie and had shoulder-length straight brown hair. Her almond-shaped brown eyes were mirrored in the child's, balanced on her hip. She turned from the stove and smiled. "Welcome to our home."

"Thank you for having me." Julie was corralled to the dinner table along with Garcia.

They were joined by a child who couldn't have been more than five years old.

"This is my son, Juan Jr. Pilar is holding our daughter, Maria."

"You have a beautiful family, Detective."

Pilar set a plate of enchiladas on the table, followed by a bowl of soup. "I hope you like authentic Mexican food."

"Love," Julie said with a smile. What time was it? Luke had to be there by now. Was he okay? Was Rick there, too?

When everyone had a plate, the little one clasped his hands together and pinched his eyes shut. *"Padre—"*

"In English for our guest," Garcia said.

Julie's heart squeezed for how adorable the little boy was as he blushed.

"Sorry, missus."

"No. It's beautiful the way you say it. Go ahead."

"Bless us, oh Lord—" he sighed before continuing "—in these gifts we receive from you. A-men."

"Amen," Julie echoed, ignoring the pain in her chest. For the rest of the meal, she vacillated between wanting Luke's plan to work and wanting it to fail. Either way, she feared for Luke's life.

Even though the food smelled amazing, she couldn't imagine being able to eat. She didn't want to be rude, so she managed to get enough bites down that she wouldn't offend the Garcias' generosity.

Seeing the sweet family gathered around the dinner table made her heart ache to have her own family someday.

There was a time—not so long ago—when she'd thought she and Luke would be holding their own child by now. The image of Hitch's angelic face stamped her thoughts.

Would their baby look anything like its adorable cousin?

Would they ever get the chance to find out?

Instead of dreaming of their future, they were running for their lives from a determined serial killer.

Not running. Not anymore. Luke had placed himself directly in Rick's sights in order to draw him away from her.

She couldn't imagine a future without Luke.

Reality hit hard.

Life could change in a heartbeat. An instant—a changed appointment—was all it had taken to alter her course forever. And yet, it had brought her back to Luke.

Was that destiny?

Would it be his to die at the hands of a monster after surviving so much?

Julie refocused. She had to think positive thoughts for Luke. Nothing could happen to the man she loved. Not again.

She didn't look at the detective when she asked, "Have you heard anything?"

"Not yet." He waited until she met his eyes. "But we will."

With everything inside her, she prayed he was right.

Chapter 17

Four hours and sixteen minutes into the mission, Luke started thinking this had been a bad idea. He'd received a coded text message from Garcia letting him know everything was okay. No matter how much he trusted the detective, his first choice would have been to take Julie to the ranch and have his brothers, Nick and Reed, watch over her.

There simply hadn't been time. Considering they'd pieced this mission together in a matter of an hour, everything had fallen into place well. Even so, not having his own eyes on Julie left him feeling unsettled and tense.

The small ranch mostly used for training exercises made for a perfect location. Four SWAT officers were positioned outside on the grounds in various locations.

Luke sat squarely in the center of the place for so

long, his legs were going numb. He stood, dropped to the ground and did twenty push-ups to get the blood flowing again. To his backside was a solid wall. No chance Rick could surprise Luke with this setup.

A dull thump pounded between his ears as a flashback rocked him. This was different, he reminded himself as he rubbed his eyes.

Luke shook off the memory. He was no longer alone. He had Julie.

Movement to his left caught his attention. A shadow crossed the window. House lights were on outside, making it brighter than inside, affording a better view. He had company.

Luke readjusted his earpiece and alerted the SWAT team that they had a guest outside the building. He raised his AR-15 to his shoulder and aimed the scope toward the front door.

His eyes had long adjusted to the darkness. He relied on his other senses, too. A noise came in the direction of the bathroom. If this was Rick, he was not in the house yet.

Luke repositioned his scope, lining his crosshairs with the center of the shower door. Adrenaline pulsed through him in audible waves. Every sense heightened, on fight alert.

He changed position, crouching next to the sofa, and then relayed his new position to SWAT. Rick set foot inside this house and this whole ordeal would be all over.

Another noise came from the other side of the house this time. Luke reached for his thermal binoculars. They confirmed SWAT's presence, but where was Rick?

Luke didn't so much as breathe as he listened for anything that would give him a position on Rick. Find that bastard in the crosshairs of his scope and Luke wouldn't think twice about doing what needed to be done, especially considering how dangerous the man was.

But there was nothing.

Luke cursed under his breath and then relayed the message to SWAT. Everything had been quiet for ten minutes. Instinct said Rick was gone. Could they get to him before he got too far away?

"This party has moved on. I'm going hunting." Luke wasn't about to give up until he knew for certain the search was over.

Ringtones sounded. Luke palmed his cell and checked caller ID. His boss. "What's the word?"

"There's been another murder."

"Him?"

"We believe so. It has his signature written all over it."

"Where?" In the hours he'd waited for Rick, could he have been saving someone's life? Luke took down the address, ended the call and loaded his GPS.

He bit back a curse.

While he'd been waiting for Rick, taking up valuable resources, the SOB had killed someone right down the street. Anger and frustration engulfed him, lighting a fire that had been simmering since Iraq. Another person was dead because of Luke's misjudgment.

The familiar sting of shame pierced him, spreading throughout his body like a flesh-eating bacteria. There was no one to blame but Luke. He'd been shortsighted, acted too quickly, and Rick had capitalized on the mistake.

Luke drove the couple of blocks to the scene. A squad car, lights blazing, was parked in front of the house. A uniformed officer stood on the front lawn of the small ranch house, taking a statement from, most likely, a neighbor.

Luke fished for his gloves in the console and pulled them on.

Eating up the real estate in a few short strides, he flashed his badge and made a beeline for the front door.

The kill had to be fresh because there was no stench coming from the house as he crossed the threshold.

Inside, the scene played out the same way the others had. A black-haired woman, decapitated, sprawled across the couch. Her arms folded, her legs crossed. Luke fisted his hands, angry with himself for allowing the monster to strike again. Did he blame himself? Yeah.

Did he take it personally? Hell yes.

It was his responsibility to catch this creep and get him off the streets. Every time he was allowed to breathe air freely and strike again, Luke failed.

There'd been an attempt to clean up the blood, but splatter marks were everywhere. A substance that looked and smelled a lot like bleach soaked her clothes. Nothing else in the place had been touched.

The house was clean, so there were no dust tracks to indicate if anything had been removed. The place was small but neatly kept.

A few personal pictures of the woman and a child at various stages of the child's life were neatly placed around the room.

The whole scene smacked of Rick.

Guilt ate at Luke's insides. If he'd chosen a different neighborhood, this woman would still be alive. Her child would not suffer the horror she was about to face. Life would go on normally for the two of them.

He'd just cost a child her mother. He swore under his breath. His fingers fisted and released.

Was he beating himself up over this mentally? Yeah. Losing another life to this monster was something Luke would always take personally.

He had to remind himself to calm down. Maintaining his cool could mean the difference between being too hasty and missing something important that might lead to finding the life-stealing jerk who was responsible.

Luke walked the house, checking every window, picture and piece of furniture for clues. He'd check and double-check everything just in case.

The officer who'd been interviewing witnesses stepped inside the house and called for Luke. He met the man in uniform in the hall.

"Did the neighbors see anything?" Luke asked.

"No, sir. I canvassed the surrounding houses after securing the area. No one saw anything out of the ordinary."

"No sudden noises? Screaming?"

He shook his head.

"What's her name?"

"Kimberly Jackson, sir."

"Thank you. Has her next of kin been notified?" Luke opened the notebook app on his phone.

"No, sir. Not yet."

"You have kids?"

"A two-year-old and a newborn."

"Must keep you busy."

"Can't remember what it's like to sleep for more than six hours at a stretch," the officer said, easing his stance.

"Ms. Jackson has a daughter. There doesn't seem to be a father. Can you do me a favor and see to it that her daughter doesn't see her like this? No little girl should have to see her mother in this condition."

"I hear you, sir. Will do. I can't even imagine anything like this happening to my wife."

Luke nodded agreement. "Any idea how the guy got inside?"

"Didn't see any signs of forced entry."

How had Rick charmed his way inside? The likelihood he'd planned this out in advance was slim. This was a crime of opportunity.

"Thanks a lot. For everything," Luke said. Another question ate at him. Why? What good would it do to kill someone here? This was outside his usual kill zone.

The logical answer nearly buckled Luke's knees. Rick already knew where he believed Luke and Julie were, based on the tracking device, and he wanted to create a distraction. Had he hoped to create enough of a diversion to snatch Julie from the scene?

How had he gained entry when nothing indicated the use of force?

Luke scanned the area.

A fresh bouquet of flowers sat in the middle of the kitchen island. A weight lodged itself inside the pit of Luke's stomach as he moved toward the yellow roses.

There was a card. He pulled a small evidence bag from his back jeans' pocket, then opened the note.

It read "She has to pay."

Rick had figured them out. He knew.

The diversion wasn't created to snatch Julie from here. Luke released a string of swearwords. The air sucked out of his lungs in a whoosh at the same time his cell phone sounded, because he already knew Rick wasn't talking about the woman in the next room. He palmed his phone and studied the screen, barely aware he was already in a dead run toward his truck. The text from his boss read…

Garcia's missing.

Julie fought the darkness surrounding her, draining her. A blow to the back of her head had left her nauseated and with a pounding headache, but she forced herself to stay awake and remember what had happened.

Her brain was mush, but a picture began to emerge. The detective had been called into the station. She and Garcia had been walking toward his car when they'd been ambushed. The last thing she remembered was the detective grabbing his chest after a shot had been fired. *Garcia.*

Julie said a silent prayer he would be okay. She couldn't imagine having to look into the eyes of his beautiful children or wife and tell them he was no longer coming through that door or sitting at their dinner table.

Pain so overwhelming and powerful it was like a physical punch assaulted her. Where was Luke?

What had happened to him? Had Rick gotten to him before he'd attacked them?

Another stab of pain tightened her gut at the memory of being thrown in the trunk of a gray Volkswagen Jetta. Looking into Rick's dead black eyes would haunt her for the rest of her life. Which might not be all that much longer if she didn't figure a way out of this car.

Didn't all trunks have an emergency-release lever?

It was hard to move with her hands bound behind her back. Her ankles had been tied together with rope. Could she wiggle enough to break free?

Rick must've been a Boy Scout, because, try as she might, she couldn't gain an inch.

There was only one of him. As much as he seemed superhuman, he was only a man. Men had weaknesses. She would find Rick's and fight him to the death. His intentions were clear. Her throat dried up just thinking about what he'd done to her client, what he would do to her.

Maybe Rick had been in such a hurry, he'd allowed Garcia a chance to live.

Julie bounced around in the trunk. A speed bump? She listened for any sounds that might help her figure out where he was taking her or give her an edge when describing her location later.

No situation was hopeless, she repeated to herself quietly as tears spilled out of her eyes. There had to be a way to escape.

Sirens blared past her. She was still in the city.

How long had they been in the car?

She'd panicked at first. It took her a little while to get her bearings. How much time had she lost in the interim? Ten minutes? Twenty?

Foreboding numbed her limbs. She had to fight it. This couldn't be over yet. Julie worked the restraints on her wrists again. She couldn't get any traction there. She kicked her feet and screamed.

"Be quiet back there." The voice was almost a nervous squeal. Freaked out?

He should be.

Julie had no plans to go down without a fight. What was the worst that could happen? She knew what he had planned and couldn't think of a more hateful way to kill someone.

Trying to reason with this guy wouldn't do any good, either.

Fear barked at her, threatening to consume her. She refused to allow it. If she allowed terror to paralyze her, he'd already won. His victims must've been scared to death in their final moments.

He could do what he wanted with her body, and probably would, but he couldn't touch her mind. She alone had the power to control her thoughts. And she refused to give him the satisfaction of knowing she was afraid.

The car came to a stop before he cut the engine.

This was it.

Julie positioned herself on her back and bent her knees.

The trunk opened and she released a scream, thrusting her feet toward Rick's face.

His head knocked back. He swore, grabbing at his nose and checking for blood. Before he could grab her, she kicked again. Hard. With all the fear and anger she had balled inside her.

He stumbled back while cursing her then disappeared. "Be still. Wouldn't want to have to knock you out before I kill you."

Julie expected to be out in the country, far from the city. But she could hear cars. A highway?

All she could see were stars against the curtain of a black sky. There was a brisk chill in the air.

She curled her legs, ready to strike again.

This time, he surprised her from the side. A quick blow to the head and she struggled to remain conscious. "He won't let you get away with this. You hurt me and he won't stop until he finds you."

She was baiting him, but she hoped he'd tell her what

he'd done with Luke. Because if her FBI agent was alive, she doubted she'd be in the back of a trunk, fighting for her life right now.

The thought of anything happening to Luke made it hard to breathe.

Another blow to the head and she wouldn't have to worry about it. She remembered Luke trying to make him angry to force a mistake. Could she do the same?

Her heart hammered against her ribs. The simple act of taking in air hurt.

Let her panic control her, and she'd be dead for sure.

What if Luke lay in a ditch somewhere? What if she could help?

She had to try.

"Come back, jerk, and give me a fair fight."

"I should have taped your mouth shut is what I should've done." His tone was frantic, almost hysterical.

"What's the matter? Don't like being rushed?"

A siren wailed in the distance.

"They're coming for you, Rick."

No reaction.

"How about I call you a simpleminded jerk instead? That is what you are. You think you're clever but you're not." She listened for a long moment.

Nothing.

"You're nothing more than a leech, sucking the blood out of innocent people."

"That's where you're wrong. They're filthy. People are dirty. Mother always said women are nasty creatures who will hurt you the way she hurt me. She was preparing me for my life as an adult. But she has to pay for her sins, too."

She tracked the voice to her left, repositioning her feet

in order to deliver a crushing blow as soon as those blue eyes appeared. "Your mom sounds as insane as you."

"Ask your FBI agent how stupid I am. Oh, right, you can't. He's dead."

The blow from those words knocked the wind out of her. Was it true? Her heart screamed no. Rick would say anything to throw her off balance. Exactly what she was doing to him. "Might be. But you won't get away with this. They know who you are. You go home and they've got you. They know your family. There's nowhere left to hide."

A hysterical laugh came from the right.

Julie quickly adjusted her positioning.

"Impossible."

"Is that so? How can you be so sure?"

"I would've seen it on the news."

"Like they'd tell those jerks." Her best bet was to stall for time.

Silence.

"What's the matter? Didn't figure that part out already? They swarmed your house. Found everything. One of the officers called you a deviant."

"You're lying." His tone sounded agitated now. "I'm the most sane person they'll ever meet. Besides, I can tell you're making it up. People wouldn't say that about me. I'm too smart and they know it. Smarter than your FBI boyfriend, that's for sure."

He'd moved closer on the right side.

She repositioned, remembering something Luke had told her about serial killers. "Sorry to tell you, bud, they know who you are. Leave here and you'll spend the rest of your life as a scrawny girlfriend to a man named T-Bone in prison. Guess what? T-Bone won't like the fact you make wigs from your victims' hair. People who kill innocent women rank right up there with pedophiles in prison."

He rose up from the side of the car, anger radiating from his slender frame.

Julie kicked with everything she had inside her.

Rick sidestepped in time to avoid the thrust of her foot. She made a move to reposition, but before she could fire off another blow, her legs were captured. She tried to break free, but even with the extra strength another shot of adrenaline provided, the grip around her ankles was too strong.

A quick smirk followed by an even faster blow to the head stunned Julie as her vision blurred.

Before she could get her bearings, she was on the ground being dragged. Every movement hurt. She raised her head to stop it from being scraped along the pavement, screaming, fighting with everything she had inside her.

"You shouldn't talk to me like that, Mother. All I ever wanted was your approval," Rick mumbled. "You've been bad, too. You have to tell me you love me. You'll do that once I cleanse you. Won't you, Mother?"

What was he talking about? She glanced around. And who was he talking to?

Julie bucked and wiggled, still screaming, but his grasp was too tight. He hauled her in front of a storage unit as if she weighed nothing. He unlocked and opened the door using one hand.

Light streamed inside as Rick shoved her against the wall, forcing her to sit up. All she could see in front of her were boxes. "Please, don't go through with this. Let me go."

Rick moved to the center of the room, his body blocking her view.

He turned around. She got a glimpse of what he held in his hands and her heart pitched. In his grasp, he held a half-made wig of black hair.

Bile burned the back of her throat. She screamed as he forced her to be still, placing the wig on top of her head.

"Be still, Mother. You mustn't get upset with me." He withdrew. A hurt look crossed his features. "Bad things happen when you get angry."

"I'm not her. I'm not your mother. Let me go."

"All I ever wanted was for you to love me, Mother. As usual, you deny me." He rose up, fury rising with him. "Why won't you love me?"

He struck Julie again.

Then everything went black.

Chapter 18

Luke had hit Redial for the tenth time in a row when his cell buzzed. He answered his boss's call immediately.

"We found Detective Garcia a block from his house." His solemn tone sent a fireball of dread rocketing through Luke's stomach.

"Alive?"

"Yes. He took a beating, but he's on his way to Parkland Memorial. The EMT said he's in bad shape, but his numbers are strong."

"And the woman who was with him?" Luke steeled his resolve, fighting against the overwhelming urge to slam his fist into something. Anything.

The beat of silence his boss gave him wasn't a good sign. "I'm sorry, Luke. He got her and disappeared."

A torpedo couldn't have pierced his heart more deeply. "Any witnesses? Any idea where he took her?"

"We have a guy who's talking. He saw a man force a woman into a gray Volkswagen Jetta and head east. We have men combing the area. A chopper's already in the air."

Luke fisted his free hand. "Who else is on the investigation?"

"I have all my men on the case. Rogers, Stevens, Segal. Everyone. Dallas P.D. put some more power behind it. We're canvassing Garcia's neighborhood, just in case someone saw something but is scared to come forward. I sent out an alert in the system. Plano, Richardson and Garland have teams ready to mobilize on a moment's notice. The BOLO's already out. I got every bit of my people available working toward finding her."

Given enough time, his boss's words would be comforting. The names he'd mentioned would put the pieces together and produce a location. The sand had drained from the hourglass, and Luke had no time to wait.

"You know I appreciate everything you're doing."

"Goes without saying. We're checking property records, the DMV. If this guy or any of his family members own so much as an RV, we'll be on it."

"Thanks for the update. If I get any leads on my end, I'll keep you posted." He needed to end the call. Right now, he wanted—no, needed—to punch something, and he didn't want to risk being pulled from the case for going ballistic.

How could he not?

It was Julie.

His boss knew about the personal connection, and Luke had half expected to be yanked. Figured he hadn't been because he'd been able to put up a good front. He was human. No doubt every agent would feel the same way if one of their loved ones was in a similar situation. The boss would, too. He sure wouldn't sit in an ivory tower and hope for the best. He'd be out beating the pavement with the rest of them.

Luke needed to refocus and recap what he knew about Rick. The guy was sneaky. Luke had to give him that. Bright. The guy liked a good diversion. While they'd been trying to lure him into a trap, Rick had murdered a woman and then got to Garcia. The noises at the ranch couldn't have been him.

Why would he risk killing so close to Luke?

Obviously, to kill again. He seemed to enjoy operating on the edge of being caught. Could that mean he wouldn't take Julie far?

Luke's cell buzzed. Nick's name came up on the screen. "What do you have for me?"

"Reed's also on the line. I put the call on conference. What do you know so far?"

He recounted the day's events.

"Man, I'm sorry. I know how much she means to you," Nick said.

"I'm already digging around in the backgrounds of everyone connected to Rick Camden, financial records," Reed chimed in.

"Your support means the world."

"Reed's contacts through Border Patrol can move mountains," Nick said.

"We'll know something in the next few minutes," Reed said. He paused a beat. "Hold on. I have news. Guess what? His dad rents a storage unit at the crossroads of George Bush and Preston. It's a Dallas address. On the southwest side."

Luke bolted toward his truck. "I know that location.

I've driven past it a thousand times. It's just off the street. The place is blocked because of the highway."

"Be careful, bro. We'll send Riley for backup. He shouldn't be too far since you'll be at Plano's back door," Nick said.

Luke tossed the cell on the passenger seat as he turned over the ignition, praying he wouldn't be too late. He couldn't lose Julie again. Not like this.

His only real question was whether or not he'd get there in time to make a difference. Flashbacks of the night he lost his men in Iraq assaulted him as he navigated through the evening traffic in frigid temperatures.

That same helpless, angry feeling enveloped him now as he neared the storage facility.

He gunned the engine and weaved through cars and trucks.

The intersection was busy, but, just as he remembered, the facility was off the road, hidden by the wall that was built to block noise from George Bush Highway onto a nearby neighborhood.

Using hands-free, he called his boss to let him know he'd arrived. He left clear instructions with everyone to creep in. No lights. No sirens.

He ended the call letting his boss know he had no plans to wait for backup.

The gate was closed and this facility did not have on-site personnel. He knew that from past experience dealing with the owners. Security would be loose. An iron fence enclosed the place and there were cameras positioned in the corners. These conditions were perfect for a man like Rick. Man? No. Animal.

A real man wouldn't hurt women.

Luke strapped his AR-15 to his back and scaled the

metal fence in one giant hop. A security gate wouldn't keep him from taking down this monster. Without sirens, he had no idea how close backup was, so he wasn't alarmed by the fact he heard none. But it wouldn't be far away.

Either way, he couldn't afford to hang around and wait.

The place was cold, dark and eerily quiet. Julie worked her hands behind her back, trying to loosen the rope. She hadn't managed any progress so far. After the last time she'd screamed, a piece of tape had been placed over her mouth.

Had someone heard her? Stopped him?

No. If they had, wouldn't she be safe right now instead of locked in a storage room, wearing a wig the sicko had made from his victims?

Tears slid down her cheeks as fear gripped her. Detective Garcia was most likely dead. She couldn't begin to think about his sweet family when they heard the news. Whatever Rob had done to Garcia, his plans for her would be much more sinister.

Where had he gone? Worse yet, when would he be back?

He'd secured her and disappeared. Painfully aware he could return at any time, she pressed her back against the wall and tried to push up.

She struggled against her bindings. Fear caused her hands to shake, making it that much more difficult to work the knot. Damn that she couldn't break free. If she could surprise him, she might have a chance.

A little piece of her prayed Luke would find her. But

what if he was…? No. She couldn't allow herself to think like that. Lose hope and it might as well all be over.

The wind howled, her heart pounding faster with every gust. Could she work the knot? Her fingers fumbled around for the bow in the rope. No use. Her eyes were beginning to adjust to the darkness. Was there anything she could use? She squinted, trying to make out shapes, but couldn't get a clear look.

Could she scoot to the door and wiggle out before he got back? Surely there were security cameras. Wouldn't someone be watching? Only one thing was certain. Sit there. Do nothing. And she was already dead.

The bindings around her ankles made it difficult to scoot across the floor. She rocked her body until she inched forward.

A gust of wind slammed against the metal door. She couldn't suppress a yelp.

There were more noises, which sounded like feet shuffling.

Couldn't be wind this time. Rick was back.

Her heart hammered her ribs as she tensed her body and clenched her fists, preparing for whatever walked under the metal sliding door.

She worked her jaw from side to side, trying to loosen the tape because as soon as that metal grate lifted, she planned to scream.

Was there anything else around she could use? She scanned the enclosure but could see only general shapes and nothing specific.

If she could scoot a little closer to the door, she could bang her head against it and make a loud noise. Anyone around would hear it. Except she was reasonably certain there was no one else around but her and Rick.

Julie managed to inch closer to the door. She held her breath, half expecting it to shoot up any moment and Rick to be standing there, that satisfied and haunting smirk on his face. With his blond hair, blue eyes and runner's build, she could see why he was disarming to women. He looked like a Boy Scout, not a murderer. Ravishing Rob. *Captivates then decapitates.* A chill gripped her, numbing her limbs.

Was that a pair of crutches leaning against the wall? Yet another in one of his many traps to disarm his prey? Blood ran cold in her veins.

How could someone be so cruel?

Movement outside the door gave her the ominous premonition that she was about to be next. Hesitating, waiting for a sign—any sign—that the person on the other side of that door wasn't Rick, she held her breath and listened. If she could manage to get a little closer, six more inches, she could make some noise. Maybe she could draw their attention. The footsteps came closer, paused, then moved on. Couldn't be him. Could it?

She banged her shoulder against the metal door, causing ripples of sound to roll through the room and the door to shake.

"Julie?" came out in a whisper, but the voice was unmistakable. Luke.

With the tape covering her mouth, she couldn't speak, but she didn't let that stop her from trying. She banged against the door again, with more force this time, and shouted—which came out like a muffled scream.

The door slid open enough for her to get a glimpse of him. Her body went limp from relief at seeing his face. Luke was alive. A flood of emotions descended on her like a hundred-foot wall of water.

He pulled the wig off, dropped to his knees and captured her face in his hands, his own emotion visible in the worry lines bracketing his mouth. He pulled the tape off her mouth. "I thought I'd lost—"

"Luke. He said you were gone." Her own emotions made her eyes fill with tears. "How did you find me?"

"My brothers tracked down this storage unit." His kiss was a mix of sweet and needy.

Her sense of relief and joy was short-lived as he immediately pulled back and surveyed the area. Luke's guard was up as he scanned the room. Enough light streamed in to see clearly.

"Where is he?" Luke asked.

"I don't know. He threw me in here and disappeared. I was screaming. Hoped someone heard me and interrupted him."

"He had to know the area was hot. Most likely plans to return later and finish the job. Even if he was caught, he'd still have his final revenge if no one found you." Luke turned to face the opening, his back against the wall as he pulled a knife from his pocket and cut the ropes. His gaze continued to sweep the area as he worked.

As soon as her hands were free, she rubbed them together, trying to bring feeling back.

"Let's get you out of here." Luke shifted his position quickly, and before she realized what he was doing, he'd cut the rope on her ankles, too. His handgun was leveled and ready to fire.

The blood rushed to her feet. She made a move to get up but landed on her backside.

"Give it a minute. Feeling will come back," Luke whispered.

The light streaming in from the door gave Julie a lit-tle perspective about what the storage facility was used for. She'd already seen the crutches, but there were other props. A wheelchair was in one corner. There was an open box filled with various ropes and handcuffs. There were tools like saws lying around. Boxes of garbage bags sat on the floor. Uniforms ranging from scrubs to local police blues were strewn around. He had everything he needed right there to get inside someone's house with-out using force.

Back where she sat, he'd spread several blankets on the floor. He must've been in too big of a hurry to tie her to the pole he'd installed.

Julie rubbed her hands together faster. She didn't want to be caught off guard if he returned. And he would come back. She needed to get the heck out of there.

Luke finished sweeping the area. "I can carry you, but that would leave us vulnerable. Can you walk?"

"I will." Julie pushed herself up and took a tentative step forward. "He's just going to let us walk out of here?"

"He doesn't get to decide." He handed her a weapon and shouldered his AR-15. "On my word, shoot. Got it?"

She nodded.

Squeezing her hand around the butt of the gun brought more feeling back. She followed closely as Luke led the way toward an iron fence to what she hoped would be freedom. Faint sounds of traffic from a freeway could be heard. If only she could move faster. As it was, adrena-line was the only thing keeping her upright.

She didn't recognize anything, but that was because

Rick had covered her eyes before. With the parking lot in view, she lowered her weapon.

A blow came from behind, striking Julie on the crown of her head.

Chapter 19

"Luke!" Julie's scream wrapped around his spine like an ice pack.

He pivoted and leveled his weapon at Rick. With the SOB using Julie as a shield, Luke couldn't get a clean shot. She'd dropped her weapon and Rick had kicked it out of reach. The blade of a knife was pressed against her throat. Luke forced himself not to focus on the panicked look in her eyes.

"She doesn't get to live." Rick's agitated pitch was a far cry from his normal controlled tone. His voice practically shook from hysteria. The guy must not have wanted to risk being too far away in case she tried to escape.

"This is between us, Rick. Let her go."

"No. I need her. She's part of this, of me. You wouldn't understand."

Julie's body shuddered.

"She didn't do anything to hurt you. She's not your mother. Just another innocent woman." Luke walked a mental tightrope, balancing between angering and disarming Rick.

"We both know that's not true. She's your wife. I should slice her throat just for that." Rick turned his attention to her. "Don't worry. I'll be quick this time."

Luke needed to get the guy to focus on him. "I understand now. What your mom must've done to you. She made you angry, didn't she?"

Rick's laugh came out as a chortle. "I wouldn't push me if I were you. I can end it all now."

"Then tell me. Why do you hurt people weaker than you? That makes you just like her." He needed to keep Rick's attention away from Julie.

She gripped the arm braced against her chest with both hands. The knife was pressed so hard against her throat, Luke could see an indentation from it. A trickle of blood rolled down the blade. If Luke could somehow signal her to bite or fight, maybe he could get a clean shot. With that knife so close to her throat, even an accidental slip could cut her jugular vein. She'd bleed out before the ambulance arrived.

Luke inched forward, closing the five-foot gap between them a little more. If he could get close enough, maybe he could grab the knife or knock him off balance. Backup should arrive any minute.

Rick took two steps back. "Stay right where you are. Don't come any closer."

"You slit her throat and you've got nothing. I'll shoot you right here and now. And that's a promise."

Rick didn't move.

"What happened? With your mother?"

"She can't cut me out."

"What did she say?"

"That I was out of the family. She kicked me out of the house, just like that. Two years ago. After everything we'd been through. Said she was done with me."

"Why would she do that?"

"I told her I didn't want to play her sexual games anymore. I wanted a real girlfriend like my brother Chad had. And she cut me out of the family."

Luke looked at Julie, needing her to stay focused. He angled his head back ever so slightly. Did she catch it? Did she understand what he was telling her to do?

She blinked her eyes several times quickly but didn't dare budge.

Good. She understood his message.

In the background, Luke heard several cars pull into the parking lot. The footsteps of what had to be several officers rushing toward them echoed across the empty space between the storage buildings.

"Make them go away. I'll kill us both." Rick was panicking. His gaze darted around and his face muscles pulled taut.

Luke instantly knew what Rick meant. He'd slice her throat and then make a move for an officer, forcing him to shoot. He didn't turn when he shouted, "Stay back!"

The footfalls stopped.

Rick wore the expression of a caged animal. He knew he was surrounded. No matter what else happened, the SOB wouldn't get away this time. There would be comfort in that thought if it didn't involve Julie. Blood trickled down her neck.

Except that none of this was good for Julie. And there was precious little Luke would be able to do to save her.

No way could he allow that to happen. He had to keep the officers back, as well. Maybe he could soften the guy. Make him think Luke was on his side. "There's another ending to this story, Rick. All three of us can walk out of here." He didn't add that one of them would be in handcuffs, but it was true.

"That's not how I see it going down." The lean man's hand shook. More trickles of Julie's blood ran down the blade.

"It doesn't have to be like this. You need help. I can arrange it for you."

Rick backed away a few more steps. If he managed another ten feet, he could slice her throat and disappear around the corner. And he would. Rick knew that Luke wouldn't let Julie die alone. His best chance of escape involved ensuring the woman Luke loved was dying.

"Make the officers go away, or she dies right here."

Luke bit back a curse. "Stay back or he'll do it. I'll meet you guys in the parking lot."

Rick took another step back. One more and it would be too late for Julie.

A distraction was needed. But what?

She must've sensed what was coming because she took a breath and then dropped down, buckling her knees. Her movement must've caught Rick off guard, because he fumbled for her, dropping the knife.

Luke lunged, wedging himself between Rick and Julie. At that moment, Rick punched her, knocking the wind out of her. Her weak ankles were unable to hold her weight, so she went down fast—a crack sounded, skull to pavement.

Luke fended off a potshot from Rick as he glanced down at her. "Julie."

Slumped on her side, she didn't answer.

Rick threw a punch that Luke blocked. He was stronger than the other man, but adrenaline did funny things to baseline strength. Not to mention the fact that Rick had everything to lose if he got caught.

A knife thrust at him. Luke ducked in time to miss the blade. He pivoted left and crouched low, getting a quick visual on Julie.

Her chest moved, so it meant she was breathing. *Hold on, sweetheart.*

Luke looked up in time to see an object the size of a coffee can being hurled at him. He deflected it with his forearm. What the hell was the jar filled with? Lead?

Another object flew toward him. He ducked, losing balance. In the time he gained his footing, Rick was over top of him.

The sound of officers rushing toward them was a welcome relief.

A jab to Luke's ribs took his breath away. The blunt end of a shoe cracked into his stomach.

Luke hauled himself into a squatting position, then burst toward Rick, knocking him back a step.

A kick to Rick's groin had him doubled over and groaning.

The fight inside him was still strong, powered by his freeze, fight or flight response. Rick stepped forward, leading with the knife, jabbing at Luke's ribs. He sidestepped and spun in time to avoid direct impact, even though he felt the blade sear through his flesh. There was enough of a wound for blood to ooze through his shirt.

"Not this time, bastard." Luke ignored the pain in order to keep his full focus on Rick.

Another jab caught Luke under the arm.

More of his blood spilled onto the sidewalk.

This time, Luke would be ready when Rick made his move.

"Oh my God, Luke." Julie must've regained consciousness. At least she would be fine.

Luke didn't dare take his gaze off Rick. Another jab and he might just hit something the doctors couldn't fix.

The telltale step forward came, but before Rick could blink, Luke had spun around and twisted the knife. Rick was knocked off balance. He turned in the direction he fell, landing directly on the blade. The knife stabbed him directly through the chest, piercing his heart as footsteps surrounded them.

Rick made a gurgling sound as blood spilled from the side of his mouth and his eyes fixed.

Luke rushed to Julie's side and pulled her into his arms with the intention of never letting go.

Julie's tear-soaked eyes gazed up at him.

He pulled back and looked her straight in the eyes. "Everything's fine now. He can't hurt you anymore. You don't have to cry."

She buried her hands in his shirt, pulled back and gasped. "No, Luke. It's not okay. You're hurt."

He felt light-headed, cold and a little nauseated.

A stoic-faced medic parted the crowd, his gaze fixed on Luke.

He took note of Julie's pallor. Blood was everywhere. Blood on her hands, her shirt, in her hair.

His blood.

He was fully awake but couldn't make his mouth form words. How did he tell her he was okay? They'd survived. That he was determined to take her home with him where he could take care of her now that this whole ordeal could be put behind them?

He made another move to speak, but darkness was closing in.

The faint sounds of her sweet voice telling him not to die registered.

EMTs blocked his view of her.

Darkness was pulling, tugging.

Fighting against the tide sucking him under and tossing him out to sea took all the energy he could muster.

Luke closed his eyes.

Chapter 20

Luke blinked his eyes open. His head felt as if he'd tied one on last night, except that couldn't be true.

He searched the room for Julie. Found her as she slept in the chair next to his bed. His heart squeezed.

A short dark-haired nurse rushed in. "Someone's finally awake."

"Yeah, guess I needed a good night's sleep."

"Or three."

"You're telling me I've been out for three days?" he asked quietly, trying not to wake Julie.

"Uh-huh." The nurse went to work pushing buttons on beeping machines.

The noise must've stirred Julie, because she rubbed her eyes and yawned.

"Hello, beautiful."

She sat bolt upright. "Luke. Oh, thank goodness

you're awake. Are you okay?" Riding a bolt of lightning couldn't have brought her to his side quicker. "How do you feel?"

"Better. My head hurts. Nothing a little aspirin won't heal." And yet, seeing Julie there, waiting, energized his tired body. God help him, but she was the light.

"How do you feel?" the nurse asked.

He wanted to ask if she was the one who'd dragged cotton balls through his mouth, but thought better of it. Her permanent frown gave him a hint that she wasn't the teasing type.

"You can give me a shot, clean me or bandage me, but I'm taking this lady beside me home." Little did they know, he wouldn't stop there. He'd do whatever it took to defend her and make her his.

He made a move to get out of bed but was instantly met with two sets of hands pushing him down.

"That's not a good idea, Luke." Julie's voice left no room for doubt.

"You should listen to her," the nurse agreed. "Before I make sure you can't."

He put his hands up in the universal sign of surrender. "No harm done."

Recent events flooded him. His thoughts snapped to his friend. "What happened to Garcia?"

"He's good. He was treated overnight and released. Told me to call him as soon as you woke up." Julie leaned toward him. "If you listen to the doctor and do everything he says, I promise to climb under the sheets and keep you warm later."

The nurse grumbled about his blood pressure as Julie located her phone and sent a text.

"Sweetheart, I don't plan to be here later." He looked into her eyes and saw home.

"Where do you plan to go?"

"With you. Home." He hesitated, praying to see a flicker of excitement in her gaze.

Instead, she lowered her lashes, screening her amber hues. "Your brothers have been calling every hour. They might have something to say about where you end up. Gran's worried sick. And coming home with me? I don't know if that's such a good idea, Luke. We've been down that road before. Remember? I thought I could fix everything by sticking in there, but what did I really do? Hoped everything would magically turn out okay. I was scared to death to try to make you talk. I didn't know how. I'm just as much to blame for what happened."

"No."

"Don't say it, Luke." Her forehead creased and he could tell she was concentrating hard on her next words. "I didn't give up. That part's true. But I let you mope around and eventually drown in your own sadness. I should've stomped on the floor until you picked yourself up. What did I do? I let you fall apart right in front of my eyes."

He made a move to speak but was met with her palm.

"It's true. I didn't know what to do, so I hoped and waited. When that didn't work, I let you push me into the divorce."

"I didn't give you much choice."

"People always have choices, Luke. I didn't fight for us before. Not like I should've."

"I appreciate what you're saying—"

"Then don't take all the blame. What happened to us was both our faults. We were young. We both made mistakes. I shouldn't have let you get away with closing yourself off to me."

Her words lifted the burden he'd been carrying on his shoulders for the years they'd been apart. "Have I told you how sexy you are when you're making sense?"

He brought his hand up to her chin. "I understand if you think it's too risky or too fast. But if you give me a second chance to do what I should've done when I first got back, you won't regret it."

"And what should you have done before?"

"Take you in my arms and never let go. No matter how dark my life becomes, you're the light. Instead of turning away from it, ashamed, I should've run toward it, both arms open.

"I was young and stupid...ashamed of myself for being weak. But I've learned a man isn't weak because he cares about the people he loves. Especially when they're taken from him too soon. A real man hangs on to the people he loves with everything inside him, until light fills him again and the darkness is gone."

Tears rolled down her cheeks. His gaze moved to the bandage on her neck and he thought about how easily he could've lost her.

He thumbed them away. "No more tears. I don't want to make you cry again."

"That's beautiful. You're beautiful."

He cracked a smile. "No. I'm not. But you are."

"Luke Campbell, you're the most beautiful man I've ever known. That's the person I fell in love with before. Who I am shamelessly and deeply in love with now."

"I love you, too." Relief washed over him. He had every intention of asking her to marry him when the time was right. And when she agreed to be his bride this time, it would be forever. "Will you move in with me when I get out of here?"

"Yes."

"Just so you understand what I'm asking, I don't do temporary."

"Neither do I."

"As long as we're being clear. I have every intention of making this permanent as soon as you're ready."

"I'll do my best not to make you wait too long."

"Take as long as you need, sweetheart. Like I said, I'm staying put for as long as you let me. I love you. I never stopped. You're the only one for me."

"Good. Because I can't imagine getting sick of you anytime soon." She leaned close enough for their foreheads to touch. "I never plan to stop fighting for us, Luke. I love you too much."

"Do you have any idea how badly I want to kiss you right now?"

She pulled back and said, "Then what's stopping you, Campbell?"

"Toothpaste. I haven't brushed my teeth yet and I don't want to send you out of the room screaming from my breath."

The nurse, who had finished fiddling with the machines, turned toward the door. "You two behave in here. He needs rest."

Julie helped Luke brush his teeth. He took a swallow of water as she placed the supplies on the counter. He opened the covers. "Get over here, Mrs. Campbell."

"Is that a request?"

"Command. Why? Did it work?"

"Very effective tactic, Campbell."

She slipped under the covers with him and he pulled

her body flush with his. "I'm afraid we can't do anything with the nurse keeping her eye on us."

He pressed her fingers to his lips and kissed each tip before finding her lips. "We can get to the rest later. And believe me, we will. For now, having you right here, holding you, is all I need."

* * * * *

SPECIAL EXCERPT FROM

ⒽHARLEQUIN

INTRIGUE

Sheriff Jace Castillo comes face-to-face with his nemesis, leading to a dangerous pursuit through the rugged Texas Hill Country and a reunion with Linnea Martell, whom he vows to keep safe... no matter the cost.

Keep reading for a sneak peek at
Pursued by the Sheriff,
the conclusion of the Mercy Ridge Lawmen miniseries,
from USA TODAY *bestselling author Delores Fossen.*

"If need be, I could run my way out of these woods. You can't run," Linnea added.

"No, but I can return fire if we get into trouble," Jace argued. "And I stand a better chance of hitting a target than you do."

It was a good argument. Well, it would have been if he hadn't had the gunshot wound. It wasn't on his shooting arm, thank goodness, but he was weak, and any movement could cause that wound to open up.

"You could bleed out before I get you out of these woods," Linnea reminded him. "Besides, I'm not sure you can shoot, much less shoot straight. You can't even stand up without help."

As if to prove her wrong, he picked up his gun from the nightstand and straightened his posture, pulling back his shoulders.

And what little color he had drained from his face.

Cursing him and their situation, she dragged a chair closer to the window and had him sit down.

"The main road isn't that far, only about a mile," she continued. Linnea tried to tamp down her argumentative tone. "I can get there on the ATV and call for help. Your deputies and the EMTs can figure out the best way to get you to a hospital."

That was the part of her plan that worked. What she didn't feel comfortable about was leaving Jace alone while she got to the main road. Definitely not ideal, but they didn't have any other workable solutions.

Of course, this option wouldn't work until the lightning stopped. She could get through the wind and rain, but if she got struck by lightning or a tree falling from a strike, it could be fatal. First to her, and then to Jace, since he'd be stuck here in the cabin.

He looked up at her, his color a little better now, and his eyes were hard and intense. "I can't let you take a risk like that. Gideon could ambush you."

"That's true," she admitted. "But the alternative is for us to wait here. Maybe for days until you're strong enough to ride out with me. That might not be wise since I suspect you need antibiotics for your wound before an infection starts brewing."

His jaw tightened, and even though he'd had plenty trouble standing, Jace got up. This time he didn't stagger, but she did notice the white-knuckle grip he had on his gun. "We'll see how I feel once the storm has passed."

In other words, he would insist on going with her. Linnea sighed. Obviously, Jace had a mile-wide stubborn streak and was planning on dismissing her *one workable option*.

"If you're hungry, there's some canned soup in the cabinet," she said, shifting the subject.

Jace didn't respond to that. However, he did step in front of her as if to shield her. And he lifted his gun.

"Get down," Jace ordered. "Someone's out there."

Don't miss
Pursued by the Sheriff
*by Delores Fossen, available January 2022 wherever
Harlequin Intrigue books and ebooks are sold.*

Harlequin.com

Love Harlequin romance?

DISCOVER.

Be the first to find out about promotions, news and exclusive content!

Facebook.com/HarlequinBooks

Twitter.com/HarlequinBooks

Instagram.com/HarlequinBooks

Pinterest.com/HarlequinBooks

YouTube.com/HarlequinBooks

ReaderService.com

EXPLORE.

Sign up for the Harlequin e-newsletter and download a free book from any series at **TryHarlequin.com**

CONNECT.

Join our Harlequin community to share your thoughts and connect with other romance readers!
Facebook.com/groups/HarlequinConnection

HARLEQUIN

Heartfelt or thrilling, passionate or uplifting—Harlequin is more than just happily-ever-after.

With twelve different series to choose from and new books available every month, you are sure to find stories that will move you, uplift you, inspire and delight you.

SIGN UP FOR THE HARLEQUIN NEWSLETTER

Be the first to hear about great new reads and exciting offers!

Harlequin.com/newsletters

Get 4 FREE REWARDS!

We'll send you 2 FREE Books
plus 2 FREE Mystery Gifts.

KILLER CONSPIRACY
LENA DIAZ

LARGER PRINT

THE SETUP
CAROL ERICSON

LARGER PRINT

Harlequin Intrigue books are action-packed stories that will keep you on the edge of your seat. Solve the crime and deliver justice at all costs.

FREE
Value Over
$20